WESTLAND

Also by Michelle Muriel

ESSIE'S ROSES

WATER LILY DANCE

WESTLAND

a novel

MICHELLE MURIEL

LITTLE CABIN BOOKS

LITTLE CABIN BOOKS
2025 Zumbehl Rd, #252
Saint Charles, MO 63303

WESTLAND

www.littlecabinbooks.com

Printed in the United States of America

ISBN 978-0-9909383-6-1 (hardcover)
ISBN 978-0-9909383-7-8 (paperback)
ISBN 978-0-9909383-8-5 (eBook)

Library of Congress Control Number: 2021946249

In memory of Wesley Van Tassel
The Wes in Westland

PART I

PROLOGUE

KATIE

Alabama
Summer 1866

I held my breath, watching the flames from my bedroom window. A plume from my past rose above the trees, blacking my sunset. "Lord in Heaven, someone's out there." I glimpsed a figure in the shadows. *Man? Woman? Ghost.*

I froze, clutching my chest, trying to breathe. Since my illness, I could not trust my mind to discern the sight real or imagined: a silhouette, tossing a torch, running into the forest.

Adrenaline replaced my frailty as I rushed to Essie's garden. My legs failed me; I collapsed near its gate. Ash defiled the sweetness of rose perfume.

"Miss Katie," Delly called after me. "Katie girl!"

Katie girl. Delly's call transformed me from forty-five to four. Delly raised me during the early days of Daddy's Westland when the small plantation grew more wildflowers than cotton. On her first day, Delly, a young black woman, marched up our porch steps, enamored with my golden hair. Mama's "wild Katie" ran into Delly's arms. Daddy laughed. Mama pried me away.

James and the men managed the brush fire behind Essie's garden, and as flames curled toward the fence—a sprinkle of rain. Raindrops hadn't splashed my cheeks since I was a girl. My tears flowed with them.

"Katie," James called. He ran to me as I pictured a thousand times, dreaming of him when my life was not my own. For ten years, we lived as husband and wife. Ten years—a lifetime and vapor all at once. "Katie, you should be in bed. Do you want to catch your death?"

"I saw the fire and wasn't thinking. I ran, James."

"I don't know how. You're all heart, darlin'."

I closed my eyes, falling into his arms.

"It's over, Katie," James promised. "The fire's out. Let's get you home."

"I tried to stop her," Delly said. She covered me with a quilt and pulled me toward the house. "Katie slip right away from me like she do when she a child."

"Drought cause the brush fires this year is all, Miss Katie." Bo, our gentle giant and protector, lumbered toward me with an unexpected smile. "You go on. We gonna fix it all."

"I'm afraid the blight has stolen Essie's roses faster than any fire," I said.

Bo's strong hands cradled mine. "But the roots still good. We save em, Miss Katie. We save em."

That evening we all sat in the parlor, staring into the amber glow of a welcome fire.

"These be the only flames I fancy round Westland," Delly mumbled.

James sat with me on the settee, nestled under our blanket. Delly and Bo quietly played cards—Bo in the parlor after all these years. My unlikely family, family they were. My daughter Evie and Essie Mae, an intelligent black child born at Westland I raised as my daughter, opened our first school for freed slaves in New York. They matured into women under my sister Lil's guidance, making me proud.

"Do you think Evie and Essie Mae come home to stay now?" Delly asked, breaking the silence. "You want more tea, Katie?"

"I want our girls home," I said, tired. I stared across the room at my mother's empty settee. A flash of sewing lessons, debates with Father, tea with a dear friend. "James, the settee . . . I want Mr. Koontz to have it with Mama's pink crystal vases and the lace doilies."

Silence.

Delly couldn't hide her sniffles. Bo cleared his throat, fidgeting to leave.

"Yes, Katie," James whispered, scribbling it on my list of last wishes.

"Don't like such talk." Delly rose with a groan and poked at the fire. "No, ma'am. Now thunderclouds come a hovering in this room."

James's laugh strengthened my heart and put us at ease. "That's just my pipe smoke, Delly." James's winks calmed Delly faster than any words.

A blur of pink silks and lemon pillows; I welcomed sleep. A tap on the door. A new maid Delly hired, Astra, entered the parlor appearing as a ghost. I hardly recognized her, but the past year, faces muddled in sight and memories. "Mr. James, trouble come," Astra said, voice quivering. "They torched our barn. We save the horses, but Tom's crazy stubborn battling the blaze. Such a sight, Miss Katie; men give up fighting that fire and watch it burn."

"Go home, Astra. Bo will fetch Doc Jones," James said, holding me tighter.

"Ain't ya gonna help with the fire?" Astra asked, eyeing James, me. "Thirty men now."

"If they're watching the blaze, Astra, they gave up," James said. "A new law rules in this valley now. Union soldiers will set this right."

"But will they come?" Astra's eyes peered into me, black, hollow. "Will they come?"

I turned away.

"I have my hands full putting out fires here." James seldom raised his voice. "Astra, there's nothing I can do now. We'll take care of Tom and build him a new barn."

Astra stood taller, scanning us, the exit. I focused on her hands, scarred and delicate, twisting her apron. "Indifference brought us slavery; it's what'll steal our homes now!"

"Enough." I searched her eyes, the years and pain in them. "No one's talking about indifference. The fire destroyed the barn. Or will you have me lose a husband for you too?"

"Yes, ma'am," Astra whispered and scampered away.

"Don't you go on feel bad bout not rushing over there, Mr. James," Delly said. "Miss Katie has a right to say that, too. Why the neighbors go on thinking you the law in these parts?"

"Because James protected us during the war," I said.

"In ways not fitting to speak on, hmm." Delly rubbed my shoulders. I closed my eyes, absorbing the strength and peace through her hands. "That war's over."

"And a new one has started," I said, surprising James. "Yes. It is time, James."

Our crackling fire filled the silence. "It ends now." James's tender touch and whisper in my ear still caused a flurry of goosebumps on my arms. I relished his kiss. "I promise, Katie."

"Time for Katie to rest. Take her, Mr. James," Delly said with a peck to my forehead. "My china doll, you have sweet dreams tonight, sweet dreams."

Peace blanketed our home, though a fire raged near Westland.

"Tom McCafferty's all right," Bo announced. "His pride's hurt for not heeding the lookout or hiring them extra men."

James carried me up to my room and tucked me into bed. "Katie, send for the girls."

"My letter is ready." It was the last loving night I spent with my husband before my sickness returned. I felt it, carefree in the rain, the heaviness in my chest, a fever. I rushed to Essie's garden because I longed to feel strong and useful again. I wanted to save it, us, believe my life was not over but beginning. All the lost years returned. Lost love, found. I wanted to believe and dream among those roses. Ten years I savored the selfless love of a good man, ten years we fought day after day to keep Westland, keep me. And Essie's roses helped me to dream again, helped all of us.

Westland, where its willows hold secrets, until the night air sweeps through their leaves, scattering them in the wind and into our ears . . . Evie, it's time to come home.

1.

ESSIE MAE

New York City
October 1866

At the start of my journey, on a stop outside New York City, a little white girl boarded the train, reminding me of Evie. She eyed my potted rose, and as children do, stopped, stared, and plopped on the empty seat beside me, my chaperon soon to arrive.

The passengers did not gasp that a white girl stopped to speak to me, a black, young woman, nor did they wonder why the conductor had not moved me to a different car. I wore my finest blue dress, sapphire, as Evie's night sky, a lavish gift from her aunt Lil and the yellow bonnet sprouting sky-blue feathers Miss Katie gave me on my birthday. My hair tucked in the soft waves Miss Katie adored, and a touch of peach blush and lip rouge, though Miss Katie claimed my creamy brown skin needed only a brisk walk for rosy beauty. But as I dabbed it on, the bit of makeup reminded me of Lil's instruction at her long-ago school for ladies. "You said nothing of how to smooth crow's-feet," I whispered to my reflection in the sterling box mirror Evie sent me for my birthday. The woman's portrait etched on top resembled Miss Katie. How we have all matured now.

"Miss, why do you hug that potted flower as a doll?" the little girl asked, wide-eyed.

Miss. I smiled to myself.

"Is it magical?" she asked, tugging my sleeve.

"You remind me of someone." I laughed.

She scrunched her nose and tossed her blonde ringlets like Evie.

Her mother arrived. "Wren," she called. "This is not your seat. Leave this woman alone."

"But it's my birthday," Wren whined. "I'm seven now, and you said on our next trip, I may choose my seat."

"Your daughter is charming. No bother," I said. The fidgety girl tugged the fingertips of her white gloves. "Wren. What a glorious name. Are you a lilting songbird?"

Wren fluttered her lashes, aqua eyes pleading with her mother. "Oh, Mommy, but this nice lady was going to tell me a story about her magical flower." She winked at me at last pulling off her gloves, and in an instant, the distracted child popped up at the call of the conductor, lured away by his musical whistle. "Mama, he's giving out whistles." She rushed to him.

"Stay close, Wren," her mama called. "Children, they skip from one wonder to the next. We travel so much the conductor is an old family friend. He always watches over Wren."

"She reminds me of someone. It's hard to believe we were once that young and trusting." I had meant to say curious, but it spilled out, my heart envying Wren's innocence and radiance.

"Curious," the woman echoed for me, watching her daughter show off to admirers. The conductor, distracted from his duties, taught Wren how to make her whistle sing. "I have seen you," the woman said to me, smiling. "I'm Abigail Fitzpatrick. You don't remember me."

"Pleasure," I said, relieved my defenses down. I nodded and shook her lavender-gloved hand. She caught herself, slipped off her gloves, and offered her delicate handshake. A flush washed over me as I gazed into her eager eyes, trying to recall our meeting. We managed the awkwardness, admiring her daughter swaying in her sun-soaked spotlight. I had imagined Abigail would grab Wren and complain about me to the conductor, but then, I have learned to believe first in the goodness of people; that most white folks were not like the ones who hurt me.

"My husband and I saw you speak at the Hayden Theater in New York. Exquisite, dear. We contributed to your school." She removed her wide plum hat, fluffing her orange curls.

"Yes. Abigail! Of course. We bought many books with your generous donation. You are gracious, but we could hardly call the Hayden a theater. A river town's hall perhaps, arranged with two rows of chinoiserie armchairs." We chuckled.

"No. You spoke with such passion. It must be difficult keeping track of your admirers."

"I have not given a speech in months and moved outside the city, to Piermont, to open a small school. I help a sweet elderly couple at their inn and cultivate flowers on their strawberry farm. They indulge my study of roses. I should say they help me."

"The Morgans and their inn are staples in Piermont. Now I know why their courtyard garden appears lush and vibrant. Haley never could keep roses. They're lucky to find you."

"I sometimes lecture at Haddock's Hall. The bustle of the city no longer thrills me." My cheeks burned, speaking about myself.

"Cape May by steamboat in the evening during the season, delicious."

"I'm entirely too busy to visit Cape May," I said in jest. Evie would have laughed at the British accent I slipped, a ruse Evie performed during our stay in London, hidden from the war.

"How are Sam and Haley Morgan? Their strawberry festival was grand this year."

I pictured the plump, juicy berries waiting for Haley's hands to whip them into sugary concoctions—their sad faces as I waved goodbye. "Dear friends," I said. "The festival is my favorite time of year, but I miss another quiet escape. Pleasure seeing you again, Abigail." I was eager to rest and dream of my days on the strawberry farm, away from my roses and home.

Abigail remained, eyeing her daughter and rummaging in her handbag.

A man squeezed by, thumping Abigail with his satchel. "Pardon."

"I should take my seat," Abigail said. "But we are going nowhere fast. This train is always late. Where's your husband, Thomas?" Her eyes twinkled, anticipating gossip.

I fanned my blush. "We are not married . . . friends."

"I've misunderstood. My husband has eyed Thomas for politics."

"It may be the other way around." I inspected a leaf on my rose, restless to sit alone.

"Forgive me. I'm an anxious chatterbox before the train departs. My card. We're returning to Mobile."

"Alabama as well." I rose, searching down the aisle for my late escort.

"My husband said many Southerners opposed to slavery left the South after the war for good. Others make trouble for those sympathizers who stay."

Sympathizer. I despised the word, not for what it meant, but the hiss when whispered in disdain by those waiting in the shadows to snuff out its true meaning's light. "Rebels are the failed leaders of the war bent on destruction of blacks and white Southern sympathizers and Union support-ers. They are the enemy of freedom."

"Yes. Yet you return?"

"For a special reason." I shook off my memories, gazing out my window. A husband kissed his wife and children goodbye. He presented his pink peonies, making her sob. "Oh, red roses and white jasmine represent sweet love, peonies bashfulness."

Abigail sighed as the couple embraced. "Peonies also mean romance, dear. Bah, I don't believe in the language of flowers as I once did as a young girl in love."

"At my school, I arrange a bouquet for my students, former slaves, every week. My favorite bouquet is one of pink roses for boldness, a sprig of mint: virtue, yellow tulips: hopeless love, and a stalk of willow . . ."

"For freedom."

"Yes," I said, surprised she knew the willow's meaning. "I am sentimental, but the language of flowers saved me, Abigail."

"And you have made me fall in love with the romantic code all over again." Abigail looked at me fondly and handed me a violet from a posy in her satchel. "Faithfulness, I believe."

"I teach my students beyond reading and writing, but navigating life's hardships, planting hope, watering their faith, so that despite deluge or drought, something beautiful will blossom inside each one."

"My dear, you teach something greater: curiosity. I dare say curiosity saved you, a curiosity to live beyond your station."

"To live period." I hadn't meant to shame her, but I also hadn't planned on engaging in a conversation on life and love, in no mood for the talk of either. I wanted to sit at my window, quiet, counting the hours until I saw Evie, Delly, Bo, James . . . and Miss Katie again.

Abigail waved to Wren. "I'm no speechmaker. My husband warns me not to discuss subjects I don't understand."

I chuckled. "How can we learn if we never discuss them?"

"Agreed. Perhaps women will lend our voices to politics someday."

"We are. We shall."

Abigail summoned Wren. "I hope you'll call on me should you visit Mobile." Wren returned, pushing her gloves into her mother's hands, showing off her new whistle. "I'll take that." Abigail stuffed the noisemaker into her bag.

"Mommy, the conductor said, the train won't leave for a long time. They're fixing something or making more steam. I don't remember."

"We await the queen of this locomotive." Abigail laughed. "Katy Dale, opera star and owner of a luxurious car furnished with red velvet seats, walnut paneling, and a bed covered in emerald silk." Abigail relished her gossip.

I smiled a "Katy" traveled with me.

"Mommy, may I please stay to hear this lady's story?" Wren asked.

"My manners," I said, a blush prickling my cheeks. "Essie. My name is Essie Mae. Wren, what story?"

Abigail searched out my window. "My husband waits to see us off. He's in politics and stays behind on business." Wren tugged at her mother's dress. The yellow satin skirt reminded me of a ball gown Miss Katie fancied, black embroidery and mother-of-pearl buttons. I looked out my window, picturing Katie waltzing with James in the moonlight under her magnolia trees.

Abigail caught me dreaming, primping the violets adorning her hair. Her elegance reminded me of the mistress I left behind; the teacher who taught me grace and opened my mind to learning, the mama I dreamed raised me. I gulped the sadness knotted in my throat.

"Mommy, I *know* Essie has a story. It dances inside her eyes when she looks at her flower." Wren waited, twisting in her pink dress, primed for a twirl.

"A rose," I said. "This is a very special rose." I enticed Wren further.

Defeated, Abigail sat in the empty seat in front of us. "I have postcards to write. I brought your blanket, Wren. Winter arrives early this year."

To my surprise Wren, squirming to sit in my lap, sat next to me waiting for a story, reminding me so much of little Evie tears watered in my eyes. "You are a beautiful girl," I said. "As pretty as my rose."

"Why do you carry it?" Wren's tiny hand clutched my arm.

I hadn't felt the pleasure and joy of innocence rising in my heart for a long time. "I grow roses. This rose is for a special woman."

"Your mama?"

Wren's question surprised me. I bit my lip, stretching for an answer. "Perhaps."

"We have a gardener who grows roses that look like peppermint sticks."

"A Village Maid rose." I closed my eyes, inhaling the imaged candied fragrance.

"What is your rose called?" Wren tugged at my sleeve, waking me.

"It has no name yet, for I created it."

"Doesn't God create roses?"

"Oh, yes." Wren walked her fingers down my arm, swirling the pearl buttons on my sleeve. She lifted the cuff and found the daisy-chain bracelet, a parting gift from a student. Her curious eyes passed over the thick purple scar curled across my wrist and forearm. I felt uneasy at her instant attachment. I slipped the daisies on her wrist, settling her fidgeting fingers as Katie used to do with mine. "God gives us wisdom to fashion our own, but it takes patience." I tapped her nose, making her giggle. "People learn about flowers to cultivate new varieties to enjoy."

"Like Mama having babies."

"Wren." Her mother snapped around. We exchanged a look, stifling a chuckle. Wren sat taller and held her finger to her lips to quiet her mama. Abigail handed me a throw for Wren and returned to writing her postcards. Wren snuggled under her blanket, ready for a story.

"But now," I whispered. "It is time to tuck my rose away to sleep."

"Essie, I wonder, do flowers dream?"

I sighed as her blanket stretched across our laps.

Passengers filed in; the train would soon leave the station. Wren's eager eyes never left mine, even after the sellers of newspapers and snacks sang their offerings, racing up and down the aisle. I hurried to think of a fable. "Long ago, in a magical forest, a young prince set out to find a special gift for his new bride. He passed a well of diamonds."

Wren gasped. "Diamonds are a brilliant gift."

"'The diamonds sparkle,' said the prince. 'But so does my bride.' The prince marched on until he passed a field of gold grass he could pluck and pay for anything he wished."

"Gold grass is a priceless gift," Wren whispered.

"'No,' said the prince. 'For my bride is priceless.' The prince came to a meadow. Tired, he planted himself in the shade by a sapling. 'You need the sun,' said the prince. 'And water.' The prince plucked the tree from the shade, planted it in the sun, and watered its roots. Out of the corner of his eye, he spotted a glorious white rose, its petals sparkled gold and crimson. But how could he think of cutting it, for it was the only one in the valley?"

Wren nestled closer, her eyelids drooping. Abigail had turned around to listen.

"An old woman passed by and informed the prince the rose was hers; she planted it for her husband gone these many years. The woman, seeing the prince had cared for the tree, said, 'I will gift you my rose, for you saved the tree my husband planted for me. This rose will bring you happiness, but you must never give it away until you find one worthy who will care for it.'"

The train's bell hastened my story. "The woman dug up the rose, and before their eyes, the wondrous flower closed for its journey to the prince's garden. When the prince's new bride saw the rose, her eyes watered with joy. 'You have gifted me the rose my father planted for my mother. We quarreled years ago. I was a stubborn child not to return and ask for forgiveness. You have brought me more than a gift, you brought me love.'"

Wren applauded, bouncing in her seat.

"More than diamonds or gold is the love of our parents. Some know not or treasure this love. Others embrace and remember. Always remember, Wren, a mother's love is as sweet as a priceless rose."

"Thank you," Abigail whispered, taking her sleepy daughter. "Come, Wren, to our seat."

Wren begged her mother to stay. "We're going to Mobile to find me a sister."

My tired eyes widened. "Excuse me?"

"Three years ago," Abigail whispered as the conductor walked her daughter to her seat. She motioned to the conductor to wait and turned to me with a nervous grin. "We lost my eldest son in the war. I return home to

Mobile. My husband stays behind on business in New York at his parents' home."

"North and South fighting each other." I sighed.

"That was always the saddest part. My husband, Reginald, makes his way in politics. We're looking to adopt. You travel south to speak?"

"To go home. We know many in Mobile." I crinkled the kerchief hidden in my pocket, hoping for a rescue now.

"We?"

"The family who raised me."

"I see." Abigail bid a final wave to her husband. "We're off. Please call on us should you visit Mobile. We are staying until Christmas. Wren would love to hear more of your stories."

"I would like that."

She shook my hand to the stares of the passengers now. "In my travels, I have learned one may find a treasured friend during chitchat on a train. I am thrilled I recognized you."

"So am I." I handed her the peppermint sticks I bought for Evie. "They'll settle Wren's stomach for the journey. I noticed her rubbing her belly while I told the fable."

"And my daughter's green complexion." She laughed. "Wren drank too much . . ."

"Orangeade."

"Yes."

"All aboard," the conductor called.

"Thank you, Essie. Wren hasn't been this happy in months. I hope you'll visit us, dear."

"I will try." I cloaked my potted roses with gauze and cradled the seedlings in my lap.

"You should place your flowers back inside your box, miss," the conductor said in passing. "Train's about to leave the station."

"Roses," I whispered. *At least the passengers aren't staring at me*, I thought. They were.

🌿

"Ready, Miss Essie?" My chaperon sat next to me, scouring his newspaper as usual.

"My royal guard." I snickered. "When will James ever let me travel alone?"

"Perhaps you will sleep this time, Miss Essie."

"A dream." I peeked at my roses and placed them in their box as the train hitched forward. Billowing smoke floated past my window.

The fourth and final year, my rose's delicate pink coloring—perfection, the tinge of lavender to the edges of the petals, as a silk ribbon framing a fancy bonnet. *A new variety, a prize rose,* I thought, proud. It takes four to six years to cultivate a worthy rose.

My life has taken as long to start anew. A seedling.

The best father and mother plant cultivates a new rose. Father rose is the pollen and provides strength and health. Mother rose births the seeds, adding beauty and fragrance. The wrong parents will produce a fragile, dull flower, the right pairing, with a bit of luck: a wonder.

As a girl, despite my reality, born a slave, I believed I was a wonder. Might my coloring change, my health and strength, if I had the right parents . . . parents at all. I have learned these twenty-five years; a mother may transfer beauty, a father may deposit good or bad, fear, faith, strength, weakness.

Loving secret gardeners raise, water, and nurture buds to blossom, produce fruit in us, and pull weeds so we may thrive. Is it mother, father, or someone else we look back to for the bits of us whole and broken, the traits that make us a wonder? I was cultivated not by father or mother, but by someone else. Most years, I raised myself.

But to roses—they cannot choose their coloring, shape, or size, or can they? Pollen from the father brushed inside mama rose, a time to wait for seed in autumn. I sprinkle Mama's seeds across the dirt in a small pot. White seeds, orange, or brown, Mama doesn't care what color her seeds are; they will produce whatever color they wish, loved and treasured. Now a test: cold, isolated, dark under earth, a moment of sleep; a seedling rises. A summer rose shines on its own. I trust it to the elements with the others to grow and survive alone.

I cannot judge the first rosebud as perfect, but it's a start, as forgiveness.

My new roses endure heat, drought, disease, the coloring dull, its perfume faint. Next year—a vibrant pink, as a streak in a sunset, shows itself to my glee. I look closer; a petal boasts an unexpected, magical variation: lavender tinge to the tips of a single petal.

Year three: my pink roses grow plump and hardy, favoring sun. It withstands disease. A darker pink, the inside of a strawberry; I tinker in secret gardening, hoping its blush returns.

Year four: my perfect roses. Girls matured into ladies. A new rose I cultivated with time and years as a life. After years of obedience, its petals choose mischief, all brushed with the lavender of its birth. A silky ribbon of unexpected delight as a rich detail on a bonnet the fashionable notice, for they notice everything.

As our train gained momentum, racing toward a home I scarcely knew, I feared I cultivated too much a new life for my roses and not myself. Like this rose, I stayed hidden. Among a class invited into, I was still invisible, feigning my way through this crowd, a people, black and white, wishing to promote their own agenda—no matter my color or fragrance, hardly treasured. I fought for every glance, every word in their ears. This rose tucked away in its box deserved a showing, judge, and award. But what of my life? Many judge me. Others have shown me proud on their stands, but I won no prizes. I carry badges of another sort, some beautiful, others worn and ugly.

2.

EVIE

The dry Alabama soil filled my fingernails. I clawed through, pebbles rolling over my knuckles, sand, and clay. "Too dry," I moaned like Essie. *Evie, it's not time for planting,* she whispered in my thoughts. "And you're getting dirt on the calico dress your mama made." I chuckled. "Grassy green to match my eyes ... but, Essie Mae, Mama made this dress too tight."

My childhood melted away as fast as a sunset.

"Mama, you forgot I wasn't a girl anymore, my sunlit hair now sandy from the years. We've all changed ... as your Westland."

With Mama gone, one question splashed about us as a raindrop through the trees: What would become of Westland now?

Five years away, my eyes skimmed a Westland I barely knew. Its hidden history, my grandparents, Alexander and Ruth Wilcox's legacy, its future, and the stains my father marked on its door. The large, white two-story house untouched by war; the path to its door still lined with buttercups and violets, its porch flanked with Mama's blue and pink hydrangeas. A new paddock for James's stallions and pasture for his cattle, James, at last, made his mark saving and protecting Westland. Mama demolished the slave quarters years ago. The cottage Delly and Essie Mae lived in when I was a child remained. Though Essie and Delly moved in with us after my father died, Mama spent her final months approving a flurry of secret improvements to the old cottage; Bo and James wouldn't let us see until Essie arrived.

The view from our hillside, unchanged. The last of fall's splendor shimmered in the trees. With every blink, through the peephole of the branches to the sky, the swirling leaves shifted in stained-glassed shapes as nature's kaleidoscope. "How I've missed you." A gust of wind; I relished the trees' applause. My nose to the breeze; ice tickled the air, odd for the season. But many odd happenings visited the South since the war's end. Westland's cornflower blue sky glistened like James's eyes. Today silver framed the white fluffs I dreamed in as a child. "Winter's coming early."

Secret benches remained, built by my grandfather, hidden for his daughter, my mother, and her forbidden friendship with a slave girl, Isabel. When I was a girl, Bo constructed new benches for Isabel's daughter, Essie Mae, and me, placed on the forest path to Mr. Koontz's farm and one at the creek, cloistering us away from an unforgiving world. The years of an innocent friendship birthed and rescued in pain, love, prejudice, and hate, repeated themselves a generation later, and Mama and I never discussed them. I grieve unspoken words.

In spring, solace warmed me under Mama's magnolia trees, plump with white and pink blossoms. Autumn, her weatherworn stone bench underneath them, invited me to take her place and waited for Essie Mae to dream again. But something had changed, beyond the sorrow of its owner, lost, beyond the pain of my past whirling a tornado of demolishing words in the shadows, coves, and orchards vast and adventurous as a child, frightening to me now.

I strolled to my favorite hideaways, inhaling earth and sky, evergreens, marshland, and an apple cove bursting for harvest. Roses no longer permeated at Westland's door; dried leaves, ginger, and cloves, from Delly's baking, welcomed me home.

Nightfall was the only time I felt a child again, giddy, restless, staring at the stars with a spark of a dream awakening. In the crisp night air, I breathed in the faint fragrance of roses. The honey spice of mums and freshly cut grass reminded me cherished memories still resided here, and love. My heart understood; my mind battled, tempting me to stay away, far away from the horrors of my childhood lurking behind roses and willows.

You can't fit in that dress 'cause you sneaking gulps of my strawberry lemonade in the night. I loosened the sash around my waist, smirking at Delly's imagined scolding.

My skin prickled in goosebumps as her eyes spied on me from behind a willow. "I heard ya sweeping," I shouted at the tree, watching a flap of Delly's white apron scuttle away. "The whole county heard you sweeping," I sassed.

"You an old maid, Miss Evie. Ain't no baby child no more a playing in that dirt. Ain't gonna stand for no sassing neither," Delly huffed. She couldn't hide the chuckle in her voice. She slammed the front door to mask her laughter, signaling she would leave me alone for now.

"Mama, the years march on, but Delly's howling never changes." I searched the sky and inhaled. "Rain's coming. You, Sky, have lost your magic today, every day since I lost Mama."

Autumn.

Past the season for strawberries, past the time for many things. The nip in the air tickled my nose; the smell of dried leaves made me think of my mother, Miss Katie, to all who loved her. Every morning her hands pressed her daughter's offerings into her diary, saving memories—a crimson maple leaf, dried rose petals, a violet from our hillside. I started a new scrapbook for her, a page of strawberry leaves and yellow rose petals from her favorite rose-bush. Still blossoming, still mingled with ruby roses—regret, thorny memories one never thinks to snip and discard, and so they sting just enough to cause discomfort, wake us from sleep, and aggravate our present. *My daddy say, even a li'l thorn cause a whole mess a trouble, Delly warned. That tiny thorn burrow in you skin, travel, and cause a mess in you heart. That's what staying in the past do.* I dug in the dirt, ignoring Delly's warnings echoing in my daydreams, my heart. *Let them bad thoughts fly away or they'll steal from you, like them li'l foxes that spoil the vines. A nibbling till not a sweet grape dangling. Evie, fore you knows it, you got no fruit left.*

No matter where I hid at Westland, at the creek, our hillside, in a forgotten garden, I couldn't escape Delly's wisdom, not in Paris, London, New York, not even in this neglected patch of dirt behind a tired willow and Grandfather's magnolia trees.

My sigh swirled with the wind. "One morning, I'd love to savor the quiet as I did when I was small—dreaming, planning, following imagined trails away from Westland. Yet, here I sit in the quiet listening to clatter." I raked the hairy roots of a strawberry plant, tucking them into the soil, smoothing a mound of dirt to the leaves. My tears sprinkled the earth, praying something plentiful might grow. *We'll plant a new bed in April,* Essie promised. I wanted to surprise her, but it was too late, too late for many things. I plopped to the ground, staring at the tiny plant for answers.

"Frost is coming early."

Essie promised she would return to Westland. She didn't say she would stay.

I couldn't sleep most nights thinking of Essie. The past two months, we didn't discuss leaving each other nor write about wedding plans we avoided, Aunt Lil's invitation to take us back to Paris, or how James might manage without us. As children, Essie claimed, I had the gift of dreaming and planning, but I wasn't that child anymore. I hadn't a plan.

It wasn't safe traveling South after the war, but James insisted, sending William to New York City to fetch Essie and me home. Mama was dying. The doctor said my return brought sunshine back to Westland, strengthening Mama to hold on into summer; she surprised us all.

Dozens of plans danced inside my mind then, including my promise to Mama to return to New York and finish establishing a school in her honor. After the Civil War, with Essie and Aunt Lil, we opened a school for freed slaves who flocked north desperate for an education. When Mama's strength failed, I returned to Westland alone, reminding me of the only time I spent without Essie—the night Grant and his cutthroats kidnapped Essie Mae to sell her as a runaway slave, though Essie had never been a slave to us. A night we never spoke on again, a thorn traveling to our hearts.

In Mama's last letter, she wrote, Rebels set fire to Tom McCafferty's barn, our neighbor, because he went against his own, sheltering Union soldiers and Confederate deserters during the war, and he married a black woman. Now gangs of rebels who never accepted the war's end vowed to keep fighting against freedom and civil rights for blacks. Martial law descended on Alabama and the Southern states. *Haven't we suffered enough death? They hate we free and hate drive crazy men to do the work a demons,* Delly wrote.

It was true. Our small community, tucked away in the river valley, wasn't like most. Our rural location saved us from most of the fighting. Yet, our fertile land and stance against Alabama's secession provided a target for agitators and unscrupulous land-grabbers. Delly said when she first arrived at Westland, Grandfather didn't own slaves; he hired men. It wasn't until my late father, John Winthrop, ushered in the horrors of slavery to Westland's land to our near ruin. But it's been years since Delly whispered her tales of

Grandfather's Westland. I suspect, with Mama gone, she'll bellow as a carnival barker her enticing tidbits of the mysteries and intrigues of its past, and I will beg her to reveal every trick and secret under the stars.

Mama did all she could to right Westland's many wrongs. During the war, she sent Essie Mae and me away to London and Paris with Aunt Lil and wrote most of our neighbors freed their slaves before the war and went against the South to save their families, plantations, and farms. Others had family living in the North. James, a Northerner by birth, appeased the Yankees. Now he's doing all he can to keep Southern rebels from knowing.

James wrote that three months ago, two men visited Westland impersonating government land officials. "We gave them a worthy sendoff," he said. I imagined this involved a shotgun, boot, and Bo's snarl. Mama's health declined. I left New York for good.

Union soldiers fill the towns now to stamp out the hatred and destruction of the rebels who refuse to believe in the reconstruction effort and educating freed blacks, freedmen. Essie and I found purpose in this battle. We wielded tablets and pencils, proud of our small school in New York. Essie and Thomas discovered a new cause: fighting the Black Codes passed by Congress restricting the hard-fought rights of freed blacks. The Southern states couldn't bind a slave by paper anymore, but by laws. Our fight had only begun.

Mama's final letter shifted in my pocket. I shuffled to the last page.

Truth is a priceless treasure, but worthless if buried. Value simplicity. Pause to smell a rose, preferably planted by your hand, for it will smell sweeter. Toil builds character; heartache tests our fortitude. The key to happiness is forgiveness, forgiving ourselves most of all.

If I could only sit with you once more in my garden, listen to my girl, a woman now, act out her stories of the big city, life, and love as we watch the sunrise, sunset, and our sapphire Westland blanketed in moonlight. I eagerly await and pray for that day when you return home.

Love,

Mama

I smoothed out the worn edges of her letter, inhaling its rose-scented paper, reading it for the hundredth time. It rested in my pocket until I traveled home. I hadn't experienced the war as most. No more the lavish galleries of the Louvre, musical Parisian cafes, and boulevards dotted with parasols, artists, and chestnut trees, but war's devastation, torched cotton fields, shattered lives, towns, and homes. Aunt Lil's Richmond fared worst of all.

"Destroyed by the Confederacy's own daft hands," Lil said. In an act of defiance, Confederate soldiers burned a tobacco plant that set Richmond ablaze. Now we must decide to rebuild together in the South, continue our work in the North, or hide again in a foreign land of indulgence and strangers. I coasted on Essie's progress until news of Mama would make me choose.

"The key to happiness, Mama, is there such a key?"

3.

ESSIE MAE

"Miss Essie," my chaperon said, finally looking up from his newspaper.

My posture stiffened, shoulder blades pinched together. I held my breath at the train's departure, learning to exhale and settle my heart as Westland inched closer. "Why, Mr. Jarrell, I wondered if I might at last travel alone."

"I shall grant your wish . . . for a moment. I spot a friend." He raced up to a man in a brown bowler and long white whiskers. The man eyed me and whispered into Mr. Jarrell's ear.

"Mysteries and secrets," I mumbled. By now, Mr. Jarrell's odd companions and habits, at stops throughout our journey, did not concern me. He seemingly knew everyone, and anyone he deemed suspicious; he found them out before the train departed. Evie claimed he arrested several men during one brief trip. "Arrested for what?" I asked. *Lil, into the bourbon, revealed Bedford Jarrell is an expert detective. Bounties, collecting rewards for robbers and swindlers, that's how he earns his living.* "Applesauce," I whispered to myself. *I've missed your stories, Evie.*

Last night, under a blanket of a blue moon, Evie's tales skipped inside my dreams, her favorite yarn about us floating on a star. My skin glittered as gold ribbon, but I scarcely saw Evie, as if a lighted planet swallowed her whole. I studied the passengers boarding the train at the third stop of many on the long journey home. *I'm too old for childish dreams.* I scribbled it in my diary for a story to share on our hillside. But this dream puzzled me. I couldn't see Evie, not a spark. *Flimflam,* Delly warned in my thoughts. *"But sometimes, God speaks to us in our dreams," she said, confusing herself in a whisper. "Sure enough. Joseph go on dreaming his dreams, get him a crown 'sides."*

"Which is it, Delly?" Evie asked, riling her. "Are dreams warnings or applesauce?"

"Flimflam," Delly barked. "Evie, you sneak and eat my apple pie fore bed like I warn ya not to and moan, 'Apple man chase me in my dream.' Head as

big as a flying balloon wonder in the sky. Now I scare myself with the thought. Maybe God say, bes not sneak Delly's pie at bedtime 'cause that brown sugar crumble filling you head with sweet mush.

I chuckled to myself, catching Mr. Jarrell's attention. Despite his peculiar manner, with two recent train robberies, I felt safe with him, unlike any other white man I had known, except for James. I trusted Mr. Jarrell because James and Katie trusted him. Though I feigned bravery, as a young black woman, traveling alone was nothing I planned on attempting. Lil's generosity provided safety. Still, Mr. Jarrell had not earned my total confidence yet.

Threats continued for black men and women traveling south. Ten months after the war ended, a ring of slave dealers kidnapped a group of freedmen in a cruel trick. A dealer hosted a dance at his sawmill for freed blacks, only to sweep them up and steal them away for slave labor in Brazil at secret places offshore as if slavery had never ended. We dipped our toes in freedom, but our fight was far from finished. When Evie writes, insisting I cannot travel alone, I accept the gift of Bedford Jarrell, as I need no reminder that I, too, was once taken.

My breath skipped as I lost myself in the silhouettes of my past, riding a plume of steam outside my window. Nightmares chased me aboard this train.

Steam swirled into the smoke of *his* campfire. *She* gazed into its red-hot embers, frantic to take herself elsewhere. The slave girl I abandoned on the road to Ashland, the one they caged in a wagon, leaving her for dead on the forest floor, the girl I left behind at Westland, the woman returning to it now. I spoke of her before attentive crowds, but *She* was not me. I conjured stories inside amber sparks that drifted in the black smoke, but I hadn't Evie's imagination. I tried, try still. *Chains, rust, bleeding wrists; a torn dress exposed my long, cold limbs. I clutched the bars inside that wagon, clanking those chains to drown out the old African mumbling a spell.*

"*Essie,*" Evie whispered.

My eyes shot open.

"*You're free.*"

I inhaled, wincing at my sore ribs. *You spent the morning hunched over, hulling strawberries for Haley's preserves and lifting crates for Sam. He broke his hand. "You're no young lad, Sammy, climbing ladders," Haley warned. "Yes."*

Think of them. The Morgans took me in for what I could give them and what they gifted me: a chance to live on my own, a chance to live free. *You don bleed like we do,* the old African slave intruded. I swirled the knotted scar on my shoulder, the one from the old man's bullet. It still ached, telling me the rain was coming.

Wren's smile chased the ghosts away.

At her wiggling fingers, I waved back, settling in my seat. "It's over." I sighed, dabbing sweat off my brow before Mr. Jarrell noticed. "My dreams are not flimflam, Delly. They frighten me." *The panic of my past might present itself again,* Haley's doctor explained. She fetched him for my heart; he examined my mind instead. I knew my soul and spirit longed for healing.

Mr. Jarrell laughed with his friend, tugging the man's beard as if testing Father Christmas's whiskers. Jarrell sauntered past Abigail and little Wren, revealing a silver coin behind Wren's ear as a magic trick, handing it to the giddy girl.

I closed my eyes to childhood, the wonder in Evie's eyes at a field of fireflies on a sapphire night, twinkling in the trees like bits of stars floating to earth. Our dresses twirl in the breeze, our tiny fingers raking through soil, planting roses, hope. *Healing from a magical rose garden kept by a queen,* Evie proclaimed, the white girl with the sunbeams in her hair. Our years at Westland and beyond it raced past my eyes as the landscape outside my window. Tears, courage, and love held my heart for this journey and our memories—the invited ones.

The freed slaves I taught in New York could never believe a wealthy white girl hidden on a small plantation suffered more scars than most; still, they lived freer than Evie. "But that white woman weren't no slave," they would say. "She free."

"Was she?" I could hardly utter a word of Evie's past while I wrestled with my own.

My students—freed slaves—black men, women, and children, fathers learning to read with daughters, mothers practicing letters with sons, looked on their teacher with curiosity, my creamy brown skin and proper speech. A former slave? Katie would never dare utter the word. Too many words existed, lost in the lemon wildflower fields of Westland. Whispered by children on a hillside, mumbled by a house slave, now free, railed by the only papa I knew, Bo, and locked away by its mistress forever. Words hung in the air as the leaves on a willow, golden, dry, ready to shake loose come autumn to drift and land, waiting for those who will discover them.

I missed Evie, but I did not relish returning to Westland and its once fertile soil, dried and unproductive; its home, too quiet and forlorn; its sky, a soft gray ready for rain. Delly wrote, warning me about my roses. *This year, we all too busy caring for Miss Katie. Them rosebuds need the drink, and the Alabama sun doing em no good at all. No good, child.*

When I left Westland, I said goodbye to my roses too. Evie found solace in her mother's secret garden. Despite the drought and war, Evie wrote, Miss Katie's flowers thrived, pristine and watered with secrets, weeded by unknown gardeners, protected by Miss Katie's dreams, and Delly's able hands. I grieved for Miss Katie and my roses, picturing my garden vibrant and plentiful upon our return to Westland after the war. Now, those rich days on that plantation play in my dreams, to erase the horrors hidden by the task, wonder, and fragrance of roses.

"Must be good reading," Mr. Jarrell said, sitting beside me. "Nice to see you smile."

"Um-hmm," I mumbled, scribbling in my diary.

He crinkled his eyes, amused, wriggling his nose to push up his glasses. "You're sweating."

"I'm fine."

"Good." He flapped his newspaper open, reading me instead. "There's a nip in the air."

"Mr. Jarrell, I'm well aware summer has ended." I searched through my diary, ripping a page. "See what you've made me do."

"Why do you insist on sitting here when you have a grand stateroom to yourself?"

"Shh, I don't want my friends to hear," I whispered, waving to Wren. He swirled a fist in his palm, shaking the tired hand awake. *He's nervous again.* I slipped a smirk. *Mr. Jarrell nervous, that's like saying Delly's coy.*

A jarring halt.

The train expelled rhythmic puffs of steam as slumbered breathing. I clutched my chest. "Stop analyzing my every twitch. I do not need protection. Depart at the next stop if you wish."

He stuffed his fingers in his vest, revealing a pocket watch twirling on its gold chain. "In the past five years, have I ever fallen for any of your excuses to leave your side?" He shifted in his seat, jostling his elbows at the crowding, eyeing my potted rose.

"Six years." I scrutinized his unspoken request.

He eyed my flower again, the floor. I placed my rose back into its box and set it at my feet. He scooted closer, shuffling a stack of papers in his lap.

"The middle of the train is the safest. The back moves in a dusty haze. You feel all the bumps and jerking in a cloud of ash. Mr. Jarrell, why are you looking at me so?"

"I rather the daisy Wren tucked in your hair. You shouldn't hide those eyes of yours under a banana brim." Bedford Jarrell, a traveling escort insisted upon by James. The able clerk to Evie's Uncle Augustus, now a respected lawyer in Mobile—rumored Pinkerton detective. He grinned, as if reading my thoughts. But then, reading people was Mr. Jarrell's gift.

I searched the landscape outside my window, calming the quiver in my chest. *Essie Mae, why are you nervous to go home? Home?* The idyllic scenes in a blur past my window reminded me of Westland. *Chocolate grooves of the farmer's plow,* Evie would whisper. *Thistle, foxglove, starflowers.* Every trip, we played a game naming wildflowers on the banks and at the station.

"What are they this time?" Mr. Jarrell quietly asked. "The wildflowers on the bank."

"How do you know I'm looking for them?"

"You always do."

"I forget how you notice me."

"It's my job to notice everything."

"You should study painting. Could you paint my portrait, Mr. Jarrell?"

"With my eyes closed, Miss Essie."

"That would make for a messy portrait."

He pocketed his watch and buried his eyes in his newspaper.

I searched again out my window, the sunset fading. "White daisies and blue dayflowers," I said, yawning. "Delly calls them mouse ears."

"It's too late in the season for daisies . . . isn't it?"

I raised an eyebrow at his correction. "Who was that man with you? Santa Claus?"

"A friend." He rubbed his knuckles again, stopping himself as I eyed his hands. "Santa is an old newspaperman sniffing out gossip on one Katy Dale opera singer."

"Lord a mercy, what scandal could entangle itself with that dainty opera singer?"

"None—unless Katy Dale wasn't an opera singer."

"Really?"

"What do daises represent?" He looked up from his papers, his spectacles slipping down his nose. "Katy's suitor invited me to a poker game. The rest of my story is inconsequential."

"Scandalous. I've met the best and worst in New York and, to my dismay, privy to the choicest gossip in Lil's parlor by consequential guests."

"Hmm, why you need my protection? I should introduce you to my Santa Claus so he can make his paper's deadline and write a choice gossip or two."

"Um-hmm. Mr. Jarrell, you squashed my future inquisitions of your *friends*."

"Lil insists you're somewhat of a savant. I say this with all sincerity."

I laughed. "I understand complex subjects. I absorb knowledge and understanding, and since a child, God gifted me with an insatiable curiosity."

"At last, something in common. You don't wait for answers. You seek them out."

"You had a scuffle. Why you rub that fist; a hint of violet rises on your cheek."

He sat taller, giving me a side-glance; he smiled too. And for the first time, his eyes took me in, as mine did his. Sudden warmth tickled my arms, my stomach. I looked away. "Miss Essie, I taught you well the art of observation. You'd make a fine lady Pinkerton."

I plucked the flower from my hair and pressed it into my diary. "You have blue eyes," I blurted. "And you asked what daises mean on our last trip—innocence."

He removed his spectacles, glancing at me, out my window, and back to his papers. He looked much younger than I remembered. Blond streaked his sandy hair as Evie's. Copper speckled his eyebrows and stubble on his chin. The sun kissed his cheeks, his nose slender as Evie's Uncle Augustus. *Evie mocks your nose, Mr. Jarrell.* I suppressed my smile. *Delly warns a blush on a man's cheeks means mischief.*

"You're fixated on my eyes. They're gray," he said, bothered. "My mother is proud I have her gray eyes."

"No." I leaned in closer, squinting, trying to distinguish their coloring. "Evie would insist . . . cornflower blue, as Westland's sky and James's eyes."

His neck inched back. I caught myself almost touching his nose and spun away to the distraction out my window. "You've noticed James's eyes?" he asked.

"Haven't you? One can't help noticing James's eyes. A blue lake swims in them."

"I haven't noticed a lake in James's eyes but wondered at the gold in yours."

I almost kicked my flower. "You look different on this trip. No Stetson, dust on your jacket's shoulders, yet shoes polished, and if you twirl the dangling middle button on your vest any longer, it's going to fall off." I glimpsed the silver pistol at his side. He never carried one before. Nerves jostled my stomach at the sight. He tugged his jacket to hide it. "No, it's something else." I lightened my manner.

He dismissed my spotting the pistol and glared at a man walking toward us. He angled his body, shielding mine. The man passed. Mr. Jarrell snickered at my hand, gripping his.

I removed it. "Since when do lawyers carry guns?" I whispered.

"I shaved my mustache," he said, failing to answer. He grinned and relaxed into his seat. I exhaled, doing the same. "In time, Miss Essie," he whispered. "Now, back to the vital question of my shaved mustache, how did you miss it?"

"On the contrary, I miss your mustache very much." I spied his holster again.

His finger nudged my chin so he could look into my eyes. "We'll discuss the matter later," he said through his teeth. I nodded. "My father claimed my unruly mustache resembled gunslingers from the Wild West. Mother claimed a bride-to-be wouldn't approve."

"And do you have a bride-to-be, Mr. Jarrell?"

He waved to another fellow and turned to me with a grin. "No. I am hopeful now that I've rid myself of the hindrance. I hear you're no longer engaged?"

"Our trips have become more intriguing . . . and chatty."

"You haven't answered my question."

I buried my head into my diary, folding my torn page. He left me alone, rustling his papers. My finger twirled the curl at my cheek, and suddenly, his fingers untwined mine from the strand, curious for my answer. "Be careful, Mr. Jarrell, on what you hear. It is true. How could I not answer, you trapping me and sitting this close?" I leaned in and whispered in his ear, "That gun you're hiding has made me nervous."

"Do you wish me to leave?"

"No . . . not yet." I dabbed the sweat off my brow again. "Thomas will marry in time, but not to me." My eyes shifted from the page, catching his blue eyes again. He folded his newspaper and tucked it into his satchel. "It is strange, Mr. Jarrell. Time has caught up with us. I'm far from that frightened girl, and you no longer appear as my elder."

"It took you two years to look at me, don't you remember? I wasn't much older than you when I escorted you on your first trip."

"I was nineteen, scared, and eager to know everything."

"I was twenty-five, a wreck with the responsibility, and caught hellfire from Lil for your haggard arrival in Richmond. Despite her gossip, I didn't play poker in Danville."

"I overheard you tell a friend you were headed for a high-stakes game in St. Louis."

"You've never said a word," he said, impressed.

"My first trip away from that plantation feels like decades ago. A time I don't relish remembering, yet, Thomas goads me to relive it in every speech. Write a book, he says, describing the horrors I strive to forget. It would help his career, you see."

"Miss Essie, waltzing around the truth isn't my forte. Thomas is a fool for demanding you relive pain for profit." He stretched to look out my window. "White jasmine?"

White jasmine, sweet love. "It's too dark to see flowers now. You've taken to mischief more than Evie and fancy riling me when I rather travel under different circumstances . . . and alone." I lowered my voice, my wall repositioned.

"My apologies." The warmth of his arm left mine. He quietly organized documents and dropped them into his briefcase. I touched his hand. His other hand covered mine.

"Mr. Jarrell . . ." I swallowed my sadness. "Thank you for trying to cheer me. Jasmine?"

"Yes." He scanned the empty aisle and back to me with a sly smile, our hands fluttering away from each other. "White jasmine, but yellow . . ."

Yellow jasmine—passionate love. "Indeed." I withheld the temptation to rap his knuckles as one of my fresh students. Abigail turned around at my outburst. I bundled under my blanket to rest, still wondering why Mr. Jarrell had a gun.

4.

ESSIE MAE

The conductor passed, exchanging a curious look with Mr. Jarrell. A routine of secret signals commenced during every trip. Mr. Jarrell's slight nod to the conductor; we could socialize together for a while. A sigh and a slap on his leg, annoyance at an associate's summons, a warning. When he rubbed his knuckles and sat taller, a suspicious man or woman boarded. Mr. Jarrell seldom took his inclinations or anyone lightly. I relished trips when he bantered, relaxing by my side, ensuring an uneventful excursion, what I needed on this trip. He never divulged the threats. He simply watched me. But on this journey home, I found myself watching him.

"You're relaxed tonight," I said. "Uneventful, I hope."

"You've read about the train robberies. I rather you rest in your stateroom."

"Lil spoils me by renting such an expensive car. They wonder who I am, eyeing my fine dress, a black woman surrounded by luxury. Even the porter cannot hide his side-glances."

"Perhaps it's because you're stunning." Mr. Jarrell turned me to him, staring into my eyes with kindness. "You deserve Lil's gift. Now, I insist we leave. I will carry your rose to the safety of your room and answer your questions."

"That rose has four years of my sweat and work into it. It stays with me." Unashamed, I studied him now, the wrinkles in his brow, eyes glistening, the breath he held. "You're worried."

He darted his eyes down the empty aisle again, scanning the scattered passengers settling in their seats. "No one will bother you on this trip while I sit beside you. But come, let's—"

"Because you're white."

His eyes widen.

I gasped, surprised the words tumbled from my lips. "Mr. Jarrell—I . . ."

Quiet, he thumbed through our tickets, his papers. "That was incredibly unfair."

Anger flushed my skin, stopping my tears. I stared at Wren's golden hair, watching her sleep without a care in her mama's lap. I needed to run and hide in the shelter of my private room, as I was used to doing since my youth, hidden from a danger that only waited for me, hiding still. "I would like to retire to my room now. I'm sorry, Mr. Jarrell. You must understand, for years, I traveled with my eyes down, staring at a dirty floor, passenger's shoes, anything to hold my interest. Now I see. I will never look down again."

"You just did . . . at me." He remained sitting, unwilling to release me into the aisle.

I stared ahead, awaiting his next words.

"One may still be blind in seeing," he finally said. "A wise mentor taught me we see what we wish to see. Sometimes this saves us. Other times, it is an ignorant, reckless way to live and judge the world—people— around us. I have protected you on sundry trips, yet you know nothing of me. This is your prerogative. I do what I'm paid to do, and so, we don't have to converse if it upsets you."

Stuck in my seat, I picked up my rose, eager to rise. "Some railroads still exclude a black woman from the ladies' car."

"And others forbid the practice. Progress."

"Yes. We rejoice at every inch."

"Inches soon turn to feet, yards, miles. Mary Miles, a black woman, bought a ticket for a ride on the West Chester and Philadelphia Railroad. She chose her seat in the middle of the car, but the conductor, stating some rule, demanded she move to the back. She refused; the conductor removed her from the train. She sued the railroad company and will win."

His story surprised me, not his words as I had heard of the case, but the tenderness when he spoke, the belief in her fight. "Yes, a few brave black men and women use the courts to advance equality. I have no delusions equal rights for blacks will take years, decades. It's no small task to change the hearts and minds of men."

"You cannot change a man, only yourself."

His quote stopped me. "Where did you hear that?"

"Miss Katie," we said together.

I stroked my butterfly brooch, swiping my finger over its jeweled wings, Katie's gift. He admired it, snapping around to a porter serving coffee. I gathered my things, ready to retire.

"Concerning your poor observation I'm white." He snickered. "My blond hair and blue eyes present the assumption. What of my olive complexion? Don't squirm, Miss Essie. I'm teasing."

"All right, Mr. Jarrell. I'll play." I cradled my rose, settling back into my seat. "Chiding has evolved into a lesson in observation. You do have an olive complexion. I hadn't noticed before, but you are enjoying my embarrassment far too much."

"My grandmother was a Cherokee Indian." He tugged his ear, his nervous tell, relishing my awe at his confession. "I wish I had known her. She met my grandfather at the outset of the Indian Removal Act. In love, she hid at a neighbor's farm, the couple's son, my grandfather, hid her in a loft. She stayed behind as her family left."

"A heartbreaking story. I know nothing about my family."

"You will in time. Augustus and I see many cases of emancipated slaves searching for their family. A woman's former master sold her son and daughter before the war. She's suing to get them back."

"A black woman is suing a white man for her children?"

"It happened years before us."

"Sojourn Truth."

"Yes. She won."

"You help black folks? In the courts? You never told me this. Thomas believes most men in powerful positions move in guilt not—"

"Thousands, black and white, lost their lives fighting against slavery, including the loss of your friend Abigail's son, a Union, not a Confederate soldier. Be mindful the next time you sling your arrow; it may miss and penetrate the wrong heart."

His truth pierced me. I exhaled, studying him. He recoiled into his usual position: aloof and indignant. "You cannot deny you have advantages." I said.

"I was an orphan until age eleven or twelve. I cannot remember, and like you, rather not recall this time in my young life. A family took me in,

Augustus offered me a job, and as you, I learned fast applying myself to an education would provide the freedom I needed to take care of myself. I hadn't a reliable father or mother to teach me, and so . . ."

"You raised yourself."

"Do we ever? Adults step in, nurturing and destructive. An abandoned child grows up faster to learn the difference. Older, trust in the kindness of people takes time—if won at all."

Bedford Jarrell peered into the deepest part of me, one I hadn't shared in years. The only one I knew who could see so clearly was a blind man, Mr. Koontz, awaiting my visit as I sat here thinking of those old days sneaking apples from his trees.

"I hold firm beliefs but realize every day good people will fight for freedom for all men and women. I have not decided if Lady Justice is indeed blind. My misjudgment of you is what ended my engagement with Thomas. He's jealous of my bond with Evie and questions why I continue allowing Miss Lil to parade me in her high-society circles. In his words, I'm a sideshow . . . ironic, in the end that is how Thomas made me feel."

"Thomas has benefitted from the circles he judges."

"I'm afraid he will soon learn attaining power is not the dream; it is not what makes or keeps us free in our hearts and minds. We must live free without it. And if God so grants a position of power to fall upon us, we must carry it in humility, utilize it in awe, and wield it carefully guided by the One who appoints it. We are but the vessel; a vase cannot make itself."

"Hear, hear."

"Truce." I held out my hand in friendship. He shook it. "Enough talk of dire subjects. I offer you this gingerbread sold to me by a seller shouting a worthy song."

He devoured the hunk, making me laugh. "Delly adds browned butter icing."

"Nonsense, Delly's *never* frosted her gingerbread."

"She did for me last month." He folded his arms, smug, reminding me of Delly.

I motioned for him to wipe the crumbs off his chin. "Lord a mercy! You've beguiled Delly as Evie's William. Perhaps you do hold a special gift. Anyone who persuades Delly to change a recipe must be taken seriously."

"That's all I had to do to earn your trust?"

"Monumental." I savored the last bite of gingerbread, dreaming of Delly's. "Thank you for helping James with Miss Katie's estate. That's quite a stack of papers." The porter strolled past with a wink. Mr. Jarrell's eyes followed the man as he hustled down the aisle. "I shouldn't have said what I did earlier. I feel jumbled inside, an unwanted tug toward being someone I'm not."

"We all grieve Miss Katie." He fixed his gazed ahead, lost in thought. "I've never met anyone like her. Katie inspired me to change one heart and mind at a time, starting with myself."

Nightfall.

I searched for wildflowers in the moonlit fields. The landscape blurred in a silver haze.

He waited until I turned back to him and said, "We are all not like the men who hurt you, Miss Essie."

I bit my lip to keep from crying again. My tears fell anyway. Out of the corner of my eye, his handkerchief landed in my palm. "Mr. Jarrell, you're one of the few in this world who knows everything about me. Everything. I must trust you." I handed him the box holding my prize rose.

"You can," he said, without hesitation, clutching the box. "I'll see this is safe in your room and leave you to your view and quiet."

"I'll go with you ... so I don't get accosted when the train turns pitch-black in the tunnel. I hate the tunnels."

"When has anyone accosted you in my keeping—forgive me, Miss Essie, I didn't mean—"

"I understood what you meant, Bedford."

"Do you know these six years that's the first time you called me Bedford?"

"Then I suppose you should call me Essie, don't you?"

I looked at the horizon. The moonlight drenched the fields in shimmering gold. Silver halos drifted in the night sky past its diamonds. I wondered if Evie was dreaming under the stars.

5.

EVIE

Westland, where its willows hold secrets, until the night air sweeps through their leaves, scattering them in the wind and into our ears. Mama's last words chimed in my mind on the hour as a reliable case clock, no foreboding whisper—mischievous—as a riddle, enticing me on the chase to solve. I left my patch of dirt to visit a blind man who sees. A blind man who knows the secrets of the willows, yet, in all my years, I dare not ask.

Daydreams played inside the forest as I walked the trail to Koontz's farm. During the war, Delly said Koontz visited Westland often, but since my return, he hasn't visited once. Koontz was away for months, keeping his secrets buried deep in the ground of his heart. Dr. Hodge claimed Koontz had a chance to see, advancements in medicine, too new for an ornery man to muster faith in anything but old ways and remedies.

Halfway down the path, his worn wooden bench sat waiting. The creek's footbridge signaled it was close. "This is where you meet Delly." I welcomed the chuckle, the thought, as I rounded the corner past the gnarly elm standing guard at his farm's entrance. I tiptoed up the porch steps, missing his rusted, tinkling trap. "Why are you stringing this old thing?" I shouted for him to hear. I unhooked the trap, bells jingling as Santa's sleigh, coiling it on a footstool. A new table strewn with orange zinnias, yellow mums, and crimson roses awaited their vase, the ornate tabletop encrusted in gold flakes, seashells, and pearls. "Magnificent."

"Sneaking peeks at my gift for ya, eh?" Koontz called. "That's my best table." His voice sounded deep and soothing, stronger than I remembered. My eyes shifted to the window. He grinned toward the ceiling; slapping at his trembling hands, waving me inside his home.

I entered.

"Been too long, child," he said softly, rocking in his chair. He flipped the collar of his pressed blueberry-checkered shirt, stuffed a forgotten shirttail into his bibs, and tucked himself under the quilt Essie and I made for him years ago. Lemon blossoms and musk sweetened the air. His head crowned with a mop of wiry gray hair sprouting as a turnip. As if knowing, he smoothed it and scratched at the stubble on his chin. He closed his eyes and puffed a tune on his harmonica, buzzing and whistling, a gliding vibrato milking his skills for effect. The song found its gusto with a stomp keeping time his winded rendition of "Camptown Races."

Doo-dah. I sang inside, smiling at this ghost story turned fairy tale.

The blue and yellow patches of the calico fabric on his quilt danced with him. He paused and said, "Ain't ya gonna sing?"

"I don't like that song."

"Blarmey! You do too."

"It's blarney." I clapped instead. "But you mean hooey," I shouted over his music.

"Blarmey. Mean what I say. Now you're interrupting my musicality. Ya gonna sing?"

"No."

He shrugged, happily riffing his tune.

"Doo-dah. Doo-dah," I croaked.

An eyebrow raised, and with a final blast, he caught himself blowing a laugh. "No, child, you could never sing. Go on and fetch the brew I fix ya."

"What flavor today?" I licked my fingers and slapped the top of a sprout on his head.

"You know I slap ya back, I catch ya." I dodged his hands and raced around his rocker. "Hee hee. Delly's right, you sassing like that little girl way back when. Tea today be Katie's favorite: rose hips, apple, and orange blossom. On your mama's last visit, she give me two cans of what she calls sweetened condensed milk—sugar milk in a can. What a wonder. You go on add a spoonful 'cause you like all them sweet things." Tears knotted in my throat as I watched him snuggle back under his quilt, waving his harmonica, pondering another song. He sighed, sensing I hadn't moved. "I hear them tears a splashing on my floor I jus sweep. Come ahead." He offered his short, awkward embrace and nudged me toward the kitchen.

Cherished memories awakened at a whiff of musty wood and honeysuckle. His potion of lemon blossoms and musk sprinkled about him was enough to remember our first meeting. Delly's blueberry bread sat waiting on his table. I left it, him, staring outside at the apple cove, imagining little Essie daring to swipe the fruit. "Would you like a spot of tea, Mr. Koontz?"

"Huh? A spot of teeeeea. You ain't in London no more. Essie Mae talk like you now?"

"No. Tea?"

"Why you think I fix it? You ain't lose your touch to rile me. When James gonna come? He likes them tables I make. Say some lady want two more. I go on to the creek and find the gold flakes and pebbles myself. That one look pretty, don't it? Feels pretty. It do."

"To think, years ago you'd say nary a word."

"And nothing like womenfolk to teach a man to yap. Fancy my table or not, child?"

"Your best yet. Where did you find seashells and pearls?"

"Ah, that's my secret." He held his harmonica in the air, retiring it in his pocket.

"You're finding gold in the creek, too?"

"I smell and feel it. Nothing like the feel a gold."

"Applesauce. Delly separates it for you but you can still swirl a pan."

"Been smelling gold round here fore you were born. Your granddaddy knew all bout that. How ya think I've been living here alone all these years?"

"I just imagined you were rich." I handed him his steaming brew, watching the cinnamon stick bob inside his cup.

"Whooeee! Still spewing them whoppers." He passed the cinnamon stick under his nose like a fine cigar. "Curious thing . . . the smell a cinnamon makes me feel like a boy. I be a fidgety young'un like you."

"That's a long time ago, hmm?"

"What'd you expect? Fine, Evie. Fine." I missed him, this mysterious, odd man with a lifetime of secrets and stories. For months, my days encompassed caring for Mama. Every minute was hers. He could fill some now, he knew. We sat in our usual quiet, slurping tea, inhaling the aroma. Just when I settled, enjoying a peace, I missed; Koontz would holler a question to begin our banter, an argument, a tall tale. "You gonna stay, child?"

His question surprised me. He usually asked about James, Bo, Delly, fishing, or if the creek was on the rise. I said nothing. Delly's bundle of cinnamon sticks and cloves hung at the window. I spotted something new, a stack of books on a table near a new sofa, the flowered sofa from Mama's parlor. "When did James bring you that settee? Those vases and dollies were my grandmother's."

"Hope ya don't mind. Bo bring em. Said Miss Katie wanted me to have that sofa and them fineries from her parlor, womenfolk always trying to change a man with frills and fluffs. But I welcomed them. I did. Why, me and . . ." Mr. Koontz slumped over, nearly dropping his cup in his lap. "Katie jus give us them pretties, that's all."

"Us?"

"Dagnabbit, child, *me*! Me." He deflated, clutching his cup, taking a slow sip. "Need to put my flowers I got outside in the vase she give me. Ain't seen Delly near a month."

"You know why. I hear you shooed away visitors. Tom McCafferty and his wife tried—"

"Don't need to meet no wife a Tom McCafferty."

"I'm ashamed you would say that."

"Why? Gotta right to dislike folks; people hate me for years."

"Mr. Koontz, you're not an easy man to get to know. If they knew you, they would like you. We all need to stick together. Folks are out there trying to do us harm."

"Them *folks* been out there my whole life. Most of em dead; I'm still here." He slammed his cup and saucer down on the table, nearly breaking them.

I took them away, curious at his manner. His chest rose and fell, trading the music of his harmonica for a steady wheeze. "Are you feeling well?" I asked. He threw off the quilt and walked to the sofa, patting the books on the table. I hurried to him, placing one in his hand.

"This valley has its own strange history," he said. "Strange history, strange folks. We don't want secession. I don't begrudge Mr. Tom go on marry a black woman. Ain't my affair. If I did, would I have Delly come all these years taking care a me?"

"No. I'm sorry."

"Nonsense. Ain't your burden to fix folks. They either fix themselves or stay away. I stay away mostly." My hand rested on his, shaking. His spindly fingers tickled mine away. With a hoot, he led me to the sofa and handed me a small green book embossed in gold letters that read, "River Wild." "Folks won't come round here no more. I see too it. Some menfolk think I'm nothing 'cause I can't see or work my land. But them men don't realize blind men see sharper than sighted men most times."

"It's true."

"Bes remember this old man knows all the secrets of this land, tending and otherwise." His tone frightened me. I never relished visiting when Koontz took to one of his moods, a strange, unsettling nature that often surfaced as I departed, careful to suppress it when I first arrived. "Yep, you're thinking. I see deep inside ya. I feel it, hear it, 'cause that silence heavy. But you won't ask me bout things, but that Essie Mae, I suspect she will. It bout time."

"For what?"

"Women wanna know things, that's all. And tell Delly to stop preaching bout cleanliness next to godliness 'cause I think most of them whitewashed folks filled with the dirtiest secrets. Why don't she ever say clean your insides." He tousled his hair, grinning.

"Lil's been visiting you, huh?"

"Well, you tell Delly, I know how to do my ablutions." His lecture was a distraction from his shaking hands, his way to settle his mind and body, unsettling me at the same time. "And I use lye soap not roses or mint— Delly picked all my lavender too." He pressed his palms together. "Lady soap . . . no ladies here except you. And you ain't—"

"Mr. Koontz."

He caught himself. His hands stopped trembling. "Child?" he asked, as if forgetting me, his place. *He's getting worse*, I thought. *The spells and temper.* Fear deepened the wrinkles in his brow, softening him. He reached for the book again in my hand, stroking the gold letters. Sighing, he stole it back and placed it on the table as a priceless work of art. "Old folks have a world a stories and learning inside, that's all. You young folks don't care to ask bout em. Think ya would, so you won't make the same mistakes we dream a warning you bout. That's why we tell our stories. That's why."

"What stories?"

"You don't know bout me, child." His thin, frail form rocked in front of the window. The way he searched outside made me wonder if he could see, but he was relishing the sun's warmth on his face. "Life I had, things I've done. Sometimes, bes we don't know, got no right to know. But I suspect, soon, Essie Mae come round asking them questions, too many . . ."

"Secrets. That's the second time you've mentioned it."

"Pollywash. Jus can't wait to see her. Ain't seen that child in a long time. Long time. Hope Essie brings me her roses."

"You mean hogwash?" I joined him at the window.

He snickered to himself, found his youth, and grabbed my hand, pulling me outside to the porch. "Pollywash. Mean what I said."

Gruff today. I stayed quiet until he wanted to speak. The codes of our relationship over the years, eggshells, a prickly cactus, a rosebud, too, open to trust and love in time. "I've watered you for years, Mr. Koontz," I whispered.

"And I stink too. Stink, stink, stink." He left me a moment, shuffling back inside.

I sat in the rocker Bo made for Delly, fondling the smooth round handles. Though she would never admit it, Delly enjoyed sneaking away from Westland to sit up with Koontz, sharing a sip of sour mash, trading yarns until the wee hours. Bo painted the porch, too, the same gray-blue as the rails Mama disliked at Westland. New white posts held up the battered porch roof and near the barn a large new birdhouse. *Bo's handiwork.*

A pumpkin patch showed itself around an old willow, a new bed of yellow and purple roses, and a white picket fence Mr. Koontz wrote about when I lived in New York. I received only two letters from him, Mama helped him write. I spotted his fall flowers: orange chrysanthemums, yellow pansies, and purple asters. Delly had taken good care of our friend.

I felt him breathing over me. A shallow breath and a soft, slow sigh. His milky blue eyes watered. "Polly," he said, his voice breaking. The small, green book with the gold letters teetered in his hand. "My wife." He pressed his lips together, smug as if silencing himself. "You didn't know I had a wife, did ya?"

"No, Mr. Koontz."

"My beautiful darling, light as a feather, but she could do the work of three men." His laughter fell upon us as welcomed rain. "I'm twisted up now, but I used to be a handsome, able man. I sport the goldilocks like you and the cherubs on my cups and saucers. I remember em."

"Goldilocks? Delly says you're still handsome. She likes you, Mr. Koontz."

"Fiddle-faddle. When you gonna call me River? Stop using old man Koontz. Don't mind the disrespect when you a sassy girl, but now you full grown."

"River."

Rose tinged his cheeks and forehead. His grin followed mine. He kicked up his heels, flashing another burst of youth, plopping back in his weathered rocker. "My Polly invented her own language. Pollywash, flippy, what she used when my temper on, and snickety pickety, when I fuss at her cooking. Polly baked the best apple pie loaded with cinnamon and brown sugar and the crisscrossy crust on top, ambrosia."

"Delly makes a delicious apple pie with cream."

"Polly pie don't need no cream. No, ma'am. Flaky crust . . . heavens, girl, Polly pies win blue ribbons. Miss me a good barn dance and a fair. You make it for me, that apple pie, hmm?"

"We'll bake one this afternoon. I hope you'll reconsider and come to Mama's party."

"Why? She ain't there." He hung his head at himself. I kept mine high, though I wanted to scold him and run away as a child. "Forgive a crazy, mean old cuss, dear Evie. Got no right a shooting my mouth like a slingshot. Don't mean no harm."

"Forgiven. I want you there, River. We all do."

"Can't promise," he whispered. "Bet it be fine. A fine night for a jig."

"Did Polly know my mama?"

My question soured him. With nowhere to run, he shuffled across the porch. "Winter's coming early. Delly say Essie's roses catch the blight. Did what I could. They'll come back."

The years proved kind to River Koontz, maybe because his secrets hadn't caught up with him until now. "Did Polly know Katie?" *As if asking him a different way would prompt an answer. Tricks sometimes worked on him, tricks that may banish me forever, tricks that may unlock truth and trust, his heart.* I yearned to know more about Mama and her youth, the stories she wouldn't share. River was blind, but by the intensity of his stare, I thought, for a moment, he could discern my thumbs twiddling.

"Why'd ya remove my tinkle trap?" he asked. "You want me to get hurt?"

"Who's coming to hurt you?"

"You."

I swallowed my tears, tugging at my sleeve. "I see today is not a good day for a visit."

"Never is, but you still come."

"You can't do that. You can't drive me away like you do the others because I have just as much hurt inside me, old man."

"Delly's right, you're acting like a child, spitting out words you know nothing bout. Now you sit there and be sweet and kind and filled with sunshine likes I know ya, you hear."

"I won't unless you answer my question."

"Why do ya think you have a right to come here and change a man? I don't ask for it. Some say it's no gift living alone, but I say 'tis! I know how, that makes me some kinda special. Ain't no harm in loving a quiet life, especially when you had a lifetime a folks yelling in your ears, folks take away your sight, steal your wife, folks promise cures for money, cures that mean nothing but loss. Don't need none ya but you still come."

"You're wrong. You need us otherwise you would've given up years ago."

"And there 'tis . . . that's why you're here 'cause that's what you wanna do: give up."

We left our corners and retreated to our rockers. I couldn't take the sound of his rocker squeaking a loose slat. "Move your chair closer," I ordered.

"Don't know if I wanna."

"Then I'm leaving. I can't stand the noise."

"You ain't the girl I know. My Sunshine who walks for hours in the quiet woods, past the trees you name that give you sparkle and life, the girl who sneaks, stealing my sweet apples in my trees. So soft, I fall asleep to giggles and footsteps crunching in the leaves. Can't sleep without em."

Tears streamed down my cheeks, their salt washing my lips, my chin. I sat, looking toward his orchard, seeing little Essie zigzag around the trees.

His chair scraped closer to mine. At my sniffle, his rough fingertips swiped a tear off my cheek and smoothed the ribbon twisted in my braid.

"Pink ribbon today, child? I feel it's pink, jus a shimmering in that gold hair a yours. Rappyunzel."

"Rapunzel. I always wear pink."

"Katie's favorite color. River knows, child. I know. Feel it deep in my soul that hurting."

"I barely remember me as a carefree girl."

"Broken you were." We sighed together. "Yes," he answered. "My wife knew Katie when Katie was a wee girl. Katie don't like sewing no more than you."

I turned to him, pleased, drying my tears, toughening up, as he required. "But Mama was an excellent seamstress and sewed the finest quilts and dresses."

"'Cause my Polly have a soft way and teach her. Little Katie enjoy being with us more than at Westland. Katie's daddy always working, expecting her to be somebody she ain't."

"Funny, that's how Mama raised me, why I ran away from Westland."

"Good to have schooling, but Katie's daddy push her hard. Alex disapproved of the company Katie keep with—well, that was years ago. Polly always wanted a daughter, suspect why Katie give me that sofa. One day, little Katie invited Polly to tea. Polly was gone all day. Your Grandma Ruth made the lace doilies for Polly. Polly gave Ruth the pink vases one birthday." He paused, rubbed his lumpy knuckles, and caught his breath as if a weight dropped from his shoulders. "Would like to smell Essie's roses again. Shame 'tis."

"What did Polly and my mother do?" I edged closer to him, praying he would answer. "I'll place your new table in Mama's parlor. Would you like that?"

"Fine, child. Fine." He clapped and sat on the edge of his seat, signaling an end to our visit. When he settled back, I held my breath as he contorted his face, remembering. "Polly used to tell Katie stories, and your granddaddy, the big-wig round here, Alexander Wilcox, talked my wife into writing a children's book using her made-up language—good memories I don't think on for a long time, child." He felt his pocket; his harmonica wasn't there to save him; he rubbed his chin instead.

"Don't stop."

"Polly painted the drawings, too," his voice quivered. After a hard swallow he continued, "I fetch my secret gold and travel to Sweet Water to buy colors for her so she could finish her book a wonder. Stars, monsters, rainbow valleys ... Polly don't do chores nor baking for months till she finish."

"My grandfather encouraged your wife to write a book?"

"Alex won't let go a the idea. He asked Lil, Lil's husband, and that Augustus lawyer to get Polly a contract for her stories. Polly gonna sell books all over, they say."

"How wonderful. Did she?" I remembered his green book with the gold lettering.

He smiled, proud, eyes to the clouds, holding the book to the sky as if thanking her. "Child, such a thing I never did see," he sang, giddy. "I watched my Polly dream and write em on paper and laugh and smile, always snickering at her secret stories. I wish I woulda told her more they be fine stories. I was too busy. Too busy."

"She knew. A woman knows the man she loves supports her, even in the quiet."

"Hmm." He moved to the edge of his chair. I readied to leave. He said, "Yellow fever come through here." He held himself a moment, rocking steady. "We fine, till darling Polly went off to Sweet Water with Ruth."

"My grandmother."

"Yep. Little bookshop selling Polly's books and Polly wanna see it in that shop window, though she'd been traveling all over seeing that green book with the gold letters sitting on the shelves and in the window displays. It bring a light to Polly I ain't seen in years. All 'cause she drawing and telling yarns."

"It was everything to her. More than stories, River; they were her heart, a contribution to her family, purpose, standing on her own ... for a moment."

"Yep ... all that I suppose. I suppose."

"What happened? Was her book a success? Is that it ... in your hand?"

"Why I don't tell stories. Too many questions an old man can't answer."

"River."

"That's what she named it, *River Wild*, nothing to do with a river at all. A fidgety boy fights giants and feeds imagined beasts apples to tame em. That story stuffed with all kinda nonsense, but in the end, it's a story bout loving, loving them things so different to the rest a the world maybe they look like monsters 'cause ain't nobody take the time to understand em. Most a the world blind to what's real. Most a the world." He passed me the book, holding onto it a second longer, releasing it into my hands.

"*River Wild* by Polly Koontz."

"Polly come home sick. Never saw a life taken so fast. Never wanna see that again." His back stiffened in his chair, but he stayed, clearing his throat, his tears. "Forgive my sad memories, Evie. Ain't a good one in the bunch."

"That's not true. It's a lovely memory, and you shouldn't hide them from yourself."

"I don't, child. I see em play every night fore I go to sleep. They tickle my insides, waking me up come morning. They calm me when my body shakes and my mind's black as midnight. But I don't trust another soul with em . . . they my treasure gold—until now."

I hugged Polly's book into my chest, eager to read it. "I'm honored."

"'Cause you battle through a war, too, girl. Here you be still standing. I used to see, Evie." He surely heard me catch my breath at his confession, grinning at my surprise. "Now, some days, I see shadows and light. One morning I saw color, yellow and blue, would like once to see the green grass, hills, and trees. I don't tell nobody that neither. You may think you in blackness now, but you walk in this house and bring the sun, and I'm thankful. Now . . . we gonna walk to the creek today or not? I got the itchy feeling today we find gold."

"Will you tell me more about Polly?"

He stood and patted the book in my hand. "For now, I'll let her tell you bout herself. It's been a long time since I heard that story. You go on read whilst we sit a spell at the creek."

"I would like that."

"I'll get my coat, Sunshine."

"Grab the blueberry bread you're hiding in the kitchen," I sassed as I knew he wanted.

He slammed a door, hooted, and rattled pots in the kitchen.

My fingers stroked the gold lettering on the book again. I peeked inside.

For River, my love, my dream.

6.

ESSIE MAE

Bedford followed me to my stateroom. I caught myself relishing his firm hand nudging my back, assuring his presence, his body almost warming mine. We walked into a traveling hotel room. Royal blue velvet curtains framed the windows; a sage duvet and pillows covered the bed. A lavish sitting area arranged as a parlor boasted a chandelier, Persian carpet, and a sage tufted sofa and chair. Bedford lifted my potted roses out of its box and placed it on a marble stand.

"Yellow jasmine. Hmm." I held the crystal vase, sniffing the sweet fragrance.

"Ah, yes, yellow jasmine means . . . passionate love? A jest I pray you will indulge."

"Jasmine reminds me of Miss Katie." I closed my eyes, taking in the floral perfume, my memory. "When Miss Katie hugged me, she held me tight." I set the vase down, examining my rose. I saw only the night passing by my window and glimpses of moonlit fields and shadows.

Bedford tipped his hat. "Enjoy the rest of your evening."

"Stay."

He turned around, surprised.

"Dinner? It's the least I can do after our joust."

He nodded, signaling to the porter. "You have your own lavatory with hot and cold running water," Bedford said, impressed. He tipped the porter, dismissed him, then lifted the dinner tray's cover, unveiling a steaming platter of roasted chicken and potatoes. He wiggled his eyebrows, presenting dessert next: vanilla cake topped with strawberries and cream.

I shook my head, amused by it all. "Miss Lil spends her fortune as if I were her daughter." I stroked the lace napkins on the table. "Please, sit."

Bedford slipped off his jacket, revealing broad shoulders, a slim waist, and the silver gun at his side. He caught me eyeing the pistol and hid it in a drawer. "I'm exhausted," he sighed, joining me. His eyes crinkled as James's pleased for the first time we dined together in private. "Lil has no children to spoil. You and Evie are the only family she has left."

I forgot every bit of etiquette Lil taught me and stared at the chicken, my silverware. I sipped my coffee, watching Bedford attack a drumstick with his fingers, pleased to do the same. "Lil's fortune won't last forever. Evie writes Lil wishes to whisk us back to Paris."

His fingers brushed mine as he handed me a glass of wine. I savored a taste, pushing aside my coffee. "I assure you; Lil will live in comfort the rest of her days."

"I'm relieved."

He removed his spectacles; the ones depicting not a stealthy detective, but schoolmaster, the strict chaperon reprimanding Evie on our first trip. He toasted me, guzzling his wine.

I scattered the string beans on my plate as a fussy child. "The biscuits need Haley's strawberry preserves." I rushed to my satchel, holding up a jar to his smile.

"Is there anyone you don't worry about?"

"Since James's last letter, I worry about us all." I slathered my biscuit in preserves, enjoying a bite. He gave me my moment, eyeing the jar. I handed it to him. "Bedford is an unusual name. Are you called by any other?"

"Many. An unfitting conversation. My full name is Bedford Sebastian Jarrell."

I turned inward again at the thought of a full name. I never had one. "I rather Sebastian. Yes, Sebastian sings. It sounds mysterious."

"Mysterious? No one calls me by Sebastian, but you may—in secret."

"Is it a code name?" My wide eyes made him chuckle as I leaned in for his answer.

He searched for spies and whispered, "Perhaps. I was named after my grandfather."

"How noble."

"Granddaddy was a swindler—a tale for another trip."

"Sebastian, that white streak in your hair . . ."

"My mother used to say this white strand of hair was a streak of lightning from God at my birth."

"A birthmark? Applesauce." I laughed at myself. "I haven't used that expression, applesauce, since I was a girl. I've uttered it repeatedly this trip."

"Trips home do that to us; the child inside reminds us they're still there."

"I like that, Sebastian. But . . . when it isn't a good childhood, they remind us of it often."

He raised an eyebrow. "Sebastian, huh? So, you've settled on my code name then."

"Because I'm the only one who uses it. Does Katy Dale have lavish quarters?"

"Gaudy, an oriental motif with fringed lamps, Japanese panels painted with geishas, red velvet wallpaper, and a leopard blanket decorates her . . . sofa."

"Sofa?"

He pushed his empty plate away, eyeing my uneaten dinner. "I investigated an incident," he said. "A society thief with social standing but no money to support it invited herself to a wedding disguised as an opera singer. After dinner, the proud papa displayed a ten thousand dollar check for the bride, his daughter. The thief replaced the check with a forgery, cashed it, and the opera singer disappeared."

"Katy Dale?"

"Perhaps." He smirked, impressed. "Too much time had passed before Papa realized the check was a forgery, and Katy Dale no longer travels south."

"And you played poker with her suitor—your man?"

He waggled a finger at me. "Beware of the person who shakes your hand and lingers. The first descent into a life of criminality is picking pockets."

"Your journalist friend with the white whiskers and the portly gentleman pacing outside this door, aren't acquaintances. James hired those men for me, didn't he?"

He held his answer, checking his watch, the door. "Not James . . . Evie."

"Evie was right. You're no attorney." I nodded to the drawer where he hid his gun.

"I am . . . with a specialized skill set. Lil insisted. Evie agreed."

"This private car was frivolous enough." I cleared the dishes in a huff.

"Essie, this was Katie's wish for you. She wanted you to return to West-land in a grander way than when you left."

"Return in luxury to devastation." I sat, sipping the warm wine he served spiced with honey and cloves. "Guards?"

"No one knows we protect you." He refilled his wineglass and added a splash to mine. "Evie and James are bent on your safety."

"My kidnapping occurred six years ago. James cannot pay for bodyguards forever. Guilt will drive them all into ruin. Guilt took Miss Katie." I stared at my fancy dress in the mirror, blue satin, yellow fringe, the butterfly brooch on my collar, lady's extravagances Miss Katie and Lil ensured I possessed. Was I the doll in their dollhouse now, as Evie was in her youth? Ugly things washed away with powders, perfumes, and fineries. "I should be grateful. I am." I breathed in the jasmine and plucked a flower to save.

"The authorities still look for the man, Trailer."

My breath skipped at his mention.

"And one other, Essie. With Katie's death and the recent threats . . . James believed it prudent."

"The fires?"

"No. Letters. I cannot say anything further, not here."

"Who am I to them? What do I know? I've lived my life in the shadows. When the war ended, I spoke truth to those who needed to hear it. I will not hide away ever again."

"You're right. I know everything they did to you, little about you. Young men six years ago, now marry, seek political office, and build businesses with their families."

"And I threaten their ruse of redemption."

"You present a reminder of unatoned sins."

"I was told they died . . . in the war."

"Grant's men and the kidnapping—"

"Nothing I care to dwell on ever again. Six years is a good time away. I have changed. The girl they raped isn't me."

"But now you return."

I slapped my fan on the windowsill. He walked closer. "I've longed for a hillside these six years, to lose myself under the stars and forget. None of the men who violated me come with me. I left them in the dung in that barn, a pile of forest leaves, under the trees . . . in a grave."

"Essie, I understand. However, it is why Miss Katie, before her death, hired me to ensure your safety now. To end this. I will find Trailer and the man sending threats to James."

My heart raced, throat closed. "I cannot breathe."

I pulled at my dress, no longer sapphire, the blue of Evie's night sky, but the brown cotton frock I wore the night Evie and I walked the road to Ashland. I wanted to rip it off. The chains rang in my ears, the old African, Sebastian's muddled commands.

"Deep breaths," he said, his hand on my back, leading me to a chair. "Deep breaths. Another sip." I desired no wine. His hands soothed mine; they rattled inside his palms. I needed to feel the gentle touch of a gentle man. I needed to know it existed.

I slipped from his tender touch. "I'm fine." My posture stiffened, shoulder blades pinched, a deep breath to settle my heart. I left the dark, studying the man before me.

"Are you all right? Essie," he called, bringing me back.

My hands slid out from his. He examined me, slowly taking a seat on the sofa, watching me, always. "The recent train robberies, do you know about them?" I asked. He tousled his hair, puzzled, catching my hands shaking, and understood. I downed my glass of wine. The memory of this elixir warmed me. I relished the dizziness, my mind blurring to the past. "I have told my story to strangers, the horrors of my past, but I wish never to feel ashamed again when speaking with you about those men."

"Essie, when you stand on the stage and speak the truth to all those people, you portray more bravery than I could ever muster."

"Thank you. What of the train robberies?" I asked again, shaking the solemnness from the room. I held up my wineglass; he poured me a smidgen more.

"Weeks ago, masked bandits robbed the safe on a train to Indiana. Weeks before, they robbed a train from New York headed for Boston, half a million dollars."

"Those were Pinkertons you spoke with before the train departed, the cowboys with the burly mustaches as James." He nodded, relieved I came back to him, lighter. I knew well how to bury my thoughts.

"Missing cornflower blue eyes, I'm afraid. You've been away, Essie. Fear or poor judgment invited an entanglement with Westland during the war.

Katie did her best. James was unaware of her dealings. As long as Katie was alive, enemies left Westland alone."

"And me. Someone was extorting Miss Katie?"

"I have my suspicions, but I need to learn more."

"I hold one secret I can never tell." I searched his expression for clues. He appeared gifted at hiding such tells, or he knew nothing of my relation to Evie. *Sisters*. A secret I vowed to keep since I was a child. Now if those trying to hurt Evie, James, and Westland found out a black daughter might inherit a portion of the estate, James would never garner the support he needed to make it thrive. Miss Katie's acceptance, and my presence, was an invitation to burn it down. "Keeping me safe is part of your *more*, isn't it? But why should someone wish to hurt me now? The man who hated me most is dead."

"John Winthrop is dead, and James killed your kidnapper, Grant. Other men who seek fortunes and vengeance live. James did what he had to do during the war to save his family and Westland. They hired me to untangle a web to keep you and Westland safe once and for all."

I slid next to him on the sofa. My old view: his shoes, the floor, watching my tears drip and scatter the dust. My fingers stroked the sofa's arm, ending in the swirl of a wooden rosette. I lifted my head, gathering myself, searching for more rosettes in the woodwork. *Four in the window trim, two at the top of the door.* "Luxurious," I whispered. "Six years ago, I cowered in a cage chained as a feral dog by men who stole me for one purpose, the color of my skin, which made men rich. I never imagined sitting with a detective, sipping mulled wine in a luxurious railroad car with velvet drapes, a soft bed, fine dining, sleeping to the rumble of a journey home." I exhaled my fear, staring at him now.

"Evie's right. You're always—"

"Making speeches." He offered his handkerchief. I took it, dabbing my tears. I offered it back. He tucked it into my hand.

"You're here, Essie, because you had the strength, courage, and will to live. Those memories will not stop you from . . ."

"Living free. You know much about my family at Westland, and they are my family."

"I've studied them a lot."

"Studied . . . an odd word."

He shifted in his seat. "The detective in me, not a skill you turn off."

"Why not witnessed, observed, or watched?"

"Ah, Essie Mae, Lady Pinkerton."

"One never knows."

"One never knows. The Madeira wine works its magic."

I leaned back, relishing the heat racing through my body. "You warmed it and added honey and cloves. Miss Katie was fond of making this on Christmas Eve."

"Yes."

"She would invite us to sit by the fire and speak on the greatest gifts in our life. James always added humor to the evening."

"Ruining it with a salty joke or two?"

"Yes. Thank you for the comfort of that memory."

He rose and retrieved his gun, watching me as he put on his jacket and headed toward the door. "Rest, Essie. We won't reach the next stop until morning. The rest of our trip is—"

"Uneventful."

"Quite."

I saw him to the door. "Good . . . a full blue moon tonight."

"Perhaps, tonight, you will sleep and dream."

"When I sleep, I do my utmost not to dream. Good night, Bedford."

"Sebastian."

"Sebastian."

7.

EVIE

River Koontz filled his belly with the best apple pie I ever made. When the sun soaked the tops of the trees, I bid farewell. Westland's fall splendor welcomed me home. Sun and aqua sky banished the gray day; garnet, topaz, and amber sparkled in the trees.

A golden halo flickered underneath Mama's favorite willow. I gazed up at the tree as if it were Mama, seeking answers, her. Gold enveloped the branches. Feathery wisps brushed my hair as I walked inside Willow's home. I closed my eyes, soaking in Willow's song, its whisper. "It's been so long." My lungs filled with the essence of autumn and my ears, a ripple and ping of leaves, a waterfall of grain. "Willow, do you carry secrets like River?" I swiped a crust of dirt off the trunk's middle, revealing a carved heart with the initials *A&R.* "You do."

A glint of gold in the soil caught my eye. "What's this?" I brushed the leaves and sprig of pink flowers aside and wriggled the key from the dirt, gold and square as a charm on the bracelet Mama gave me. "Where did you come from?" I checked my bracelet for a missing trinket.

"Child," Delly called, startling me.

I pocketed the key and scurried back to the side of the house near Mama's magnolias, pretending to busy with my strawberry patch.

Delly bounded down the porch steps with unexpected zeal. She searched the willow, hands to her hips, and found me, quickening her march. The war and our years apart took its toll on us, but not Delly. She still marched with a swagger, holding her strong shoulders and her Bible high. Her plump cheeks forced a grin amid grief and at my sass, and one Sunday she even pinned a daisy in her short salt-and-pepper curls. "Evie, James don't want you walking alone to Koontz's right now." A sack swayed in her hand, a blanket tucked under her arm. "Dinner's ready. James ain't sleeping again and ask me to fix breakfast. Whole house upside down."

"River misses you. He wanted me to tell you."

"River! That old man jawing bout them old days; I warn him not to, ain't the time for it." She caught herself, hiding worried eyes into the quilt she cradled.

"Mama's not the only one burying secrets."

Delly's eyes fluttered to the trees. She rubbed her forehead, sighed, and studied me with her sad brown eyes. "I see ya don't get far planting strawberries." She dropped her bundle in the grass. "You sneak inside you mama's willow, too. Listening for stories?"

"Rubbish." Delly shrugged and sauntered away. "What stories?" I called, stopping her.

"That old man tell ya stories? Delly know all the good ones, that the truth." Delly held my wrist in the air, watching the charms on my bracelet jiggle. "Shucks, you go on sneak you mama's Christmas gift for ya, too, supposing you give Essie Mae hers when she come."

"Mama threatened to cut down that willow. Why?"

"Miss Katie say the proper home for weeping willows be near the creek so they can grow as tall and wide as they please. Katie's daddy tell her stories inside that tree, and it's where I catch her sleeping under the stars. When Katie a girl, she think that old willow made a gold the way the sunset shimmer in the fall leaves."

"Then I'll never cut it down." I rose, eyeing Delly's bundle on the grass, her.

"Child, that's the bes thing you say all week." We locked arms and strolled to Mama's tree. "This weeping willow drop a lush canopy a leaves to hide under. Alex and Ruth used to hide in there, escaping parties."

"I never noticed the carved heart with their initials."

She patted my arm, relishing our closeness. "You ain't never been curious bout Westland's past, but that's what young women do, busy dreaming and planning futures."

I grabbed Delly's hand, navigating inside the tree. My fingers traced the heart as I pictured my grandparents, young and in love. "Why would my grandparents hide in here?"

"Mr. Wilcox had the bashful sickness something fierce. And that man wobble like a newborn foal—can't dance a step. Oh, child, I turn plum red, the shade a Ruth's gown, on the night I catch em in here carrying on like young lovers." With a moan, Delly's memories ended.

We walked back to my strawberry patch. I spied James watching us from the front porch. He waved, hung his head, and moseyed back inside the house.

"When you two gonna have words?" Delly asked. "James waiting—sorrowful sight . . . him sitting in the parlor alone with his memories bout you mama."

"And drinking."

Delly's spine stiffened. "Trash talk, no good thing to be thinking nor saying. That man miss you mama something we don't understand. We all lose the cornerstone a this plantation, and we fluttering away from each other when we needs fly together figure this all out."

"James and Lil ask too many questions I don't know how to answer."

"I scold em it too soon. Don't know why a body gotta rush away a life when it gone, trousers on fire searching for papers on Westland and what to do next."

"I thought that's why Mama hired Bedford."

"They playacting busy bees like you. Don't need to make sense right now I suppose."

"Little has ever made sense at Westland." *Unspoken words,* the remedy my family applied to our broken hearts. After the war, when I returned to Westland, a lifetime of unspoken words burdened us all. "Why didn't Mama ever talk about my grandparents or her childhood?"

Delly looked back at the front porch. Mama's chair rocked at James's parting touch. "It look so sad without her," she said. "Katie don't like talking bout when she a girl. She carry the guilt, 'cause she never stood up to her daddy and married you father to please him. When she a young woman, into mischief with that Isabel; Mr. Wilcox send Katie away in anger, thinking it for her own good. Katie and her daddy almost don't mend things fore he pass."

"Mama married my father even though she loved James."

Delly scrunched her apron in her hands anxious to leave. "Ain't fitting talk for today but that partly true why Katie marry you daddy. Bible say, you know a tree by its fruit, well, the love between Alexander and Ruth bore fruit that last a lifetime here. Katie find it in time . . . love . . . long enough to know what the real kind be."

I smiled, wondering what Delly knew about romantic love, but she knew plenty about the love that counted. I plucked a gold leaf off her shoulder. She winked and stuffed it in my pocket. We stared at the tree, waiting for each other to speak. I wasn't used to awkward silences with Delly. But she swayed and wrung her hands, patient, skittish, unwilling to let an inch of distance fall between us. "Do you think that kind of love still resides at Westland?" I asked.

Delly's soft hand slipped into mine. "I know it do. Gotta dig deep, tend it, water and nurture; it'll grow again."

"Essie says a plant's roots tell if it's good or bad. I have wondered what the roots of my family hold." I spotted a yellow ribbon curled on Mama's stone bench. *How did that get there?*

"Funny thing bout trees, they grow with us. We watch em sprawl in the sky, and—"

"They watch us."

"Um-hmm. Li'l girl I know used to tell me stories bout the trees. Time back, she say she gonna write em down for old Delly to read, used to preach to me bout having dreams, too. The kind you set you hands to do, not them flimflamming ones in you sleep. Jus hope she find some again . . . dreams whilst she here."

"I'll try, Delly." We searched the trees again, looking for the cardinal flitting between the branches. My eyes shifted back to the ribbon. *Delly's mischief*, I decided. "Why didn't you ever mention Polly or grandfather encouraging Polly to write, or that Koontz even had a wife?"

"Ain't my stories to tell. You a wiggly young girl never had a mind to ask."

"I'm asking now. Mama left a lifetime of stories—she won't ever tell."

"This day come too soon." Delly sighed. "You got questions I can't answer, won't ever answer." A fierce protection for Mama resounded in her voice; her watery eyes bore into mine.

"I have always known I'm not the only one burdened by what Mama leaves behind."

"Every night I pray you let go a that dark past and see the light shining on today."

"Will you share more stories about my grandparents, how grandfather built Westland?" I stretched to see if Mama's chair still rocked. The wind obliged a second longer.

"Come inside. I'll tell ya all the stories you want."

"Delly . . ." She closed her eyes. We listened to the rustle of the leaves. A pile whirled under Mama's rocker. "Maybe we should cancel the wake—all those strangers."

"You've been gone five years, Miss Evie, them strangers be Katie's neighbors and friends and have a right to say goodbye." She squeezed my shoulders, plucked a hanky from her pocket, and dabbed my tears to toughen me up. "Party what you mama wanted."

"I don't like goodbyes."

"No, you never did. We blessed than most. House still standing, land yours for now."

"What do you mean?"

"Jus reminding you a what we still got . . . more than most. You mama wanna party, and we go on do it like she plan, though nobody round here got the mind for it. We don't even suffer through them rations. Two counties away, them scallywags stealing homes and acres, and we got that barn raising at Mr. Tom's 'cause the old one in a heap a ashes. We all holding on to each other, Evie, that's how we survive, that's what you mama wanted."

"I've lived most of my life surviving." I stared past Delly to the horizon. "The fog over McCafferty's place resembles smoke smoldering."

"That's the third fire round here, finally get the law to come to our quiet valley."

"Quiet for how long?"

"James say them evil men know what they doing. I pray Essie Mae arrives tomorrow. Oh, child, we all tired a waiting."

"Trains are always late." I fanned out the roots of a strawberry plant. Delly asked for it. I dropped it in her palm.

"Firm crown," she mumbled, examining it. "Yellow roots, this a good plant. Ain't time for planting. Why don't you finish planting them tulip bulbs up the drive?"

"I didn't plant any bulbs."

She scratched her head, confused. "Suppose old Bo planting them surprises. Lord a mercy, he don't keep track a colors. Katie always like her flowers jus so."

"Remember when Mama asked me to paint her holding tulips? I didn't have the skills."

"That's what a loving mama do, believe in us more than we believe in ourselves." She handed me the strawberry plant with a gentle pat.

I snipped the frayed roots as a lock of hair, quiet.

Delly exhaled at her effort, bending to my level. "My rickety back," she grumbled. A smudge of dirt from her fingertips tickled my chin. She wiped it off. "What a lady doing in the dirt for anyhow? Least you mama use a blanket when she planting." Delly shot up, making me snicker, flapping her checkered quilt across the grass.

I smoothed it to her sniffles. "Mama's quilt for her picnics with James. I helped sew it."

"Sure enough, them crooked stitches all yours."

"You scold I'm no baby, but here you go coddling—"

Delly stomped her foot, folding her arms in a huff. "I take care a five girls on this here plantation; you all still girls to me." Delly's voice cracked; a scrim of tears watered her eyes. She turned away; swiping at them, miffed they fell in front of me.

"A fine day for thinking," I snipped, hiding my tears. "A fine day . . ." My touch on her shoulder slid into her tender embrace.

"I know, child." Her strong hands squeezed me, ending in the swirl on my back I missed. We rocked together; our sobs rose and fell. Her fingers lifted the hair swept over my face. She needed to see my eyes. I buried them back into her shoulder, soaking her dress with tears.

"We too old to fool each other now, acting like grizzlies so we hush them sad tears away. But they gonna splash and drip like the rain we need till it time for them to pass. That the truth. No harm missing you mama, no harm at all." She set me upright. This time, I wiped her tears. The grin I needed to end my day, shown in selfless love and joy.

Delly wriggled away, grabbed her sack, and handed me a corn cake wrapped in an embroidered napkin, Mama's. We admired Westland, James's new barn, Bo's painted front porch, and as if reading my thoughts Delly said, "Katie don't fancy Bo's blue railing. Liked the cedar she did."

I traced the embroidery on Mama's handkerchief, noticing a loose thread.

Delly stole it, poking the stitch. "Sewing lessons you hate as a girl do you good to fix this." Delly slapped my hair, smoothing wisps across my cheeks. I closed my eyes, soaking in her laugh. "Prissy Miss Lil strutting round the house clucking bout my cooking. Them dresses and hats she wear too fancy for round here. She won't last a month let alone move here for good." Delly clapped her hands over her mouth. "Now, why you planting . . ."

"Delly." She smirked, eyeing my hands on my hips now. "Lil move to Westland? She never told me."

"Maybe we all tired a being scattered like them dandelion fluffs you blow in the fields when you small. Come now. Ain't time for planting strawberries; they ain't gonna grow."

I stopped her from cleaning up my tools. "I want to show Essie Mae I planted them; surprise her." A cool breeze made me shiver. Delly placed her shawl over my shoulders. I bundled underneath it, sitting back on the blanket.

She scooched beside me. "I'm too old popping up and down on this here blanket, ain't no young girl like you picnicking with a beau."

"I'm in no mood for your poking around about William and the wedding again."

"I stopped asking. Katie used to sit here, and I catch her dwelling on things that don't matter no more 'cause ain't nothing we can do bout that sad past we thinking on."

I pulled Delly close, resting my head on her shoulder, taking in the scent of gingerbread and lavender. "How do you know I'm dwelling on sad memories?"

"One thing I know bout Westland girls, you pretty, bright eyes can't hide when they sad. They get to glazing and pouting and soon them li'l pink lips follow. Gonna hurt a long time missing you mama. But Evie, you gotta life, jus turn twenty-five, you a grown woman."

"Old spinster, huh? Our first birthday apart . . . without Essie."

"Yet, all my Westland girls stay children in they mind till something come knock the sense in em to grow up. Life do that, but you mama kept you hidden here, like Katie's mama do her. So you ain't full grown in your 'motions, excepting that bossy peacock Lil."

"Motions?" I asked, chuckling. "What's motions?"

Delly rose in a bluster, lifting me off the ground with her. She gathered the blanket, shoving me onward. "Don't you start with that schooling. Emotions. Time for supper!" Delly walked away, paused, and caught me back at my patch of dirt, planting more strawberries.

"I walk around Westland feeling eyes on me," I said. I hadn't the stomach for food or talks with James and Lil regarding Mama's last wishes. And I surely couldn't do any of this without Essie.

"James hired his Indian friends, all kind a folks sneaking round our land now."

"Did James catch those strange men prowling at McCafferty's again?"

"He said soldiers lock em up. James say we safe, we safe."

"I don't trust Tom McCafferty, but I wouldn't wish him harm."

"Bes get used to Mr. Tom, Miss Evie. Neighbors gotta stick together in hard times. Bo say James do business with him now, the only way we survive. You jus don't like Tom 'cause he knew you no-good daddy."

"John Winthrop wasn't a father to me. No man ever was."

"Bes not let James hear you say such words. James a loving stepfather. I know you right bout John Winthrop, but it ain't a day to be dwelling on them evil times."

"Isn't it?"

Delly's eyes widened, warning me. Mama spoke of keys to happiness, setting truth free, but Westland hadn't a door for any such key. Trust is what I longed to visit Westland.

Delly retied her apron, looking toward the barn.

"Stop worrying about me, Delly. It's expected . . . memories of my father race in my mind now." I offered her a plant and trowel.

Delly moaned and stretched, bending to the ground, taking the trowel with a snicker. "Oh, child, my old bones snapping and popping like we walking breaking sticks in the forest." Her strong hands held mine, guiding them over the strawberry's roots.

"You haven't planted with me since I was a child."

"Um-hmm. Even then, you got no mind to garden. You picked the driest earth at Westland. Lord a mercy, never mind it's too close to the house."

"I'm no child, Delly. You shout it every day."

"Do not," she said, taking my hand. "But you can be for a while since you here." Delly's hands fumbled the plants from mine, sneaking me another grin, wiping her tears. "Don't throw the soil on the leaves. Leave the crown right here so the blooms come. We pluck em off that first season. Then the tendrils spread out like so, and we tuck em in the ground for the daughter plant between em." I stared at her handiwork, the roots knotted and twisted like a ball of yarn. She scattered the dirt at her feet and rose with a groan. "Tamp the soil down so the water don't puddle and drown it. That's how we do it next spring."

Delly forgot her age, kneeling back beside me, eager to plant the next two. As she handled the tender roots, planting for me, for the first time since my arrival, a spark of hope ignited in my heart, a hope Westland could be my home again.

"Next May," I whispered, "rows of green leaves crown the soil. A row of ladies curtseying in green satin gowns, eager to dance under the sun and stars. In time, ladies blossom bearing flowers and fruit."

Delly stopped planting and grinned. "Plump red berries shine as the blush on you face when the menfolk flash winks you way. You give old Delly hope, reciting pretty words a what you picture here next spring. Means you see yourself here, too. You can't hide or stay away forever, right, child?"

"I could try."

"Then that be the shame you mama never count on, me neither. We raise ya to shine and shine some more till you get tired a dancing. Even if that fiddle stops you keep dancing till *you* say it time to try something else. But you ain't trying, Evie. You ain't doing nothing but letting sorrow and the pain of you daddy steal you song, you sunshine. I know what you fighting inside you mind, 'cause time back, Delly fight it too."

"Westland looks different to me now."

"Take a good, long look. It won't be here forever . . . neither will we. Go on. Clean up. You jumpier than a grasshopper at a square dance. And don't you get mad when Essie Mae scolds us for planting strawberries when frost coming."

"Sometimes we need to attempt things that don't make sense to anyone but ourselves."

"How bout after supper, you walk old Delly to the creek. We sit a spell on the bench Mr. Koontz made for you girls and you teach me to catch some catfish."

"Night fishing? Lil will shout, ladies wouldn't dare. I feel all a child today."

"Old Delly feel it too. Scared as the day I first skip up them porch steps to meet you granddaddy. But that a story for another day. You go on be whatever you dream. Years ago, brave girl teach me that. And Miss Lil might surprise ya and come fishing too."

I paused, spotting another carving on a magnolia tree: *A & R. Alexander and Ruth.* "I wonder what Mama's doing right now?" I clawed at the dirt again. Before I knew it, Delly's firm hand squeezed mine, wobbling in the grass next to me.

"Lord say no more tears in Heaven, but I suspect He go on let Katie cry a happy tear or two 'cause she watching her daughter shine brighter than the sun. That the truth." Delly's shadow swayed and paused, bending over to retrieve the ratted roots of two strawberry plants strewn across the grass. "And I'm gonna ask bout William. Woulda been a grand sight, two weddings at Miss Katie's Westland. Old Delly fancy a handsome man to care for her. Rub her feet come nighttime, whispers in my ear, smelling lemon and cedar on his cheek from the cologne I buy him for Christmas." Quiet, she helped me up and brushed herself off to my burst of laughter. "Who say old folks got no dreams a spinning in they heads."

"Romance?" I laughed. "We better get you all decked out for Mama's party."

"Lord a mercy, old Delly with a beau, squeezing my behind in a fancy green dress with the crinoline." We belly-laughed together, tears splashing our cheeks with joy. "That's my girl, laughing be good medicine for broken hearts. Good healing medicine." We bounced toward the porch steps, stopping to scrutinizing patches of dirt ready for surprise tulips. "Bet old Bo planted red tulips all them love books you got him reading." Delly chuckled. "Lord a mercy, child, what am I gonna do with a love mush giant got no mind for chores but courting."

"I have a solution—Delly and Bo. Bo and Delly."

"Oh, child, you set my blood to boil gonna burst my heart with that trash talk."

"But it's good to laugh, isn't it, Delly?"

"You mama do the belly chuckle at that one for days, sure enough."

"Sure enough."

James greeted us, tickled by our manner. "*Halito*! Evening, Sunshine."

"Come, child, Mr. James ate up all the bacon, but I saved ya my fried taters."

"I knew I smelled em. Evie deserves a treat tonight." James kissed my cheek. A welcome surprise. Our awkward distance, since Mama died, inched closer together.

Guilt, regret, and grief visited Westland. Delly was certain to remind us: love and laughter still thrived.

Delly rushed into the house at Bo's call, leaving me standing on the front porch. James ambled down the drive, stuffing his hands into his pockets, kicking dirt as a boy. He paused at the tulip beds and smiled. I wondered if he had planted them. I wondered. *Did you plant purple or yellow?* I wanted to ask him. I left him alone, hungry for the first time in days.

8.

DELLY

Driest summer in years, now all that come to Westland be the rain. Thunderclouds over Evie who can't stomach a bite a food or the thought, her mama ain't gonna hold her again. And sprinkles and mist on old Delly's heart 'cause I can't stop my crying. I catch Evie fussing with her mama's letter, crinkling and crackling that paper like a squirrel rooting in the leaves, she reading till the pages worn. I know what it say 'cause that's the last letter Katie lemme read fore she send it.

I can read.

Essie Mae say, till my eyes squint and focus deciphering them letters, reading set ya free. I jumble my words and ciphers, but I know how to count my money so the peddler can't swindle me, and add the worth a the gold nuggets Mr. Koontz sneak in my apron pocket for helping him make his seashell tables and housekeeping. I can figure I need sixteen green apples and four yellow to bake four pies for a barn raising. Best thing: I read fast the Good Book myself so nobody can tell me it say something it don't.

Now, Delly don't go thinking she wiser than the preacher, but when he say the Bible say God helps those who help themselves, I say, "I can't find them words nowhere . . . and I spend years a looking." Then preacher man say, "Well, it jus mean we to care for ourselves. *Then* God . . ." And I stop him right there, humble-like, mind you, and say, "But, preacher, we can't help ourselves sometimes, that's why we need God."

Then his face turn the shade a wrinkly, overripe tomatoes and he say, "Well, God . . ." Twisting his eyebrows on his forehead like I do the braided bread, forgetting his answer 'cause I'm staring back, humble-like, mind you, waiting. He squint some more, and I squint back, spotting a twig sticking outta his brow ready for a sparrow to perch. He finally say he got more learning on me lessen I wanna take his place and preach on Sunday. I say, "Sure do. God give us gifts, and we need go on and use em. But I suppose sometimes we do help ourselves—can't go walking for miles less we wear the right shoes."

Now, my mind's flip-flopping like Evie's—what we all do now without Katie setting us right with her wise words. So I get quiet, a sitting under Katie's magnolias, 'cause I feel all love and peace on that li'l stone bench. With the whispering breeze, I hear my answer: "I wouldn't have to believe in nothing if I could do for myself first, and the only thing keeping me free: believing."

Evie losing that belief, and I promise her mama I do all I can to help her get it back.

Miss Katie gimme schooling in secret back when. She break the law to teach us, and neighbors whisper bout her—till they need her help, especially after the war. This li'l valley counted on Westland. Westland's cotton days long gone, but Katie know how to make a profit and help our neighboring farms do the same, but only if they used hired labor. She rally folks against leaving the Union, too, and her sister, Lil, spark trouble with her mischief politics and funding to end the war. Lil say *sabotage*—word sounds all mischief to me. A word moaning like a hurricane wind, 'cause Lil say, we'll reap a flood a trouble if the wrong folks find out.

After the war, Lil's politicking save Westland. We prove to them Union soldiers we loyal round here, so they don't take our land. They ask Mr. James a bushel a questions. Bedford say siding with Yankees invite trouble to Westland after Katie pass. Katie be our guardian angel, least that what we believe till James find out her secret dealings.

We in the jubilee after them evil days gone and peace fall on Westland. Katie wield a magic, and we living in our own world. She always say most folks won't never understand her sitting quiet with me on the front porch or teaching me to read, heeding my warnings like I'm her mama, and Evie and Essie Mae loving and protecting each other as sisters. These the secrets we carry 'cause hateful folk try to tear us apart. "They fear what's different," Katie said. "They won't take the time to understand." It take years a pain and healing, forgiving and learning, to build a home at Westland. "Remember, Delly," Katie said, "some men hold the highest learning and the most ignorance."

And most folks don't know Westland birthed in love. They see the big house, fancy parlor, and roses, but they don't know all the pain we suffer, too, more than a heart can hold. We all show the scars, but Evie and Essie Mae best at hiding em.

Now I watch over Evie. We don't do a good job when it count—when Evie a girl. Thieves: Grief and Regret steal our hearts for years—Miss Katie's, forever. When a body can't forgive theyselves for things they wish they shoulda done to stop an evil thing . . . that a poison kill a mama faster than the plague. The blight come in all kinda ways; it be a slow, long theft a Westland's prettiest flower.

Miss Katie say one key might help Evie move outta the past for good, one old key to a garden gate far side a Westland. A garden nobody set eyes on till Miss Katie took ill and our girls come home. Evie find a comfort there, so I tend it for her. But all sorts a ghosts a prowling round Westland trampling on roses and dreams. Some days, I think they real.

Black folk I know, even kin far off, say I needs leave Westland now I'm free. But where old Delly gonna go?

Westland my home.

Bo ain't leaving neither, especially 'cause Mr. James give him a good profit from this idea Bo had on selling hay instead a cotton—Johnson grass, best feed for cattle round. Whoooeee, crazy idea might work. Essie write to me bout Katie's orchard and selling the fruit, and I peddling my flower soaps. When the war end, all kinda plans and dreaming stirring at Westland to lift us outta that sad past. Not from Evie—now that James a widower, he spout crazy talk he gonna sell Westland. Don't rightly know what Mr. James up to so I say, "Mr. James, the only good that comes from secrets, is when we go on and tell em."

"Pluck em up by the roots so something good can grow."

"First time in months you say something that makes sense."

James get mad and race away like we all doing now 'cause it prickly round here missing Katie, and all them unspoken, angry, blaming words. Miss Katie fond a planting roses all round Westland, Essie Mae, too, but something else a growing in this black soil—secrets—and it's time old Delly dig em up, that the truth.

A flickering flame.

Gold and amber shimmer in the parlor, one gas lamp, no fire, and Mr. James sipping whiskey in the dark. I spy on him like Evie, and sniff the air like she do, too. Bourbon, that sharp cedar and vanilla make my nose twitch. Tobacco chased away my fresh roses. Katie don't let him smoke inside, but it's his home now. "You want I should fix you something to eat?" I asked.

James startle a bit then slid back down on the sofa, puffing his cigar. Don't mean to glare, but I feel my eyebrows crinkle at the sight. I stood quiet. He snickered, put out the cigar, and drink another slow sip. "Should've smoked outside," he said. "You had the parlor smelling of roses for Essie. Open the window and bring in more flowers. Sunrise, it'll smell sweet again."

I don't say nothing at first 'cause tears balled in my throat. "Mr. James, you go on do what you please. You hungry?"

"It's too late. I promise I'll eat up all the breakfast."

"We ate it for supper. But I make my pancakes. That'll please ya, hmm?"

He gulped his drink, smacked his lips, and slunk back on the sofa, sprawling his legs over the pillows Katie made him. I slid them under his legs and sat on my rocker with the fancy rose cushions. I let myself dream a young Katie hugging her mama's pillow, the one with the pink roses and gold fringe. Katie used to giggle when I tickled her toes with the tassels. "Fine blue moon tonight," I whisper, thinking it good the moonlight chase the shadows from James's face. "Good you roam outside today. See ya checking the hay again. You worried bout them fires, Mr. James?"

"Just checking." I barely heard his whisper.

"Lord a mercy. Turn a field a cotton overgrown with weeds—"

"Johnson grass."

"Into a meadow a hay that'll make the money."

"Those weeds, darlin', are Westland's gold."

"God give us the land and He give us them weeds . . . gold, huh?"

"That crop will fetch more money than cotton. We cut the grass right before full bloom, makes a tasty feed for livestock, plenty of protein. Now we sew oats."

"Why, Mr. James, you like all that farming. Never woulda thought."

"I never would've thought many things, Delly."

Woulda set my hands to my needlepoint, stay with him all night, quiet, but this the last time we alone fore Essie Mae come, and I got words to say and he ain't drunk like last night, so I go on and say em. "When you gonna tell Evie?" I asked.

He stood up, scuffed his boots to the window, and opened it, inhaling the cool night air. "Not a magnolia blossom on the trees," he said, "but I still smell them, her."

I waited, silent, my heart breaking at the sound of a grown man's tears. That's the way it 'tis the last few nights, and I feel bad for using the tough love now.

I look away to my needlepoint: roses and a garden for Essie Mae's home-coming gift. I can't see nothing but James's shadow floating across the floor back to the sofa. He sat on the edge, staring at the rug; his boot trace a vine and flower in the carpet. Then he eye me for an answer, for something, words he know we need to say.

He bristles. So do I. We sigh together, ready to swallow our medicine 'cause it time.

"Mr. James ..." Now my tears fall, and we let each other sniffle, respecting the love we lose. "I know you hurting worse than a body can stand, but you—"

"I don't know where to start, Delly."

I can't do nothing but look out the window searching for the moon smiling inside maybe Katie ask God to let it shine for us tonight, casting that morning glory blue, she love, across the floor and sofa. "Start with the truth bout Katie and Westland, and that we all better fight like grizzlies to keep it. You gonna let that man, after all these years, jus walk in here and steal it?"

"Evie's not interested in Westland. She's afraid to stay, afraid she'll want to." James threw up his hands, pacing in front a the fireplace. "I can't compete with Paris and parties, and all the things she needs as a woman. I don't even know how to try."

It's better staring at my needlepoint than him, so I go on and work it. "I come in here 'cause since Katie die, you die too." Don't like saying that word, *die*, so when I says it, I think, *go be with the Lord*. "You gimme leave to speak my mind?"

"Always."

"Most folks think we crazy here the way we tend to each other. Odd family, I once heard Mr. Koontz say. Oh, he don't know nothing bout them girls. But family . . . least we that, ain't we? That's what Katie make me believe, girls, too."

"Nothing's changed."

He give me comfort 'cause we don't know what'll happen after Katie gone. James jus losing his way 'cause he lose a woman he wait years to love. "Been working at Westland forty-one years," I said.

James dally at the fireplace, twisting my lavender bundle I made for Evie to help her sleep. He smiled, fondling the white ribbon, and handed it to me like a long-ago suitor. His handsome, sparkly eyes make me grin, but it ain't no time for grinning.

"Katie jus four," I went on. "Mr. James, I still dream I'm skipping up them squeaky porch steps for the first time, tall and straight in my fine brown dress, finest my mama could sew. I see Ruth, prettiest white woman I ever see, raven hair and shiny skin, blushing pink blotches on her cheeks. She sings, 'Welcome!' high and happy, and smiling, holding Katie's hand."

James listening, but his eyes scan the room, avoiding mine, and the bourbon make him numb and sleepy.

"Katie's older sisters, Sally and Lil, hiding and giggling, but Katie brave." I chuckled. "Katie don't know me, but she jump in my arms, and I drop my traveling case, and squeeze that child, rocking her. Don't think Mr. Wilcox like it, but I heard him laugh. Never told him that."

"A sweet memory," James said, gaping at me like a lost boy.

I sucked in a deep breath 'cause he don't wanna hear no more crying. "We be few working at Westland then, but we weren't no slaves. Mr. Wilcox hire me. My daddy lemme work. Daddy played the fiddle and learned his numbers and reading. Bet ya never knew that."

"No, I didn't." The smile in his voice pleased me.

"I mostly forget my young days, but lately, they splashing round in my mind, flipping outta the water like a hungry catfish, snagging my attention. Katie always gimme leave to speak my mind, no matter the hell she take from that man. John Winthrop bring the devil's hell to Westland." For first time, in a long time, my voice shake, and it feel like that catfish flopping in my belly now. James quiet, looking out the window, searching for the moon.

"Evie wanna believe Katie blind all them years, me too," I said. "Katie a brave, bold woman running Westland, but fearful and blind when it matter. Guilt steal her away from us. But how can we judge that woman living with that man. We can't . . . 'cause we weren't standing in her shoes." James stay quiet and sip his whiskey. At his sigh, I rise to leave, but he stop me.

"Finish, Delly. Please."

I sit, catching his bloodshot eyes now. "My daddy woulda never believe his child come here living large and happy. Took one man to turn this heaven into hell. One man, James."

He come and caressed my hands and said, "Those days are over."

I soften my stare. "How many times we say never again?" We listen a moment to the frogs and crickets. "So much hate and dying; my family scattered like seeds. I prayed every night they find good soil to blossom in. I pray, but I don't wanna leave. Westland's my home."

"Delly, we've been listening to your wisdom for years. Katie counted on it . . . so will I."

"The day that fire try to eat up Essie's garden, Katie say she see a big yellow cowboy hat through the trees—you know the only damn fool who wear that hat, too."

James said nothing. He shuffled back to the window, inhaling the air, too crisp now it make him cough. He eyed the fireplace then me. Don't need no blaze with the glare he give me, boiling my blood and chilling my spine all at once. "Katie also thought she saw a woman, Delly. Even she couldn't trust her mind or sight at what she saw that day."

"She ran, Mr. James, 'cause she see somebody. Sickness take her heart, not her mind."

He slammed his palm on the windowsill then stumbled back to the sofa, stomping that vine on the rug he trace fore. The wind howled. I let him stew as I closed the shutters. "Why you go on make things harder than they need be?" I asked. "Westland be Evie's home, she jus confused, been away gallivanting in Paris salons with Lil. She hurting like you."

"You won't take no for an answer, but it's her life."

I fell in my rocker with such a moan; James rushed to my side. I shooed him away with a chuckle to his sly, handsome smile. Oh, the years don't make James no old man. His hair more silver than brown, like a fox, that burly mustache a his speckled with gray, but he as handsome and strong as the day he first strut in this house a puffing his chest and boasting his cowboy bunkum. His blue eyes glistened. Katie say they ocean eyes; I say, they a pale blue as the moon them two lose theyselves in falling in love.

He gazed at me now, smirking at my dreaming, and for a second, I see the happy man we miss. In a blink, his frown back. He lit another lamp, standing there thinking, yipping at the burn to his finger from the burned-out match. "I respect your history here, Delly. I do. But Westland was Katie's dream, not Evie's."

"But it could be we show her it worth staying and saving. Nobody round here trying. We make it through the war. You gonna give up now?"

"In every nook and corner, I see Katie."

"Good."

"With all the hell we've been through . . . maybe it's time we moved on from this place. Go North." He circled the parlor, stroking the tables and armchairs like they Katie. His fingers smooth the daisies on the quilt she made for me. He unfolded it and tucked it across my lap. "If it wasn't for William, soldiers would have burned down Westland," he mumbled.

I set my sewing aside, nestling under my blanket. "Fire ain't out, James. Long as them ashes red, fire ain't dead. You go on back North, but that fire will chase you all."

"What are you saying?" He hissed a rattler's warning.

"John Winthrop's barn burn down five years ago, but them memories flaming in that sorrowful girl's mind."

"Which girl?"

"Both. Maybe I go on poke my nose in you business 'cause I love you all like my own. Years a secrets too much weight on old Delly's soul. I ain't gonna carry em no more. My daddy say, a true secret, the one aching in you soul, be that secret only you know. But a secret between two folks—one always gonna hold it above the other 'cause that the sad nature a sin twisting you up in knots, holding a power over you."

"I've been trying to figure if this place could ever survive without a secret. No good comes from poking at snakes. You might find a rattler. Best leave it alone."

"Why, that's what I call ya, James the Rattler! Oh, but you ain't no snake, jus hiss like one. Evie can't figure her place here no more." I eyed his whiskey glass. James don't drink much in front a me. Ashamed to say, I wanna join him. Somehow, he read my mind like them circus swindlers Evie write bout, and poured me a sip. I drink it too.

"Leave or stay ain't my decision to make," I said. "But Evie needs to know the truth."

"Some secrets are meant to stay in the dark." Now the drink sapped him, the silly, tired way he look and stagger. He flopped on the sofa again like a rag doll, folded up and done.

"No, sir." I said. "No disrespect, but the dark only good for three things: saying my nighttime prayers, dreaming in them stars, and sleeping."

"What good will it do now?" He asked the ceiling—Katie, not me. "Dark good for drinking and thinking, now go on, lemme have my quiet."

"You bes be careful 'cause Evie think you acting like *him*. You know it."

His piercing blue eyes grow dim. "I never wanted harm to come to her."

"Oh, James, we all hurting, but that child . . ." Another moan. I rise to leave, but his big hand pat my arm, so I stay. He lost and broken the way he lean against the mantel staring at me, waiting for my words. "Katie kept Evie a child. Lil coddle her during the war. That's why Evie refused William. She don't trust in a good man's love. We don't think she'll ever marry."

"Afraid of living . . . stuck . . . suppose I spent years that way."

"She a child in a suit a armor. Evie and Essie deserve the truth. We *promised* Katie."

Used to all kinds a pouting and tantrums from my girls, but James set his lips flopping outdoing em all. "Take it back," he said, pouring another drink.

"What fool words you spilling now?" I tucked a pillow behind his head and covered him with my quilt, his eyelids already closing.

"I'll never be like him—I'll never be like my brother."

"Good you know it then. Enough drinking." He handed me his glass. I hid the bottle while he rested. "Tomorrow." I grab my needlepoint to go outside and dream under the moon.

"I heard you tell Evie, God turns mourning into joy. Wondering when that might be."

"Go on preach to mean old Delly."

"You smell like lemon blossoms in the moonlight."

"Hush. I act mean and ornery 'cause ya make me."

"Almost forgot. I have something for ya." Sly Mr. James pop up outta sleep like the Jack-in-the-box I hide from Evie one Christmas 'cause it scare me to pieces. James dug behind the pillows and set a silver box in my hand, displaying Katie's favorite brooch.

"No, sir," I cried. "Evie should . . ." I moved that li'l pin fore my tears splash on the gold vines and pearl flowers. "Katie wore this every day since you two married." He clear the tears in his throat, coming in close smelling like musk and tobacco, pinning it on my collar. I rush to the mirror, petting the gold flowers. "Oh, Mr. James, my swollen eyes can't cry no more, but here you go making em pour like a sprinkle a rain."

"Best kinda rain, too." His smile bring peace to my heart. "Katie wanted you to have it," he said, still grinning. "So do I."

"Feel like I'm wearing both you hearts, twined and blossoming."

"And stop worrying," he said, yawning, sprawling on the sofa. "I'll handle Evie my own way. You talk to Essie Mae. You have truth to tell her, too. I don't envy us."

His words singe my stomach like a hot coal frying that catfish. Sly Mr. James beguile me with flattery and his foul whiskey for courage; my warm bubbly feeling turn cold and flat. I got my own truth to tell Essie Mae, truth I fear will send her away for good.

"Yes, sir," all I croak.

I leave him sulking in the dark so I can do the same on the front porch in Katie's rocker. I rocked, searching the stars like them girls wide-eyed wondering, feeling a child myself, and the tender squeeze of a man who love me once. I don't think on him in years, but it pleasing. *Samuel.* And when the breeze blow, I savor Katie's roses. "Katie girl, all you romancing with James on this here porch seeping in my memory. I miss you, child."

My bones ache warning me a storm's brewing—storm already come.

I looked out at the yard, picturing Katie dancing barefoot in the grass, free. Her hair's down like we fancy, flying behind her, painting gold streaks in God's heaven. Though He shine, for a second, I think God let Katie sparkle, too.

"I see you," I whisper, dreaming. *Sitting in Katie's rocker again, so I might feel her one last time and watch her rocking next to me. Don't tolerate a quiet house much now. Don't like it at all.*

"Katie was so proud of you, reading and writing in that diary."

I hopped up and sat in my own rocker, the wood soft and weatherworn. "You know I can't take the fright like I used to. You stalking in the night worse than Evie."

James slid in Katie's rocker, fondling the arms wishing they were hers. "I'm sorry, Delly. I might be glad when the house fills with guests tomorrow, a little too quiet around here now."

"I don't mean no harm, jabbering in the parlor. Evie needs a daddy and you it."

"When she looks at me—something different glistens in her eyes."

"Child got a whole lot a thoughts bouncing round in her mind. Like when her daddy die, now John Winthrop walking round here living 'cause she let him."

"I should've never let her go to New York. She needed a doctor, someone to talk to."

"All them Indian ways—where's you courage to be there for her now." I push my boldness 'cause Katie ain't here to hush me when I need hushing. "Evie reminds ya too much a Katie and all you miss. Guilt too."

"Might be right about that. Too much damn guilt hovering over this place." He held up a ruby leaf, grinning, showing me its heart shape. He set it in my palm. "It'll be nice having the girls home. Bedford will have much to tell us."

"Lil yammering bout taking Essie Mae and Evie to Paris again."

"Might be for the best." James stood, taking in Westland, pointing to Katie's favorite places, ending with the stars. His shoulders stiffened like his body get a chill. He sat in Katie's rocker again, stroking his mustache, thinking. "Evie looks at me like this is all my fault."

"She's thinking the same thing, that you blame her."

"Evie knows I love her. I'm no man of soft words like Katie. Katie is Westland. Who am I? A worn-out cowboy made for roaming. The thing that kept me in one place . . ."

"Katie."

Midnight chill soon chase us inside. For now, our rockers creak with the frogs.

"Who's going to take care of Westland if something happens to me?" James asked. "How can I keep us safe? How can I sleep, when wolves stalk us day and night? I have to end this." His final sigh scattered his hope across the floor. He stood, pushing out a soft moan, stretched, and bid me a wave. "Time for sleep. Tomorrow's a big day." He patted my hand and gave me the smile that makes me silly, telling me we all right. He search the stars again, me. "It's not Katie's dream anymore—it's ours. I have no right to claim Westland, but I can't fight for it alone. Good night."

I scan the sky, squinting to see them stars, but the clouds rolled in tucking them to sleep. The moon dim, too, and the black sky send a fright into my heart.

We all got the sin nature in us. We make mistakes and do bad things sometimes a purpose, most times 'cause we ignorant. But a man with no conscience, lusting for power at the pain a others, has no mind for right-doing nor living. He so slippery, that snake make ya think he the threat, but he jus a white feather on a cherry hat flittering in the wind making ya look the other way. I ain't looking 'cause I learn, that snake slithering at you door, be in you house, and you bes crush and pitch it the swamp with the other dead things or it gonna swallow you whole.

Devil a charming man in a cherry hat with a white feather, and I ain't looking, no sir. Could be a lady, too, with the saddest tale, or the fattest purse; I still ain't looking. But now, how to rid Westland of this snake that's another story, 'cause most times, there's a whole nest of em, and what John Winthrop bring to Westland: snakes and snakes some more.

The slippery ways a John Winthrop come slinking outta the grave through folks trying to come round here to finish what he started—steal Westland.

We all know this day coming, but we so busy sweeping secrets away, we forget to mind the front door. That's how the thief walks in. All them dirty dealings from John Winthrop's stealing ways, come crawling back to Westland. He cheat too many folks, and now they gonna try to cheat Miss Katie.

No secret to keep from her husband, but stuffing secrets inside, all Katie know 'cause that the whispering lie: *it'll keep my family safe.*

During the war, James make deals with the Union to protect Westland, all the while he in the dark bout Katie's secret dealings, some only Bedford know—what old Delly's heart fear most. Bedford Jarrell come to Westland after the war, working with Katie's brother-in-law, Augustus Lamont, the soft-spoken Frenchman we nearly miss when he visit. But Augustus know the law, and Katie got in trouble with the wrong people. All I hear the day Bedford first arrive.

Bedford warn Katie that John Winthrop had dirty business with dirty men waiting to get theirs. Chaos after the war made it ripe for swindlers. They hear a woman running Westland, thinking we weak and prime for plucking. Katie and Augustus too smart for carnival tricks and had the law lock up most of em.

But there be another, a no-good thief from Katie's past, a man in the big yellow cowboy hat we know gonna try to slither in and take Westland someday 'cause he promised he'd do it when he left.

Delaney Houst.

Evil men wait a lifetime to get even.

John hired Houst, a young drifter, to work by his side no matter Katie like it or not. When John left Westland, he put Houst in charge. Houst, poisoned with envy, get to dreaming maybe Westland and Katie his now— till James arrive. Fore Essie and Evie born, John abandoned Katie without a word for two years. James wanna marry Katie. When John come back, James vanished. John hear the gossip from the hands bout Houst's fool ideas, so John don't trust Houst to stay behind at Westland and look after Katie no more. Houst travel everywhere with John Winthrop, teaching that fool his card tricks 'cause cardsharping that boy's gift. John start winning money; in a snip a time, Houst steal it away.

Now, James trusting that Bedford Jarrell and his detective ways, sneaking round here asking questions, will save Westland—or Bo and James will force a hand. Old Delly can't sprint, but I race in my mind and heart to the good Lord, and God gimme a plan 'cause I listen.

Just hope my heart can take the earthquake coming to break up this sad, dry land. It's coming, and ain't nobody ready for it.

9

EVIE

River Wild split the wind when he ran, with his basket of apples, to a faraway land, where the river was soft and sweet to drink.

I devoured Polly's stories until midnight, cherishing the small books in ruby, sapphire, and emerald embossed in gold containing a treasure of imaginative colored drawings.

Priceless. I had earned River's trust.

"Been thinking, child," River said before I left. "Polly would want you to have this." He handed me a large envelope stuffed with Polly's unpublished stories and sketches. "Delly said you're writing again. Maybe you'll finish these and they'll give ya your sunshine back. Use em, Evie. We give ya leave."

I hugged him, my dream awaking at his belief and kindness. River stood on the porch; his wave followed me as I cut through the forest. I looked back at him, wondering how his wiggling fingers waved again after mine—if by rote or some other magic.

The path of the great magnolias, a pergola of roses, and a stone mermaid appeared in Polly's tales, making me wonder how many times Polly and River Koontz visited Mama's garden. River said Polly used friends in her stories. Who was Daisy, the little girl in *River Wild*? Was Bo the golden bear, and Grandfather, the phoenix that lighted the night sky and Polly's way? Who was the plum and ruby dragon that told the children stories? In another tale, a beast so fierce, only the song from a kind, selfless girl tamed it. Was the songstress Mama?

When I asked River, he only laughed and said, "Sometimes, a little stuff and nonsense soothing in a selfish, cruel world."

The harsh filter of a hard River Koontz.

How did I view the world? Returning to Westland, I observed rebirth all around me, yet, through a film of distrust, bitterness, and suspicion.

I needed answers. I needed hope.

Mama's garden.

The last of spring's glory in my garden, Mama whispered in my dreams. Do you hear its music, my Evie?

"Yes."

Barren. Shut off for so long. But now my daughter has come home, and so it sings.

Spanish moss tings in an oak at the slightest breeze. A choir of crickets hides in waves of forget-me-nots and cherry tulips. Mama held me tight underneath a sprawling oak. "I hid with them," she sang, a glimpse of childhood twinkled in her eyes.

"So did I, Mama."

How my garden shines dressed in morning dew.

I sneaked outside while the house slept; I had not. By James and Delly's midnight rumblings, no one slept last night. I savored the misty, pink sunrise on another day brimming with questions, half-smiles, and grief. Studying the pastel sky, I imagined Essie's whisper carried with the wind, *I'm coming home.*

In the chill, I faintly smelled new roses—Essie's roses. I needed to smell them again, spiced honey, red wine, vanilla cake, and the palest pink rose; its fragrance I called Peace. I couldn't wait to see Essie Mae, tell her about River and Polly, and dream with her again. After all these years, she would have to teach me.

But now, a cruel blow from drought, fire, and disease—in many corners, Essie's rose garden displayed a graveyard of sticks, blackened thorns, blooms curling between dried flowers and ruffled bronze leaves. We pitched in, removed diseased canes and burned blackened leaves and debris, praying enough rosebushes survived so Essie Mae could start anew. None of us relished seeing the sight nor believing its metaphor. For Essie's roses ushered in rebirth, possibility, and hope amid the ugliest in nature, in life. It was as if, without Essie, her roses lost their way, their will. Perhaps we did, too. We took heart in knowing Essie would see the rosebuds, striving to bloom, promising her garden merely overslept until next season.

Barefoot in my morning dress, toes tickled by wet grass, I thought better of it, slipping on a pair of old boots, a worn cotton frock, and Mama's woolen shawl. Still, the morning felt strangely warm. Westland couldn't decide to embrace an Indian summer or relinquish to the encroaching winter wind.

I missed the sounds of the country, its stillness, where the swish of grass underfoot keeps time with katydids and crickets. The warm, moist air eased my chill. Memories in the house as of late turned frigid; my soul hungered for the sun. The minty leaves of two willows waved good morning. The waft of churned soil and autumn blossoms made me pause. Shadows of the leaves floated across my boots. I welcomed the sun. "A sticky morning." Overgrown willows deterred visitors, concealing Mama's sanctuary for years. I scarcely remembered venturing into my mother's garden as a girl. When Mama's strength returned, we visited twice. Once with Essie, though to our surprise, half-way inside, Essie Mae disappeared.

Delly explained, "Some places startle our souls so much, it's too painful to think on making new memories jus yet."

"I wasn't allowed inside this garden as a child," Essie said, though she later confessed she hadn't wanted Mama to see her cry.

A stone path led me to a splintered wooden bench outside Mama's garden. Ivy now covered the walls; red climbing roses escaped over the entrance. I froze. The smell of cloves, violets, and roses lifted my heart. "Mama."

I sat on the bench as the sun finished rising; the house now, too. I imagined Delly's pancakes wafting upstairs, rousing James, and his soft order to leave me to my wandering.

I stood and stretched, ready to leave, my stomach growling at the thought of pancakes and warm maple syrup until I spotted the garden's gate cracked open, its key inside the lock. "Bo," I called, peeking inside, admiring Mama's favorite bench under a pergola of a bloom of pink roses. Antiquated now, its flaking mint-green paint clung to our dresses, the iron bench of grapevines where Mama told me stories, the bench where Mama and Isabel sat with child—Mama pregnant with me, Isabel carrying Essie. *I do believe that's why you take to mischief and spying.* Mama chuckled in my thoughts. *Why, sometimes I wondered if our babies could hear all our secrets. I wondered.*

A new wooden bench sat across from Mama's iron one, Bo's handiwork, and Mama's invitation for Essie and me to join her. Throughout my life, the hidden coves and gardens of Westland traveled with me. My body need only graze a cool shadow under the cedars, and the scent of wet grass, rain, magnolias, and roses transported me home.

I pushed open the gate, listening to the tiny chimes ringing as I walked inside. "I suppose River strung those as a warning, hmm, Delly?" Life all around. "No wonder Mama loved it here."

Mama's garden was vastly different from Essie's. For one, it thrived. No one knew how it survived the drought this summer. Delly hadn't enough hours to tend to it while she cared for Mama. Bo spent his days with James on their new crop. James hired help for Delly, but no mention of a master gardener. Lil may have hired laborers unbeknownst to us—Lil's way. In the end, Delly said, "Think the good Lord know you need to see you mama's flowers fresh and pretty 'cause they all love, they all her." River boasted his horse, Shasta, knew the way to Westland by one simple command. Delly would hear Koontz's wagon arrive, excited at his visit, only to find River sleeping at the reins.

Ivy hugged a statue of a boy dancing with his dog; stone mushrooms decorated the path to a pond scattered with water lilies. I spotted an impression on the grass. Perhaps Delly rested after gathering flowers for her soaps, or James stretched across the grass, remembering Mama. Many new faces buzzed in and out of Westland. I felt ashamed I hadn't understood Westland's importance to our neighbors during and after the war, and the employment Mama provided to freedmen and women eager for a chance. Two years ago, Mama hired January, an attractive, shy woman who caught Bo's eye, her skin the color of black orchids kissed with moon glow. "That January a clumsy child," Delly complained. "With a kind heart," Mama added.

Nelly Walsh served the longest and remained at James's request. *A young lass who boasts an Irish temper and coppery curls*, Mama wrote. Nelly made us laugh, and the tender way she cared for Mama and the house seemed familiar, too. Cloistered with Mama, I scarcely knew January, or Bo's hires, Grady and Judge and Judge's wife, Grace.

Now, too many voices and hands strived to change Westland, repainting benches, erasing memories, planting new gardens, and uprooting dead ones.

January, and a few others, worked at McCafferty's now, but I often saw them roaming the grounds on the weekend or on special occasions. Delly required help, but James waited—waited for me to run Westland and make my own decisions on laborers and ventures. But Westland was my mother's dream, not mine. Five years away, five years of her marriage to James, five years of unspoken words toppled onto my shoulders, and the years living in seclusion and luxury away from war, into my conscience.

10

EVIE

I wandered the gravel path to a cove of holly, no longer shrubs, but trees. Silvery clusters of Spanish moss cuffed an oak's limbs as the lace on Mama's sleeve. "'One must consider sundry particulars when planning a garden as this,' my father said." Mama retraced her girlhood steps. "Drainage, soil, evergreens, the colors of roses and bulbs, and the mood of this garden."

"Mood?" I asked her.

"Daddy insisted on a *quiet* mood planting white, blue, and purple flowers. I argued, 'Romantic—red and pink roses, white and lilac hollyhocks, moonflowers and peonies. Daddy laughed. 'Why, Katie, choosing flowers is the easiest part,' he said. 'I'm considering the trees' shadows casting on the grass, the flowers they'll shade. Roses need the sun.'"

"I never realized," I said, thrilled to see Mama's cheeks bloom with color.

Mama led me to two ceramic garden seats painted with white lilies against a turquoise glaze. "In truth," she said, smiling. "Daddy planted this garden for Mama."

"And its tall fence?"

"To shelter Isabel and me from a cruel world . . . and his prejudice. When my father died, and I remained at school, Isabel finished what he had started."

"Roses."

"Yes. Over the years, this garden transformed into much more. I regret abandoning it after you were born."

When Mama spoke of Isabel, the color faded from her cheeks, her breathing labored. I knew then it was our last visit to her garden, locked up inside and lonely for too many years, as us.

Honeysuckle arches led to a short stone wall curving past a row of juniper trees. I found no carvings, only a blanket of moss atop its pillars. A Chinese lantern teetered in a dogwood. Past the stone wall, the garden was mostly overgrown and mysterious. The stone path ended at the yew that once formed a maze where I played with my mother.

"Bo," I called again, glimpsing a silhouette cloaked in mist and foliage. "January?" January tended Mama's orchard, but she never visited Mama's garden without Delly. *A forgotten statue dressed in ivy*, I decided.

My skin tingled at a sudden chill. I stopped at the stone wall, searching tree trunks for my grandparent's initials. I spotted one carving on a sycamore: a *K* and the start of a second letter I couldn't decipher. I scrubbed the dirt, revealing a jagged line as if something interrupted the carver. "An argument or distraction—Evie Wilcox, it could be anything." As I said Wilcox for the first time since Mama died, I honored her thoughtfulness, legally changing my name from Winthrop to the legacy of my grandfather, Alexander Wilcox, and erasing any legal trace of John Winthrop, my late father. I respected James, but Winthrop was a surname that brought pain, no legacy I desired.

James led the charge on erasing Winthrop from Westland. "Pondered it a long time, darlin'," he said. "My middle name is Adam. What'd ya think about me getting a new last name? James Adam."

"And a grand laugh we'll all have when Delly introduces me as Miss Evie Adam."

James winked, signaling his mischief. "I believe I know a new surname that'll suit me fine. We'll all think on it and have Bedford draw up the legal papers so it's final."

"You would do that for me?"

"I would die for you, little lady."

My dreams of becoming Mrs. William Reed faded. Mama's boxwood maze reminded me of a suitor in London during the war, Conrad Alby. *"You cannot hide in my mother's garden all day, Miss Evie,"* Conrad called, chasing me through its maze.

"A noble, handsome gentleman," Lil boasted. Conrad stood taller than James, lean, strong, and graceful with a head of auburn hair with enough wave to hide an endearing pair of red ears. Essie never warmed to Conrad. She had forged an attachment to William I never managed. I believed I loved William, a child's notion of love. I fancied more the escape from Westland, from myself. The war had changed William in ways neither of us committed to understand or heal.

With the gentle breeze rustling through the trees, my last words to William tumbled across my mind. *"Your family rebuilds in Richmond. How can you ask me to return to a place that nearly killed me?" I asked.*

"I thought that was Westland," William said, walking away.

"You haven't asked William why he's changed or what happened to him during the war," Essie scolded. "His father sends him to Europe. Will you let him leave?"

"William closes his heart. He only feels obligated to our engagement. I've released him." Essie stood as Delly, hands to her hips, and scrutinized me with her all-knowing stare. "I don't care if you unearth my secrets. I don't love William. I cannot."

"William closes his heart, or do you, Evie?"

"I don't belong in New York, and I can never return to Virginia—neither can you."

"You're still afraid."

"And what of it? What about Thomas?" It was my turn to watch Essie squirm. The years had not relinquished our childish game.

Essie threw up her hands in defeat. "Thomas is a different man. William loves you."

"And Thomas?"

"Thomas weds ambition now."

"Mama refuses to understand I don't need marriage or children to find happiness."

"God has settled that for us, hasn't He? No children."

I shook the past from my thoughts, wandering back toward the garden's entrance. I hadn't grieved Essie's truth—barrenness. At times, I felt relieved. But could any man love me if I could not bear his son? I didn't care. This made me an oddity among women, especially in Lil's circle. But Lil had no children. In the time of Reconstruction, I relished my own and wore my independence as a glorious gown, all the rage in the salons of Paris and London, vulgar in the genteel South.

The sight of a hummingbird flittered away dark thoughts. It hovered near the purple asters and black-eyed Susans that sparkled near the walkway as a flash of fireworks. I paused, reluctant to sit on Mama's bench. My eyes closed to the trickling fountain James fixed for Mama so she could lose herself in the past to the splashes and giggles of two unlikely friends. A missing swash of lavender made me smile. Delly laid a lavender bouquet on my nightstand, but I still couldn't sleep, watching my days with Mama, and our years apart, play before me.

Yellow climbers framed one of several arbors. "You've blossomed fatter than Essie's pink ramblers. How?" I ran my hand over Mama's bench; paint flakes drifted to the lawn. "Bo, Mama wouldn't let you repaint this, would she? She fancied the timeworn paint marking the years."

"I tell your missus year ago, bes paint that bench fore she get sick. That paint chipping up and feeding the birds. Ain't no good thing." Her voice sounded soft and childlike.

I turned around, startled at the woman before me. A tall, thin black woman, gardening tools stuffed in her apron, long black hair in a thick braid draped over her shoulder. *Rapyunzel*, Koontz snickered in my thoughts. She wore a floppy straw hat tied with a green silk scarf that hid her face. She bid me a curtsey and snickered.

"Who are you?" I asked, searching the path for Bo. *No one's there.*

"Maybe I ain't even real like ya think." Her smile was off-putting; she winced as if in pain and arched an eyebrow, mischievous. She held a watering can and sprinkled a bed of purple grass, eyeing me, curious, unapologetic for her intrusion. "Hope Delly don't mind, but purple grass in autumn attractive in that corner yonder."

"What are you doing in my mother's garden? Did you come with January?"

"This your garden now." She waved me off to stave my temper. I slowly approached her. "Suppose you don't want me painting that bench," she snipped. "Nobody want nothing to change round here."

I gasped as she cut one of Mama's prize roses, a pink blossom with a hundred petals. "Delly say you call this Mama's Pink. This year, it sneak a pale yellow inside them petals. Miss, I work at the McCafferty's, but you wouldn't know 'cause you don't live here for a long time."

"Few know of this garden. Does Delly know you're in here?"

She snickered, eyeing my hands stuck to my hips as Delly.

I fumbled them behind my back.

"Maybe, maybe not." She rolled her eyes to the sky. "Nice, dry day. No rain . . . oh, we need the rain." She dropped her shears, examining the purple grass, plucking a stalk, and handing it to me. "Delly ask me to come fix things round here for the party. See, you gone, Miss Evie." I looked at her, surprised she knew my name, watching her tug two weeds with thickets from a patch of fiery chrysanthemums. "Don't much like the orange. I fancy the white mums, though."

"You must never paint that bench, do you understand?" I sat on it now, arms folded in a huff, claiming it.

"A pergola covered in sweet pink roses a grand place for sitting, and, my, a fountain, too. But I gotta feeling that place over yonder, under that big white magnolia, be a favorite."

I stretched, looking behind her at the spot, unimpressed. She shrugged her shoulders. I had hoped she would leave now. She stood her ground anchored as a statue. "Mama said that magnolia tree is a hundred years old," I mumbled.

"Could be. You see, that li'l stone bench ends at the path of the great magnolias. A walk so fine in spring, a canopy a pink starflowers and white blossoms, fat as teacups, and purple tulip blooms fill the sky. Near the end a spring, them pink and white petals cover that stone bench, and it look like a fairyland the way all them magnolias blanket the grass like a fine carpet. Sometimes I dream I'm sporting a pair a gold shoes skipping and floating over that path a petals, 'cause I think gold shoes make it finer."

"Gold shoes." I chuckled. "Indeed."

"And the smell, child." She inhaled, gazing at the sky. "Heavens, you ever walk that path, breathe it in, see the branches fluffed with pinks and white magnolias against the aqua sky?"

"Maybe next spring." I sighed, stirred by a path I never explored. If not for the magnolia tree and the stone bench underneath it, I wouldn't believe the path of the great magnolias existed at all. "Such a story."

"Stories are the sweeties of life, miss. What kinda life ya live if you ain't got no stories, no sweet ones, hmm? Oh, I know lots, Miss Evie. I don't take to flowers much; I a dancer."

I slipped a smirk as she twirled, trowel and shears, rattling in her apron pocket; a packet of pansy seeds burst onto the soil. She gasped, snatching them up, shoving them in her pocket.

"Where did you dance?" I asked, humoring her, but my uneasiness hadn't left me. She eyed me as I wrung my hands, my dress.

"Wish I had me a pair a new boots like that, but my mister don't like me working in no mud much. He say I a fine lady."

"I didn't come to work in the mud."

"Only need for boots like that." She bid me a low kick and shimmied her knee in the air, laughing. "Oh, I be a good dancer. This a bad dance in Paris, the can-can. Ya know it? They lock ya in jail for that dance."

"Stuff and nonsense!"

Her feet tiptoed and stretched across the grass in a skip and a hop that made me giggle. I was in no mood, but I couldn't stop watching her, the way her charcoal hair slipped from its braid and swirled around her neck. The delicate way she waved her fingers through the air. She bowed to a red rose. I had often viewed fine dancers in Paris; she wasn't one. No ballerina nor opera extra, but the kind who slipped on stage at night in the clubs frequented by men and women who cared not for gossip, but sought it out. A dancer in a magenta corset frilled in black lace, wearing garters and heels high-stepping to blaring trumpets, screeches from a chorus of dancing girls, and whistles from men.

"Lord a mercy, haven't shuffled my feet like that in years. Old Bo gonna get me he know I'm in here."

"Are you from Paris?"

"Child, I'm from nowhere and everywhere." She gathered herself, re-braiding her hair. I gawked at her, glimpsing her uncovered cheek. She quickly concealed it with her scarf. "Yep, ya thinking," she said, amused. "Today's a fine morning for thinking. See, I come to McCafferty's after the war. The new president, after Lincoln shot . . . President Johnson say black folk need a contract with white folk for hired work or he'll lock us up. Black codes—new laws stealing our freedom. Lady, like me, hears all kinda useful conversations."

"Contract? That doesn't make sense."

"Oh, but I know lots, miss. My mistress teach me. Take this rose." She plucked a petal; I winced as if it were my hair. "This ain't as sweet-smelling as I fancy, nor the color, but I grind this petal with my pestle and mortar, make a li'l soft ball, get a nice string and needle, and poke it through, while it soft, mind ya. Soon, I string near fifty a them rose petal beads for a necklace that'll keep the perfume for years and years."

"Why would you do that?" I bundled in Mama's shawl, feeling a chill. The woman eyed me again. The heat had risen with the sun.

"I set them rose beads out to dry, and that be as fine as a string a pearls 'cause it smell like heaven. Don't need an oyster to hide in to make me pearls."

"What does that have to do with what you said about a contract?"

She sighed, shifting her sunhat on her head just so. "McCafferty hire me on and others. See, this genteel land long gone, and most owners don't know how to work the land. But they keep that ugly stuff far from pretty li'l things like you."

"I'm not a thing. I don't want you here."

She sashayed to Mama's bench, sifting out mint paint flakes from the grass. "Don't know why you got so many benches when the grass'll do. I paint it you want."

"I said no."

"You bes wear a straw hat like mine, tuck some daisies in it. I wear the scarf, silk from Paris 'cause Delly say it more pleasing than my scarred up face. You don't care bout yours?"

"My what?" A rock dropped in my stomach at the mention.

"Scars."

I avoided her odd gaze, wishing I wore a scarf, a veil. No one ever mentioned my scars before, except for the youngest children in our school back in New York. But when they asked about them, they were sweet and curious, not hurtful, ominous.

"But they sunburn," she said, noticing I had recoiled from her touch. She stepped away.

I found distraction in the fountain, losing myself in the water's trickle. Pink camellia petals floated near a stone mermaid. For a moment, I drifted with them.

"And turn purple lessen you use the salve, miss."

She's a half-wit, I told myself, biting my lip to stop my tears. *Why would my mother hire her?* After the war, at Mama's insistence, James provided opportunity to freedmen who held a skill. The workers Delly and Bo trained remained. But when Mama grew ill, most of the hired hands drifted to McCafferty's because James wouldn't offer lodging and stable employment. In the upheaval and aftermath of war, James trusted few, keeping new ventures at Westland small and simple. "I suppose Delly doesn't mind your sass," I said. "I do."

"Don't mean to sass. That how I talk . . . plain. When you live a lifetime a pain, miss, got no time for fancy words and fluff, but I know how to use em. I learned. Know all sorts a things. Wanna test me?" She found a round white rock and offered it to me.

It glittered in the sun, but I pitched in the fountain. "I would rather . . ."

"Sweet flowers are slow and weeds make haste. That a good saying. My mistress used to call me a weed 'cause she say sometime things I say like weeds, choking out all the good, especially the gossip, once you pluck it up, it jus come back."

"Thank you, but—"

"Roses and honey soothe a sore throat; rose petals help a sour stomach. Did ya know?"

"No."

Her posture inched taller proud she piqued my interest. "See, miss, I know things. Little bout gardening, but I help harvest the fruit with January and Nelly; that Irish redhead don't burn a temper like they whisper, least not to me. But Nell don't like pears 'cause she gotta bad tooth."

"You tend Mama's orchard?"

"Lord, child, not by myself. I can show ya . . . tell ya all bout them fruit trees. Bet I can show ya things round here you ain't never see, hmm? You like pears?"

I rose at her statement; a flush washed over me. She stepped back, searching again behind her shoulder down the misty path. "I know every inch of Westland," I scolded. "There isn't anything you can show me! Now, please . . . I would like to be alone." I collapsed on the bench, surprised by my manner. But I hadn't slept, I hadn't dreamed, and I hadn't patience to banter with a madwoman.

"Yes, ma'am."

I escaped in the fountain again, watching the pink petals wobble atop the water relieved her footsteps faded away.

"But you wrong," she said, stomping back. "There's a whole world I can show ya. No matter. You'll ask in time."

I hung my head, spying her retreat. "I don't like pears," I whispered, swiping a tear from my cheek. I held in the others.

"Believe Miss Katie grow Bartlett pears," the woman said softly. She skipped back, ending in a twirl before me. "Proud pears 'cause they ripen early so you gotta gobble em up or they go bad and winter pears for baking."

"I don't like pears," I repeated, restless. I shifted on Mama's bench, my hand scraping a flake of paint. "Damnation."

The woman wiggled her eyebrows, smug. She grabbed my hand and scraped her fingernail over my palm, searching for the splinter and wriggled it out. "Bet ya never even ate a pear, least not how I fix em. For my mister, I bake a pear with sugar in a crust served with a dollop a cream pudding."

"I might try that."

"I tell ya my secret, miss, if you don't speak it to nobody. I use honey and vanilla in my pear marmalade. I'll slather it for ya on them scones Miss Lil teach me to bake."

I wasn't part of this Westland, of fine pears and baking scones and strangers in Mama's garden. Jealousy crushed the lighthearted feeling I held upon my entrance. The woman hummed as she swiped dirt from her skirt. She dressed too fine for gardening. She offered some comfort to Mama, I was certain, housing an endless array of tales within her. I caught her gaze, not long enough. Her eyes darted from me to the roses and entrance, then behind her shoulder as if expecting someone, anxious they might catch her. I followed her glance to a wheelbarrow loaded with pots, bulbs, and buckets of pulled weeds. As my mind wandered, she left me alone, sprinkling another drink over the purple grass.

"Hmm, gonna take time for you to like me," she whined. "You will. Lessen they keep a pretty thing like you away from me, too."

"Astra!" Bo's welcome, thundering voice made this dancer shrivel. She grabbed the watering can with a final spin for my attention, leaving me with a wink and wiggle of her fingers. Bo glared at the wheelbarrow, her. She left it tucked behind the shrubs.

"You call on me if you want I should paint that chipped up bench," she said. "Don't be afraid a change, Miss Evie, 'cause change coming."

Bo towered above Astra, silent, as the woman floated past him, sliding her hand across his back. "What did James say bout running off alone, Miss Evie?" Bo asked, eyeing the wheelbarrow again.

"I needed the quiet this morning. Besides, no one knows about this garden but us—at least that's what I thought until our surprise intruder."

"Delly looking for ya," he barked, staring down the entrance, ensuring Astra left. Bo walked to the gate, puffed his chest like a cardinal, and closed the door. "Don't trust that old man Koontz, ya hear? You mama warned you bout him. Bes stay away."

"Applesauce. Besides, I've been here all morning. But the way you're acting, I might as well be with cranky old Koontz."

"Delly say she gonna fix ya warm lemonade and put ya to bed 'cause you ain't sleeping." He ambled back, his voice soft and mellow, eyeing me as he sat on the opposite bench. "I knew where you be, but I don't tell her. Here." He handed me a yellow sunbonnet, Mama's. We traded smiles as I tugged it on my head.

My sunhat made me think of the woman who hid under hers. "Bo, who is she?" I swirled the bonnet's ribbons into a knot, smiling to myself at Astra dancing the can-can.

"You don't pay that Astra no mind. She troubled. Miss Katie hire her a year back."

"She's not right. I get a feeling . . ."

"Sorry, Miss Evie, she ain't supposed to fuss in here. But a garden like this . . . Delly need help. Astra weren't to come till tomorrow, make it pleasing for when Essie Mae come."

"Astra . . . do I know that name?"

Bo avoided my stare; he rarely did. He kicked at the purple grass. I didn't like it either. The book he carried shifted in his hand. He sat next to me on Mama's bench, as he did every morning. "That woman say things?" he asked.

"She said she was a dancer and something about a contract with Tom McCafferty."

"Astra be Tom's wife. Least she say she is. Some days she say she a mama and got three children, but she don't. Sometimes she say she a teacher but—"

"She isn't. She speaks well."

"Near we figure, she be Tom's wife, not legal. She come after the war. Folks say Mr. Tom lonely after his wife die, and maybe he send for her or Lord knows the stories. New folks come in and out all the time these years."

"Mama never mentioned her. She's beautiful, from what I can see. She hid the right side of her face with a green silk scarf."

"Pleasing looks, suppose one thing the evil don't steal from her."

"Evil?"

"Stories. Suspect you come face-to-face with hard truth teaching free blacks in that New York." Bo left my side to sit across from me. I buried my thoughts, tugging at the fringe on Mama's shawl. "James say, new folks, new changes round here makes ya uneasy. Don't blame ya, child. But he never let no harm come to ya now." Bo patted the book he held. "Me neither."

For the first time in a long time, we locked eyes. Bo's fierce stare held a promise of protection I had only witnessed once before. The years hadn't softened him as I imagined; Mama's passing did. James once whispered I had won Bo as a little girl in how I loved Essie Mae and again in caring for Mama.

"I've been away too long," I said quietly. "Mama needed me."

"Old Bo a hard man, Miss Evie." His hanky floated over his face. Dressed in his Sunday best, ready to fetch Essie Mae in Sweet Water, he rolled his shoulders back and yanked his jacket's cuffs, his large, muscular frame stressing the seams.

Quiet fell.

I admired Mama's garden, eyeing the purple grass. "It can stay," I said.

With a tip of his straw hat, he understood.

"Well." Bo slapped his leg, shattering the silence. "Suppose no time for my reading lesson this morning," he said, disappointed.

Another smile.

I couldn't help thinking of Astra. The scars I noted across her wrists and the jagged one, a thick red slice across her cheek, mirrored the small scar near my eye. I learned to watch for facial scars during the past six years; Essie made me learn. The clearest memory Essie had of one of her kidnappers, a man they never caught, Trailer, was a thick red scar, ear to chin, across his cheek. I shuddered at the thought.

"Mama's garden is a wonder I regret I missed in my youth," I said. "Memories are a wonder, too, Bo. They come crashing in on you whether you invite them or not. Delly's right, regret is a weed that will choke everything good beginning to grow inside."

Bo saw me thinking and looked back toward the gate. He was easygoing with routine—without it—edgy and distant alone in my presence. Mama or Delly usually accompanied us during our lessons. Today, we sat alone, magnifying Mama's absence.

"I bes finish readying to fetch our Essie Mae. Delly won't gimme peace lest I leave early. I say trains always late." He stood with a groan, his boots scraping the gravel as he left.

"Bo," I called, stopping him. I swallowed, weighing the consequences of my next words. "Why didn't you leave?" Bo reached for the gate, thought better of it, and faced me. "Why didn't you leave Westland?" I bowed my head, trying to hide my tears; they dripped on my dress regardless.

He swiped his brow with a hanky again, sauntering back to me. His shadow falling across my body felt as protective and comforting as James's. "Ain't no day for such talk," he insisted.

But the threat of more unspoken words, as another secret about to be buried, soured my stomach. "Everyone may think I fancy pretending myself as many things depending on the hour, as Astra, but I'm no child. I haven't been for a long time. Why did you stay with Mama when you had your freedom?"

"Did I?" He found a pair of shears resting in the grass and snipped a red rose, savoring its perfume. His plump nose sunk into the silky petals. When his eyes met mine, they shone slick as dew. "Nobody free a Westland. Wherever I go, it woulda follow me. Some good, bad. Old Bo don't know too much. I know bout building things, farming the land, but not the heart." Chilly red petals brushed across the top of my hand; his rose sat beside me. "You ain't to blame, child. You ain't to blame."

I cradled my face in my palms. My sobs turned into shaking at this giant's tender touch. His boots lingered near mine, shuffling, fidgeting. "Hushaby, girl. No time for crying. No more time for them sad tears."

As a child, when Bo first spoke to me, I thought it was the magic of Mama's doing, but I hadn't taken the time to listen or ask anything of him.

When I returned home, Bo approached me, skittish like a nervous colt. But that first day we locked eyes, I knew there was more inside of him; he did, too. He longed to learn, and this proud, strong, bold man, never caring about his age or station, asked me, a white woman, to teach him. Bo longed to impress the closest thing he had to a daughter, his Essie Mae. He wanted her to know a man, a hardened man, the result of the evil of others could and would change.

"You let me in, Bo," I cried. "But sometimes I think my father stole my heart."

"Fool talk. You here, ain't ya? Pity like that bucket a weeds, useless, girl."

"Who's setting the fires, Bo?" He pursed his lips, quiet, eyeing me as he slowly sat before me. "I've heard whispers Ned ..."

"Whoa, child," he whispered, looking back toward the entrance. "Careful. That kinda talk shower trouble on folks." He searched the pergola of roses above, taking in a deep breath and exhaling. When he studied me again, his eyes glossed with pain. "War ain't over when the whispering starts, plantations taken away with a whisper. We seen it. That old slave got nothing to do with Westland now. That a long time ago."

"Ned's free. My father ... the evil he brought. He sold Ned's wife and children."

"Miss Evie, you digging in this garden for answers; it the wrong place, on the wrong day. You march in circles talking to everybody but James, so you mind swimming in that dirty swamp." He left his book on the bench and scooped up a handful of dirt, crumbling the dry soil in his hands. "Do you think I set the fires, Miss Evie?"

I rushed to him. "Never." He sighed and patted my hand. I followed him back to our benches under the sweet roses. "I'm sorry. Whoever's doing it is getting their wish—dividing us."

"No, ma'am, don't need no fires to do no such thing. Snip a gossip all it take. Last I hear, Ned take off to New Orleans. He a good man."

I spied the book teetering in his hand. *A different story*, I thought, curious. "Good folks go bad all the time," I said.

"'Cause they don't got people like you to remind em they matter."

"My father had me."

"Years ago, I walk round this earth believing no such thing as good. That maybe I born to jus figure out how to survive this hell till God take me to Heaven. Time I don't even believe that 'cause a what men do to me, womenfolk, too. No hope, till Essie Mae born."

"Sometimes I think Essie's an angel."

"I think it every day."

"What changed you, Bo?"

"Maybe you think old Bo getting soft, but I say love, the real kind . . . and Miss Katie. No perfect person on this here earth."

"But you blamed Mama, too. She could've stopped the suffering."

"And that's why you hurting. You ain't missing you mama, you missing saying it her fault and asking why she don't do nothing bout them evil days we all suffer through. But, child, we here . . . in a garden, and you teaching me to read, and I . . ."

"What, Bo?"

"I stay." He held his lips and nodded. "I . . . trust. Don't know if that word trust real when I a boy, then a man. Suppose better I old least I finally know it's real."

"Delly boasts you're one of her special chocolate eggs she makes for Easter."

His hearty laugh made me chuckle. "Hard on the outside, mush on the inner. You see my scars . . . they hard, too, but they jus on the outside now. What bout you, Miss Evie?"

It was my turn to rise. I wandered to the purple grass, watching it dance with the breeze, its leaves dripping droplets on to the others. "Scars." I sighed. "Yes, I have a few, but they faded with time." I marveled at a lavender rose starting to bloom.

"Don't know where them purple roses come from," Bo said.

"They're lovely. I've never noticed them before." Another rosebush surprised me: peach and white petals. "Funny, this rose is perfect on the inside, but look here, pluck one petal."

"That got a rot."

I returned to Mama's bench, discarding the withered petal. "I wouldn't put it that way. It's one rose in the midst of hundreds."

"But it hurting . . . needs mending."

"From within." I folded my arms and nodded, giving him his due. "How is it, Bo, out of all my family at Westland, you're teaching me the most?" I sat up straight and rubbed my tears away, staring into the book he held. "That's not *The Legend of Sleepy Hollow*."

His grin banished the dark clouds I brought into Mama's garden.

"Bo," I wailed. "That's Jane Austen!" When he hid the small book inside his palm, I laughed a good chortle that seemed to make the flowers open and stretch toward the sun. I laughed and laughed, and soon, Bo's low, mellow chuckle blended with mine.

"Fool, girl. Why do I come?" Bo asked. "Ain't gonna read this here book now. But Miss Lil say it'd be a nice surprise I read this for Essie Mae tonight."

"Oh, a splendid surprise. And what about this January I'm hearing so much about? She's a sweet, handsome woman who might love to hear you read Jane Austen, too."

"Gonna bolt on outta here you keep sassing. But Miss Lil right. Ain't no gift for Essie Mae, hearing me read for the first time bout a headless horseman. Gimme nightmares."

"We don't have much time."

"Already practiced. Wanna hear?" His sparkling, eager eyes brought tears again to mine. I left him, skipping away before they fell. He followed me in a zigzag befitting my childhood, and we sat again, sharing Mama's bench. "This need painting, Miss Evie."

"Today, I rather sit elsewhere than paint that bench."

And so we did. We walked a short distance to River's creek, retiring on the bench Koontz constructed. It made me wonder about Bo's mistrust of River. Bo had a reason, a past I never questioned. There would be time now.

Rippling water replaced my sobs, and the song of learning tickled my ears. "Read on," I encouraged.

Bo searched for spies, cleared his throat, and unfolded a small pair of gold spectacles. I sat, impressed, watching his large hands fit the glasses on his nose. He licked his thumb, struggling with the thin pages, and glanced up at me to make sure I was listening.

"The family of Dash-wood," Bo started slow and steady.

The thought of Bo reading Jane Austen stretched a grin across my lips so wide it ached behind my ears.

"The family of Dashwood," he started again, "had long been settled in Sussex."

"Fine," I said. "Crack on."

He glared at my interruption, balancing the dainty book in his able hands. "Their estate was large, and their res . . . res-i-dence was at Norland Park, in the center of their property, where, for many gen-er-a-tions, they had lived in so res . . . res."

"Respectable."

"Respectable a manner as to en-gage the general good opinion of their . . ."

"Surrounding acquaintance."

He slapped closed the little book proud of himself. "Essie Mae's eyes gonna grow the size a melons, she hear me read this."

"The best gift ever."

"Gotta few surprises . . . now, child, you ain't go peeking near the old cottage, have ya?"

"No, sir."

"When Essie come, I show ya then. Gotta another surprise I'd like to show her myself."

"Your cabin. You built a fine home for yourself. You should be proud."

He squirmed in his seat, pondering the book once more. "Jus one chapter—can't read much more a that lady book."

"You might surprise yourself and fancy that story."

"I walk ya home. Miss Evie, think ya like to know—that's the first time Astra speak so much and happy to a stranger in years. You got something that bring out the ease in folks. I know."

"Good. Do you like pears?"

"Nope."

"Me neither."

On the walk home, he peeked back inside the pages of Jane Austen's *Sense and Sensibility*. Bo found his words, his rhythm, and his reading shone brighter than the sun, its fragrance sweeter than any rose in Mama's garden.

11.

ESSIE MAE

Before the Civil War, slave labor built the railroads; now, at the time of the South's reconstruction, crews of hired white and black men rebuild them, forty-five thousand miles of tie walls, stakes, and iron rail crisscrossing the land. I imagined Bo's muscular hands driving spikes into the rock, blasting mountains, grading earth, and laying ties. But I had wished I could see him owning a railroad. *Someday*, I promised myself. A black man or woman will own a railroad, serve as an engineer, and design the metal giants.

In my years traveling by rail, no matter my destination, most of the passengers' stares looked the same: curious, offended, indifferent. They didn't know I was a former slave. They did not know if allowed to attend their university, I would graduate with honors. And they did not know I spoke in theaters across the North, taught at a school for freedmen, and cultivated my own variety of roses. And they certainly never knew I was raised on a small Southern plantation by a beautiful white woman who opened my mind to learning.

Railroads take people away and lead them home.

I pulled at my dress, hoping the yellow silk wasn't too fancy. Bo never cared for frills and fuss, but I hadn't seen him in nearly a year. I wanted to stand proud before him. I pinned on my butterfly brooch. Bedford held my rose, nodding to my diary left on a table. I grabbed it and straightened my dainty blue hat with a final glance in the mirror. White ribbons fell over my shoulder. My hands shook as I attempted to tie my hat's bow to the side, as Miss Katie did. "The closer we get to Westland, I feel as two Essies," I said. "One, a country girl in a calico cotton dress who teaches school on a strawberry farm, devoid of lavish hats and jewels."

"A daisy in your hair," Bedford said, handing me a stack of magazines.

"I've grown fond of her. The other Essie squeezes herself into Lil's satin ball gowns, fit for parlors in New York and Paris. I flap my fan in secret code to Evie to maintain my sanity among strangers who ogle this diamond brooch Miss Katie gave me on my birthday."

"You favor the strawberry farm over Westland or Paris?"

"Sebastian . . . No, I suppose I should call you Bedford now that our trip has ended."

He came in close and adjusted my hat's bow, tugging it to the side. "Surprise me with a whisper of Sebastian in private every now and again. You have made me forget I must be Bedford now. We share another similitude: the conundrum of our two selves."

"Similitude?" I nodded, impressed. "Evie guessed you were a detective. I never believed her stories. I'm still uncertain."

We joined the sparse passengers in the dining car for the final leg of our journey. I smiled as Bedford's hand guided the small of my back as we walked down the aisle to a private plush seat and view of the countryside.

"Uncertain, hmm?" he asked. "Ruminate a while longer. I spot a friend." He tipped his hat and winked as I scrutinized him. "Don't worry, Miss Essie. Everyone at Westland eagerly awaits your return. You'll charm them once again as you have me."

Bedford shook hands with a short, squatty man who straightened his cravat and tipped his bowler upon noticing me. I sat alone for the first time in days. Few travelers continued south, least of all to Sweet Water, an idyllic small town resolute on rebuilding after the war. Abigail and Wren left us a day ago. I reread her card, eager to visit them in Mobile before Christmas.

I shuffled through the magazines I promised to bring Evie, my eyes bouncing from fashions and articles to the meadows bathed in sunlight outside my window. My heart fluttered at a woman's call to her husband. "Thomas," she shouted. *Thomas.* I flipped through my magazine, glimpsing an ad depicting the rage in bathing costumes and a shocking illustration out of place next to it. I read the article explaining the horrid image, held my breath, and buried the paper underneath my satchel. "Not now," I whispered.

Thomas.

The rumble of the train rattled through me. Imagined violins; a waltz took over—a moonlit terrace in New York City—my last argument with Thomas twirled inside my mind.

"Another one of Lil's affairs." I had complained all evening.

Thomas's raucous introductions to the elite muted the elegance. I escaped outside onto the terrace, admiring a waterfall of ferns and petunias spilling from an urn. "A warning for straying guests? Petunias mean lonesomeness. Ah, but you say think of me." I floated my hand through forget-me-nots overflowing a brass planter. "Miss Katie, I miss our quiet days, sitting on your front porch and sipping strawberry lemonade," I said, lost in the champagne bubbles fizzling inside my flute.

Thomas found me. "Hiding again?" he asked, indignant. "Lil's asking for you."

"This is the closest I've come to a garden in this city, splendid flower arrangements." I found my steps, gliding to a tree of yellow roses. "Look, a tinge of red inside their petals." I examined them. "No. It's what I wanted to see. They remind me of Miss Katie's favorite roses."

Thomas sighed. "You danced with Harry Polk, the publisher I mentioned. That's good."

"I had no idea who he was. Harry invited me for bourbon in the study. I told him the only bourbon I touch . . . Bourbon roses."

"He'll appreciate your wit."

"I was horrible and tired. I don't belong here."

"You mean *we* . . . because we're black."

"If you think that, you haven't been listening to me for months."

Thomas handed me a forget-me-not. "You've lost your confidence."

"My voice."

Thomas's caress still thrilled me. His boyishly smooth face, I fell in love with years ago in Richmond, now aged with muttonchops and a wisp of a mustache.

"New York's fashionable society gathers inside," he quipped. "The most prominent socialite in the city invited us."

"Invited Lil."

"Her husband is an important businessman who supported abolishing slavery. He paid millions to equip the Union Army." Thomas held his vest, cocking his chin toward the crowd.

"You've grown accustomed to wealth—Lil's wealth." He said nothing. I shuffled back toward the party, reluctant to leave the terrace's solitude. "Their ballroom resembles the Louvre, every space covered in portraits, gilded cartouches, and cherubs."

"Lazy cherubs have worked no magic between us tonight."

"Cupid flings arrows in the music room. Evie is smitten with Conrad, who visits from London."

"Poor William."

"Oh, Thomas, look at us. We don't belong here. I miss your tall topper. Now, you strut in coattails and you fancy starched shirts with red silk cravats."

"You haven't traded your satin ball gowns for cotton. I'm glad for it."

I mustered a smile. Thomas did not. He inspected me, disappointed, always.

I knew this look—guilty, arrogant of never standing before men to be sold, nor working the fields until their hands bled, nor having no name, a spouse lost—sold. *"They glare because we're supposed to act like simple-minded women, married women, not individualists who speak out and think for our-selves."* I grinned at Evie's reminder. *How could I judge?* When I first arrived in Richmond, under the guise of Lil's prestige, I pretended I was educated and wealthy, shunning my eyes from the slave auctions and suffering—until I became *them*.

"That Thomas was a naive fool." He laughed at himself.

"I have given many speeches to once-overs from men like you. I dismissed and excused belittlement, laughed it away in extravagant parlors, and assaulted it with clever daggers."

"Lil boasted about you furthering your education."

I bristled at his sarcasm. "I never agreed to Lil's scheme, ill-conceived but innocent and for my betterment," I said, defending myself. I escaped to the railing, searching the sea of concrete and shadows. "You exhaust every advantage and association to rise higher. Why shouldn't I? Oh . . . I see. You don't want me to rise, do you? Least of all, pass you."

"That's not fair. I taught you and elevated you to this place."

I forced a laugh. "Lord a mighty, how I loved your confidence once. You have not made me, Thomas. No man ever will."

"Loved?" His airs deflated. "Marry me. Help me enter politics to make lasting change."

"The girl you left before the war and found again now strives beyond learning in the back of a schoolhouse on a spare evening. While I hid with Evie and Lil in Paris away from the war, the first black woman, Mary Jane Patterson, earned a Bachelor of Arts degree at Oberlin College. Rebecca Lee Crumpler became the first woman of color to graduate in the United States with a medical degree—the first black female doctor. I hope to meet her someday."

"Why not give more speeches? These women will desire to meet you."

"You're stuck on the past. You're missing our present progress." We caught the attention of a few onlookers. "The Thomas I knew would never concede suffering is our only story worth telling. Our triumphs in education and profession will advance freedom and opportunity. Past suffering is a chain that keeps one bound. I know; I long to free myself from it."

"And so we must tell the horrors, or they will happen again."

"You sell tragedy. I aim to offer hope beyond it."

"Then write your words to advance our cause. Harry Polk is a respected publisher; he's ready to offer you a contract for your book." Thomas handed me the publisher's card.

I studied it, him. "What book?"

Thomas bowed his head.

Lively music echoed from the ballroom. I searched for Evie dancing with Conrad. "You won't accept I'm happiest living a simple life." I chuckled at myself now, fluffing my lavish gold gown, and removed my ridiculous feather hat. "We stand costumed in wealth because Lil is gracious with her fortune, but I am not made for this. I thrill as you, but not at them—at the sight of a boy's sparkling eyes when he comprehends he has learned how to read. Life isn't meant to live in a trunk or on stage, in parlors, smiling and performing witticisms and speeches on command for strangers who tune out after the first minute."

Thomas stroked my cheek and whispered, "Essie, we have a seat at the table. When will we have this chance again? Yes, Lil's fortune bought us freedom and rescued us from the South. Why go back? We have a responsibility to use our voices and education to lift others."

I slipped out from his touch. "I have! But how can I lift others if I'm flat on the floor? You refuse to see me, the real me, as I ignore her, too."

"In all these years, you have never asked how Lil found me."

"Lil rescued you. You owe her your life."

We looked at each other surprised, distance falling between us. "Lil hasn't told you," Thomas shouted. "You're not the only one who has to reconcile with the past." He walked away. I thought for good, only to turn back to say one last hurtful word. "Miss Lil said you could pass for white and enter one of those fine schools. Maybe you should."

I searched his dead eyes, once brimming with optimism and love. Beyond the shelter of Lil's walled garden, the horrors of slavery had changed us. But it was something more. Ever since we left Richmond, Thomas saw me, as he required. Through a white gauze that made me innocent, clean, and pure. I hadn't realized until his stare changed this night.

"You didn't hear a word I said, Thomas. You used to listen. Has the war, the years, changed us so very much?"

"You left for Paris."

"I came back."

"Ghosts came with you."

"I will not apologize for your unwillingness to see me as I am, to see *her*."

"Who is *she*, Essie Mae? Who is her?"

The music, my world, stopped. The clouds hid the stars. I longed to hide with them.

"One who was broken," I answered, ". . . beaten . . . raped and left for dead." Each word a labor, as if I had lost the ability to speak, and yet, they were the words my lips formed. I heard no sound to them, none. "You cannot make peace with her; yet, you demand I do."

"It is why I study law—to help our own."

I rushed away from him. Nowhere to run, I clung to the yellow rose tree, the only semblance of comfort here. "Who is our own? Look at me, Thomas. Do you hate the white in me, too? Sometimes, the way you look at me, speak of me—I pray someday, we will live in a world where one says look at the fine, smart woman teaching children to read and write. Do you know the kind young man who runs the school in Piermont? Not a black woman, nor white, nor black man, nor brown—we are names, gifts, souls, spirits—not colors, Thomas. Names."

"I never meant to hurt you. You speak so much of Westland and those people treating you like family."

"And that's wrong? What about Lil, all she has done for you? You are crushing her now." I grabbed his hands, and for the first time in months, I held hope for us, hope he would come back to me, hope I could make peace with *her*.

"They don't own you anymore."

Five words carved a canyon between us.

"Neither do you. After all these years . . . you are still jealous of Evie."

"I longed to take you as my wife," he said through his teeth. "I waited for you for years."

I slipped his engagement ring off my finger, hiding it in my palm.

He watched me, silent. "What if part of your story is false?" he asked, looking through me, waiting for my answer.

"What do you mean?" I tossed away his question, hiding my secret inside the rim of my hat, bending and twisting it until a white plume floated to the ground.

"What if Evie wasn't your sister?"

I froze.

All at once, the past churned inside my stomach, rising to my throat. I choked it down. "What gossip are you spewing to get me to stay?" The hat twisted inside my fingers. He watched me mangle it as I revealed the secret Miss Katie warned me to tuck away deep inside my heart. I couldn't hide my tears. Thomas had lost my trust, me.

"You're not even curious?" His voice sharp, wounded. "I heard Lil talking years ago. But I never said a word, did I?" Noticing me backing away, he softened. "And you never told me the truth. You never thought I was worthy enough to tell me the truth."

"There is nothing to tell." My answer flat, indifferent.

"But there is, Essie Mae. Evie is not your sister." He watched for my reaction.

Don't flinch. "Enough. I don't know what you're talking about." He knew by my glare I wanted to know everything he presumed. *Trapped.* Lil, laughing with her friends, waved at me until she saw me rubbing away tears. I looked to the skyline, bleak and frigid, buildings and factories. I missed the escape of the trees . . . our hillside. "It looks like Paris."

"Essie, look at me, please. What if Evie isn't your sister? You could live your own life."

My thoughts swirled, dreading if a snip of his gossip were true, what it would mean. *Westland. Miss Katie. Delly . . . all my life I've wondered who I was, but now.* "Miss Katie says . . ." I exhaled, calming myself, feigning a smile as Lil dazzled the guests, watching me from afar. "Miss Katie says those often boasting the most intelligence, know nothing that matters."

I could not fool Thomas.

"You don't want to know anything about the truth, or who you are," he said. "So many of us seek answers we'll never find. What about me? I believed the lie, Lil as my mother, because I had nothing else to believe in. I might have a sister, brother . . . a father who searches for me . . . I'll never know. And neither will you."

"That's a cruel thing to say."

"If you won't believe me, ask Lil—Delly."

Delly. I laughed his threats away, but I knew Thomas well. Something or someone had made him sure of himself, but what, who?

The stars finally shined for me. My tears blurred the night sky. I couldn't suppress the urge: flight into a forest, an old man's apple cove, Miss Katie's roses, mine. I prided myself in knowing many things, but I knew running best.

"The girl you loved died that night," I said. "She's never coming back. I'm sorry, you've waited for the wrong woman. You cannot tell me what my story is and how I should tell it. It's over, Thomas. I'm leaving the city. No more speeches. The Morgans invited me to stay on at their strawberry farm. We started our school there. Evie will return to Westland. I will soon join her. She needs me." I handed him his ring.

He shoved it in his pocket as if he found a dime. "So did I."

The train's rattle on the tracks morphed into the sound of clinking chains.

I rubbed my wrists, tugging my sleeves over my scars. "Leave me alone. Please."

You don bleed like we bleed. She got her scars, old man. Leave her be. She in pain, like we all hurtin'. "Stop." I closed my eyes, focusing on the train nearing the station, its howling whistle, bell ringing. "Stop . . . please."

"Essie." A flash of red light burst across my eyes as the past melted into the wheat fields outside my window. I quickly pulled my hands off my ears, resting them demurely in my lap. Bedford patted my shoulder, then sat across from me. "We'll be pulling into Sweet Water soon," he said happily. The warm tone in his voice chased all others away.

I rustled my skirt, my hands fumbling for the magazines I could conceal my thoughts in once more. I remembered the shocking image I saw out of place. Yet, the picture strangely gave me hope it found its way onto the pages, into the sight of those who needed to see beyond fashions and gossip. "Thank you for the magazines, Bedford," I said, my voice shaking. "Evie enjoys them. Miss Katie kept stacks in her study. I bet Evie's poring over them now."

"Why?" Bedford eyed my fumbling hands, me. He looked away as I dabbed my tears, checking to ensure my rose stood upright safe in its box.

"Because they were her mother's." At my sigh, Bedford studied me again and smiled. I stilled my breathing, gazing out the window, trying to spot wildflowers on the bank. *Globe thistles look like the blue pompoms Mama crocheted on our winter caps*, Evie said in my thoughts. "Many mornings, I heard Evie rave about Paris fashions and James bemoaning their insignificance. Oh, but this stack expanded my knowledge during this trip."

"How so?" Bedford asked, leaning back in his seat, gesturing for me to enlighten him.

I nodded, accepting his challenge. "In Paris, it is no longer necessary to conceal most ladies wear false hair. The Paris exhibition will be grand. They showcase a piano with a violin attached."

He deflated, relieved at my laugh. "I should like to see that . . . the piano, not false hair."

"For seventy-five cents, I may send for Poppy's Freckle Banisher." Bedford folded his arms, amused, motioning for me to continue. "This potion will surely tempt Lil."

"Never. Lil's freckles, and the three on your nose, are endearing."

I raised a finger at his interruption. "Lastly, bead trimmings and buttons the size of small butter plates on dresses are fashionable in New York."

Bedford grabbed a magazine, scouring the pages, his spectacles down his nose.

"I almost forgot," I said, "spectacular news: of six hundred and twelve young ladies who fainted last year, more than one half of them fell in the arms of gentlemen. Only three had the misfortune of falling on the floor."

It felt good to share a laugh. Yet, Bedford turned serious as he pocketed his glasses and tucked the magazines into my tote. I held his stare, swallowing the lump in my throat.

"And the article that triggered your trembling hands?" he asked, leaning closer.

"The recipe for Family Cake with rose-water icing. Family Cake, what a name."

Bedford stared into me. My hands rattled together. I hid them under my shawl. "They're getting worse . . . your flashbacks," he stated.

"A Cruel Punishment . . . the title of an article about a black girl in Richmond." I bit my lip, my anger rising. His gentle gaze invited trust. I hungered for it. He leaned back, giving me space, a moment. I stroked the image of an abused black girl. "A man sent a photograph to this magazine." My throat closed to a whisper. "An illustration of a thirteen-year-old black girl displayed the scars of her punishment: a hot iron on her back by an evil woman."

"Essie. I am sorry. You don't have to—"

"The Freedmen's Bureau will investigate. This monster, the girl's owner, locked the girl in a room for a week, burning her with hot coals on her back and head. The pain drove the girl mad. They arrested the woman. Shouts of a good Southern lady resounded. I'm astounded they printed this story . . . an illustration of a tortured girl next to a bathing costume. Sebastian, in truth, I couldn't hear another heartbreaking account from my students or their parents. I can't even listen to my own. I can't remember . . . but I hear it sometimes . . . him . . . the old African . . . that painted and bloodied man . . . his stare through me, his longing, and I slap him away."

"For how long?"

"I never imagined returning to Westland. I was going to tell Evie before she received her mother's last letter, before she went home. But when James wrote to me about the fires . . . Evie needs me. She has always needed me."

"Someday she won't. You'll live your own lives. But come, Essie Mae, you've been so excited to see them. Think on that. Think on the good, yes?"

"I'll try, Bedford. I'll try."

"Sebastian."

"It's getting confusing, isn't it?"

"Not one bit."

12

ESSIE MAE

"It won't be long," Bedford said, noticing me admiring his watch. He handed it to me.

"Lovely. I have never seen a gold watch enameled in black and scrolled with white flowers."

"I was told it was my grandfather's. A fine man I wished I had met."

"Is there a photograph inside?"

He slipped it from my fingers and closed it, returning it to his pocket. "Perhaps another time." He tugged his ear. His rare nervous tell recently flourished around me.

"I see. Well, you've given Lady Pinkerton another mystery to solve. Bo thinks he has a secret. He always counts on the train's delay and has a drink with a barber who's an old Choctaw friend of Miss Katie's. Bo sneaks in a shave, too, and when he kisses me, I inhale the faint smell of roses on his smooth, chubby cheeks."

"A shave sounds refreshing." Bedford left, whispered something to the conductor, and reappeared with his short, squatty friend. The man removed his hat, revealing a pompadour of black hair. "Miss Essie, this is Sal," Bedford said. "Sal's been a great help to me in the matter we discussed. He will arrive at Westland in a few days with, I anticipate, good news."

"It's time," Sal said, before I could ask questions. "*Bellissima.*" He kissed my hand. "But why does she stare at me, *mio amico?*" Sal asked Bedford.

"Forgive me," I said. "I'm happy to see you won that blue bow tie with the white dots."

"*Signorina?*"

"Monsieur Lecour's haberdashery in Paris, *si?*"

Sal's eyes brightened. "How did you . . ."

I grinned at Bedford, who motioned for me to explain. "A spirited exhibition, convincing that artist to buy a hat instead of Monsieur Lecour's last blue necktie," I said.

Sal nodded his head, looked up and down the aisle, and squinted at Bedford.

"Lady Pinkerton," Bedford said, patting Sal's back.

"Five years. I recognize the men who follow me," I said. "Honestly, how Miss Katie afforded this operation, I'll never know."

"*Signorina*, please," Sal whispered, tugging his bow tie. "Bedford, it's time."

"Time for what?" Our burly newspaperman resembling Father Christmas muscled in.

"Miss Essie, this is Mars," Bedford said, reluctantly.

"You may call me . . . Santa Claus," Mars cheered, relishing Sal's snort.

"I meant no disrespect," I said, blushing. As if rehearsed, the men studied me as I twirled a strand of hair. I untangled my finger from the curl.

"Can you blame her, Mars?" Bedford searched out the window, Sweet Water in view.

I examined them now. "Mars is an unusual name."

The newspaperman admired me, amused, stroking his whiskers. "The wife says Mars means god of war. You look familiar."

I scarcely heard the men bantering back and forth, lost in the blur of Sweet Water outside my window. *You look familiar, the man said.* I had forgotten the newspaper article written on me years ago. My brutal kidnapping made the papers. My kidnapper, Grant, though dead, had managed to vanquish the truth, or so his father ensured. *This woman exaggerates a fantastical tale for profit, slandering an honorable gentleman of high standing from one of the wealthiest families in Alabama.* My story disappeared with the war, reappearing when the popularity of my speeches intrigued newspapermen like Mars. Thomas made sure of it.

Bedford jostled my shoulder, waking me.

I inspected Mars now and Bedford's silence. "God of war hardly squares with Santa Claus." I brushed off Mars's suspicious gaze.

"Boyo, Miss Essie is as sharp as you implied."

"Wren was thrilled to meet you," I explained. "You know children and their imaginations."

Mars held his belly while he laughed, caught himself, and elbowed Bedford. "I'm a craggy newspaperman, miss. Missus on me for years to shave this white beard, but in my line of work it pays to appear . . . congenial, nostalgic. Your wee girl cost me my box of chocolates."

"I thought you left us for Richmond," Bedford said.

"A tip leads me to a prominent funeral."

My stomach fluttered at the mention.

Sal whispered into Bedford's ear. Bedford raised his eyebrow at Mars.

"Who wired you to attend the funeral for Katherine Winthrop?" I asked.

"A dear friend," Mars said without a hitch. "Oh, the bloodcurdling insults I'll suffer for losing her box of chocolates. Pardon my vulgarity, miss."

"A saying I've heard too often."

Mars grinned, enjoying my brief inquisition.

"Will you accompany us to Westland?" I asked him.

"No, Miss Essie, I arrange my transportation." Mars lost his jolly demeanor and squinted at Bedford, hinting for an invitation. Bedford's grin changed to his customary poker face.

Sal busted in. "A sleigh and reindeer. Come, now."

The train halted. I fell back into Bedford. "Ready?" he asked, protecting my rose.

I steady myself. "May I have my rose now?"

Mars tipped his hat and left.

"Sweet Water," the conductor called.

I looked out the window for Bo. Bo saw me straightaway. His big wave and grin soothed my fluttering heart. "There's Bo!" I squeezed past Bedford and Sal down the aisle.

"Is it clear?" Bedford asked Sal.

Sal stopped my flight and exited first, elbowing his way through the crowd to the baggage. He spoke with a black man who looked my way. Bedford nodded to them, and Sal and the man headed for the saloon. Our Santa Claus slash newspaperman disappeared.

"Been waiting, child." Bo's mellow voice resounded through the chatter.

Bedford stepped aside, clutching my rose as I jumped into Bo's arms. "I've missed you," I cried. Bo held me tight. I breathed in the rose water on his cheeks, slathering them with kisses.

Bo stepped back to admire me. "Look at ya. Essie Mae, you a grown woman. Prettier than the last time I see ya."

I twirled for him. "A haircut and a fancy new suit, you look handsome." Bo hadn't changed in a year, though his eyes looked tired. I took him in, his smile I missed, and his overwhelming, protective presence. I no longer needed Bedford's escort. Bo would keep us safe.

"Don't wanna wear em," Bo grumbled, pulling his jacket. "Tight in the wrong places. Miss Lil bossing. Delly in a fit." He tossed his hat to my laughter.

"Evie wrote Lil's fussing in Delly's kitchen."

"Sound like yowling cats. Don't mind leaving the house a spell. But, child, Delly got the chicken on and lemon pies in the icebox."

"Good!" I tilted my face to the sun, inhaling fresh air. Roasted peanuts and freshly baked bread reminded me of my visits to Sweet Water with Evie and Miss Katie. The sights, sounds, and smells of rebuilding overtook the soot and clamor of the train departing the station. Fresh cut pitch pine and cedar bloomed from a new lumber mill, awaking my senses. "Progress," I whispered. A tingle of hope shot through my body.

"You all right, Essie Mae?" Bo nudged me toward the carriage. Quiet, I grabbed his hand as we walked on. Bo stopped, shifted his eyes to Bedford on our heels. Bedford eyed me, cleared his throat, and handed me my rosebush tucked inside its box.

"My manners," I said, giving Bo a peek at my roses. "Bo, you know Mr. Jarrell."

Bo glared at Bedford and darted his eyes to my trunk left behind at the station. "Yep. Wait here. I go on fetch you trunk he forgot." Nose to the air, Bo sauntered away, stuffing his thumbs into his vest.

"I didn't forget," Bedford shouted at Bo.

"Look at him." I sighed. "I wanted to stand proud in front of him; he wanted to do the same. And an open carriage ride to Westland in this sunshine. Bo thought of everything."

"He thinks I haven't." Bedford folded his arms, unimpressed. The horse whinnied and fidgeted. Bedford calmed her.

"That's old Star." I smoothed her black mane. "Evie named her for the white streak across her forehead. A shooting star."

Bedford lifted Star's forelock to see the mark and smiled. "I have a white streak too, Star, hidden in my sandy hair. I've learned, old gal, folks think you're quite distinguished with a flash of lightning in your hair. But it works no magic on Bo."

"Time back, Bo rarely spoke a word to anyone. He takes some getting used to."

"Oh, I know." Restless, Bedford sauntered back to Main Street, watching Bo speaking with an elderly man. Bedford raised an eyebrow at me.

"Mr. Merketts isn't a threat, just a talker," I assured him. "Delly wrote Bo's building him an armoire." I stood awestruck at the bustling town. The flurry jarred my memories of a sparse, tranquil Main Street. "I've listened to Miss Katie's stories about Sweet Water for so many years; I know everything about this quiet little town."

Bedford placed my rose in the carriage and stroked the horse's cheek. "Tell me."

I pointed to a man wearing a white apron, talking with a mother and her little girl. "Mr. Able Colburn, soft-spoken proprietor of the general store, gave Miss Katie a painted music box on her eleventh birthday. On Abel's birthday, Katie gifted him a basket of her finest pears, and two of her daddy's cigars, to the angst of Abel's wife who bragged to the town her Able had at last given up the vulgar habit."

"Of eating pears?"

"Smoking. There, another Sal." A plump lady dressed in a tan dress waved to us as she watered her flowers. "Miss Sal Fontaine, quite the Southern belle in her day, sews immaculate wedding dresses. I always wondered how Miss Fontaine came to live in Sweet Water."

"A mystery I'm sure Lady Pinkerton will solve."

"*Halito*, Essie Mae! *Halito*!" a man called, waving from outside his barbershop.

I waved at Nicholas. "*Halito*, Young Bear."

"Choctaw?" Bedford asked, surprised.

"Yes. His mother, a princess among the Choctaw people, stayed behind during the Treaty of Dancing Rabbit Creek. Many Choctaw lived here peacefully among the settlers."

"A half-breed." I spun around at Bedford's disdain. He ignored me, monitoring Bo, still engaged with Mr. Merketts. I stopped myself from scolding Bedford's remark, remembering our conversation on the train and his reluctance to speak on his Indian heritage. "I'm sorry," he said.

I patted his arm. We had enough debates for one trip. His hand found mine lingering cuffed inside his forearm. I swiftly removed it. "Young Bear, Nicholas, is the barber who splashes Bo's cheeks with rose water." Uneasy, Bedford eyed the saloon. "Happily, the Harding Saloon no longer stands. No one has fond memories of it. The theater is new."

"The Dunabee Playhouse?"

"Lil," we said together.

I walked a few steps to take it in. "Her late husband, Sir Randolph Dunabee of Gloucester, sounded like a tall tale from an adventure book."

"Lil's the proprietor of a theater in Sweet Water."

"Evie wrote this winter Lil hosts *Romeo and Juliet*. Naturally, the production will showcase the most elaborate costumes Sweet Water will ever behold."

"Naturally."

"Lovesick Juliet can't remember her lines, and Romeo has revealed an insufferable lisp."

"No. I cannot hear it. But, thoft! what light through yonder window breakthhhss?"

"That's not funny."

"Oh, it is." Bedford stepped back, marveling at me as Bo. "Look at you."

"What?" Anxious, I fiddled with the sprig of jasmine in my hair.

"You're intrigued . . . and happy."

"I wasn't sure what I would see—charred streets, ashes where gardens once grew, burned shells of buildings. But the people are rebuilding, aren't they?"

"Inspiring proof, not all is lost and desolate in the South."

"I wish this were so. Lil's home destroyed, Richmond . . . the fires around Westland."

"We will stop them. I learned as a boy who grew up with nothing I could either view this world in despair and give up, or see beyond my poor situation, and cling to hope . . . and work hard to give myself a fighting chance."

"You are an unabashed optimist . . . Sebastian," I whispered.

"I try."

"What you two whispering bout?" Bo barreled between us. We followed him, watching him load my trunk onto the carriage. Bo eyed Bedford's satchel, me. "Bedford's coming with us?" he asked.

"Absolutely!" Bedford livened.

Bo surprised me as the two heartily shook hands. Bo chuckled. "Mr. Bedford, don't you go on think I forget you owe me for that last poker game you lose, James, too. Them IOU papers work on them city folk, not old Bo."

"Just wait until we play again," Bedford said. "I have some tricks up my sleeve."

"Better not be no aces."

"You two!" I shoved Bedford, relieved, marveling at the ease between them.

"How's James holding up?" Bedford turned solemn, hands to his hips awaiting Bo's answer. Bo glimpsed Bedford's silver pistol at his side. I had forgotten it. Bedford winked, easing my worry. His jacket fell across his hip, concealing the gun.

"Bes he can I suppose," Bo said. "One minute James laughing, next he shooing us all out the house. Don't know how he'll act when you come home, Essie Mae."

"I understand," I said.

"And that Evie restless till you arrive. Bedford, why you coming now? James don't say nothing bout you riding along."

"I have news."

"Suspect we all hoping ya would."

"What's going on, you two?" I asked, drifting to Star. "Star's anxious on this trip."

"So are you," Bo huffed. "You travel with this man for days and he don't tell ya?"

"Tell me what?"

"Bes say it," Bo said, nodding to Bedford.

"I did, Miss Essie, in a matter of speaking." Bedford's manner changed to all business now. He held up his satchel containing the contracts and papers he studied aboard the train. "Augustus put me in charge of Miss Katie's estate and Westland, its affairs, that is."

"I don't understand. I knew you were helping James, but not in charge."

"Does this matter?" Bedford asked, stunned at my suspicion.

"I don't know yet." I removed the jasmine from my hair. "You've wriggled yourself into a handsome position at Westland. I suppose if Miss Katie trusted you all these years, we must too."

"Must?"

"You earn trust, Mr. Jarrell. It's not gifted."

"Mr. Jarrell?" Bedford picked up the jasmine I tossed and handed it to me.

"Bes she know, get the sour business out," Bo interrupted. "James can't find the deed, Essie Mae. Already had men show up last year snooping round on gossip James a Yankee."

"He is."

"Think it save Westland from them government folks out to steal it, too," Bo said. "But Miss Lil tearing up the house looking for them legal papers."

"Miss Katie wouldn't have left it to chance," I said. "Are you saying Evie may not inherit Westland? What about James?"

"Hush, now." Bo took my arm and lifted me into the carriage. "Too much barking in the street bout things nobody understand. Bes crack on."

"Bo's right," Bedford added. "We'll discuss it tomorrow. Don't worry, Miss Essie. I'll have it sorted. I've wired Augustus. He's more than confident we'll have a solution."

"Now I understand," I said. "The fires—someone is threatening Westland . . . to steal it?"

"Since the day she born, Essie Mae know things," Bo said. "Don't know how but she do. Hear that bird singing? Townsend's Solitaire, she'll say, says it every time."

"Bo, you're changing the subject," I said, unmoved.

"Come, child, enough chatter. We get on the trail." Bo gestured for Bedford to board the carriage. Bo's eyes rolled to their corners and back to me: the warning of my youth; he hadn't another word on the matter.

Bedford waved to Sal, whispered to Bo, and raced across the street to Sal and his fellow standing outside the saloon.

"He'll be back," Bo muttered.

"Bo," I called.

"Yep, got one of my uneasy feelings bout that Bedford, but what we gonna do?"

"You've been with him longer, Bo." I eyed the saloon. Bedford scolded Sal, hand under his jacket I imagined on that pistol. "Do you trust Bedford? Did Miss Katie?"

"We got to."

"That's no answer."

"Do you, child?"

"Yes, I do."

"Then what we whispering bout it for? You worse than Evie, always scheming." Star was eager to trot on the wagon trail. "But it's good to see my Essie Mae, got surprises for ya, too."

"And who's this January Evie wrote to me about?"

Bo jumped off his seat in a bluster, searching across the street for Bedford. "Sugar! What that man doing now? And Miss Evie bes not spoil my surprises for ya. She promised."

Bedford lingered outside a flower shop now.

I hid my blush from Bo. "Sugar? It didn't take long for Lil to make you mind your p's and q's."

"Don't know nothing bout no peas and cues but suppose Miss Lil right, sugar better than the word I thinking on. Essie Mae, one thing you gotta do fore anything else."

"Comfort Evie."

"Yes, child, but mostly I's thinking, throw that damn harmonica that child honking in the creek when she don't be looking. Jehoshaphat! Don't know how a tone-deaf child think she can whistle them songs on that old harp. Won't let Koontz teach her neither."

"Where did you learn such a word, Jehoshaphat?"

"When I boy—and never you mind. You and Miss Lil ain't the only folks spouting them big words round Westland now."

"Ready?" Bedford returned, winded.

Bo snubbed him. "Been waiting."

Bedford boarded the carriage and handed me a yellow rose. "Red inside the petals."

"How lucky. It's lovely."

Bedford settled next to me, removing the satchel Bo had stuck between us. "*Homma.*"

"What did you say?" I inhaled the rose. *It can't be.* I sniffed it again and smiled.

"*Homma.*"

"James's Choctaw word for rose."

"You can't visit Westland without learning a few Indian words."

"You ain't never give no rose to Evie nor Essie the last time," Bo said, taking the reins.

"The rose wasn't for Miss Essie," Bedford sang, revealing another rose from behind his back. "It's for you, Bo." Bedford tickled Bo's ear with the flower.

Bo swatted it away. "Humph. Essie Mae, hold tight to that rosebush in you box. It ain't a smooth ride to Westland like them old days. Walk on, Star. Walk on."

Silence fell as Star led us onto the wagon trail to Westland. "I'll bet you my piece of gingerbread that's the most Bo will say the rest of our trip," I whispered to Bedford.

"Deal." We shook hands. Bedford lowered his hat over his eyes.

My hands were still shaking. I took a deep breath, happy to lose my bet with Bedford as Bo's deep voice prattled through stories of Westland as a seasoned gossiping lady.

"Did what I could with them roses," Bo said.

"I know." I wasn't thinking of my garden, but I let Bo talk to cleanse it from his mind.

"I start some replanting to surprise ya." I barely heard him speak.

My eyes grew heavy, but I couldn't sleep now, taking in the forest.

Bo turned around, chuckling at a sleeping Bedford. "Guessing, Mr. Detective Man trust us, huh?"

"Suppose he does," I said, surprised Bedford had let his guard down, falling asleep.

"So dry round here, none of us believe rain gonna come."

"It's coming," I said. "I smell it."

"What are you watching, Essie Mae?" Bo asked.

"A butterfly. I never saw one at dusk. I imagined Evie would concoct a fantastical story on its journey in a matter of minutes."

"Sure enough." Bo laughed. I was glad for it. "Truth is, Essie Mae, that dreaming spark leave Evie's eyes since she come home. She don't even say that word."

"What word, Bo?"

"Home."

I closed my eyes, breathing in the evergreens, a tear escaping. The old African wasn't welcome here. He tried his raspy whisper in my ear when Bo wasn't looking, and his stories ended, but then Bedford's hand covered mine chasing the nightmare away. I didn't even mind when his fingers swirled my scars.

13.

KATIE

Alabama
Summer 1866

I dreamed of autumn when the sunset cast the hills in a flash of gemstone colors. The drought at last over, cinnamon and ginger sweeten the air, Delly's pumpkin pies fresh out of the oven, baked with pumpkins from River Koontz's garden. River might visit us if he smelled the spices and browned crusts across the way. But Delly and Evie spoil this once bitter man with roses, cake, and tenderness, a tenderness that departed River's home long ago.

Songs and stories used to ring from River's farmhouse. A woman's loving touch sweetened it, too. His garden immaculate, porch adorned in roses, a home scented with gardenias and satchels swaying near open windows filled with secret spices and flowers Polly swore tamed the beasts lurking in the nearby wood and River's wooly, fidgety fidgets when the moon was full. As a little girl, I thought Polly floated out of a fairy tale. Her face graced with the chiseled features of a Greek goddess, hair in golden waves shimmering peach in the sunlight, her cheeks in perpetual blush. She once confided a famous conductor in Paris had asked for her hand, and how she ended up homemaking with a hermit farmer in Alabama was a story worth writing someday. Polly never desired riches, though they came to her in doses to the awe of the beast she declared God placed her on this green earth to tame— her River Wild.

It was difficult to believe a gruff man as River Koontz had won Polly's affections, but he was different then. Neighbors gossiped how this timid, European goddess could marry a brash soul as River Koontz. But River and Polly, young and in love, determined to make something of the land as my parents dreamed. Many whispered the electric, tempting word that set a crazed spark in every man who heeded its call: gold. And my father claimed, River Koontz knew well how to find it.

"Polly's my treasure," River said with a hoot, brushing off the rumors.

"He's wiser than he lets on," Bo and James said, convinced something was afoot with River. But Westland had its own giants to slay and secrets to protect.

In autumn, my heart sang, for Polly set aside her writing to teach me, a young, rebellious Katie. I abhorred Mama's charm school, as Evie had rebelled against mine. Polly intrigued me, luring me to learn beyond sewing and domestic doldrums; she ignited my imagination. "The arts," my father moaned. "Ruth, I have committed to expanding my daughter's intellect beyond domesticity. But we cannot deny Katie is apt for business."

"You dream of a son," Mama said.

"Katie will run Westland someday. Her mind works in facts and figures, not fantasy."

Daddy was right.

"At least she sits and listens to Polly instead of running wild in the forest with that child." *That child.* I had not thought of her in years, or perhaps I did, for she forever hid in the secret spaces of my mind.

For Polly, imagining was life's essential. "An imagination will transport you to places when you're stuck right where you are," she would say. "Whatever you imagine, you could do if you apply yourself and learn."

My father knew me. I was eager to learn as a man. He began instructing me on the business of Westland. Lively debates on social and economic issues replaced fairy tales. Polly found a new pupil—Isabel—a young black child who would soon find herself at Westland. *That child,* Mama referred to, was Isabel.

Before Mama died, she confessed her own fantastical tale. In their early days at Westland, Father came down from the mountain with a wagonload of gold, plucked from a creek as children pluck apples from a tree. "Nuggets the size of eggs, real golden eggs," she claimed. Not with glee—regret. "Gold transforms respectable, studious men into lunatics faster than the drink. Your father was no miner. He stumbled upon a few silly nuggets with luck." She sighed.

"I do not remember Father speaking of gold," I said.

"You and your sisters were too young. It was my fault. Alex was determined to impress my French father and assure him his daughter had not left her family and luxurious life in Demopolis to live poor and alone in the country."

Mama said Father kept his gold a secret, so much so, no one believed my mother when she finally told the tale after his death. In the end, gold had not catapulted my father's wealth; his keen sense and knowledge for investing did.

The story goes, one night, my father ventured to the hills one last time with a hired hand, Luby. A storm kicked up, and Father returned home— alone, holding a child. Luby had hid his daughter in the wagon; most believed so Luby could run off with my father's gold. He would never believe Luby had planned to rob him and flee, but that strangers must have threatened Luby to divulge the secret route to my father's claim. In those days, one whisper of a gold strike, and hundreds of men descended upon quiet valleys and river towns as wolves to a kill. When Father discovered a little girl hiding in the back of his wagon, he confronted Luby. What happened next, my father could not recall, only that in the pitch-black and storm, someone had struck him on the head. When he awoke, Luby had vanished.

Men found Luby's body the next morning. A doctor from Sweet Water revealed, if not for the fall, cholera diminished Luby's chances to live much longer. My father, Alexander Wilcox, had long taken care of his neighbors and the locals of Sweet Water; they respected him. He was a generous man with an upstanding reputation, and so, in his grief, no one dare suggest a heinous crime. Prospectors did not descend upon Westland seeking gold. No one believed it existed. The law ruled Luby's death an accident on a stormy night that caused a rash of flooding. Luby's daughter swore that in her father's weakened state, she saw him fall on his own. Father abandoned all delusions of gold, never exploring the hills again. When he died, the rumors of hidden gold on the Westland plantation turned legend. It wasn't until I married when Mama uttered the tale. Regrettably, the only whisper my late husband, John Winthrop, needed to hear.

"So, it was true. Daddy found gold. Mama, did you believe his story?"

"*Some* gold," Mama insisted. "That was years ago, and it is depleted," she said, as if suspecting others were listening. "Of course, I believed your father, dear. Men, including Luby, had tried to rob him. I never believed Alex would hurt another man. It was raining," she said to herself. "Luby was ill, and it was raining."

And the little girl who hid in my father's wagon?

Isabel.

Isabel was too young for my father to take in. Polly arranged a home for the child in Sweet Water. Father supported Isabel until her return four years later. Isabel was fourteen, a resourceful young girl who knew how to housekeep, cook, and sew. A few months after Isabel's return, my father hired her and asked Delly to take Isabel under her wings.

Children excel at pretending their happy endings. But no gift of imagination could write a happy ending with Isabel. As I matured, my father had forbidden my friendship with Isabel, sent me away to school, and banished Isabel to Koontz's farm and Polly's charge. Daddy left me at the train station with his tentative embrace and said, "I discern something in Isabel you cannot." He never discussed the matter again.

During my final year at school, I received a curious letter from our family doctor, Willow Jones. He wrote if I could not find the courage to return to Westland and make peace with my father, I should strive to rectify a dire situation and insist on Isabel's return to Westland. *Polly Koontz has taken ill and River's irrational behavior has become a danger to Isabel and his son.* On the same day Dr. Jones's letter arrived, I first met James—an awkward, charming encounter. Months prior, I had also met James's brother, John.

The last of the Wilcox daughters to marry, John had beguiled my father and Daddy arranged the marriage. At first, I refused. My father visited me, promising, should I marry John, and return to run Westland, Isabel could come back under Delly's watch. After our years of estrangement and missing Mama, I longed to go home.

Now, tossing in my bed, I reminisce as my mother. When I dream of autumn, I wake, and my heart quivers, reminding me my days are growing shorter. Still, I wonder about fairy-tale gold, and if I could remember the path to my father's creek, where one could pluck a golden egg from the stream. And I wonder if Isabel, the little girl in my father's wagon, remembered it too.

My last visit beyond Westland's gate was a quiet ride with James to the covered bridge over Chancers Creek. I tossed my coin and made my wish. "A country-dance," I whispered. "Remember me in song, dance, and joy." James promised, nestling me into his arms as his young bride. "No wearing black in mourning," I said. "Not a swatch, you hear, unless it flitters as lace on a fancy dress sleeve. Black is for crows, coal, and midnights, not celebrations."

"'Cause our Katie going home," Delly sang, our tears sliding together as her cheek pressed against mine. "Don't much like that talk," she said, tucking me into bed.

Bright-colored gowns, fiddles, an accordion, and mandolin—joyful stomping music. I will even imagine Delly dancing a jig. An old-fashioned country-dance; yes, this would please me. Tables stretched with gingham for the buffet. Our neighbors will add to Delly's bounty. The entrance fee, smiles and laughter, the way I remember my best days at Westland.

An outing to Sweet Water was the time I needed alone to plant the seeds of hope I prayed would blossom and restore Westland to the ideals and vision my father instilled upon its origin. I had convinced James, Bo, Delly, and Evie to take the trip into town as a much-needed break from my care and their work at Westland. Dr. Jones arrived, my willing accomplice convincing them to leave. "A quiet home will do Katie good," he pressed.

James was reluctant.

"But you negotiate the prices for the supplies we need," I said. "Summer is almost over. I want you to go." I needed to be alone. "James, you promised."

James threw up his hands in surrender. "Doc, you go walking, like Katie will beg ya, take the shotgun." I held my tongue. Dr. Jones nodded. "You're in good hands," James said. "Doc here is a finer shot than any of us. You sure, Katie?"

I smiled and nudged my husband toward the wagon.

James tucked his hat over his eyes. "As you wish." He kissed me and left.

I watched their caravan, a wagon and barouche, drive away. Evie and Delly looked back, waving kerchiefs. A slow lope past an oak; they vanished in a cloud of dust.

It was time.

"Has Augustus arrived?" I asked the doctor. "We have little time."

"He's waiting for you in the study."

"We will need a witness. Please, come."

My brother-in-law, Augustus Lamont, a reserved Frenchman, won Mama's French heart. My sister Sally was hardly ready for the eyes of a sophisticated, older gentleman. Augustus, an unusually tall man, had a head of hair Evie imagined she could spin into gold. He appeared as delicate as Sally, thin nose, high cheekbones, and a complexion too fair for the Alabama sun. Eleven years since Sally's death, Augustus led a quiet life in Mobile as a distinguished, respected attorney.

"Sign here," Augustus said.

My once immaculate script fell shaky on the page. "You will not say a word until the proper time?" I asked, blowing on my signature, staring into it until it dried. A tear escaped.

Augustus nodded, took the document from my hands, and offered his embrace. For the next hour, we reminisced about Sally.

"I haven't the time to remarry." He laughed.

I had never thought he would.

"Katherine, I must ask you . . . you are certain this is what you wish, *oui*?"

Dr. Jones interrupted, "Katie's of sound mind, if that allays your fear. I can attest to that."

Augustus snickered. "No need. Nothing can keep Katie down. Nothing."

"Thank you for everything, Augustus." I exhaled. "Come back and visit when James returns, you hear. You will not rush back to Mobile?"

"*Non.* I shall visit our old friend, River Koontz, and return later this evening. How is River?"

"Balmy as ever." Our laughter chased the solemnness from the study.

"It's getting late if we're to finish, Katie," Dr. Jones said.

Augustus handed me my stack of papers. The two men watched me fumble and fold them with my trembling hands. "Let me, *ma chéri*,"

Augustus said. Warmth glistened in his eyes as he tucked the papers into an envelope, presenting them with a smile. "I pray it works out the way you wish, Katherine."

"It will. It must. Westland will not survive if it does not. James would rather it burn than let that man take it. See you soon, Augustus."

"You are your mother's daughter. Such courage," he said. "I will do everything in my power to protect Westland."

"I know you will."

The sun hid behind the clouds, cooling off the day. The perfect time to visit my garden. I insisted on a walk; it would be my last. I inhaled my treasured rosebush bursting with yellow and ruby roses; the gift from Isabel decades ago and tribute to her child Essie Mae. Everything about this morning was sublime. The breeze skimming my face, the smell of the trees and roses, the sight of a few turning leaves.

"Dr. Jones, it wasn't that long ago James looked at me the way you are now, but your gaze is meant for another, yes?"

"You're still a beautiful woman, Katherine. Is it wrong for me to notice? I'm pleased the color has returned to your cheeks."

"I am grateful you came." I twirled a strand of hair as a nervous Evie, relishing the red rosebuds tucked in my chignon. The doctor smiled, noticing them. I felt foolish, my golden hair now streaked with white.

"I left the South years ago, promising never to return," he said, looking over his shoulder. "I cannot erase the horrors . . . the war, my cowardice."

At the gate, I stumbled into him, winded. "Regret." He steadied me. "That monster isn't welcome here. You are no coward and cared for many."

"Forgive me. I know better than to discuss our sad pasts." He surprised me with a sweet kiss.

A blush bloomed on my cheeks. I savored the spark of youth. "Careful, Doctor, I haven't been kissed like that in this garden in years."

The raven-haired Willow Jones garnered the attention of Southern belles near and far. He held the stature and appearance of Evie's young William, debonair, a nervous habit of flicking his black mane as a wanton stallion, and alluring green eyes, though Delly would argue juniper blue. A quiet, humble man, Dr. Jones married his calling until the sight of a red-haired lass in the meadow at Westland caught his eye. Now, silver invades his raven locks.

My father had set him on the course when Willow was but a greenhorn country doctor. "I agreed to his doctoring you children," Daddy said, "because Mother insists any man named Willow must hold an exorbitant amount of caring and compassion."

"Willow sounds like a wizard in one of Polly's stories," I said, to my parents' horror and sister's giggles.

"Why, I've seen James kiss you as a prince," Dr. Jones said, interrupting my memories.

"Ah, but I said kissed in this garden."

"You can't blame James for being a man with an aversion to lingering among roses."

"No." I turned inward. "When I reopened my garden after the war, when my girls came home, James hadn't a desire to set a foot inside. Yet, he often lingers in Essie's garden."

"James busies rebuilding Westland. This offers you hope."

"Always remedies and prescriptions of hope."

"Yes, Katherine. It is often the best medicine."

"Today, I plant all the hope I need to rest and gain peace."

Willow removed his jacket and rolled up his sleeves. "Shall we get to it?"

I stared into his eyes, thankful. In a flash, I was the little girl he treated for a swollen ankle after a tumble in the forest, the mother with a sick child he consoled, the friend he cared for, sitting at my bedside, nursing my fever. It was my turn to make him blush, sneaking a tender kiss to his cheek. "Thank you for caring for me and my family these many years."

"I wish I had done more for your parents. I wouldn't be a doctor without Alex."

"You have done more than was fitting. We shall never forget that."

When Dr. Jones opened the gate, for the first time in months, the sight of new roses and rebirth overtook me. "My garden is splendid," I said, catching my breath. I kneeled beside an old favorite rose Evie named Mama's Pink and inhaled its sweet perfume. It made me feel young and strong again. "You need water."

Dr. Jones found my secret, a cart hidden behind the fountain, and brought it to me. "Perhaps, this symbolism will give you the peace you need to get well," he said.

"I am proficient at burying secrets. But this is one I pray is found at the right moment."

"I will do my best. I promise you."

I sat on my bench fighting sleep as he dug the hole and placed the strongbox deep inside the ground. "My heart is in that box." I rose, held his hand for courage, and patted the strongbox as a final goodbye. "My heart for Evie and Essie Mae; it is the only way." My tears watered the earth. "And the key?"

"I've tucked it at the base of the tree as you requested."

"The willow? It must be inside my willow near the house."

"Yes."

"Then, it is safe. Westland is safe."

"I don't understand why you won't tell them now."

"I can't. I promised."

"I must return to Ashland. Dr. Hodge will take good care of you. I have my own secrets to make peace with, Katherine."

"We all do."

Roses and grass swirled in a blur. Dr. Jones rushed to me and led me back to my bench under the pergola of budding pink roses. We lost ourselves for a moment in the blue sky above.

"Are we ready for the gardener?" I asked.

He smiled and walked toward the gate. "How I loved you," he said before opening it.

"Careful, Doctor. My roses work their magic." I relished our play.

He sat beside me. "You returned from college no longer a girl asking me endless questions. You spent weeks impressing me with your newfound education and spirit."

"I was a fool," I said, losing my laugh. "Why didn't you say something?"

"I, a man in mid-life, you merely starting; we made our choices."

"I never loved John. I married him to win back my father."

"You never lost Alex. He adored you and only meant to protect you."

"That irony haunts me."

He sighed. "I've broken our rule again, haven't I?"

"Mama used to say, regrets are as sticky as honey. No matter how hard we shake them, they'll only disappear with a rush of water, life."

"A dear friend once told me forgiveness is the antidote for our regrets, forgiving ourselves most of all."

I cherished he remembered my words. "You waited a lifetime for your true love, and I, to forgive myself."

"If I hadn't accepted your invitation to return to Westland, I wouldn't have met her." He ambled to the fresh mound of dirt, scattering a handful of dried leaves over the soil. "Katie ... I'm sorry. I shouldn't have left Westland after John died. I'll never forget the look on Evie's face that night I entered her bedroom, tended to her injuries. The whole of hell resided in that man."

I closed my eyes at the thought. "You feared you couldn't save Evie's leg, but you did."

"That was all Evie." In a blink, his tender gaze hardened. "Today isn't a day for our regrets, but I was a coward leaving you, Isabel, and Evie. I've failed wherever I was called. Perhaps River is right, I'm no brilliant doctor."

"That's not true. Look what you've done for him."

"They do not train us to understand nor heal what took place here."

"But you came back and you will, in time, make your peace, won't you?"

"Yes."

"I have shed my burden. It's time for you to do the same. We cannot change our past, least of all Evie's."

"But her memories will come rushing back now after you ..."

I held up my hand, stopping his words. "Now you need a prescription. Doctor, freedom isn't free. Whether or not Westland is Evie's home, I have ensured she be free of it—him." He nodded, forcing a smile. "Please, fetch the gardener."

When Dr. Jones left, I smiled at his earlier kiss and confession, banishing regret with thanksgiving for James and Evie's return home.

A sheepish woman entered. "Missus?" she asked, holding a rosebush. "Grow this one special for ya. That old man know the flowers."

I gasped. "Lavender roses." Its blooms captivated me. "Beautiful, Astra. Plant them there, next to that fresh patch of dirt."

"Yes, ma'am. But might need a li'l more sun. Wouldn't ya like it by the magnolias down yonder? So many roses grow here already."

"No," I snapped. "I'm sorry. No. This is fine. Fan the roses out so they will grow and hide the dirt." Astra looked at me, confused. I wanted to plant them myself without questions and explanations, but I needed to save my strength for my daughter and Essie. I turned sleepy again, watching Astra plant the new lavender roses. "Fine," I said. "Not too much water."

"Has Essie Mae written to you about her arrival?" Dr. Jones whispered.

"No. I wrote and told her to stay in New York. Essie has the school, her students, and troubles with Thomas. I couldn't ask her to return now. She's barely holding on, poor child. She will visit when it's time."

"Come now, Katie. Let's get you back into the house to rest."

"Miss," the gardener called. "If you like, I can paint that bench for ya. That paint chipping up in the grass ain't no good."

"No. Leave it alone," I insisted. "I can't erase the past anymore. Leave it be, you hear?"

"Yes, ma'am."

I had used the last of my strength to bury one final secret I prayed Evie would find. It made no sense as I thought it, but in time, it would. Sprouts will stretch through the earth, rosebuds bloom, curiosity, too. I counted on that most of all. Curiosity and a new hope stretching between the roses; they had to. They must.

"Westland, where its willows hold secrets, until the night air sweeps through their leaves, scattering them in the wind and into our ears."

"What's that, Katie?" Dr. Jones tucked me close, walking me back to the house.

"Something my father used to whisper to me when he told me stories inside the willow. I loved those quiet days with Daddy when I was a child. When I grew older, I thought I no longer needed his wisdom. I resented him for sending me away to school. I hadn't known it was for my betterment. 'How many women receive an education?' he would ask."

"Our minds don't belong in the past. To grow stronger, you must think on the future."

"Oh, Willow, I must focus on today."

"You haven't called me Willow since you were a girl."

"How odd it is we soon catch up to our elders."

"Elders? Watch it now. Come, time to go home."

"Yes. Yes, it is."

14.

EVIE

The warm night air blanketed my chills. The past few days my skin tingled hot, then cold, convincing Delly to call Dr. Hodge until James intervened.

"She needs rest," James said. "She needs us to leave her alone."

"She alone," Delly said. "Too much. That's what making Evie weak and forlorn."

"Losing her mama did that all by itself."

I abandoned the flurry of preparations for Essie's homecoming, tickled as I spied James setting the table, cradling Mama's fine porcelain as a newborn. "Forks on the left?" he asked, gaining no reply.

"Yes," I called through the open window, ducking out of sight.

I welcomed the distraction. "Lord a mercy, I fixing a feast," Delly sang all day, cooking our favorites: fried chicken, buttermilk biscuits, roasted potatoes, and for dessert, Mama's lemon icebox pie. I suspect whining for Delly's chocolate cake convinced her I wasn't that ill. The front porch was mine. I stretched my chin to the sky, tiptoeing on the bottom rail, seeking answers in the stars. Delly decorated the railing with Mama's roses, honeysuckle vines, and potted violets. It smelled like springtime, with a hint of cinnamon spice from the gingerbread she baked this morning for Essie's journey home.

I closed my eyes, picturing Essie's carriage ride to Westland. The cool shadows of the mysterious wood, creatures hiding in the pines, wildflowers she begged Bo to pick for me, and the stories they shared about forgotten years. Faraway hills, a horizon of garnet sugar maples, golden sycamores, and evergreens. The splendor of fall might entice Essie to remember the good. Nearing Westland, her memories play: our secret outings, hideaways in the forest, treasure hunts, a forgotten trail to old man Koontz's. Mrs. Bixley's storybook cottage and the little egg farm where we walked twice a week, fetching eggs for Mama. I wondered if the walnut grove still stood and how tall the trees had grown without us. Did a crust of dirt hide our carvings in the lonely pecan tree at the edge of Westland?

"You didn't have to come back, Essie Mae," I told the stars. "Not for me." *For Miss Katie,* I imagined Essie's whisper with the breeze.

I rearranged Delly's potted violets for no reason, fussed with the roses, and set Mama's rocker into motion by my light touch. I hugged the railing and closed my eyes again, imagining the wagon trail, trips into town, marveling at the bustle of Sweet Water. "Surely, you've crossed the bridge nearing Kootnz's farm by now." The covered bridge across Chancers Creek that doubled as a haunted house on Halloween, the end of my walk with James when I pitched coins and made wishes, a thoughtful stroll where Bo and Essie spoke of new horizons beyond it and freedom.

Just before the entrance to Westland, its orchard and willows, my grandfather's lake laced with pink water lilies. Ruth's Lake where we made fools of ourselves ice-skating in winter, picnics and fishing in spring, and long summer swims that tuckered us out before sunset.

The treasured places of our childhood might bring hope upon entering Westland's gate. But a heaviness overtook me as I thought of the dark spaces within it. One memory bombarded all others, and I suddenly had the inclination to pray it would drift far from Essie Mae's mind. That awful night, the gunshots, intruding pitch-black, and silence until Delly's screams announced Essie's bloody arrival. The wild horseback ride Essie traveled on the trail to Sweet Water to fetch James. But it was Mama and James who happened upon Essie dangling from the horse she rode to save me from my father's imprisonment; save us all.

Unspoken days, unspoken words hovered above, blurring the stars. *You don't belong up there. If I look at you, I'll never stay.* The front door slammed, startling me back to the present, where my heart and mind belonged. "I'm sorry, child," Lil said. "I didn't mean to frighten you, dear." Lil's coy glance coaxed my slight smile. The way her eyes smiled reminded me of Mama. She primped her mound of chocolate waves and smoothed the lace hugging her curves. Aunt Lil's touch wasn't as soft, but it came lovingly and often. Her voice, imposing and gruff, but her own and offered comfort.

Lil guarded her grief with duties and joyful recollections, but she was ever-present, ensuring I knew, without doubt, I was not alone.

Down as Mama fancied, Lil draped my hair over my shoulder. "My mama used to say, God washed Katie's hair with starlight. When we were children, it was so blonde it looked almost white. You look so like Katherine," Lil said, beaming. "And we are all thankful for that."

"I don't have Mama's grace or wisdom to run this place."

"You could learn. So could I?"

"You would stay?"

"I don't know, honey. James needs me. Lost profits, wild spending, Westland's books are atrocious. I presume, in my sister's weakened condition, she neglected them for years. What will we miss out there, hmm?" Lil held me, taking in the stars.

"When I returned to Westland, Mama would hardly let me stay."

"Katie grew stronger. She believed in your work in New York and the new school." The rustle of her dress glided away and back toward me.

I kept my gaze on the stars, holding my tears. "Five years away, during a war no less, is hard to reconcile, Aunt Lil."

"But you're home now."

I envied Lil's assertiveness. "Home. I hadn't time to dwell on dark memories, caring for Mama, now they've come flooding in my mind." A violet found its way between my fingers. I hadn't realized I picked it.

"No one is promised a life free of tragedy, but one can and should move beyond it."

"I've tried."

Lil glided her finger across the nape of my neck, sending a chill through my body. I faced her, no longer hiding my tears. "Have you, Evie?" As a magic trick, a lace handkerchief floated before my eyes. I shook my head, refusing it, rubbing my tears with my fists as the tomboy she failed to tame. It was Lil's turn to stargaze. "It is too quiet tonight," she said, rattling her fingers atop the railing as if playing the piano. "Have the frogs and crickets abandoned us? Where's Delly's howling? Child, toot that harmonica; it'll rile Delly for sure."

Delly and James developed an aversion to Lil's brass since she arrived; I drew strength from it. "You always comfort my heart," I said. She never tolerated fuss, but I fell into Lil's open arms again. She smelled of Mama, magnolias, and lemon blossoms. "Soon, the house fills with tears and laughter."

"I hope laughter tonight. I miss my sister, but I am not meant for mourning. Before my Randolph died, he asked me to remember him with a celebration too. Oh, the doing kept my sanity. Katie gardened, you write stories, and I plan—everyone else's life." She snickered to herself. I nodded, standing taller, braver. "The house will brighten when Essie Mae arrives." Lil inspected the violets and roses strewn across the railings. "A fine display. Delly knows the flowers, though the mugwort and juniper wreath, oddly superstitious."

"Mugwort? I found a sprig of those tiny pink flowers under that willow." As I pointed to the tree, the key dangling on my charm bracelet reminded me of the gold key, now hidden in my pocket, I found inside Mama's willow.

"Weeds." Lil backed away from the wreath, holding a sneeze. "The mugwort is a tribute to my French mother. Your Grandma Ruth believed a wreath of mugwort and juniper protected us from evil men. It repels insects, not men, and makes me sneeze." Lil floated her hanky to her nose, fluttering her lashes.

"Essie would remind us juniper means tranquility."

"So it does." We breathed it in. "Now, let me look at you. Where have you run off to the past few days? Are you sleeping in your mother's garden . . . in the potting shed?"

The mention of a potting shed piqued my curiosity. "Is it really still there?"

"Ah, the spark I've waited for, dear." She held her answer, savoring my anticipation and vanquished melancholy. "You've not ventured beyond your mother's bench and fountain, have you? I don't blame you, child. Neither have I. We shall together, hmm? The potting shed was my favorite hiding place when we were girls. It's stood unused for years." Lil's hand rested on Mama's rocker as if Mama sat in it. Her palm stroked the headrest and slipped behind her back when she caught me looking. "Evie, you cannot hide those black thoughts from Lil. Who saw you through them?"

"You." I relished her soft stroke to my chin and swift kiss to my nose as Mama.

Dressed for one of her evening galas in aqua silk, Lil hummed a waltz and grabbed my hands, her plump fingers warming mine. We whirled across the porch, taking in each other and Westland. Our waltz finished; she caught her breath and curtseyed.

I bowed and readjusted the posy in her hair. "Violets. Mama's favorite."

"Roses, child," Lil said, winded. "Forever roses."

I moped back to my railing and the stars. "I feel irreverent in this pink gown."

"Black," we said together, "is for crows, coal, and midnights."

"I saw you wrapping your pearls for Essie. She'll love them, Aunt Lil."

"With the volume of Jane Austen my Randolph gave me on our wedding day."

"And how did you convince Bo to read a Jane Austen novel for Essie Mae tonight? He refused to read *The Headless Horseman*, spoiling the joke I planned."

Lil pulled me to the rocking chairs as a gossiping girl. "Balderdash," she shouted, leaning back into Mama's rocker. "Jane Austen will do Bo good, for I have learned he sets his sights on January, a striking but lonely woman. Not a peep, you hear. Our chatty giant will turn mute." Delighted, she flung her rocker, nearly tipping backward.

"What have you done, Lil? Bo asked me why folks don't confess when they're in love."

Lil's rocker stopped. "No." We burst into laughter. "Imagine Essie Mae's talk with him on their ride home. "No. I cannot imagine it. I merely suggested romance is replete with love games. Darling, a Cheshire grin stretched across Bo's face."

I spied inside the house. "I said lovers hide their feelings at first."

"I can only attest to his most shocking interest in romance; it is the magic of Katie's secret garden that softens Bo's heart."

"He's smitten, but he rebuffs January as a child and insists he's a worn-out man."

"Posh, Bo's not much older than James." Indignant, Lil rose, playing her part. "I warn Delly not to hire that girl from Mr. Tom," she growled as Bo. "Clumsy. That woman always spills soup on me." Lil raised a finger. "January isn't clumsy, Bo, but smart as a jackrabbit."

I chimed in. "Look like one too." I bobbled my head like Bo, making Lil snort. "With that wiggly nose a hers. Why is that woman always scratching her nose?"

"You make her nervous." Lil doubled over, laughing, staggering back to a rocker.

"Shame on us." I sat next to her. "Bo rather play cards with James."

"Bo's a wounded man who has lost much. Someday he'll find a piece of happiness."

"Bo mentioning love will surely jolt Essie." I shook my head in disbelief.

Lil pinched the color into my cheeks. "No matter our age, we still desire someone to love. We dream of it."

"Do you, Lil?" I tucked a red rose behind her ear. "Who do you dream of?"

"Hush, child. I didn't come out here to gossip about me."

The quiet returned.

"I wish you would. All we talk about is Mama, Westland, and how to keep it."

"A pressing matter."

"Maybe we should start fresh. Maybe James is right."

"How do you know? You won't speak to him. Honestly, dear, you would think I hadn't taught you a thing about manners and respect."

"I talk with James."

"You talk at him." She let me think on it, jostling the mugwort wreath on the door. "Evil men," she whispered. "Since you've come home, I've heard nary a word between you two. Oh, a nod, a smile . . . thank goodness. Therefore, come ahead, James," she called.

My heart jumped.

"He's been waiting for you all day, darling," Lil said. "We cannot have this tension when wolves gather, waiting for us to fight each other instead of battling them. No mugwort or juniper will chase them away, only our solidarity and communication."

"I don't even know what I'm fighting for." My face flushed at the sight of him.

James closed the front door, stroked the evergreen wreath, and took a deep breath of fresh air and a posy of Mama's roses on the windowsill. He sipped the last of his drink and handed Lil his empty glass. "You see, that's what I've said. Little lady, if you don't know what you're fighting for, how can we? Thanks, Lil. You best go inside. Delly's asking for ya."

"I gather she requests my opinion on the soup." Lil sniffed James's glass, shook her head, and barreled through the front door.

James let the silence fall, taking in Mama's roses, her empty rocker.

"I've always thought it funny," I said. "Lil commands attention with a few graceful steps into a room. At Westland, she stomps through doors like Bo."

James winked and approached me, hesitant.

I settled at his soft embrace. "You smell like a campfire and marshmallows," I said.

He squeezed me and walked back to the front door. "Then I best change this shirt. Delly demanded I smell of sandalwood and lemon blossom soap tonight."

"No." I stopped him. "It's only the coat."

We traded smiles.

"Just like your mama." He laid his coat across the back of Mama's rocker and walked closer. In the moonlight, his crinkling blue eyes sparkled with love. I would miss Mama crowing about James's handsome looks: the burly mustache Delly begged him to shave just once, his strut and jingling spurs, fierce protection, and gentle wisdom. Tonight, grief aged him. His wrinkles appeared deeper and his eyes bloodshot from sleepless nights and bourbon.

"You do smell of sandalwood and lemon blossoms."

He swiped his mustache, hiding his blush. "Women's concoctions."

"Delly's thrilled selling her soaps in Sweet Water. It was kind of Mr. Merketts to consign them. Mama was overjoyed with the changes and opportunities blossoming at Westland."

"You haven't spied Bo's surprise for Essie, have you?"

"No. I can't wait to see that old cabin. James, you've made wonderful improvements to Westland. Mama was so proud. Westland still stands." Regret slipped into my voice. "A miracle, when others lost everything during the war."

He followed me to my favorite spot at the railing, the side of the house facing Mama's magnolia cove and stone bench. We stargazed together. "Remember the night of the falling stars?" he asked. "Hope you'll stick around for the next one. Next month, we'll witness a show, stars falling like fireworks all night long."

"The stars . . . children of sun and moon." James admired me, pleased. "Diamonds falling from the sky."

"You do remember our good times, huh, little lady?"

"I'm sorry I didn't come to you today. Delly was busy and—"

"Rough few days for us. With Essie Mae arriving any minute, feels like the day has just begun." His clap startled me; he started to leave. "I hope things turn out how you wish."

"I don't know what I wish."

The creak of the front door; his footsteps faded and soon scuffled back. "But here you are, losing yourself in the stars like your mama. That's good."

"Is it?"

"Your mama used to say thinking's always good. It's when you don't think things through when trouble comes."

"Trouble?"

James loosened his collar and searched back inside the house at Delly's humming. "Shh. Not tonight," he snipped. The pain in his words unsettled my heart, making me face him. "We'll sort it out tomorrow. All the words we need to say."

"Mama left much unspoken." I pressed him. "Have you found the deed?"

James wandered away. "No. Augustus arrives tomorrow, Bedford tonight with news."

"Augustus promised us the threats from the Union to seize Westland have passed. You satisfied the government's loyalty pledge. Mama paid, though it's insufferable to think she had to pay again for land she owned."

"There was a war on, Evie. The South lost. The government will take any land they wish. Suppose so did we once."

"Surely Mama left Westland in your hands now. I wouldn't want it any other way."

"I didn't marry Katie for Westland, darlin'. I married her for love. And . . . there is the complication of Essie Mae to figure."

"Complication? I don't understand."

"Essie is your half-sister, so Katie believed."

"Believed?"

He waved me off to finish. "That must mean something to us and the damned folks starting trouble. Katie wanted to provide for her. I imagine Essie has a say in Westland's future."

"Mama didn't reveal her wishes to you? You kept the list; I saw it."

"Tokens for her friends." Quiet, James lost himself in the stars.

"You're right about Essie," I said. "I never thought of it that way. There's no question we'll take care of her, but no one knows about Essie Mae, do they?"

"The wrong folks have a gift of sniffing out scandal—and using it."

"Is that what you think Essie is . . . a scandal?"

James shook his head, his eyes groggy. "You know better. I don't have pretty words like your mama to smooth over harsh things that need saying. Augustus will help us. He'll explain soon enough Katie's will . . . and wishes. Ain't the time for it now, Evie. Last I'll say on it." He peeked in the window at the bustle inside.

I hadn't wanted to speak to anyone regarding Mama's will. I wasn't ready for what it might require of me. "Selfish, Evie," I whispered to myself. "I'm sorry, James. I only thought of what Mama's death means to me, not to you or anyone else, least of all Westland."

"Lil thinks we've been avoiding each other. Is that why?"

"I haven't meant to. These decisions shouldn't be crushing, but they are. Nothing with Mama's Westland comes easy."

"I know, little lady." His agreement surprised me and lightened my heart. "Supposing Delly's right, the only good that comes from secrets, is when we go on and tell them."

"Pluck them up by the roots so something good can grow."

"Right. I didn't want to bring this up tonight, but there's a lot at stake. Folks don't give up the chance at free money when a relative dies."

"An odd way to put it. Is Lil troubled? Augustus? My grand aunt, Charlotte, in Paris, is she worried?"

"No, darlin'. Lil signed over any claim she had to Westland years ago."

I strolled back to my railing facing the magnolias, picturing Mama sitting underneath them, me as a child resting on her lap. I took a deep breath, noticing James's new barn and Essie's roses beyond it. "My father."

The sounds of the night stilled. The scent of roses sickened me.

James rushed to me. "No." He couldn't hold my stare.

I recoiled from his touch. "My father is dead, but the evil he left behind lives."

"Evie, your mind's drifting to a place you shouldn't go. I won't let you. Katie always knew she would never leave Westland. Her daddy planned this land would fall to her. He made sure of it, in her education, and well . . . made certain. Your mama worked hard to do the same for you. But you have to want it. Nobody fights for something they don't want."

"I know someone is making trouble for you." James stroked his mustache again, searching around the porch I presumed for the whiskey glass Lil took away. "I'm not blind like Koontz. I see my family hiding evil from me in the guise of keeping me safe. This is what Mama left me, always. Maybe it's time we leave."

"If that's true, hate wins," James said, disappointed. "But I won't fight by myself."

"I never asked you to."

"How many times do you have to leave Westland to realize freedom isn't out there, it's in here?" He pointed to his heart. "And here." He tapped his head.

"Why didn't you leave? With all the horrors here, why didn't you take Mama away?"

"Where? Separating Katie from Westland would be like trying to separate the stars from the night sky." A glare slipped; he knew by my puzzled look. I didn't fear staring into his eyes for answers as I did when I was a child, ashamed, uncertain. "Tomorrow," he whispered, clutching the railing. Our row exhausted him. "Essie's coming home," he said, tears in his eyes.

It wasn't until now, in my stubborn selfishness, demanding explanations all at once, I saw the weight James shouldered over the years. "Yes." I smiled, relieving him of the task for now.

"Darlin', I don't have the schooling to understand such things. And I ain't used to soft words and feelings." He checked his watch, sighed, and searched the sky again. "I miss her. Missing Katie has us all twisted up. A surprise or two will help," he said to himself, walking to his coat and pulling something from the pocket. "I planned on giving this to your mama this Christmas, but . . ." He handed me the small velvet box.

I opened it, gazing at the glistening brooch in my hand as if a star had fallen and James captured it. "It's breathtaking."

He pinned it on. Frenzied thoughts stilled as I pictured Mama wearing it.

"Lily of the valley means a return to happiness, doesn't it?" he asked, hopeful.

"Yes," I said, impressed. *A return to happiness.* "Mama would have loved it. I remember the brooch you gave her when you visited Westland . . . when I was a child."

"She wore it every day."

"Turquoise flowers, pearl centers. Mama brightened every morning, pinning it on."

"Naturally, anything of your mother's is yours."

I searched his eyes, the sparkle nearly gone. "But you would like to keep it?"

"I pinned it on Delly last night."

"Oh, James." I ran to him as little Evie, a shooting star falling into his arms.

"Hush, darlin'," he whispered, pulling away. I held his arm as we strolled our short distance back to my railing, admiring Westland in the moonlight. "Your mama couldn't talk about Westland without mentioning the blue light of a big chestnut moon."

"Tell me more about the night the stars fell."

His shoulder pressed into mine. Mama's porch wasn't made for distance.

"I was a young man back then, the country in a holler over the night the stars fell. Most panicked, screaming it was the end of the world."

"The honest truth?"

"Honest truth, little lady."

"Did you know Mama then?"

"No. We were youngsters. It was a clear, cool night in November. Not a cloud in the sky on the night of the falling stars, so they called it in newspapers all across the land."

"How magnificent and strange, so many people saw the spectacle together."

"I never forgot it, like seeing Katie for the first time. I thought those falling stars twinkled in her eyes as if she'd seen them, too. Bet she did."

"I wonder if she watched from her window."

"So many stars fell steam covered the windows. This front porch, more likely, marveling as she watched, fearing, too, all those streaks of lightning, falling stars—thousands of them. I ran to the fields and stood alone under a sky snowing stars. Not a little one stayed in their beds as if Christmas came early. One star and another, for three hours, stars flashing and falling every second; fireballs, yellow streaks, and white tails blazed the night sky so bright I couldn't find the moon. A constant blaze in the black sky; you'd think you could hear fizzes and hisses, but it was quiet, Evie. So silent and still it scared me. My pa found me, laughing and crying, thinking the country was at war, a sky painted with flaming arrows. Streaks of white light held in the sky long after the stars had disappeared. Pa coaxed me back inside the house. I didn't wanna leave. I wanted to melt with the stars."

"Except for a blue meteor called the Serpent."

James grinned, comforted, I remembered. "My family moved from place to place. New York, Mississippi, but in this year—our first proper home, a farm in Missouri. How I ended up in Missouri from New York, I don't know."

"I would love to hear more of the stories that made you."

"Stories don't make the man, Evie. Man makes the stories. Remember that." I treasured his kiss to my cheek, our quarrel forgotten. "That December," he continued, "was so warm . . ."

"Indians made maple sugar well into winter."

James and I turned around to her sweet, calming voice.

"No one tells the tale of the night of the falling stars better than James."

"Oh, Essie!" I shouted, running into her arms.

We were twelve, holding each other, rocking, her firm hand swirling on my back.

"It's good to be home," she cried.

"Home," I whispered. The word stirred my soul. I let it sink into the soil of my heart, praying Essie's hope would graft into mine, blossoming a new life and fresh fragrance to dispel the sights and smells of withered memories.

"*Chuka*," James whispered his Choctaw word.

"Them the best words I hear all week," Delly cheered. "Crying when you two left, crying still. Won't say we don't need the water with this here drought, but sometime flowers need to survive without it. And they do, children. They do."

Essie jumped into Delly's arms. Delly held and rocked her until I muscled in. "You two full-grown can't fit in my arms together like ya used to."

James hugged Essie next. I stood back, watching Essie bounce between them.

"Bedford." James nodded. "Thanks for seeing our Essie Mae home."

"Pleasure to see you again, sir," Bedford said. "Likewise, Miss Evie."

James corralled us together. "Don't stand on ceremony here. Delly's made a feast and—"

"Her dinners are meant to be eaten piping hot," we all chimed together.

"Fine voices," Lil said, opening the door. "I'll give you that."

15.

DELLY

No need for lamps or a fire; my Essie Mae light up the parlor all by herself, sharing stories bout that New York City, teaching school, and the new rose she take four years to make. Evie and Lil cluck bout fancy things they miss in the city.

"Wine at Delmonico's," Evie said, gleaming like a star.

Evie fuss bout wearing her pink gown with the white lace trimming her mama make, thinking she bes wear black. I say, "Pooh, ain't no wrongdoing wearing the colors a God's rainbow, seeing how Katie sitting under it now."

"A world's fair in Paris," Lil sang, leaving to fetch the mulled wine.

After supper, we gather in the parlor 'cause it Katie's favorite place in the house. At first, Essie quiet, taking in all she miss. Her eyes glisten, watching James and Bo laughing and funning with Evie. Essie admire the parlor, stroking the scarlet drapes, running her palm across Katie's new settee covered in lilac damask. She see a vase a yellow roses, gliding to em like they Miss Katie, stroking the petals, breathing them in. "Heavenly," she said. I catch regret skimming across her eyes like a stone rippling atop the lake. It skip from Essie to Evie, so they stroll to the window, lost in the moonlight, whispering. Always whispering.

I see something else too, Bedford's steely gaze following Essie Mae round the room, changing the way he usually watch her protective and suspicious-like. Tonight, when he think no one looking, and that ain't often, Bedford smile a smile I only see once fore—on Mr. James when he grin at Katie them first days he stay at Westland, days I wish woulda last forever.

The parlor look like Katie decorated it tonight. Jasmine on the mantel, her mama's pillows lined up on the sofa like paintings on the wall. Now, her embroidered and silk pillows mussed 'cause we linger, catching up on our memories, except for James. He make excuses all evening to sit outside on the front porch and pop back in at the swell a laughter. He say, he jus wanna listen to the sounds a family again, but I catch them tired, sad eyes welling with tears. Essie Mae sneak outside, supposing they have good words 'cause she coax James back in to stay.

"You really make your own flower, Essie Mae?" I asked.

"Sure did. And you'll all see it tomorrow."

Bo puffed his chest out proud. "On the ride home, Essie Mae keep that rose in a box tucked in her lap like it a pup."

"I can't wait to see it," Evie said, tapping Essie's mystery rose box. "Is it your yellow and orange rose? That one smells like cloves. It's pink, Mama's Pink, isn't it?"

Evie sneak her fingers under the rim a that box, so I thwack em like she sneaking icing off my party cake. "Ain't it enough Essie Mae pile gifts for us like it Christmas?" I scold. "When we gonna open em?"

"Hmm," Essie said, teasing. "Pink? Maybe, Evie. You'll see it tomorrow."

"It's a beauty," Bedford said, stuffing his thumbs in his vest. We all look at him, then at Essie, thinking the same thing. *Why this man get to see this sight fore us?*

Essie squirm, tugging at her dress and scratching her neck like she do when she muster a fib. "Well . . . he . . . Bedford—Mr. Jarrell," Essie stuttered. "Bedford kept me and my rose safe, and I'm thankful."

James save Essie, wrapping his arm over her shoulders. "So are we."

Bo, he stay in his corner for now, clearing his throat, looking at Evie, and hiding that green book under James's newspaper. Bo ain't working in the field, but he sweating like he do, a wringing his hands, making Essie start to wonder.

I set the tea table, making room for the mulled wine. But I can't stop looking at Essie Mae, pretty as can be, smirking and winking at us in a white dress sprinkled with ruby roses, a red velvet ribbon swirled in her hair. Essie wear the butterfly brooch, Miss Katie give her. It flickering in the light like it go on fly off her collar. I pat my brooch, Katie's turquoise pin James gimme. Essie see me across the way, look in my eyes and see Katie's flower pin on my dress, and flash the grin from ear to ear I love.

Essie Mae finally home, so is Katie. *Homegoing. Well done, my faithful servant.* I smile 'cause I picture Katie as that gangly tomboy I raise, shaking her head saying, "Oh, Lord, but I make too many mistakes." But it's what she waited a lifetime to hear—well done—'cause she beat herself for all the pain her daughter suffer, barely enjoying life and a good husband with all that guilt. Guilt the sin a this earth.

My laugh fill the parlor, and they all jus staring not knowing what my mind dreaming. I sit in my rocker, watching my family, the one God gimme. And when God give a body a family, He don't worry bout no blood kin or nothing. He see fit to melt our hearts together no matter we look the same or not. 'Cause sometime, it ain't the family you born into, it's the people who love ya and stand by you side. God made the heavens and the earth, man, woman, beasts, fruits, flowers, and all the wonders, like how a ladybug land on a blade a grass. He know full well how to make a family, so I don't ask Him no more bout that. What God bring together, no man can tear apart, least not while old Delly here praying them evil men away, that the truth.

Evie boast her yarns, acting happier than I see in months. Essie Mae, a proud, beautiful woman now. Evie ain't far behind 'cause losing her mama make her grow into Mr. James's boots soon enough. Evie always wear his boots when she young; maybe it pave the way for her to run Katie's West-land. Least I hope it do.

I chuckle to myself. Essie Mae come behind me and smash a soft kiss on my cheek. Like a magnet, she stick right back to Evie, whispering. The smell of them flowers dressing the parlor ease my mind and the crackling fire warm my heart. Giggles and rumbles sound good to me, filling the parlor with the music I miss. And in this song, I hear a whisper, *trust Me.* "I do, Lord," I sing to myself. "I always do."

Bedford's eyes sparkle when he spy on Essie, she standing in the middle a the room, chirping stories and handing out gifts. I catch Bo's glare at me now 'cause he see it too. I shoo Bo's frown away, holding my belly laugh 'cause that big man jealous.

"Bedford," Bo called. "Come finish the game less you out."

"Just getting started," Bedford said, sitting at the table, plunking his money in the pot.

"Gambling tonight?" Evie asked. She weren't scolding, wanting to play more likely.

"Delly," someone yelled, waking me.

"You gonna make my heart burst all this hooting and hollering," I said. "I dozing in my rocker—deserve it too."

"You deserve a prize." Essie pulled me to her table a gifts, bout time too.

I stopped her from twirling me. "Old Delly ain't a top, Essie Mae. My back ain't fit for spinning." I open the hatbox she gimme. She fit the wide hat on my head so I get to strutting.

"Delly, give us a dance," Bo howled, clapping.

"Now you go on plopping them purple and scarlet feathers on my head make me look like a hussy a strutting outside a saloon." I chuckle. "Hen-house hussy, that the truth." The thing wobble off my head, hiding my eyes. Essie swoop in and fix it.

"This style is all the rage in New York." Essie tilted my hat jus so.

"Delly, it looks mighty fine," Evie said, showing off her new hat; it like mine but sprouting yellow and blue feathers.

"What's a rage?" I asked.

"The fashion," James said with a wink. "Can't live in a house full of women and not know that. Get to stepping," James cheered, clapping with Bo.

So I did 'cause I make James laugh and forget his troubles. A fine dance it was, too. "Lord, child," I said to Evie, trying to jig with me. "You still can't clap nor keep a rhythm."

For a lady spouting grace and manners all the day, Lil caw like a peacock, squawking her return, carrying a silver platter holding a pitcher and glasses. Lil stumbled, sneaking too much a that wine. Handsome Bedford take the tray. "Story goes," Lil called, waving us like her little chicks to come and gather.

We hustle, filling the chairs round Lil now. Evie sneak her third jumble and serve the cookies as we waited on Lil's next words.

"One day," Lil said, chomping a cookie. "Katie caught me wearing a pair of Daddy's old trousers. I argued with Mama that my dresses were too tight. I grew faster than most girls."

"Supposing I don't got nothing to say on that 'cause I a glutton for my jumbles, too," I sassed. "Lord, child, you could eat near a dozen in a day."

"Honestly," Lil huffed, cramming another jumble in her mouth.

We all snicker.

"You wore Grandfather's trousers?" Evie asked. "How old were you?"

"Old enough, dear. Unsightly, but comfortable tied with Mama's sash."

"Sure enough," I said. "Remember how you scared you daddy and his friends? They come all the way from New Orleans to talk Mr. Wilcox into buying a racehorse."

Lil flapped her fan. "Of course, Mama would not have it—"

"The racehorse nor that child wearing menfolk trousers?" I butted in. Lil gimme a bug-eyed glare; I give a good one back.

"Daddy was so tickled by my rebellion and display of individuality," Lil went on. "He often allowed me to wear trousers in the house when Mama wasn't home."

"But you missing the bes part, Miss Lil," I said. She shoo me away, but I go on cackle and finish. "Lil be dressed in a lace blouse and her papa's trousers, a twirling that pink sash that hold em up. Them menfolk march into Mr. Wilcox's study, and there she be. Lil stuff her daddy's pipe in her mouth and say, 'How y'all doing?' But she don't know little Katie sneak up behind her and pull them giant trousers down. Lord a mercy! That child wearing red bloomers nobody know she has. Lord a mercy!"

"Honestly, Delly," Lil fussed. "I don't recall red bloomers or a pipe."

"Figure you forget em so I tell it straight," I said. "I can go on in the attic and fetch them red bloomers you want."

"Delly," Essie said, hand on her hip, giving me that mischievous squint I miss. "How do you know red bloomers are in the attic?"

Nothing I plan on but now they all doing the belly laughing at me.

"Maybe I see em one day . . . maybe I wear em," I said.

"Sounds like the Katie I fell in love with." James served the wine.

I help him. "Them menfolk from New Orleans never came back."

"That night," Lil finished. "Mama served me an extra scoop of rice pudding. My trousers act ended Daddy's ventures in horse racing."

"Red bloomers, eh?" Bedford asked.

"How I missed your stories, Delly," Essie said. "And cooking." Essie Mae closed her eyes and sighed. "Sugar ham, pancakes, and blueberry bread."

"Guess I know what I'm making for breakfast tomorrow."

James held up his glass. "A toast to our magnificent Delly; our angel in the kitchen, angel to us all."

"Hear, hear."

"What do them chefs cook in the fancy restaurants in New York?" I set my hat in its box.

"Awful junk," Evie said. "Tongue toast with pickled walnuts."

I almost spit my drink. "Lord a mercy."

"Evie, you never ate that," Essie said, pouring bourbon for the men.

"Monsieur Batteux served it," Evie said. "I refused to eat one bite and asked for a steak."

"Good for you," James said.

"New York City has pesky peddlers on every corner," Essie said.

Evie make a show waltzing to Bedford, all mischief. "Bedford, I met one selling a potion guaranteeing the growth of whiskers," she sassed.

Bedford shrugged his shoulders at Bo who couldn't stop cackling. "I can grow a thick beard, Miss Evie."

"Evie, you jus forget Mr. Bedford shave off his squirrel tail mustache last month," I said. "He got the blond whiskers is all."

"Practically white," Essie chimed in, "like that streak of lightning in his hair."

"Lightning?" Evie asked, searching for it, mussing Bedford's hair. He give Evie a playful shove. James rear up a li'l, but I like seeing all this mischief in the parlor, Katie would, too.

"Well," Lil shouted, "I haven't met a Yankee, aside from James, who will not dispense with the vulgar word monstrous. I'm monstrous hungry, monstrous tired . . ."

We look at Lil like she a monster with a bunch a worms wiggling atop her head. "Too much bourbon," I whispered. Lil snuggled under Katie's quilt on the settee.

"That's nothing," Essie Mae said. "In a little coffee shop in Piermont, a Yankee hostess, Darla, serves a fine cup of coffee—but don't ask her to sweeten it."

"Why?" Evie asked.

Essie answered, "She'll ask, 'Long sweetening, or short sweetening?' A man asked for long sweetening, assuming that meant a spoonful of sugar. But Darla dipped her finger into a honey jar and stirred it into his coffee."

Evie choked on her drink. "Finger and all?"

"Yep. Short sweetening wasn't any better. Darla holds up a lump of maple sugar, bites off a hunk, and plops it in your cup."

"Whooeee, if that ain't a daft Yankee," I hollered, startling Lil.

"Why, Delly," James said. "I might take offense to that."

"You ain't no daft Yankee, and you don't need no long nor short sweetening 'cause you all sugar." I get the silly wink in my eye at that man's flirting.

Essie Mae finished handing out gifts.

James rang his glass for our attention. "Essie Mae, on behalf of your family welcome and thank you, darlin'. Your gift was coming home," James said, a quiver in his voice.

We rush Essie with hugs and kisses.

"Our turn," Bo said, his booming voice drop a quiet over us.

That peacock Lil bust in and wrap pearls round Essie's wrist. They pretty against her skin, but Essie trembled when her purple scar showed. "I've always loved these, Lil," she said, covering up that scar straightaway.

"I make ya two dresses and a new quilt," I crow like Lil.

Essie squeezed me. "Thank you, Delly. They're beautiful. I've missed your soft dresses."

Evie come barreling into Essie next, cuffing a charm bracelet on Essie's other wrist. "It's gold with hearts, keys, and roses. Mama gave me one to match." Evie jingled her bracelet, showing us. "See there, inside the heart charm is a dried petal from one of your roses."

"It's marvelous," Essie said, holding onto Evie not wanting to let go.

Bo cleared his throat, and we all turned to see that giant man standing in the middle a the parlor, holding his li'l green book. Never saw old Bo nervous all my days, but he look at Essie Mae, and I think she knew, staring at that li'l green book, trying to make out the gold letters on the cover, biting her lip like that young girl trying not to cry.

Evie motioned for us to sit and give Bo his audience. We did, not a whisper, not a snicker, jus the quiet Bo earn.

"*Sense and Sensibility* by Jane Austen." Bo's voice strong and proud.

Not a sniffle or cough, held in now. The parlor fill with fidgeting, 'cause none of us wanna show the other we a mess with tears.

"The family of Dashwood," Bo started again, "had long been settled in

Sussex. Their estate was large, and their res . . . residence was at Norland Park."

"Oh, Bo." Essie couldn't stop herself, running to that big man, bombarding him with her hug. And it the best gift of em all. Love.

I ain't never felt so light in my heart I almost float off the ground.

Bo took a deep breath, pocketed his gold spectacles. We twitter bout how proud we be Bo learn him to read. We beg him to read on. He read three chapters. Woulda like to sing my hymns a bit longer, but couldn't stop laughing, thinking that giant, tough man reading them love books.

Essie Mae grin so wide, ain't seen that smile in years, the smile when she a li'l girl, looking at Miss Katie like she her mama them years the evil left this house and Essie move in.

My girls finally tell us they tired, exhausted in they mind and hearts, but I spy them, like I do when they small, a sneaking downstairs after we retire. And what do I see? They're not sneaking pie or cake, but sipping whiskey, giggling, 'cause they full grown. I can't blame em 'cause that peacock Lil standing in that parlor with em. Surprise she don't light a cigar. Lil stumble upstairs to bed. Don't know how she made it, all that carrying on, a jumping up one, tripping down the other. Then I see the thing that make my heart flutter, a good one, like I see them butterfly wings float to a flower.

My girls wrap themselves up in James's coats, the two he leave by the door. Evie and Essie Mae look like li'l cowboys. They search up them stairs, and behind they shoulders at me, but they can't see me 'cause I hiding. And I see them hold hands, a skipping out the front door.

I know where they going. Only way Essie Mae go on see her rose garden, be in the dark, in the moonlight, hoping it cast enough glow to make her remember that dream in full bloom. She won't see the blight, nor the burned fence from the fire, or the dry ruffled petals. Them two will jus close they eyes, sniffing the air like it be my apple pie bubbling in the oven. So I pray, Lord, let em smell that dream and let em taste it. Let it sink in they souls bothering till they do something bout it. Then they'll open they eyes and smile, cry, too, 'cause it happen.

They smell hope. They smell a dream bout to blossom right fore they eyes.

16.

ESSIE MAE

"It made my skin crawl," Evie growled, flailing her arms, making her shadow a monster.

"Don't start with those ghost stories," I said. "I just wanted to view it in the moonlight."

"Are you sure you're not too tired? We can go back. I felt Delly spying."

"Evie, we're not children."

"Yeah, but Delly's glare and knack for sniffing out mischief makes me feel like one."

"Me too."

"Suppose that's why we're sneaking."

"Who's sneaking?"

Evie's giggle calmed me as we tiptoed through the brush, looking over our shoulders for spies. We teetered into each other, navigating the clumps of earth. Evie searched the sky for the harvest moon.

"We missed our big chestnut moon this year," I said.

"Choctaw . . . you remember. It's good remembering happier times."

Evie grabbed my hand, leading me on. The trail to my rose garden appeared overgrown; creeping myrtle filled the cracks on the stone path. Reading my thoughts, Evie squeezed my hand and said, "Bo did the best he could, Essie Mae. But with Mama . . ."

I kissed her cheek. "It's all right, my sister." *Sister.* A word reserved for secrets and in private, but its sound awakened my senses and lonely heart. "I missed you," I whispered.

"I missed you too, Essie."

My heart raced at the sight of my garden's entrance, a trellis tunnel Bo had constructed, its canopy covered in pink climbing roses. "It still stands. He's trained the roses perfectly." I paused, inhaling their perfume. "Delicate as I remember."

"I'm happy they survived. They're showing off for you."

In the distance, flickering flames quickened our steps. I gasped.

"What's this?" we said together.

Fastened on poles and swaying in the trees, paper lanterns set the garden aglow in candlelight. I noticed scorched earth, new fencing at the back of the garden, the absence of my horseshoe of tall cherry roses, and a missing wooden bench I made for Evie in the spot I called Evie's Cove. I held my tears, careful not to reveal an ounce of disappointment. It wasn't the sight of the fire's destruction, but the thought, hate visited this sanctuary, our hideaway from it.

I looked away. Evie held my hand tighter as we stood in my garden, taking in the candle glow on the sparse roses below. "We'll make it new again," she promised. "A grand rosery."

"We'll plant hedges of Bourbon roses over there, and a shrub of Blush Noisettes will grow nicely up the new fence."

"I'll ask Bo for two wooden barrels to plant your favorite China roses, the ones resembling carnations, pink and crimson petals."

"You remember."

"How could I forget?"

The joy tonight wasn't visiting my rose garden in the moonlight as if reacquainting myself with old friends; it was the glimmer of hope dancing inside Evie's eyes.

"That's the first time we've planned anything together in years," I said.

"I didn't think of it like that."

"Maybe we should."

The door inside. My spine stiffened. I walked through it first. Evie waited for her invitation. I offered my hand, and she jumped over an invisible line, stepping back in time, reliving the magic. She pointed to the top of the entrance, a weathered arbor, frail white roses clinging to the posts. Her hand-painted wooden sign held on. "Essie's Roses," she whispered.

"Smells like dreams."

I breathed in hope, for I faintly distinguished the sweet perfume of my roses tainted by the remnants of arson. I listened now. Evie closed her eyes, listening, too. Crickets, a squirrel scrambling down an oak, acorns dropping, dried leaves swirled and crackled across the lawn to a new space in the garden: a stone patio. A wooden swing graced a corner of the patio over-looking the garden, and a stone bench sat underneath a small magnolia tree. Miss Katie's cherished blue moonlight mingled with the soft yellow glow of the lanterns on the patio. *A garden dance floor as a Parisian outdoor ball*, I imagined. My roses needed tending, a gardener dedicated to starting over. *Me?* Evie tugged my hand, banishing doubt.

The wind kicked up, scattering petals across the beds. Leaves tumbled as acrobats flipping over our shoes. We smiled at the rustling behind trees and bushes.

"Surprise!"

My heart leapt at the chorus of laughter. A harmonica blaring "Camptown Races" made Evie clap and search the shadows for our old friend, River Koontz. But the flash of a silver harp came alive in James's hands.

"I wondered where my dusters ran off to," he said, revealing the handsome grin I hoped for all evening. It hadn't come until now, relishing Evie's bouncing as if his music hooted on.

"James!" Evie rushed him with her hug. I followed.

"Hush." James squirmed from our clutches. "This was all Delly's handiwork."

"Honestly, I don't know how young ladies catch their beauty sleep at this hour," Lil said. "I'm no young lass, but the Sandman calls." She kissed us and marched back toward the house.

"Suppose Lil's right," James said, tipping his hat. "Not too late, ladies."

"Wait, James," Evie called, standing underneath a swaying lantern, engrossed by the flickering flame. "Thank you. It's magical. You've challenged the fireflies to flash in autumn and outshine the glowing roses."

"Evie, look." I pointed to a small rosebush spotlighted by Delly's swaying lantern.

"That's right, child," Delly said, arms open, rocking me to frog songs now. "You left here crying; come back crying. Old Delly like jus one day with dry eyes like this here soil been all summer. But a sprinkle a rain do it good. So go on. Go on."

Curious, Evie eyed the new roses, squinting at me for an answer.

"That's right." Delly slapped her hip, proud. She patted my tears with her hanky. "You come gliding back to Westland, tall and straight, like Miss

Lil teach ya, but Delly know, inside you still them li'l girls. And that's okay. Don't need to rush em away too fast."

"That's a cutting from Miss Katie's favorite rosebush." I inspected it. *My mama's roses*, I thought. "It's taken nicely." I couldn't wait until morning to see the coloring. Its cinnamon and honey fragrance tickled my nose, my memories.

"It'll grow in no time, won't it, Essie?" Evie asked.

I breathed it in. "A beginning."

Delly plucked a yellow rose from her pocket and handed it to me. "These roses tease us over the years," she said, yawning. "One year, we think them intruding yellow roses in that red rosebush gone. Then we see a yellow bud striped with red. We bring the orange tinged beauties in here. Bo think they'll turn ruby next spring. Maybe yellow ones will bust in, maybe peach."

I held her lantern to a small bud. "My own variety. Oh, Delly."

"Don't Bo get his hug now?" Bo bounded out of the shadows. "You don't think we'd let you two sneak off in the night."

Unlike at the station, he lingered in our embrace. "Bo, it's beautiful."

"Lost some favorites, Essie Mae," Bo said, sitting on his new wooden swing. "Roses might not be as bright, but we got the trellis and arches up a ways. Evie and Miss Katie surprise ya with stone statues a two girls and an angel yonder."

I barely distinguished the statues near a bed of lavender, their bases entwined with ivy.

"We'll make it sweet and plush again," Bo said, resolved.

"I don't have to see my roses," I said. "I remember them."

"Bo and the men work like honeybees, paving this fine sitting place with stones, seeing how the fire ate up them three beds." Delly cleared her throat at Bo's growl. Though the evidence of a fire remained, acknowledging the act appeared taboo. I agreed.

"It's perfect. A garden swing."

"Cleared land by that old oak," Bo said. "Ready for new roses, yours."

Tears welled in my eyes at the anticipation in his, the longing I would stay.

They swayed and grinned before me. My family. The one God gave me, Delly often reminded. "Thank you all," I said. "I could have never imagined this homecoming. I take heart in knowing sometimes, the end of a dream is the start of a new one."

"Essie Mae, Evie tells me we have a bona fide horticulturist in our midst," James said, beaming. "Katie was proud of you. You know full well how to grow roses and more." James checked his watch in the light. "Now, you think you two might sleep tonight?"

"If you'll play another song," Evie said. "Please, James. It's been so long."

"Whooeee. Look, Mr. James," Delly said, mimicking Evie's pout. "Evie puffing that bottom lip like she do when she small. Essie Mae, too."

"It still works." James snickered, pinching Evie's chin, winking at me. "One song, if you promise to get some shuteye tonight."

"We promise," Evie and I chimed together.

"Fine voices," Lil said in the shadows. "I couldn't leave this sight."

"Well," James called. "What are you waiting for? Get to stepping."

James's silver harmonica shimmered and danced in the moonlight as Evie and Delly clapped and stomped together. Evie did her utmost to copy Delly's dance, succeeding, her inhibitions warmed by whiskey and wine.

"You're a fine dancer, Delly," I shouted over the whistles of a lively march. Delly had us form a circle; she curtseyed to Lil and pulled her in it. Evie skipped in the middle, tripping up the stone path and back to our circle with a kick and a hop like a dancing girl.

"Fool, child," Delly wailed. "Either you got the spirit or you drank too much a that mulled wine Bedford make. Keep a stepping!"

I watched from afar, clapping to Evie's wild dancing. "It's the can-can," she cheered, nearly kicking Lil. I searched the garden, disappointed I couldn't find Bedford, surprised I even thought he would come.

"What about you?" Evie hollered, pulling me into their fever pitch until we all tired, and the music stopped.

"Been a long day." James turned inward again, scanning the perimeter of the garden, worried. "Not too late." He tipped his hat and slipped a kiss to Evie's cheek and mine. Lil took his arm; they waved Delly on.

"I'll walk you girls home when you ready." Bo covered his face with his hat and rested on the swing.

"What you two gonna do if Bo fall asleep?" Delly laughed. "Can't carry that big man home, can ya? Lord a mercy. Ain't shimmied like that in years."

Delly fanned her face; her laugh echoed in the distance as she cuffed arms with James and Lil on their stroll home.

Evie and I gazed at the flickering paper lanterns. But in the quiet, sweat washed over me. The past clamored to ruin my present. Evie's touch brought me back. We grinned at Bo's snoring and walked a few steps to sit on the stone bench underneath the magnolia tree.

"Are you all right, Essie?" Evie held my hand. "You're trembling."

I slipped my hands from hers. "It's nothing . . . tired from the trip. This magnolia is new."

"Bo planted it last year." Evie eyed me, concerned. I focused on the magnolia. "After we left Westland for New York again, he added this stone bench."

My hand brushed a ribbon on our seat. "How did this . . ." I held it to the light.

"The yellow ribbon I gave you when we first met. That's the second time it's appeared. Someone's mischief; Delly no doubt, planting surprises, guiding us to remember the good."

"Happier times." I rubbed my eyes, exhausted. "An evening of surprises . . . has it been like this since you arrived? Surprises, gifts—oh, Evie." My heart dropped. Evie bowed her head and tugged at her sleeve. "Forgive me. You cared for your mama."

She squeezed my hand, forcing a smile. "Let's not discuss it tonight. I longed to laugh and dance again. Perhaps we shouldn't now, but . . ."

"No. She wanted us to be happy."

Evie snatched my ribbon, tickling my wrist with its frayed edges. "Without me, your trip was a bore with our mute Bedford Jarrell, wasn't it?"

"Not so mute this time." Evie perked up at the mention. "I met a plethora of intriguing characters, an opera singer who wasn't an opera singer but a swindler."

"Did Bedford arrest her?" Evie scooched closer, her eyes greedy for gossip.

"He turned mute on the opera singer. I met an Italian man named Sal and a little girl, Wren. Wren reminded me of you. I told her one of your stories. Oh, and Santa Claus."

Evie scrunched her face, dismissing my last claim. "I missed all the fun.

Bedford droned on how intuitive and cautious you were, that you didn't need protec—"

"Protection? Did he?"

"Damnation, that Bedford. Mama insisted before she . . . you're safe, that's what counts."

"Bedford explained Miss Katie's last wishes for me, traveling in luxury and comfort to Westland, but, Evie, you can't protect me forever."

"Mama longed for you to think of her as a mother, yet, you still call her Miss Katie."

"Too many years dreaming about Isabel as my mama, but I had wished Katie was mine."

For the second time during the evening, Evie fiddled with something in her pocket. Caught, she revealed a gold key. "I found this under Mama's willow." She handed it to me. We held it up to our charm bracelets. "Lil thinks it opens the potting shed in Mama's garden."

"I didn't know a shed stood in her garden."

"We haven't walked beyond the magnolias." Evie held out her palm, anxious for the key. I tucked it in her pocket. "I thought Thomas might come."

"It's still dangerous traveling south. And William?" I shoved my hand in a pocket, finding James's tobacco pouch. "Dresses and dusters."

Silent, Evie swirled her palms together, making whirling noises with the crickets. Finger in the air, she directed my attention to a lone cricket's serenade, a five-whistle song.

"The other day, Delly dropped a pearl of wisdom from her shell." Evie sprang up, hand to her hip. "Child, though you an old spinster now," she mocked as Delly. "You nursing a lonely heart all these years 'cause you think it's better than a broken one." Evie settled back on the bench, snuggling beside me.

"I believe God whispers words to Delly for us." I studied Evie. "I'm seeing Delly in a new light. She's lived a life I don't fully know."

"Secrets."

"No. It's something else, close and private. Delly was young once, too."

"Now you're against me? There's nothing wrong with choosing to live as a modern woman and alone. Lil's independent."

"She supports herself. Lil wishes she had daughters, why she spoils us."

"I'm talking about ideals, a mindset. I'll never be weak-minded like my mother."

"Your mama ran Westland."

"Did she?"

All this time, I guarded myself from dark flashbacks, only to watch them fall on Evie.

"Maybe I'm not fit for marriage," she continued, "or raising a family. Maybe I don't desire it. Does this make me a monster, an odd thing?" She avoided my eyes, taking in the garden, squirming to leave. I grabbed her hands, making her look at me. "Essie Mae, I can still spot the flecks of gold in your hazel eyes."

"Even in the dark?"

"Especially in the dark."

"You're still in denial about William."

"Claptrap. No more questions on love unless you explain . . . Bedford, hmm?" Evie folded her arms and bore her emerald eyes into mine.

"What do you presume?"

"We're not in Lil's parlor."

"Mr. Jarrell escorted me as he always does to Westland. That is all."

"Mr. Jarrell?" Evie snorted. "I've watched you two the past five years. Bedford tolerates me but you."

"Because you yap too much." I turned my back to her.

Evie dropped her chin onto my shoulder. "Nope. Bedford's changed."

I spun around, unable to hold Evie's stare. She reveled in the win. "Conveniently so." I hid my blush, strolling to mounds of soil where my magenta roses once bloomed. "A good place for my new varieties; you should see the roses I cultivated at the Morgan's."

Evie looked through me, letting me escape the subject of Bedford Jarrell for now. "Will you return to Piermont . . . to the Morgan's, your work?"

"It's my first night back. We'll sort it out."

"That's what I thought." Evie looked about the garden, her eyes watering, the magic lifting. "Lil wants to rush me away to Paris again—and you."

"It's nothing to decide tonight."

She raised an eyebrow at my consideration of Paris. "Bo's planned another surprise for you tomorrow," Evie whispered.

"I hear ya," Bo shouted, startling us. "Bes not give it away, child. You promised."

Evie stuck her tongue out, reminding me of Miss Katie's last letter, confessing her concern that Evie had remained a child in her mind, but she treasured the trait in Evie's heart and imagination. *Tragedy hasn't matured her, Katie wrote. Clinging to this immaturity, Evie refuses to embrace life.*

My breath skipped. I sat back beside her.

Evie's hand rested on mine, cold, soft. "Bo could hear a fly land on a piece of lettuce."

"Evie, Bo reading was the best gift I could have ever dreamed."

"Then it's good . . . you're dreaming again." Evie offered me the yellow ribbon.

I tucked it in my pocket. "And you?"

"Not so much."

"*Sense and Sensibility*, the first book from your grandfather's study for me to read."

"Essie Mae, you're being modest. *Sense and Sensibility* wasn't your first book. Your intelligence had surpassed anything I could teach you."

"You opened my world when you taught me to read. Do you remember your dream?"

"Which one?"

"Writing. Sharing your stories. Evie, I met a publisher in New York. You should have seen Wren's eyes when I shared your tale about the prince and the rose."

"I've forgotten it." Evie held her small gold key to the light, staring into it for answers. "We may forget our dreams, but they never forget us. It doesn't matter how old we are."

I spun Lil's pearls on my wrist; they felt tingly and numb rolling over the purple scar. "Dreams are gentlemen and ladies, Lil would sing. They will present themselves again at the right moment."

Evie wandered the garden now. She looked lovely in the moonlight, even hidden underneath James's old coat. She swayed with the lanterns. I looked back at Bo, awake now, keeping us in his sight. I joined Evie, walking down the path, admiring the statues.

Evie paused at the angel. "I prepared . . . but Mama grew stronger. She surprised us. My mind's a jumble. James and Lil are in a flurry regarding Westland . . . the fires . . . I don't know if I trust Bedford. Do you? Can we trust him, Essie Mae?"

I didn't want to answer. Not yet. "Evie, you don't trust anyone. Neither do I. That's our problem. It's not supposed to make sense right now." We locked arms and joined Bo.

"Delly almost danced her knickers off."

The silence fell until we looked at each other and blew a laugh, startling Bo.

"Evie, you're going to be all right. We all are. We must carry on."

"A party for Mama . . . it's good. I see that now. Westland holds a complicated and storied past. It was never just Mama's or ours. It's beyond land, legacy, or home. Westland fed families and kept farms afloat during the war, now." We ambled to the barren Evie's Cove. "We're fortunate James doused the fire. No one was hurt."

"Last year, Evie's Cove was lush and vibrant beyond my dreams."

"We needed it to be."

"In one moment, life may change. What we do next makes all the difference. Remember, Evie, indecision is a decision."

Evie knocked into me. "That'll take me a few days to decipher, Miss Speechmaker."

"You gave a fine speech on Westland."

"Mama's words. You'll grow more roses, won't you? You grew a splendid rose garden for the Morgans. I miss Sam and Haley and their strawberry farm."

"When I heard the harmonica, I thought it was River."

"I tried, Essie. Can you imagine River dancing? You're disappointed he didn't come."

"I understand. It's hard to believe River visited Westland after we left."

"Much has changed."

"I can't wait to see that old curmudgeon. Lil said his fits are worse and perhaps I shouldn't rush to visit him. She got into the bourbon and called old Koontz a poor bastard."

"Essie Mae, she did not."

Bo stretched, moaned, and pried himself from the swing.

We took his place.

"Don't know why you two sassing bout such things," he said. "When you should wait till tomorrow and visit him. Time to go home."

"And who is this January I've heard so much about?" I asked. "I thought she was going to spill the soup on you tonight."

We watched Bo snuff out the lanterns, and at the last one, Evie busted out a laugh.

"Don't miss you mischief sassing, that the truth," Bo said, crinkling his nose at Evie. He flashed his lantern at us. "Wearing James's dusters like fool women, sneaking out the house. You lucky I tell my men don't bother none if two folks come sneaking in this garden. Now, you ain't gonna do that again 'cause I got no time to be following ya round all hours."

"January is a frosty month," Evie said, busting another laugh.

"Not as cold as your saddle I have James keep ya from riding." Bo nudged us along through the trellis tunnel, around to the side of the barn.

"Beans."

"Some things haven't changed." I laughed. "And that's a good thing."

As we cleared the brush, strolling on the path back home, I smiled inside, listening to Evie and Bo make amends. "Miss Evie, you know I only funning."

I marveled at the two bantering back and forth, forgiving each other in an instant as old friends. *Yes, much has changed ... and that's a good thing.* A chill swept over me as they walked ahead, bathed in moonlight. Bo caught a tripping Evie, and his soft pat to her back warmed my heart. I looked behind me toward my roses. "You're not as ravaged as I expected." As plans for new beds and flowers scrolled across my mind, a flicker of hope ignited that Westland could welcome me home ... perchance for good.

But a different flicker caught my eye, a streak of a candle's flame through the trees.

"Evie," I called, thinking better of it.

"What's wrong?" Evie asked. "No time for hollering, Essie Mae. You'll wake the house."

"It's nothing," I whispered, telling myself it was only a firefly, James enticed from fall's slumber, drifting to my garden.

17.

EVIE

Mama rested under a willow in a cove near our hillside. She prayed Essie and I would return here and dream again. This time, she dreamed with us.

We dressed the parcel of land as a memorial to Mama. Bo built a handsome reflecting bench. Essie promised to plant her new pink and lavender roses. Even River offered his respect: a wooden cross embellished with dried roses, seashells, and gold flakes.

"Fitting, the hills glistening fall's glory for Katie; I don't have enough pretty words for her," James said. "She wouldn't want the fuss, and we all know it."

I tried focusing on the preacher's words, but I couldn't help gazing at Essie. She stared past Mama's grave to the forest we escaped into as children. I nudged her and whispered, "Your roses." Essie bowed her head, clutching her roses tied with the yellow ribbon from our youth.

James motioned for me to speak. I glimpsed two late-blooming morning glories in the grass next to Mama, losing myself in the imagined task of pressing them in my diary.

"Evie," James spoke up.

The smell of fall leaves and a coming rain lulled me to sleep. All waited, clicking the noises of crickets, rustling in gowns, and slapping trousers until the wind swept through the trees, introducing them to nature's applause.

"Mama possessed grace and beauty in sorrow and joy," I said. "We loved her and will miss her with unimaginable sorrow. But she wouldn't want showers of tears or praise. We promised her no crying. And breaking a promise to Mama was like thinking it's a good idea to give a porcupine a bath." I found my smile.

Delly hooted. "What a picture." She hushed herself until our muffled snickers escaped.

"That's my Katie," James said.

"The best way to honor Mama is to live, not in the past, but today," I continued. "For many, Miss Katie was Westland—its brightest days. Mama strove to leave a legacy of freedom, opportunity, love, and peace, and to defend it until her last breath." I looked at Essie for courage. She raised her chin, smiling as her tears fell.

"Go on, honey," Lil said to me.

"Before leaving Westland at the onset of war, I brought Mama to this hillside. She dreamed this, her family together again, taking in this view. In the spirit of her mentor, Polly Koontz, Mama fancied more this storybook willow, declaring Mr. Willow presides over the path to and from this tranquil place. Westland and willows go together like Mama and James. Their deep-rooted love, entwined in our hearts, forever inspires us. I don't have all the right words . . ."

My courage failed as I lost myself, not in the hillside's majestic view, but in the love and compassion shining in my family's eyes. The weight of their loss, my grief and fear of the future, toppled upon my shoulders. I wanted to run into the forest now. I missed River. I missed wisdom, safety, and surety. James rushed to me, and before all, our disjointed bond melded. I sobbed into his strong chest Mama relied on; the force of his firm hand steadied my steps.

"I didn't mean to break my promise, Mama," I said, pressing my lips into a smile.

"The bond a child and mama messy," Delly said. "And it hurt, but it also a fine painting you keep in you mind, a treasure to give ya courage—worth more than a wagonload a gold."

Delly's words sank into my spirit, settling my soul. "Mama showed us what life could be when we open our hearts to change . . . and forgiveness," I said. "Her last letter offered me comforting wisdom I'd like to share." I caressed Mama's letter, unfolding the worn paper laced with perfume. The last page trembled in my hand. I took a deep breath. "Truth is a priceless treasure, but worthless if buried. Value simplicity, pause to smell a rose . . ." Essie stood beside me now, bolstering my courage. "Preferably planted by your hand, for it will smell sweeter. Toil builds character; heartache tests our fortitude. The key to happiness is forgiveness, forgiving ourselves most of all." Teardrops trickled down my chin.

Delly faced me now, bearing her firm hands on my shoulders, matching my watery gaze. "No man or woman on God's earth can stop the rain. Rain bring rebirth, remember that."

"Thank you, darlin'," James said, swiping his mustache and my chin.

"I thought I could be brave," I whispered to him.

"You were, little lady," he said, tucking me close.

"I pray for the strength to follow Mama's example," I finished, slipping next to Essie, her fingers locking with mine.

Delly cleared her throat and said, "God raise us from the soil at our birth, and He raise us to His sky in our death. You free, Katie girl. You free." She paused, rocking on her heels, dabbing her eyes with her kerchief. She looked up at the clouds, tucking her curls underneath her grand new hat from Essie. Years of love and admiration warmed me, watching Delly hug her Bible, radiant in her plum dress, its tiny yellow flowers shimmering in the sun.

"First sound we make coming into this sinful world be crying," Delly said. "We gotta learn to sing. Katie teach us that. Good Lord don't say we won't have no hard times nor plenty a crying whilst we on this earth. Why would He, when that the first sound we make in this life?"

Delly walked a few steps to take in the hills. "Yes, fitting. We stand with the trees rooted in faith. God say the oil a joy for mourning, the garment a praise for the spirit a heaviness; that they may be called trees of righteousness, the planting of the Lord, that He may be glorified. Joy ain't bubbling jus yet, but it will. It come in the memory a this star come to earth. Our angel."

James leaned over and kissed her cheek. Delly beamed.

"Amen," I said.

"Beautiful, soothing words, Delly," James said. "Thank you." James nodded to Essie. "Fine roses, Essie Mae. Katie would've loved them."

Essie stepped forward, presenting her roses. "I named them Miss Katie." She grinned. "That's what a grower does when they cultivate a new rose. I raised this flower, as Miss Katie raised me, with love, care, dedication, attention, and concern. Its coloring, the pale pink gown, flowing with lavender ruffles, the dress she wore when James visited, every time."

"Every time," James whispered.

"But don't let its fragility fool you," Essie said. "This rose is hearty. As Katie it grows tall and graceful, but weathers cold days and unexpected storms. It will not wither in drought, but blossom. Its fragrance reaches deep beyond a floral perfume. It offers an essence, prompting joy and peace as Katie. No matter its surroundings, it radiates; it dances."

"Dear, those are the most stunning roses I have ever seen," Lil said.

Essie offered me the bouquet. Pale pink roses, lavender kissed the petals' edges. I inhaled their sweet perfume, marveling at Essie. The scent reminded me of Mama—violets, wildflowers, rose water on her cheek. We placed the roses at Mama's grave together. Essie pulled a handful of petals from her satchel and scattered them across the dirt. Dots of pink and lavender flittered with the breeze as Mama's dress on a moonlit walk with James. I had no tears left now, only pride as Essie's roses transported me to her garden, our hands spreading the cocoa earth together at the base of a pink rosebush bowed in blooms.

"Don't know how you do such a thing," Bo said to Essie. And for the first time in a long time, tears glided down his cheeks.

"Mighty fine roses," Delly said. "They do look like Katie's pink dress. Glad you home."

"Essie Mae, I ..." I fell into her embrace, engulfed by the arms of James, Delly, and Bo encircling us now. Nowhere to run; I was thankful.

Bedford stood aside. When he caught Essie's gaze, he nodded to James and left, walking back to the house.

Lil twittered about "wild little Katherine," who, in defiance to their mama, ran through fields with Isabel, sending a whirl of gossip into parlors when they were children. James spoke more words than I remember about Mama's kindness, love, bravery, and resilience in working and living on Westland's land. "The heart of this place," he said, "isn't in the name, history, profits, or business ... it's here, now ... it's you. The crop Katie was most proud of, love."

James hung a wind chime in the willow. The crisp breeze made it ring.

I closed my eyes while Delly sang "Amazing Grace," but thoughts of Mama's last days intruded. She held on, but I wasn't enough. The war, and its horrific aftermath, the illumination of detestable secrets, and the blow of facing them in her fragile state, stole her strength.

"I miss River," Essie whispered. "Why didn't he come?"

"Maybe he'll surprise us tonight."

"Always whispering." Delly busted in. "But I'm proud of ya. We all go on to the house for lunch and finish readying for the party."

"I'm worried about River." Essie searched the hillside and the forest again as if River hid behind the trees. "It's not like him, avoiding me."

"Nobody likes to say goodbyes, child." Delly hushed Essie's concern.

"Thank you, everyone," James called. Bo and Tom McCafferty joined him, engaging in whispers too.

We watched the crowd stumble down the path to their horses and carriages lining an old forest road. "Do you remember the first time we walked up here?" Essie asked.

"I tore my stockings in the thickets while you walked the smooth path up the other side. You always outsmarted me."

After goodbyes to the small gathering, we walked the trail home. Lil filled the quiet with stories about Mama. I scarcely heard them, watching James walk ahead alone.

"I'm worried about James," I said as men entered the house.

"I'll see to them," Lil said. "Help for James."

Delly scuttled around the porch, watering her flower arrangements. "Too early for bourbon, Miss Lil, go on serve the coffee. I hid the whiskey too."

"Evie. Miss Essie." Dr. Jones shook our hands and nodded, his eyes twinkling with Southern charm. "My condolences." His voice broke, noticing Mama's empty rocker.

"Thank you, Dr. Jones," I said, "for everything you've done for my family over the years. Mama counted on your friendship. She spoke nothing but praise regarding you."

"I would have done anything to keep Katie safe . . . well, and happy."

"Mama found peace in your presence here. Will you stay for the party?" I asked.

"No. I shouldn't have returned." Dr. Jones looked at Essie, his eyes teary. "Restrictions on traveling . . . my wife, you see, stayed behind in Virginia. Oh, she wanted to come."

Dr. Jones wouldn't stop staring at Essie, gaping at the scar across her wrist. She hid it and waved to the parade of carriages. He cleared his throat, mussing his salt-and-pepper hair. In his sixties, Dr. Jones was still as trim and handsome as James, but I never saw this look from him before, cautious, ashamed.

"Perhaps another visit," I said. "You will visit often, won't you?"

"I will try." He looked back at James, who watched us from a nearby carriage. "James waves me on. Evie, Essie Mae, James will need you now more than ever."

"Yes, sir," we said.

Dr. Jones took our hands again; his sparkling blues stuck on Essie. "I am sorry. You look so like her," he whispered.

"Who?" Essie asked.

"Your mother."

"Doc," James called. "Sam's off to Sweet Water. He'll take ya into town."

"Very well," Dr. Jones shouted. "Goodbye, Evie. Miss Essie."

"Wait," Essie called to him. Dr. Jones hadn't heard swept up in the camaraderie of men.

I held Essie's hands as we watched the good doctor ride away.

Essie's hand rattled in mine. "That was a curious thing the doctor said to me."

"I lost count of the curious things people confessed to me today," I said, reassuring her. "Why couldn't they bother Lil or Delly?" I snapped, scuffling up the porch steps.

"Don't you think it's odd the words Dr. Jones chose?" Essie chased me.

"You've hung around Bedford too much, interrogations and suspicions."

Essie poked my shoulder for my attention. "Dr. Jones said he would have done anything to keep your mama safe and happy. What did he mean?"

"What of it?" I caught my edge, forcing a smile. "Willow Jones is the kindest man I have ever known. And a good doctor to us. You don't know him like I do, Essie Mae. You don't."

"I'm sorry, Evie. I merely thought . . ."

We hushed at the creak of the screen door.

"And handsome," Lil said, joining us, disappointment in her glare.

"Willow Jones made Southern belles swoon for years. Yes, he loved your mother a long time ago." Lil pleasured in our collective gasp.

"Lil, did Dr. Jones know my mama Isabel?" Essie asked.

"Yes, but I was speaking of Katie, dear." Lil's eyes widened. She shook her finger at us. "Willow was our family doctor since we were girls and when Katie had Evie." Lil shooed away the gossip. "Come along, ladies, there's much to do for the party tonight."

Essie grabbed Lil's sleeve. "But . . ."

Lil held her breath, staring into Essie's curious eyes. "Time enough for questions another day, Essie Mae. Mugwort." Lil groaned, removing the wreath on the door as she escaped inside.

"What's going on, Evie?" Essie asked, plopping on Mama's rocker. Noticing it was Mama's, she popped up. I stopped her and sat beside her in Delly's chair.

"I says it," Delly said, reappearing. "Someday all this secret foul mess gonna spill out." She tapped a fan on my shoulder.

I snatched it. "We don't talk about those days." I fanned my flush.

"But they talk bout you. You jus ain't listening. But old Delly hears em howling, stirring up the troubles we pray to forget."

"Delly . . ." James rescued me. "Lunch ready?" He walked to the edge of the porch, admiring his setup for the party. "You ladies like the dance floor?"

"Lord a mercy, the party! No time for jabbering. Sandwiches ready." Delly stopped her flight indoors. "Girls, Katie be proud a them words you say. Essie Mae's roses Heaven's flowers. You fine women. Remember that, hmm?" Delly kissed our foreheads.

"Think I'll sit out here a spell." I handed Essie Mama's fan.

"I'll help, Delly," Essie said, bundled in Delly's arms, jostling through the front door.

Mama's chair rocked next to mine. I admired Westland, inhaling the fresh air, unwilling to enter the flurry of a stuffy house making a party. I scanned the horizon, orchard, wheat fields, and road leading away from Westland. In the breeze, the willow's golden leaves swayed and pinged. I wanted to hide inside its branches, but the sight of the dance floor and colorful Chinese lanterns strewn above lightened my heart.

"Lil outdid herself, hanging streamers and swags like the Fourth of July. We'll host a fine party, Mama."

"Evie." James's deep voice startled me. "Honey, I didn't mean to make you jump."

"I'm sorry. I thought you went inside."

"Enjoying the view. Take a turn, Miss Evie?" James tipped his hat and offered his arm.

I rose and curtseyed. "I'd like that."

He motioned to a winding path. It snaked through the orchard, behind the barn, past Essie's roses, to Mama's garden. "Sun's hot this afternoon." He plucked my hat off the railing and placed it on my head. We walked on.

"You cut this trail for mama." James's sweet cologne made me grin.

He caught me inhaling. "Hope I don't smell like a campfire today. Delly made sure of that. You smell like lemons."

"I woke up early to help Delly zest and juice lemons for pies."

"Folks pitching in and bringing fixings like a barn raising. Mrs. Mirabel and Tom McCafferty's wife decorated the refreshment tent. River promised to bring his apple cider."

I perked up. "River's coming?"

"He's invited. Now, you asked me if I cut this trail, wore more likely. I lost count the number of times Katie and I walked this path admiring Westland."

We paused, taking in the land.

"I'm proud of you, little lady ... the way you spoke of your mama."

"Essie's new rose would've made Mama speechless. Worthy of a silver cup, she'd say."

"They took our breath away."

When we reached the orchard, James stopped, leading us back toward the barn. "They're harvesting pears and apples. If I had my druthers, we'd be riding."

"Star's getting too old for the drive to Sweet Water."

"Nah, she's as young as springtime, loads of steps in that mare."

"Honey's itching for a ride ... Mama's plucky palomino."

"Katie loved that horse. She spoiled Honey. So do you."

We passed the back of Essie's rose garden. James ran his hand along the new fence.

"Why didn't you leave?" I asked, my hand sliding off his arm. He stopped and offered his arm again. I peeked through the slats at Essie's roses.

He sighed, lowered his hat to hide his eyes, and walked on.

I raced to catch up. "What did Mama do, James? Essie mentioned threatening letters. You're mum on the fires. Who was threatening Mama and Westland?"

James swiped a handful of straw off a bale and tossed it away, keeping a strand to chew. "You need to know when I say. Ain't today, little lady. We just buried your mama."

"I'm not a child."

He took me in; the glint in his eyes calmed me. They crinkled at my smirk. "On the hillside, in that fancy yellow dress, I saw you as little Evie asking for a twirl."

"Wearing your boots."

"They might fit you now."

We turned the corner into the stables, checking on Honey, Star, and the other horses. Honey popped her head out of her stall at the crunch of our footsteps. James sneaked her sugar. Star appeared next, sniffing the air. "You got yours this morning." James snickered.

"Animals always set me right," I said, stroking Honey. "What are we doing?"

"We're two adults in a world of hurting about your mama, my wife."

"So, you're just going to sit in a dark parlor drinking her whiskey."

"What did you say?"

Honey nudged James's back for more sugar. We left, returning to the path home.

"I didn't mean it like that," I said.

We walked in silence to Mama's stone bench underneath the magnolia trees. James surprised me, inviting me to sit beside him. "I waited for Katie my whole adult life. She'd say, 'I don't remember what I felt when I first met John; I only remember what I didn't.' I should've pursued her. I was a fool. She met me before John."

"You never told me that."

"You never asked, darlin'. My brother fooled your granddaddy."

"John Winthrop tricked everybody." Mentioning my father soured my stomach. He knew so, always, but this time, he didn't change the subject for me or himself.

James wrapped his arm around me. "Tricked is the word. Of all the fool places . . ." He laughed at himself. "I spied your mama at a library in Richmond. Prettiest girl I ever saw."

"What's a cowboy like you doing in a library?"

He tipped his hat down again, hiding his eyes. "Trying to meet Katie. A business partner of mine held a meeting. Ah, my way of business was the open road and a handshake. I knocked into your mama, made her drop a pile of books. She was always reading."

"That's Mama."

"She agreed to meet me for lunch that afternoon. She was so young, and yet, she wasn't."

"And bold," I said, surprised.

"Delly taught her well. Katie held her own in the big city. But that afternoon, Katie's daddy, Alex, met with John. Alex was the most distinguished man I had ever met. I brushed my boots and trousers, even slicked my hair, to Katie's laughter. A few months, Katie gave way."

"Gave way?"

"Stubborn, independent; she gave me a chance." James rose and circled the trees. "I hadn't seen my brother in years. John probably thought I was dead, and here we fought for Katie. A rough cowboy against a huckster who beguiled Alex with fake manners and culture, who busted himself into highfaluting circles like a bull; Lil helped John."

"She regretted it and didn't discern his true nature."

James stretched his arms over a branch. "Regret eats us alive. John won."

"You did."

He avoided my eyes, checking his watch. "John found money or stole it, presented a fine game to Mr. Wilcox. I asked Alex for Katie's hand."

His confession took my breath. I bit my lip to keep from crying.

"Alex left Richmond without a word, weighing my proposal. He raised

Katie to lead, run his Westland someday. He needed assurance his daughter married well, a Southern gentleman with social standing."

"But you and your brother are Northerners."

"I didn't expose John. I tucked tail and ran; never saw them again, not until John abandoned Katie years before you were born. After two years, John returned. I left . . . for her."

"Money. Mama said Grandfather fought to prove himself to Ruth, who came from a wealthy French family. Yet, he never gave you a chance. I'm told Alex Wilcox was a wise, honorable man, but my father beguiled him with a child's judgment."

"That's what you call a bluff, darlin'. Never knew what John was good at until that day."

"Bluffing?"

James winced in pain. "John made an easy living out of it, had a teacher of sorts, a young man they say had the gift for poker, Delaney Houst. Katie swore gypsies or a magician dropped Delaney at Westland. He just appeared and knew every trick, flattery, and swindler's game."

"What about your father's farm in Missouri and the shooting stars?"

"A good family raised me for a time, not long, little lady. Good Lord left it up to us. John chose wrong every time. Truth is, I don't rightly know if we have the same mother, ashamed to admit that."

Compassion overwhelmed me at his confession.

"I tried with John," he continued. "From what I recall, my pa abandoned Mama. I left with her. John fled with a wealthy woman, his mama. Hell, she spoiled him with fancy suits and chocolates like a child, while my mama, a Choctaw, taught me good in this world despite him."

"You both never said a word."

"Why would we? The sins of the father showering down on the son—life isn't fair, Evie, but it's what you make of it. I stayed to take care of my mama, and when I was a young man, I made my way the best I knew without much of an education. I discovered my own gifts."

"Horses."

"Reins, ropes, and cattle; this rugged country was my business. A good boss paid for my schooling. Did my utmost, but my education was under the stars, in the meadows and mountains. Delly warned me a rough cowboy hadn't a chance with the likes of Katie."

"You proved Delly wrong, didn't you?"

"John wasn't the honorable choice. But Alex knew he could control John, never me. Alex was hell-bent on preserving Westland and anointing Katie its new owner."

"Westland wasn't a cotton empire. From what Delly said, it barely hung on."

"Not cotton—gold."

"The rumors are true."

"Your grandfather ran a successful cotton plantation without slave labor, but it yielded small profits compared to the hills. Alex concocted a fool plan to sell shares, but the gold ran out, flooded. The law almost jailed him, where Ruth Wilcox shined as the true owner of Westland."

"I don't understand."

"Alex struck gold, but the claims he sold had nothing, and he knew it. And there's the question of robbing Koontz from expanding his farm, mine a little of that gold, too. Maybe a handful of nuggets were all Westland yielded, but Alex secretly expanded Westland's boundaries to include that creek, legally. Koontz hadn't a chance."

"Why would my grandfather risk losing Westland and jail?"

"What drives a man to do desperate acts faster than gold? Love. Alex obsessed over securing his daughters' futures. Ruth set things right. The floods brought Alex back to her."

"Near the end of her life, Mama scarcely spoke of this, and her story changed."

"She was afraid to tell the truth."

"What is the truth?"

"Buried with her." James rose with a groan and stared at the house.

Delly marched outside, searching for us. "There you be," she called. "Lunch waiting."

We waved. She hustled inside.

"What about the hand who died the night of the storm?" I asked. "Luby. Maybe Grandfather's ways upset folks."

"Some say a fight erupted between them. Others said it wasn't safe for an inexperienced miner. Alex almost didn't make it. Men took his gold. He was lucky they didn't kill him."

"Mama insisted there wasn't any gold."

James tired of my questions and left me under the magnolias. I chased him.

"Maybe that's exactly how Ruth Wilcox wanted it," he said. "Loads of rumors nobody believed were true. But it just takes one."

"James . . . my father believed it, didn't he? Gold, hiding in Westland's hills. That's why he married Mama."

My question stopped him. He looked around and motioned for me to be quiet. "Suppose John wanted to believe he'd get rich off Alex's gold. Alex blamed himself for Luby's death, and now Luby's daughter would have to grow up without a mother and father."

"Who was Luby's daughter?"

"Isabel."

Mama's favorite rosebush caught my eye, Isabel's roses. "That explains Mama's attachment to her."

"I don't believe Katie ever knew the full account. Suppose no one does, little lady. Truth is, there's no gold on Westland's land."

"A curse. Ruth kept Mama from her father's dark secrets. Mama kept me from mine."

"Nothing dark ever hovered over Alexander Wilcox. He fell into a fever that has robbed many men. Ruth nursed Alex back. He invested in Westland beyond cotton. Right-headed again, Alex aimed to provide for and protect his daughters. Katie's sister Sally was the first to marry, a Frenchman who was an attorney and a man of letters of noble breeding."

"Uncle Augustus."

"Lil became Southern royalty and built her own empire with her husband until his death."

"And Mama?"

"Katie joked she was born funny that way, no desire to marry. She fought her daddy on everything. Isabel was the last straw. Isabel had no business in Katie's life. Though Alex never owned a slave, Isabel was born of one, then rescued."

"But my grandfather did own slaves. I found the receipts in his study."

"He saved them; purchased the freedom of every black man and woman on the plantation, or hired straight out."

My anger kindled at James's rosy depiction. I pointed to the overgrown lot that once housed my father's slave cabins, now demolished. "And the slave quarters?" I asked.

"John Winthrop brought evil to Westland. I stayed away for too long. I blame myself for it. Why today, I suppose I drink Katie's whiskey in the dark. As long as Katie was here, it made sense to overturn Westland's past, now . . . we may lose it. Maybe that's best."

"Freeing certificates . . . do you think this erases what my father did? It makes it worse!"

"A big part of me wants to walk away, but I'd be leaving your mama. I did before and regretted it all my days. No more running." James tapped a paper lantern, making it sway. "Fine dance floor," he mumbled. We stopped at the porch steps, reluctant to go inside.

"James, you've always given me the space and respect I needed. Don't carry this alone. I know what it's like to push everyone away."

"*Chulosa.* Enough truth for one day. We'll sort it out tomorrow . . . the good and bad."

"There's more?"

"Always more—but isn't that Westland?"

I stood at the bottom step, watching James leave. Just as he neared the front door, I asked, "Does Essie know about Luby and Isabel?"

"Essie always knows," he said, touching Mama's rocker, watching it rock without her. His hat landed in her seat before he walked inside.

I stopped Mama's rocker, staring at the door. Delly hadn't come to fetch me nor Essie. "James . . . always demanding they leave me alone. You've done that since I was thirteen."

Bitterness swallowed the joy from Mama's service. I sat in her rocker and tilted James's cowboy hat over my eyes, longing to sleep until this nightmare ended.

18.

EVIE

We gathered at the brick walkway leading to the cottage where Essie Mae lived with Delly until my father died and Mama took her in. James and Bedford stayed behind, whispering in Mama's study. Bo swaggered ahead, proud. Essie skipped keeping pace. A glass dome in the distance, Essie gasped. I giggled at the sight of the new white picket fence.

"Hmm," Bo grunted, eyeing me.

"I didn't tell," I whispered.

Delly swatted me from behind. "Always whispering," she hooted, marching on my heels.

Essie held her breath at Bo's surprise. A new greenhouse.

"A small conservatory to exhibit your flowers, dear," Lil crooned. "A worthy family gathering place for tea, reading; I may even take up painting."

"Lord a mercy," Delly moaned.

"Wait until you see the wicker furniture, darlings," Lil said, prodding us onward as geese.

"Mama Goose, we come to see flowers in that steamy glasshouse, not chairs." Delly snatched Essie's hand first, waving off Lil. "Ashamed to say, I beg Miss Katie to buy two lemon trees. Oh, child, wait till you smell the blossoms."

"A winter garden." Essie sighed, brimming with joy.

I clasped her other hand. *See not with eyes, but heart, a future.* Essie squeezed my hand as if she too remembered Mama's words.

"Think of all the roses you'll grow, Essie Mae," Delly said, hopeful. "I show ya the corner where I make my soaps. Be fine, you creating new roses and me my soaps, huh?"

"Mama sure changed this old cottage, didn't she?" I asked Essie.

"What do ya think, child?" Bo asked. "Saved some a your best roses in there."

Essie ran into Bo's arms.

"What we say bout crying." Delly stroked Essie's hair. "You short, soft curls remind me of you mama's, child."

Essie gazed at us, tears streaming down her cheeks. "It's stunning . . . a dream."

Lil sighed. "I miss my greenhouse in Richmond, always worth the effort."

"Sure enough," Delly said. "We be buzzing refreshing it every fall, scrubbing mildew, repainting, fore Essie bring in her flowers for winter."

"A worthy addition to Westland," I said. "Thank you, Bo."

"Bes thank James, too." Bo folded his arms, squinting at me, coaxing my confession. "You know you go on peek when the building done. I catch ya."

I rolled my eyes at Essie. "Well, it's Essie's surprise. I suppose I helped a little."

Delly huffed. "If gobbling up my rice pudding whilst you flirting and watching them men set the glass panes, helping, you sure enough helped— me, clean my pot and make that butterfingers farmer drop a window with all them winks you give him."

"Squinting." I stomped my foot as a child, making Essie laugh. "That farmer resembled Conrad, didn't he, Lil?" I hustled behind Bo before Delly whacked my rear.

Lil stood alone on the stoop, clapping for our attention. "Come, ladies. The greenhouse will not show itself."

"You go, Miss Lil." Bo caught my sleeve. "Got something I wanna talk to Evie bout."

Essie stood before Bo, her eyes bright and teary. "Thank you," she whispered. "Bo, there is a chance I might not . . ." Essie looked back at Lil. Bo rubbed his chin, staring into the grass. "It's grand. I love you," she said. "I appreciate everything. Everything." Essie left Bo with a kiss and scurried inside the greenhouse at Delly's call. Bo stroked his cheek, grinning.

"I haven't seen Essie this happy in a long time," I said. "I see Mama's poinsettias inside."

"Delly gonna bring em and her pecan fudge to the Christmas festival in Sweet Water this year." Bo stared at the greenhouse, enjoying the laughter of ladies. "Guessing you won't wanna miss that, huh, Miss Evie?"

"Perhaps." I focused on the grass now, spotting a four-leaf clover. "Hey."

"I fix the sleigh," Bo hollered, bobbing and weaving for my attention. I gave it. "Doc Jones think Alabama gonna get snow this year. Honey bucking to take us for a ride."

I smiled at him, picked the four-leaf clover, and handed it to him. "I used to fear you once, and you, me. Mama longed for change at Westland. It has in many ways. Look at us." I walked to the side of the cottage, impressed by the greenhouse and the stone terrace outside its back door. "Westland is more than buildings, isn't it?"

"Why don't you go on and stay, child?"

"Look at them buzzing inside. I can hear them now; Lil imagines a hothouse parlor. Delly moans about wicker furniture and potted palms too highfalutin for Essie's studies."

"Child, you bark I'm mute, but you talking and mum in you own way. Now, close you eyes. I got something for ya."

I squinted at him, suspicious. Bo held my stare, pursing his lips. "Fine, but I don't know if I can take another surprise."

At Bo's whistle, I couldn't help peeking, giddy at the gray-and-white border collie January released, bounding our way. January waved and walked back toward the orchard.

"Bo, he's the cutest puppy I've ever seen!"

The plump collie hopped and snorted at my feet.

Bo stepped aside, proud of himself. "He act like a pup, but he two. Dog do more cuddling than sheepherding, why Mr. Bixley give him away."

"How could he part with him?" The dog slid his head under my hand for affection.

"I build Mr. Bixley a fine tea table for his wife." Bo snapped his fingers; the frenzy of puppy kisses and whimpers ceased. "Sit." The collie sat eager to spring up again, his penetrating stare into Bo's. "Take a bow." At Bo's command, the dog stretched his front paws and lowered his head at my feet.

"Oh, Bo." I laughed, giving in, caressing the pup's white flame down the middle of his gray face. "What's his name?"

"Sky. What you always be dreaming in."

Sky tapped his nose on Bo's fist for the hidden treat.

"Look at those sweet brown eyes. Thank you, Bo. Sky's so soft."

Bo chuckled, looking toward the greenhouse for the ladies to reappear.

Sunlight shined on a new structure at Westland. Inside, the glasshouse appeared spacious as a new beginning. We watched their animated flurry. Potted ferns and flowers framed and colored the windows as stained glass. Lil, Delly, and Essie gathered around a table of camellias and fuchsias. Essie smiled, covering her mouth in glee, pointing to shelves of crocks, pots, bulbs, and roses.

Bo cleared his throat, a reminder of his aversion to silence.

I couldn't wait to go inside the greenhouse, but something bothered Bo. It would be hours now, Essie taking in rooms, examining flowers, listening to Delly boasting about her new soaps and success selling them in Sweet Water. Stories I eagerly listened to all summer until Essie's return. Lil coos, "Oh, the Brussels carpet and swinging lamps with wine-colored globes." She provided sundry varieties of the best roses from Paris, London, and New York for Essie's study. "I'm certain you'll show your new rose at the flower show in London next year," Lil promised.

Essie waved to us, overwhelmed by our love and effort without her commitment to stay.

Bo directed Sky to my side. The dog wandered back to Bo, confused. "Go on," Bo ordered. "Miss Evie need ya now. Lil do the fluffing and primping. Sky nip my fat fingers thinking they sausages."

"Sky doesn't like baths?"

"Oh, he love em. Lil say Sky a show and parlor dog. I say something else."

"I bet you did." Sky flopped on the grass, claiming my shoes. "Sweet boy."

"Evie, my soles stomp this land from one acre to the next, but these boots don't dance."

"I caught you and the men stomping a fine jig in the barn, embolden by corn whiskey."

"James in a heap a trouble, won't say nothing."

Tingles shot down my arms at his words. My heart hadn't room for more grief. I snuggled Sky, opening my heart to him. "James is quiet. Augustus will sort out our trouble."

"Men threatening to seize Westland lessen James prove it his. Don't know bout legal papers, but Lil say without em, they might take it this time."

"Mama had the lawyers draw up papers. Her husband—"

"James got no papers, and you mama never give him Westland."

I edged my neck back, agitated. "You're mistaken, Bo. Bedford hasn't said—"

"Mr. Bedford wait till you bury you mama. Suspect we'll all have words tomorrow."

My soldier's posture crumpled. "I'm exhausted, Bo. We have Mama's celebration, Essie's here. I trust James to fix it." I patted his arm and stepped toward the cottage.

"Long as you mama here, they leave Westland alone."

I stopped. "You believe James would let strangers steal Westland?" Bo couldn't hold my stare. "James isn't fit to fight, is he?"

"Five years a war, girl . . . you think it easy protecting this land? We fight them raiders off Koontz's farm. Never mind seeing ashes from fresh camp-fires in the hills, we ain't setting."

"Mama never said a word."

"Miss Katie fill out them government papers swearing we loyal, and Mr. James prove hisself a Northerner, supporting the Union in the war."

"How?"

"Bes he tell it. But they ask who Mr. James be to Miss Katie."

"Her husband."

"Then they whisper that word that take a plantation in the night? Trea-son. Bedford have words with James we don't hear, that's it. James got no legal papers to prove they married."

Sky pounced up and nudged my leg to keep me from fainting. "James married Mama at Westland." The sky and grass blurred. Bo steadied me. "Bo, tell me Mama divorced my father. Augustus wouldn't be so careless. Tell me."

"You daddy's dead. He don't get Westland."

"You're doing a mighty fast jig right now."

"Knowed a man do a fine waltz—up to Westland's door years ago, saying you daddy owe him a big debt, and he ain't never letting it go. Say Miss Katie bes see to paying it."

"I recall several drifters claimed my father owed them money after his death. It wasn't Mama's affair, and Augustus jailed the frauds."

"Delly confess Katie pay one, kep paying him. One taste a honey all it take for the rest a the flies to swarm."

"I best go inside. They'll wonder." I wanted no more mystery and heartache.

"Evie."

I turned around at his call. Bo looked exhausted and worried. He played with Sky for a second and glanced up to see if I would return. I froze. *Mama, too many secrets.*

"I was gonna leave Westland, Miss Evie. Last year."

A blow hit my stomach at Bo's confession. I rushed to him. "This is your home."

"Government folks come round promise acres to black folk to farm. I says James got him a good plan on that Johnson grass, but I like to build, Miss Evie. You let me."

"There's no letting. You work hard, and you have a gift."

"Supposing you don't mind I black. Since ya come home, I take to you sitting next to me every morn in Miss Katie's garden, teaching me to read and something happen in my mind."

"Bo, if you ever want to leave Westland, I will help you. After all you've done . . . I wouldn't be alive if you hadn't . . ."

For the first time, Bo touched my face. He set his large palm to my cheek and softly placed a finger to my lips. "When you a li'l girl, you go through pain like old Bo. You weren't no slave. You jus a li'l white girl . . ." Bo swallowed hard, distracting himself, fluffing Sky's coat.

I held my breath, tears falling.

"I see to it," Bo said, his voice nearly a whisper, "that you daddy never hurt ya again. I got no place to go where folk pay me mind like you do."

I stood taller, a fire in my belly. "Don't you ever say that, you hear? You never say that again. My father died because he was a sick man."

"In twenty year, I don't cry a tear, not one. Near close when Essie Mae go on leave me that first time. I'm like you—don't feel nothing. Don't got no kinfolk. Hate try to kill ya, too. But I ain't leaving Westland, thinking it try again."

"This is what you needed to tell me."

"It ain't over, Miss Evie." Bo held his breath, exhaled, and turned back to me. "Bad men come. Hear from Mr. Tom the night that fire ate his barn; they ain't gonna leave Westland alone. Way we live here, black folk and white, schooling and working together, war ain't over to them lessen we be kept like dogs again, lessen slavery come back in a new way. James say, sure enough, we gonna win this fight once and for all."

"If those rebels discover James's support for the Union . . . and Aunt Lil's money funding to end the war—no." I shook my head. "Essie said Bedford promises the law sides with us now."

"When the law coming? Last time, Bedford say, Army got no soldiers to waste guarding a plantation for maybes. Ain't no trace a strangers coming and going to these parts."

"Someone's setting the fires, Bo. We need the soldiers here."

"War make a mess a this valley. Ain't no law, girl. Folks stealing, killing, running farmers off they land. Things be calm for a spell, then the fires. We get word sheriff lock up three men and send em to Mobile for the trial. Tom and James say, they the ones setting fires."

"That's wonderful news." I sighed, relieved.

"Bedford don't trust it. Law round here still be the shotgun I hide in them azalea bushes in you mama's garden and over there till we know." He pointed to a small wagon near the porch.

"That pup isn't for showing or cuddling, is it?"

"Sky protect ya. He knows what to do. Got him a keen sense; smells and hears trouble."

"That dog nudged my leg when I nearly fainted. He doesn't herd sheep?"

"He guards em. Time back, James send you away to keep ya safe."

"Now you want me to stay to keep James safe?"

"No, Miss Evie. I ain't asking, jus telling what I know. James ain't right in his mind to tell ya. I promise Miss Katie I get the words out bes I can."

"James asked me to travel to Paris for Lil. She deserves to grieve for her sister in her own manner. A few weeks away . . . James says—"

"Shh." Bo held his hand up at Sky's growling "Astra! Woman, get outta them bushes."

"Ain't hiding, mean old Bo. Come fetch ya is all." Astra showed herself, fidgeting and twisting by the small wagon. "Keep that mutt away from me," Astra said, frightened.

"Sky's a sweet boy, Astra," I called to her, holding him back.

"He growling at me. Tom holding a meeting." Astra eyed Sky.

Bo snapped his fingers, and Sky sat at my feet, quiet, fixated on Astra.

"Jackson see two men prowling last night," Astra shouted. "Indians."

Bo nodded, waved her away. "Them Indians our friends. Go on now. Bes be careful next time you snooping round, I fire ya. Go home."

Astra raised her chin eyeing me, folded her arms, and glared at Bo. "Tom says the party a bad idea. I come to help 'cause Delly ask. You send me away? I never come back."

"Then get!" Bo shouted. "You know them men."

Astra approached. Bo waved her away again. She still hid her face underneath the green scarf draped over her sunhat. "Jus wanna see the greenhouse. I wash them windows."

"Then ya sees it," Bo growled. "James say the law jail them men who set Tom's fire. You jus don't knowed 'cause you a half-wit. Now get on."

"Bo," I said, surprised by his rudeness.

"No, Miss Evie. I handle things my own way now. James gimme leave."

"That's not our way."

"It's my way. Maybe good you go on to Paris whilst we take care a things ain't for womenfolk to see."

"Good day, missus." Astra curtseyed and whimpered away.

"Good day, Astra," I called to her.

"Fool woman. She don't come round till you come home."

My conversation with Bo ran through my mind. I clutched Bo's hand, frightened, thinking of his words about my father.

"What's wrong, child? You white as a moonflower."

"Do you think Astra heard us?"

"No. She come after 'cause Sky snarl. See, I train him."

I held my chest, taking in a deep breath. "I'll be glad for a party tonight."

"Built the dancing stage in front a the house. You get tired, you can sit and watch."

"I bet you never thought such a thing was possible at Westland, did you?"

"What's that, child?"

"Being happy."

"You all go inside yet?" A quiet, demure voice asked. "Don't mind saying, I pick the teal drapes and the ruby rug. Oh, they too fine for a humid greenhouse. Morning, Miss Evie, Bo."

I smiled. "January, you're a ladybug landing on a leaf the way you crept up on us."

"Ain't do no creeping, missus, but the ladybugs be plentiful this season."

"Bo knows all about ladybugs," I teased. "He's the only one who can hear them, too."

"Hear?" January asked, patting Sky's head.

"Miss Evie talking nonsense," Bo said, kicking dirt. "Jehoshaphat, who gonna pop outta the bushes next?" He sidestepped, searching toward the greenhouse, nearly falling over Sky.

"Astra slip away from me whilst we in the orchard. Hope she don't cause no trouble."

"It's all right, January," I said. "You look mighty pretty today."

She bowed her head, glancing at Bo. "Hush, Miss Evie. Little ladybug tell me, you think my skin shine as a black orchid in the moonlight. Don't know nothing bout black orchids, but I know it be a full moon glowing for the party tonight. We all excited to help. Ain't never hear live music nor seen a shindig in these parts for long time. We make it grand for Miss Katie."

"Thank you, January. Delly shouldn't have said a word. I meant it as a compliment."

"I thank ya, Miss Evie. If anybody has the courage to tell me I look like a flower, why, it'll be the nicest words I ever did hear." January noticed the dirt on her hands and scrubbed them with her apron.

"Why don't you come inside with us to see the greenhouse and meet Essie Mae?" I asked, to Bo's disapproval. He pulled the back of my dress to Sky's bark.

January stuffed her hands in her pockets, swaying and looking behind her toward the orchard. "It family time now, Miss Evie," she said. "I bes finish my work. Harvest day."

"We'll see you at the party," I said, encouraging her.

"Miss Evie, Miss Katie a kindhearted woman. Do anything you ask ya need my help."

I walked up to her and held her hands. January swiftly looked at Bo. "Mama wrote about you often, grateful you came to work at Westland. I understand Tom McCafferty took on many of our workers when Mama's condition worsened. You have a home here, should you wish to stay. I've spoken with Tom. He'll give you leave."

January peeked at Bo and smiled. "I would like that, Miss Evie. Think I jus bout train that orchard to my liking. Fruit fat and sweet this year." Overcome, January giggled and ran off.

"Bo, you didn't say one word. Why not?"

"You doing all the talking."

"Mama's right. Time changes us all for the better if we let it."

"You go on say them words to me when you stuck stubborn bout leaving Westland."

We walked to the cottage's front porch. I peered inside the wagon, unable to spot Bo's hidden shotgun. He stopped in front of it, blocking my view. "What I can't figure," he said out of nowhere, "why the man in that story I read for Essie Mae, Mr. Edward Ferris—"

"Edward Ferrars?" I pressed my hand over my mouth to stop my laugh.

"Act like a hot coal burn his tongue when he round Miss Elinor. Why don't he go on tell her the truth?"

I burst a laugh. "*Sense and Sensibility.* A few chapters, hmm?"

"Maybe I read four. What does 'when his natural shyness was overcome' mean?"

Stunned, I marveled at the power of a beautiful woman to change my once mute giant. "Do you remember when James first arrived at Westland?"

"Sure do. He a bold man, but he can't say a word to Miss Katie, none that make sense."

"James overcame his shyness, didn't he?"

"Meaning, he figure what to say to Miss Katie to maybe—ask her to dance?"

I played it straight. "If you ask me, the trouble lies in the feet."

"Feet?"

"Approaching a lady in the first place. James had the words. He needed the courage to walk up to Mama and ask."

"Ya gimme something to think on."

"I'll tell you a secret. Sometimes, a woman's so bold, she'll grab your hand, and you'll be twirling before you say Jehoshaphat."

"You filled with bunkum today. We bes go inside fore Lil come hollering."

"Bo, you've helped us see Westland anew. Delly's thriving; maybe we could too."

Bo offered his arm. "Shall we, Miss Evie?"

I happily held on, but I couldn't thwart my belly laugh. "You chased my fear away. Bo, I trust Bedford. And I think Jane Austen is making a fine gentleman out of you."

"Miss Lil harp, it ain't too late."

"Perhaps you'll find your voice as Mr. Ferrars and ask January to dance tonight."

"Don't dance, Evie. You'll learn soon enough."

"Um-hmm. The moonlight and January don't know."

"Hush now. I ain't reading no more a that *Sense and Sensibility* book. Don't rightly understand all them words and fool white folks' doings."

"I think you understand more than you know. Come, Sky."

"Look at that. Sky don't need no asking; he go on dance for ya, Miss Evie. Look at that!"

Fueled by our praise, Sky pranced around us in a circle and bolted into a frenzied race back and forth on the lawn and up the porch steps. At Bo's whistle, Sky bowed again at my feet, wagging his tail, asking me to play.

"We wondered what was taking you so long." Essie opened the front door. Sky showed off for her, blissfully rolling in the grass on his backside, then running right into her arms, slathering her cheek with kisses. "Pretty boy."

For the first time in years, something lifted off my heart. Fear. I pondered Bo's warnings and confession, but they didn't frighten me. Westland took on new life in the morning dew, the sunlight glistening on the panes of the new greenhouse, on the faces of my family, standing together as a portrait I wished Mama could see.

"Or could she?" I whispered, skipping up the steps as we piled inside to imagine a new beginning.

19.

DELLY

Chinese lanterns aglow over the yard and dance floor, making everybody giddy like children. I imagine Katie watching us, shining a grin so wide, it light up Heaven. Essie Mae and James finally visit Katie's garden, sharing private words that make James stand taller. Maybe Essie gonna stay, but I don't let my mind think too much on that yet.

I fix my blue-ribbon desserts James beg me to bake every Sunday, but I don't the last two 'cause he getting the belly on him; I past the age caring. We fry the chicken, smoke the pork, and bake the sugar ham Essie favor. Not a black sash, frown, or sour memory I'll let spoil the evening. Some prissy girls gossip we should act forlorn. But the mamas scold and remind em, Katie order our merrymaking. I stand taller, too, like a fancy lady in my French green gown the color a Christmas firs with sparkly trimmings.

James don't let me serve, declaring I'm a guest tonight. But I can't help checking on the tent James and the men raise for the refreshments. Long tables covered in the gingham I scrounge outta storage. Evie and Essie Mae make posies for the tables, and a centerpiece a yellow jasmine has special meaning: the passionate love Katie hold with James. Like my girls, I breathe in the night's wonder and can't help wishing this be one a my girl's weddings the way the tent smell a home cooking, orange blossoms, and sugar.

The music sound sweet, floating up in the trees. Couples crowd the dance floor, waltzing under gas lamps and moon glow. Evie lose herself in a flickering paper lantern. A sight in rainbow colors and a Polly fable come to life. Men and ladies flittering like fairies, lighting up the valley. The moon cast Katie's blue, making Westland shine a magic worthy of a story.

Our morning sorrows turn to joyful surprises. Bo showed Essie Mae his cabin he built, hoping maybe he get him a wife someday. We all know it January. Bo don't know it yet, but we do. It fine that big man tiptoeing round that lady. And January don't spill nothing tonight, strutting between folks, handing out refreshments with a hop in her step every time she see Bo. I figure our sneaking mischief get them two on the dance floor soon enough.

The menfolk lawn bowling as the pink sunset linger. James laughing with his men and passing the beers. Giddy girls whispering bout the menfolk they wanna dance with. Soon James leave his men to talk business with the McCaffertys, not too much. I ain't in pride, but I proud of 'cause, like I promise, not a frown or tear invited nor come.

"Oh, child, that peacock Lil think she a young filly, floating up to the gentlemen and showing us how to polka. But it a fine sight, I say. Fine."

"Lil knows how to enter a party," Evie said.

"Where you hiding all this time, Evie? Folks asking."

"I heard Jackson tell Bo something spooked the horses. I checked on them, spoiled Star and Honey with love and sugar."

"You mama used to do that at her parties."

"She did?"

"One time Katie ride off on Honey; James had to fetch her. Lord, child. I miss her." I held up my finger fore Evie scold me. "Ain't crying, smiling. Katie leave us a treasure chest a precious memories." Evie stared at the guests as the band played a polka. "Now my girls gotta find smiles again."

"What do you mean? I haven't smiled this much in months."

"On the inside, child. On the inside. You gonna show us them wild city folk steps?"

"If Evie dances the can-can, they'll hear the cheers in the next county." Essie give Evie a playful shove.

"Shush, Essie Mae. This isn't a fitting time for that dance."

Essie fluff her short curls, stretching her neck, swiveling, searching for someone. I know who it be. "There's no law stopping us here," Essie said. "Maybe in Paris, not Westland."

"Don't know nothing bout fancy stepping, but I sure enough know when Evie's feet get to moving, they crisscross outta time with the music, she look like a frog hopping on ice."

"Hogwash, Delly. I'm a fine dancer." Evie hop and clap outta time again.

I sneak behind her, snatch her hands like she a li'l girl, and clap with her. "Um-hmm. One, two, one, two. There ya go, child."

"Evie dances fine with a steady oompah-pah." Essie snickered.

"My thinking, folks who got no rhythm, ain't free inside. Then one day, something snap in they head; they quit caring who be looking or whispering and hop and skip 'cause they free."

"A lovely sentiment," Evie sassed, rolling her eyes. "Essie Mae, you've seen me dance."

"I love you, but I make it a point not to see you dance."

Evie stop her clapping and swing my hands. "Why looky there, child, swinging our hands in time with the music. Sure enough, Katie woulda loved us celebrating her life."

"Even when a cloud of uncertainty floats over ours," Evie snipped.

"Frowns ain't invited," I warned. "Go find a handsome man to dance with; they asking."

"A lady never dances all the dances." Lil busted in. She look like springtime in her sky-blue gown, rosebuds stuffed in the pile a curls I fix on her.

"Evie and Essie haven't danced yet." I locked arms with Lil, swaying.

Essie Mae sneak in with a squeeze. "Delly, go on and dance for us."

"Capital idea! Watch my star pupil now." Lil grab my hands, making me show the girls my waltzing. I prissy in my fancy green dress. I past the age, stuffing gardens in my hair, so I sport my new feather hat, proud and sassy.

"Delly, you're a vision," Evie sang. "When are you going to dance?"

"Soon as a man ask me." I giggle into these silly women, thinking this what it like standing among Southern belles. "Can I sneak sips a champain?"

"Champagne," they chimed together. Lil swoop away and swoop back, fetching me a glass. She handed it to me.

I lift it to my nose but the fizzes make me snort. "How you drink it without tickling?" I sip to laughing; it taste creamy and tickly.

Lil tilt my hat and said, "Remember, a lady never drinks—"

"More than one glass of champagne," Evie and Essie Mae said together.

"Fine voices, I'll give you that. Excuse me. I think I'll ask Augustus for a dance." Lil fluttered her fan, handed it to me, and left.

"What you say bout a lady asking a man to dance?" I asked Lil, fanning my blush and fluttering my eyes, but that makes me dizzy.

Lil wink and raise an eyebrow at us. "I didn't say a word."

First time all day, I hear my girls giggling, taking me back to them days they sneak round the house hiding and spying. "You come back for more ham, Mr. James?" He sauntered to us, looking handsome with that grease jelly slicking his hair till he plop his hat back on his head. "Oh, why you go on hiding that handsome head a hair."

James wink and pinch my cheek. "If Westland and willows go together, suppose my hat ain't partial from parting from my head." He look at me with smiling eyes. "Delly, why don't you get on that dance floor, show us how it's done."

I catch myself twisting in my dress like Evie. I dust my sassy look off too. "Think most them white folks won't like it." Evie pinched my elbow 'cause I break my rule frowning.

James hold my hands, making me grin silly. "Then they're not guests worth having. They might surprise ya. Everyone here loved Katie; they love you, too."

"That gimme comfort; I see so much hate, but friends here stuck together in tough times."

"Ones you cared for time and again during the war," Essie said sweetly.

Evie bring the sour. "I've heard whispering we're acting disrespectful carrying on."

"Big mouth Miss Maybell. I remind that li'l snip, I nurse her through the croup when she a babe and bake her cakes for the beau she trying to catch, that man with the crooked ears."

"You didn't," James said, chuckling.

"Did. Miss Snip hook Crooked Ears 'cause a my butter cake and strawberry preserves."

James pat my shoulder to calm me, Evie the other, and Essie Mae a swirling my back.

"Truth is," James said, rocking with me to the music. "Our friends came to celebrate Katie's life. Made the announcement to their smiles. Ladies, we've experienced life and death together in this valley; they know that, too."

"Them hard days." I sigh, wanting more a that champagne. "That's why Katie want us happy now." I searched the crowd. "Where's that Bedford fellow, Essie?"

"Look, Essie Mae," Evie said, pointing at Bo and January relighting lanterns together snuffed out by the breeze.

"Lord a mercy." I can't stop my laughing. "January can't serve a bowl a soup without splashing somebody. What Bo doing giving that child matches?" Saying matches gimme a chill, like I shouldn't say nothing bout lighting fires.

"Bet ya five dollars, I'll get Bo to dance with January tonight," Essie said.

"You two planning mischief and the party ain't stirred up yet. Wait till the band really gets to playing, that a fine fiddler. My daddy used to play."

"Delly, you never told us," Essie said, wide-eyed.

"You children never ask, but I got stories, more than that old Koontz."

"Do you think River will come tonight?" Evie asked.

I slip my smile, making them light up like daisies in the sun. "You two the prettiest ladies at the party, flashing mischief in you eyes for old Delly, warms my heart."

Bedford sneaked up on us and handed me a posy a yellow jasmine. I tucked some in Essie's hair. "Now you ready. Go on ask her."

"May I have the pleasure of this dance, Miss Essie?" Bedford asked.

"You told me you can't dance, Sebastian."

Essie's whisper set my hair up on end.

One a James's men called Bedford, so he don't get to dance with Essie jus yet. "Excuse me. I'll be right back, ladies," Bedford said and bowed.

"Mr. Bedford, you sure look handsome tonight, don't he, girls? But you been saying you be right back to us all night," I called. James laughed make my heart light and free.

"Mama wanted us to be happy." Evie rocked on her heels now, swinging her clasped hands with Essie.

"Evie, what do you say we show em how it's done?" James tossed his hat and grab Evie's hand, pulling her toward the dance floor.

"But you don't dance," Evie shouted, looking back at us, shining a smile like her mama.

"I do tonight."

I grab Essie, and we all get to stepping. Don't matter, I ain't dancing with a fine man like James, 'cause I got my Essie Mae in my arms, twirling and swirling under the glow a magic lanterns. Our friends move outta the way, and I see a beautiful thing, not a frown nor crying. And I close my eyes, letting thumping music make me young again, dreaming Katie watching us from the stars.

20.

ESSIE MAE

Lil brought Paris to Westland, lighting Miss Katie's magnolia cove in small blue globes as the spectacle of a Parisian outdoor ball. *A tribute*, I thought, *to the matriarch of Westland*, though lately, it appeared the mantle fell on Delly in grace and wisdom. White globes illuminated the walkway and porch steps as starlight. But a row of old swaying lemon and magenta paper lanterns flickered my past: stolen innocence and girlhood naivety. *Dreams survived that night, Essie Mae. Did they?* I dabbed the sweat off my brow before Evie noticed.

Evie fanned us as we watched couples promenade. "Double shuffle, gliding step," she muttered. "Hogwash, I can dance in time. Conrad never complained."

"Do not bounce, Essie Mae, Lil whispered to me," I said. "Glide. Glide."

The crowd thinned; our evening nearly over. We hid behind a willow spying on Bo, who mustered the courage to ask January to dance. Among trusted friends, in the middle of a fever pitch, Bo stood awkward clapping as January twirled.

"Wish Bo give us a real jig," Delly wailed. "Flapping his arms like a swamp crane."

"Why, Delly, I do believe you're jealous," I said.

"Humph. Do me a fine jig, that the truth." Delly rubbed her back and rested on a bench near the dance floor. James joined her. "But, Evie girl, you found the rhythm. You free, child?"

Delly poked Evie's ribs, and before we knew it, Evie bolted to the middle of the dance floor next to Bo. "Watch how free, Miss Delly," Evie shouted.

Evie glowed, raising her arms with a carefree spin. The air charged with hope tingled my skin, making the hairs on my arms rise as I admired her. Hands to the sky, Evie flicked her wrists to the music, despite the guests' curiosity.

"What's Evie doing?" James asked, tickled.

We couldn't take our eyes off her.

"You go, child," Delly encouraged. "You dance you own way now."

Evie swirled her arms like a whirligig, flapping her wings, ready to soar. She stomped one foot and then the other, hands clapping to the banjo's rhythm.

"Too much wine, Miss Evie?" January called. "I'll fetch her, Miss Lil."

"No," Lil said, hushing the crowd. "Let Evie dance."

Evie floated above them. Before my astonished eyes, William appeared. Evie hadn't noticed. Eyes closed, she waltzed with him, graceful, the two scattering the guests in a whirling waltz. "Come out the wilderness," Evie sang. "Leaning on the Lord. Leaning on the Lord."

I walked closer, squinting at Evie's partner. It wasn't William, but James. I shook my head, laughing at myself. It was what I longed to see. I sat next to Delly and whispered, "I thought I saw William."

"Lord, child, you drink too much champagne? That woulda been a grand sight."

Lil shouted, "What a treat, folks; the newest dance steps from New York City."

A rumble of laughter from lingering friends, Evie curtseyed, relishing their applause.

"Did you see, Delly?" Evie asked. "The music made me dance. Something made me . . ."

"Free," I said, envious.

Frenzied fiddles introduced a country-dance.

"This child got the spirit," Delly said. "And looky there, I think it's catching."

"Jane Austen, indeed," Lil boasted, pleased. "Land's sake, Bo's dancing with January!"

My heart jumped. I wanted to cry. "He's smitten," I said, astounded.

Evie stuffed her formerly freed arms into her chest, leering at the pair. "I'm worried."

"Mama Hen." I laughed. "Yep, a day of surprises—you and Bo are two peas in a pod."

Evie moaned. "I just don't want Bo getting hurt."

"Dear sister, your burgeoning friendship with Bo is the best gift. I dreamed it once."

"Westland's changed, Essie. Everyone's working hard to keep us here."

"Get to stepping, Bo," I shouted. We ducked behind the tree.

Evie grabbed my hand. We bobbled through the crowd, rushing onto the front porch for a better view. "Where in heavens did Bo learn the gallop step? Look at him." Evie greeted Sky.

"Delly's happy. She grieves Miss Katie, Evie, but inside she's . . ."

"Free." Evie slouched in her mama's rocker.

I sat in Delly's. "Delly's always lived free."

Evie gazed into my eyes at my words. *Live free.* "Bedford's tried to ask you to dance three times, Essie Mae."

"I hadn't felt like dancing ever since Delly told me Ned passed through Westland."

The ruckus on the dance floor paused. A gentle breeze quieted the clamor.

"Essie, I'm ashamed I wondered about Ned causing our trouble. Mama gave him money to go north and tried to help him find his family."

"Ned lost everything, his wife, and sister, Nancy. Like so many freedmen, he's searching for family. I admire his courage and wished I could've seen him."

"I don't know what's true anymore." Evie rose, losing herself in the guests' jubilee. "Westland could be a healing place, couldn't it? Look at Bo."

"And January." At the start of another lively tune, I stood beside her. "I can't stop watching them."

Evie turned quiet, glancing toward the magnolia trees cast in blue.

"Miss Evie danced in time." I swayed into her.

"I felt free, Essie. Freedom . . . we've chased that word since childhood."

"Sometimes, I think I'm running away from it."

"You taught us to open our minds and hearts to change, or no matter how hard we pray, a miracle may shine right before our eyes, but we won't see it, blinded by hate, pride, revenge."

"Evie Wilcox, quite the speechmaker."

"Wilcox. The more I learn about my grandparents, Alexander and Ruth, I'm proud to be one. Still, questions hover over Westland. I don't know what to do."

"Sure you do."

Evie bristled. "At the greenhouse, Bo confessed he doesn't trust James's state of mind to make the right decision or fight. Aunt Lil dropped a stack of papers on Mama's desk regarding Westland's debt, taxes, and claims to seize it—take Mama's Westland, Essie."

"James has never backed down from a fight."

"I catch them frowns! Thwacks a coming," Delly shouted from her bench.

We covered our ears. "Delly's right. We should thank Katie's lingering admirers. Evie, don't worry."

"Augustus reads Mama's will tomorrow. My stomach's in knots at James's coming *news*. I must worry. Where will they go? Bo, Delly, January, and James? Have you thought of that?"

I let go of Evie's hand and sat in Katie's rocker. "When Grant locked me in that cage with the old African, I told myself that wasn't me. *She* wasn't me. And when James rescued me, I spoke with Jeanie, the woman who tended my wounds, promising myself, I will never be her."

"Who?"

"Essie Mae, a slave. I would never be her again. I would never let another man rain terror down on me as not to speak or fight back. Go to Paris with Lil. You were happy there."

"Delly's waggling her finger at us."

"Evie, you're my sister," I whispered. "I will never abandon you, but I must find my way. Do you understand?"

"The greenhouse is a dream. Look at that pup. Sky's watching them all, taking in those silly folks. Come here, boy."

"He's watching you." Sky dipped his head under my hand, begging for affection.

"If that Border collie wasn't so sweet, he gives me the creeps." Sky tilted his head, looking at us, puzzled, and plopped at Evie's feet. "See, he senses how we feel, nervous, sad."

"When Bo showed me the improvements to his cabin, he taught Sky how to find me, under the guise of a game of hide-and-seek. At Bo's command, Sky found me every time."

"Sky's smart. Bo played that game with me, too. We know why."

"Yes."

"You know the rules, darlings," Lil said, staggering to us, winded.

"Frowns and tears banished," we said together.

"Fine voices, I'll give you that. Our evening soon ends. Katie would be mighty proud."

Two hands slipped on my shoulders. I rose; they patted me gently back down in my seat. *Sebastian.* "I'm not trying to steal your rocker, Miss Essie," he whispered. "Shall we?" He bowed and offered his hand.

I popped up, excited to dance.

Evie failed to hush her muffled giggles. "Wait! Essie Mae, do you see what I see?" She stepped to the edge of the porch, astonished at a dancer in the crowd.

"River!"

Evie stopped me from bolting onto the dance floor to greet him. "Let's watch," she said, bouncing with the music.

"In my day, we call this the Chorus Jig," Koontz hollered, flailing his feet in the air as if hopping across hot coals. He calmed himself as the banjo and fiddles wailed. Delly grabbed River's hand, and the two walked in a circle, kicking up their heels at the end. "And this called Speed the Plow. Come on, everybody." River hooked arms with Delly and off they went. "This is the Rustic Reel." River held Delly, sashaying back and forth in the middle of the dance floor; the crowd clapped, cheering them on.

"River came, Essie Mae," Evie said.

"Hey, Evie," I said, walking down the steps, observing him closer. "How is River . . ."

"Dancing!"

The song and River's shuffling lasted forever. I couldn't wait any longer. I wanted to hug the old man. But before I stepped forward, a carriage pulled up to Westland's drive. Bedford spotted the late arrival next.

Sky growled.

Oblivious, Evie and Lil stood near the dance floor, egging on River.

"Santa Claus?" I whispered to Bedford. "Why is Mars driving that carriage?"

Bedford didn't speak, but held me back as we watched the woman saunter up the path.

Evie and Lil noticed her next, swiftly returning to my side.

A woman in a black dress flickering in gold trimming floated like a firefly to Miss Katie's front porch.

The music stopped.

Delly bounded in a swift march to stop the woman before she greeted us. James guided a tuckered River to a bench, then made an odd signal in the air with his fist. I heard a rustle in the trees. I tried to make out the woman. Evie did, too. The woman wore a black veil.

Sky's barking and snarling distracted us. A snap of his fingers, Bo quieted Sky. The woman nodded at the guests as she strutted past the dance floor, tipping her black hat to James.

Evie squeezed my hand so tight I yelped.

"Who you be, woman?" Delly yelled. "Party's over. We ain't buying no more jams or fruit this week. Jus turn round you painted face and go on home."

"I didn't come to sell anything, Delly," the woman said, her voice smooth as silk.

"How you know my name?" Delly asked.

The woman stepped out of the shadows, lifted her black veil, and smiled at Evie. "It's Lila, Evie Winthrop," the woman said.

"Who's Lila?" Bedford asked Delly.

I swallowed. Bedford noticed my tears, shaking hands and body.

Delly reared up and said, "Grant's sister, the devil that kidnapped our Essie Mae."

Evie slowly walked down the porch steps to greet Lila and slapped her face.

I ran.

21.

ESSIE MAE

"Essie Mae," Bedford called, chasing after me.

I barreled through the crowd, slipping past James's grip.

"Let her go," I heard Delly call.

Bedford stopped to speak with James.

I glanced back at the newspaperman perched atop Lila's coach. Mars, the man from the train I jokingly called Santa Claus. I stopped, looked inside the coach; a man in a yellow cowboy hat laughed at me, lit a match, and tipped his hat.

I ran faster.

I could so easily, reaching my familiar hiding place. I tripped behind the barn and fell, startled at a panting Sky at my face. "You scared me, boy." I raced through the arbor to the safety of my rose garden. "Bo told you to find me, didn't he?"

I held my breath. *Long deep breaths, in and out.* The tool the Morgan's doctor gave me to calm my runaway heart, my mind. I collapsed onto the stone seat under the little magnolia.

Sky sat still, sniffing the air.

"Calm down, Essie Mae. Lila was paying her respects. I shouldn't have left, Sky. I shouldn't have run away."

The garden looked dead and black. The paper lanterns, James surprised us with—unlit, motionless. The clouds hid the moon. I couldn't see my hand, only Sky's brilliant white scruff. "Come here, boy." I cried into him.

If my mind conjured nightmares appearing real before me, at their worst, my feet ran without permission, and by memory, hid me.

Born of a slave, raised as a ghost, saved as a child, ravaged as a woman.

"Let her go," Miss Katie whispered. "Let her go."

"Who?" I asked.

"The battered, broken young woman. If I hadn't done so, I would have never opened my heart to James, known how . . . felt worthy."

"I loved you, Miss Katie. I should have told you, thanked you more. I should have . . . now you are truly free."

I closed my eyes to stop the terrors, recalling my morning. "Take my mind elsewhere."

I woke before sunrise to catch the mist over the valley. In the still house, the creak of the stairs, as I remembered, echoing on the middle of the fourth step. I sneaked past Delly and the sound of her spoon slapping inside the bowl, stirring the batter for breakfast. The aroma of frying bacon and pancakes would soon wake the house.

Adventures on our own were magical as children, now vital, but lonely.

On the Morgan's farm, I fell in love again with the countryside and my roses because I was somewhere else, cloistered with nature and an elderly couple who knew nothing of my past. Their embrace held no remorse, shame, or hesitancy; it came full on in an honest love my soul craved. Surrounded not by fear, but by my students hungry to learn and make something of their new life. I could be anyone . . . anyone but *her*, far from luxurious parlors, balls, and an audience's applause, out from under Lil's care and Evie's concern. Separation from Evie frightened me until one morning I awoke in love with solitude. Living with the Morgans, I felt whole again, even at the cost of feeling lonely.

After five years and the fires of war, our hillside appeared the same, but my vision had changed. I no longer heard Evie's giggles, Delly's call, Miss Katie's whisper, but my own inner voice confirming Westland was no longer my home. Westland was never my home.

"You don bleed like we do."

I gasped at the sound of clinking chains.

"Who's there?" I shouted. "This dog will get you."

But Sky hadn't growled or moved. He looked at me, curious, whimpering.

"Go away!" I dropped to the ground, hiding behind a bush. "Leave me alone," I screamed. Curled in a ball; hot tears soaked my skin. Sky nuzzled to move me. I closed my eyes at the sound. *Chink. Chink. Chink.* "I heard them."

Sky scampered away, leaving me alone. I wasn't anything but alone.

Footsteps.

Clink. Clink. Clink.

"Essie!" he called. "Essie Mae."

I shot up and ran into Bedford's arms. "Someone's in here."

"Wait here." Bedford drew his gun, searched the garden, and rushed back to me. His jacket fell upon my shoulders. "It's all right, Essie. You're safe."

My breathing stilled. I couldn't look at him. "Take me back," I said, ashamed.

"Rest a moment. James is dismissing the crowd. It's over."

"Why did Grant's sister come to Westland? Why did Lila come here?"

"It happened so fast. After Evie slapped her, Lila ran back into the carriage."

"That newspaperman, Mars . . ."

"He works for me. I didn't know who Lila was, but I thought Houst might visit tonight. Bold. And that's exactly why he did."

"That man in the carriage?"

"An associate of John Winthrop, a ghost from Katie's past. I can't be sure. I counted on Houst's arrogance, but I wasn't certain he'd face us. He hasn't yet. But this is monumental. If it was Houst, we've got him."

"You said Houst wouldn't be foolish to visit Westland so soon after Miss Katie's death."

"Something or someone lured him. We'll find out. I have a feeling our newspaperman worked his magic. Essie, I promise you, you were safe the entire evening. You all were."

"Is Evie all right?" Dizziness left me. Bedford came into focus. I came back to him.

"Evie's fine. Lil took her inside. They're worried about you."

"I shouldn't have fled. I feel so foolish."

He caressed my hands. I missed our train ride, catching myself wanting to stay alone with him now. "And we should have danced and danced." He smiled.

I stood, searching for Sky. He sat near the garden's entrance. "That's some guard dog."

"Bo trained him well. He ordered Sky to find you."

I regained my footing and walked to my garden's new patio, the swing in motion. "I couldn't see the blight before. My roses appeared magical under James's paper lanterns. Evie lost herself inside the lanterns tonight. She always did."

"I'm sorry. I should have warned you this could happen."

"The last time I hid in this garden was from Grant, who raped me." I said it to shock him, knowing better. Bedford looked at me without pity but compassion. "Evie loved Grant in her own way. She saw us. I ruined her life."

"No. The last time you stood in this garden was the night of your homecoming. You glowed with the lanterns. I saw you."

"You didn't come in."

"I was there."

"Like on the hillside, the morning we buried Miss Katie. Why didn't you stand with us?"

"I stood where I need to." Bedford guided me back to the cold stone bench.

"We both hide from the world. I preach freedom—a lie because I don't embrace it for myself. I punish myself like River, and I don't know why." I stumbled. Catching myself, I leaned against a tree. "I broke a promise to Miss Katie," I said, steady now.

He let me go.

I wandered my garden. "She asked me to recite her favorite words from the first speech I ever gave. She even had me perform it for her in the parlor during my last visit to Westland, arranged chairs, and summoned the entire house to listen. But I didn't want to say those words at her service in chastisement or pride."

Quiet, Bedford sat watching me.

"I should have kept my promise. When I saw Grant's sister walk up that path . . . I felt it all over again."

"What, Essie?"

"Insignificance."

"What were the words Katie wished you to speak? Say them now."

"You're trying to calm me with a task." I took a deep breath. "It's over. I'm fine now."

"No, I want to hear them."

Darkness lifted.

Moonlight scattered itself across my sparse roses. I plucked one. I couldn't smell it but feel its silk across my cheek. "A rose is the most exquisite flower loved for its fragrance and beauty. But be careful where you touch . . . its distracting blossom makes you forget it sprouts thorns, that when touched, prick the skin and when you bleed, you bleed its red. Whether black, whether white, we bleed the same."

Bedford stood to the calls of James. "In here," he said. "We'll come to you."

The chatter beyond my garden ceased. Sky disappeared to Evie, I presumed, who waited outside the gate.

"Wait," I said.

Bedford came to me. "Those words are you. No one else's."

"Thank you." I handed him his jacket.

We walked to the exit in silence.

I could absorb the quiet now, but couldn't help looking back for a stranger in my garden. "Sebastian, I'm not crazy. I heard someone. I heard chains."

"I know." He revealed the rusted shackles and steadied my steps. "I won't let any harm come to you. I promise. Trust me."

"Essie," Evie shouted, running to me.

"I trust you. Someone is playing games," I said, stronger.

James greeted us and helped me navigate through the brush. "You all right, Essie Mae?"

"Yes. I'm fine now."

"Lila said she came to warn us," James said.

We stood in front of the barn, looking toward the house. The crowd had departed, lanterns snuffed out.

"You all right, child?" Delly asked. "Disrespecting woman won't ever come back. I see to it."

"That man in the carriage . . ." I wobbled again. James and Bedford cradled my arms.

"It's been a long day," James said. "Don't worry, Essie Mae. Bo's seeing to the trouble."

"That man don't look like Houst," Delly said. "He wear the hat, but we don't know."

"Lila came to warn us?" I asked, finding my strength. I stopped short of the path home.

"We'll talk about that tomorrow," James dismissed. "We're all tired."

"No," Evie insisted. "We'll talk about it now."

James tipped his hat back and stared into Evie. "Evie, I've said my peace."

"I haven't. Lila said she came to warn us. Essie Mae, she knows where Trailer is hiding."

I eyed her, skeptical. "The last of my kidnappers the law couldn't find. How would Lila know?"

"She described Trailer, Essie . . . his scar from ear to chin on the right side of his face."

I froze at Evie's words. "How would Lila know?"

"Mr. James right." Delly scooted me onward. "Too late for this evil talk. We remember the good. A grand party. Do it for Delly, hmm? Think a old River dancing his jig."

"All right," Evie said. "Answers come tomorrow, or this is over. I will not care about selling Westland and leaving this land, you hear?"

"Child, that's what they want," Delly said. "They trying to scare us off this land, scare you into not living life. You ain't been here to know that. We have. And this ain't the first time, so you gonna get some sleep and get right. Mr. James says in the morning. Morning 'tis."

Evie hadn't an answer. She stood defiant, soon melting into Delly's arms. "I wanted—"

Bedford held up his hand for us to stay quiet.

James halted.

We all watched Sky race toward the stables.

"Fire in the carriage house!" Bo shouted.

PART II

22

EVIE

Delly confess Katie pay one, kep paying him. One taste a honey all it take for the rest a the flies to swarm. Bo's words tumbled in my mind since his confession at the greenhouse. James and his men rode three days searching for the man called Houst, the ghost haunting Westland.

No fiddles or yowls at Koontz's jig could quell my horror at the sight of my father's decaying carriage in flames. The once polished barouche Essie and I scouted, signaling his departure, the one I dreaded spying from my window upon its arrival.

Essie fainted at the inferno. When she came to, Bedford escorted her to the house. I stayed, watching the fire billow and swirl, eating up a past I believed buried.

"Mama kept my father's carriage?" I asked Bo, pacing close to the smoldering ash. I threw off Bo's hands, pulling me away. "Don't herd me like Sky. Lil's nipping at my ankles to forget this, but it won't work."

Bo bowed his head, sifting ash with a stick. "Jus trying to . . ."

"Protect me? Bo, if I'm to run Westland, this is my business now."

"Miss Katie give you daddy's carriage to Tom McCafferty years ago, but Tom sell it. Someone must've brought it here."

"Who?"

The men doused the fire swiftly. Bo made them haul the charred carriage away as fast. "Miss Evie, Jackson say it a game that got outta hand," Bo said. "He confess the men drinking and smoking, pretending they swells, something went wrong."

We didn't believe Bo's story.

"That Lila and Houst be the cause a this," Delly said.

James said nothing. He tipped a paper lantern on the porch, making it sway, and retired to the parlor, waiting for his men. They rode off in the night, and for the next three days, scoured the hills, neighboring farms, and Sweet Water for Houst.

"I don't know how Katie's mixed up in any of this, Evie," James said, disheartened. "Houst was before my time."

"Supposing a good thing 'cause James woulda run that cardsharp off for sure," Bo said.

As the days passed, my uncle's delay tempted me to wonder if losing Westland was the best thing for us. Essie and I cloistered in the house with Delly. When the men trickled back, I at last pondered this word—*home*. I remembered dancing at Mama's party, feeling free. *Freedom's not merely a feeling, Essie once said. It is a sanctuary, position, God's gift, and only good if you're willing to fight to keep it.* A stranger threatening to steal Mama's Westland ignited my fight, the belief—Westland could be my home again, a healing home, and I wasn't going to let James fight to save it alone.

James warned River of the trouble. Koontz still hadn't visited, except for the night he surprised us with his jig. I hadn't thought much about it until Essie's reluctance to see him. Last night, I saw it churning in her mind, something . . . questions. Essie's night terrors and flashbacks worsened, taking her away to that horrific night she described on stage as a narrator, not the young woman who endured hell at her kidnappers' camp. We didn't speak of Lila. Essie wouldn't visit her rose garden, or say if she could overcome Westland's painful past to stay.

And I didn't ask.

Aunt Lil needled me about Paris. I decided I should go so Essie could return to the peace of the Morgan's strawberry farm in Piermont. "If Essie Mae will not accompany us to Paris, which I hold hope," Lil said. "New York is safest for her now."

"Bunk. Essie's spirit is stronger than all of ours put together. We'll fight." I just hadn't figured how yet.

Rest and an unlikely companion brought our Essie Mae back to us, Sky, our spunky, strong-willed Border collie.

"I think she see herself in that dog . . . learning to trust folks again, giving home and love a chance," Delly said.

I agreed.

At the word of Bedford's arrival, Essie's spark returned. We gathered in the study awaiting Uncle Augustus, his news on the state of Westland, and the reading of Mama's will. Delly wrung her hands and mumbled all morning about digging up secrets. The anticipation I held regarding Mama's last wishes turned to trepidation.

The rain fell in a curtain of billowy drops pinging across the window. "Red sky at night, sailor's delight. Red sky in morning, sailor's warning." I lingered at the window, watching for Bedford. "Why couldn't a red sky in the morning signal adorning or worth exploring?"

"Hearts a soaring," Delly said, forcing a ripple of uncomfortable laughter in Mama's study. She sneaked up behind me, watching the sun attempting to stretch beyond the clouds. Her soft sigh brought tears. When I turned around, Delly grinned, stroking Mama's flower brooch pinned on her dress.

"Anything but a warning," I mumbled, closing the curtains.

"It stopped raining," Essie said.

"We need a good rain," Bo whispered. He looked dapper in his Sunday best. Mama had asked we dress in pastels for her homegoing, but today, I wore black, respecting her memory.

As I took in my family, I felt Mama's love and faith bubble inside me, opening my eyes to see Westland had transformed into a healing place for years. Quiet, their eyes followed me as I wandered to the basket of Mama's handmade Christmas bows. I swirled a stack of red and gold foil paper. "For Mama's poinsettias."

"Evie," James said softly.

I skipped my fingers over the spines of Mama's books, smiling at her volume of Jane Austen. James's eyes shot away when I glanced at him, warming myself by the fire. Delly served tea, silent. Documents and letters covered Mama's rosewood desk. "She still has it," I said, "the owl letter opener." I spied Mama's letterbox, wondering if a threat hid inside. Grandfather's case clock chimed. An hour, two arguments later, nothing resolved.

James and Bo whispered. Lil reached for my hand as I passed my old writing desk Mama had repositioned near a window. "Mama did this, didn't she?" I asked Delly. Delly had arranged my worn writing tablet, pencils, paints, and childhood journal holding my stories on the small white desk.

"You tell me you imagined a tale," she replied, "bout a boy who hid in the forest talking to the trees . . . and they talk back. Figure maybe you write that one for old Delly."

We traded smiles. The room sighed.

I contemplated a fresh start, sitting behind that desk, writing and drawing again. *Something's missing*, I thought, thumbing through my old journal.

Mama softened Grandfather's study with her touches. Japanese fans replaced antlers on the wall. The fans reminded me of Lil's charm school, the day she stuffed her bread loaf feet into a pair of wooden clogs. *Getas*. Eyes followed me as I admired Mama's floral lamps, silk pillows, and perfumed satchels hanging at windows. *Polly Koontz's influence*, Mama said.

Essie stood off in a corner, swirling her finger over the gold spines of the books she swiped as a child. We watched her entangle her finger in a curl. She ambled to Mama's museum: walnut shelving displaying Grandfather's Venetian glass and Mama's blue and white porcelain.

Delly and Essie admired curiosities. "See there, Evie?" Delly pointed to a painting.

"My painting, Mama holding tulips," I said, my voice breaking. "When did she hang it?"

"Last year. You never wander in her study too much."

"No, the business of Westland wasn't for Evie," Lil quipped.

"If it was, I wouldn't have let it fall into disarray. I'm not as ignorant as you presume."

"Hush, child. No need for sassing," Delly scolded. "We all prickly, wanting to know the same as you."

"Run Westland," James huffed. "Thought you'd be glad to run away from it now."

"You're a fine one to speak on running away." I slammed my journal on the desk. "What's going on, James?"

Delly stepped between us. "No hateful words gonna help us now, Mr. James."

"Then maybe you're setting fires," I said to James. "To get rid of it."

Bo towered over me, glaring, ashamed. "Could think the same bout you, but we don't."

"Stop it," Essie shouted. "Look at us, blaming each other for hateful acts.

You should be ashamed, Evie, Bo, all of you. If Evie didn't want Westland, she would have told Miss Katie."

"I'm sorry, James, Bo." I hid my shame, flipping through my journal.

"Essie's right," Bedford said, entering. "What's important now, focusing on the cause of this—Houst." Bedford whispered to James. James patted him on the back. It kindled my anger.

Essie Mae hadn't allowed the moment to swallow her whole. She snickered when Bedford twisted off the middle button on his vest. It landed on his shoe. "I warned him," she said, trying to calm me. "Tugs at his buttons like you."

"Explain," James said, flicking his watch open and closed, staring into Bedford.

Bedford held up the dangling gold chain of his watch. "It's time," he whispered.

James stilled, admiring the details of Bedford's pocket watch, opening it and handing it back to Bedford. "You win," James said.

"She does."

Bedford sat in Mama's chair, giving James the floor.

James darted his eyes at me and away, pulling the bottom of his formal jacket, squirming to toss it. "That's a handsome watch, Bedford, but I don't have elegant words to dress up what I gotta say now. Darlin' . . . Evie, there's no excuse but hurting in the words I said. Forgive me."

"I understand. Forgive me, James."

James nodded, leaned on the edge of Mama's desk, and raised his hand to stop my embrace. The only time I had ever seen fear in James's eyes was the night my father died. The night James found me, at thirteen, bloodied and beaten in my bedroom by my father's hands.

James waited a long while before any words spilled out.

We took our seats.

Delly dabbed her tears and said, "You go on, James."

"What I know," James started, "ain't no easy thing to tell. More days go by, more our predicament twists and turns, making me wonder how a stranger got a foothold on Westland's land." James nodded to Bedford to continue. "Bedford."

Bedford nodded, scanned the room, and began, "After the night of

Katie's party, Augustus returned to Mobile to distressing news. Don't be alarmed. I have assured Augustus we have complete trust and support from the United States government. Soldiers arrive any day."

"Good news," James said. "Until then?"

"As executor of her estate, Katherine instructed me to withhold her last wishes until the matter of her blackmailer is resolved."

"Blackmail?" James asked, charging at Bedford. Bo held James back. "Bedford, you kept this from me?"

Bedford stood his ground. "No, sir. Katie did."

"Let him finish, James," Delly said, leading James to sit beside her.

James exhaled and poured himself a sip of whiskey. "Go on."

Bedford stood behind Mama's desk, rummaging through his stack of legal papers. The room stilled as he put on his glasses, reading to himself. "James, you're a loving husband who protected and honored your wife's reputation. Katie, in her naive way, attempted to do the same."

James returned by Bedford's side. "You're in an awkward position, lad, working for Katie in confidence, talking to her family now. Speak what Katie needed your voice to confess."

Essie reached for my hand.

Bedford removed his spectacles. "Two months ago, a man identified as a former hand at Westland and John Winthrop's confidant, Delaney Houst, claimed a debt so great after John's death that in her final days, Katie had sold Houst Westland."

I rose. "I don't believe a word. Mama would never sell Westland."

Augustus barreled through the door, dropping his satchel on the desk. "*Bonjour*. Houst surely knew John Winthrop died years ago, but he only recently discovered Westland still stands after the war, and the government hasn't confiscated it, so he presumes. Several entanglements exist. Apologies for my delay."

James greeted Augustus heartily. Delly poured my uncle tea.

Augustus sipped his tea, studying our expressions. "*Merci*, Delly."

Essie jostled my shoulder as I sat daydreaming at Augustus, remembering him from my childhood as a golden-haired prince from a fairy tale. Today, Uncle's piercing eyes inspected us as if we were criminals on trial. "Bedford just started, Uncle. Will you sort the trouble now?"

Augustus sighed and gazed at me. "*Oui, ma chéri*, but today will not be easy nor pleasant. Katherine insisted you must all have hope for in the end I promised her, I would do all I could legally to protect Westland."

"Did Mama sell Westland?"

"No. However, Westland is not out of trouble yet. But first . . . Bedford." The two murmured over documents again.

"Come on, now. My pound cake settle our insides," Delly said, buzzing about the room.

Essie's habit of kicking a chair leg hadn't disappeared with age. She caught herself and slapped my hands from fiddling with the lace on my sleeve.

James paced, pausing to peer out the window.

"I sent the servants away, James," Delly said. "Nobody here but Sky pawing at the door."

"Sky wanna know we all right," Bo said, eyeing Essie, me. Bo let the dog in and sneaked him some cake. Sky weaved through our chairs, found his rug, and drifted.

Augustus knocked on the desk for our attention. "Family, I am here to read the last will and testament of Katherine Winthrop, legally known as Katherine Evelyn Wilcox, daughter of Alexander and Ruth. However, as Bedford indicated, at the request of Katherine, no will shall be read until the manner of her blackmailer, Delaney Houst, is legally put to rest."

A rumble swept through the study.

"Surely Westland goes to James, her husband," I said.

Augustus waved a paper in the air. "Perhaps. However, though John abandoned Katie years ago, he legally remained her husband at the time of his death, and as such, John Winthrop's debts fell to Katherine. We appeased most of his creditors, but one."

"I didn't marry Katie for Westland," James said. "We wed without, waited long enough."

"My sister knew better," Lil said. "Any scoundrel could claim John owed them money."

Augustus continued, "They did. Thankfully, news spread of my firm's reputation and relentless pursuit and success in jailing the frauds, thwarting further schemes. No one knew Houst was blackmailing Katie until after the war when the payments ceased."

Delly handed me a fresh cup of tea. "Go on drink, Evie. You pale as cotton. That Houst always threaten he gonna get Westland someday."

Augustus opened Mama's letterbox; it was empty. "As her lawyer, blame me. When Katherine dismissed Houst, I had him arrested for robbery and extortion. He lost everything, and I lost track of him until I received word Houst died during the war. When I saw the payments continued at war's end, without my knowledge, I confronted Katherine. She confessed a dreadful mistake. She had paid Houst, now an enemy of the United States, in gold to protect . . ."

"Me," Essie said.

Bedford stepped in. "It's a bit more complicated, Miss Essie."

"Delly, how did Houst know my father?" I asked.

"Houst come round years back when Mr. Wilcox run things. But Houst jus a rough boy then, making trouble in Sweet Water. Mr. Wilcox, he gotta reputation for helping orphans, giving em schooling and a job. But Houst disappear, then show up with John Winthrop years later. Don't know why, till Houst never leave John's side."

"Is Houst the gifted gambler you mentioned, James?" I asked.

"Yes, darlin'."

Bo finally spoke, "Houst an ornery boy, but come back to Westland a slippery young man, earning him dollars for gossip he hear at dinner or drinks in the parlor, sweeping the porch when the master and mistress whispering private words, and swiping our money with his poker tricks. We all say Houst no good, but nobody listening to the slaves John made us."

I bristled. "Didn't Mama know better than to keep a man like that on?"

"Houst knew you daddy's secrets," Delly said, "Blackmail start with John Winthrop."

"John hired Houst to keep him close," Bedford said. "Houst's true gift, bluffing. Played a good game with John, sneaking into the secret aspects of his life with the delusion someday he would own Westland and marry Katherine."

"This scum overplayed his hand." James couldn't tame the rage in his voice. "I warned Katie, you pay one, you'll pay them all . . . if she had only told me."

"You know why she didn't," Lil said.

Augustus handed me a paper embossed with the seal of the United States government. The words blurred on the page. "Someone informed the Union army, traitors lived at Westland. The government could seize it."

"We had a letter from the Union general I supported with supplies during the war, proving loyalty," James explained. "Lil's activity also aided the Union . . . and William's."

"William?" I asked, shocked.

"We'll get to that, Evie," Bedford interrupted.

"Mama had no sons fighting in the war."

"Evie you were engaged to William Reed, a Confederate soldier, were you not?" Augustus asked. "The owner of the plantation and their heirs must prove loyalty. With Katie's payments to Houst, the Union had their proof Katie supported a war criminal until I intervened. I petitioned for leniency. Katherine meant to protect you. I proved Houst's blackmail started years before the war, and the government accepted our defense."

"Why didn't Mama reveal her blackmailer? Why did she pay Houst for years, Uncle?"

"I presume, at first, it was after Essie's birth, to protect the child from John. Houst was an ambitious young man, one of two who torched Westland's cotton the night you were born."

"Near the end, Mama had fevers and delusions. You could be wrong about everything."

"Katie weak in heart," Delly defended, "but also in her mind and spirit for failing to stop that secret evil John be doing, bringing slavery to this plantation, enslaving his own child."

"Evie." James blocked my escape.

"I can't do this." I ached to leave at every mention of my father.

"Please. We face this together." I let James guide me back to my chair.

"Houst witnessed John abandoning Katie several times during their marriage," Bedford said. "He knew Katie would never divorce him. Houst hadn't a clue of James or her remarrying."

"Never met him," James said. "That's why Houst had the guts to show up the night of Katie's party, spy Westland's protection and if it appeared as prosperous as he remembered."

Augustus nodded. "Houst could claim Katherine was paying off her husband's debt to him. It was your speeches, Essie Mae, and our court documents on your horrific kidnapping that proved to the Union Katie committed no treasonous act but one of desperation to protect her family."

"I brokered a deal with the Union," Bedford added. "Houst for the release of Westland and all debts owed fabricated or otherwise, and protection for our valley until the fires ceased."

"What crimes did Houst commit?" Essie asked.

"Along with blackmailing four high-ranking officials, including a client of mine, who shall remain nameless, Houst ran cotton through the blockade, making a fortune by paying off crooked Union soldiers in charge of the shipments out of Montgomery. Houst split the profits. The government wants Houst and the soldiers he bribed; if they're still alive."

"At five hundred dollars a bale, Houst planned on stealing Westland's cotton," Bedford explained. "He hadn't known Westland no longer produced. He played every angle, threatening to steal Westland using his accusations of treason. Remember, Houst's gift ..."

"Bluffing," I said. "With no lucrative cotton crop, he's not after Westland, is he, Uncle? He wants the land because he believes the bunk my father said about Grandfather's gold."

"We don't know what Houst is after. But he discovered Katie's involvement in assisting Confederate deserters. Houst believed she kept a book on the soldiers who joined the resistance fighting for the Union. She holds no book. That didn't keep Houst from adding this to his hand."

Bedford scowled. "Houst is holding a junk hand. That's his play, throw everything at us, keep us guessing and afraid. He's stuffed aces up his sleeve ... don't know what they are yet."

"I won't deny we supported the Union and glad of it," Lil boasted. "From what I found, Katie only made three payments to Houst in gold. Where it came from, we do not know."

Bo and James exchanged a look, making me curious. I wondered if the color in my face drained again as James's.

Bedford stood before me, looking at me in pity. "Perhaps, that is enough for one day."

"Not nearly," I said, planted in my chair.

"Evie's right," James said, sitting next to me now. "Go on, Bedford."

"I needed confirmation the man blackmailing Katie was the real Houst. Katie hired me to find him. My lead came in New York. Houst ran an exchange and ticket swindle there with a woman. We never found her. Houst played his first hand, insisting he had a legal claim to the estate and promised to take us to court, but we called his bluff. If Houst dared to visit Katie's party, it's the first we've heard from him in months."

"Bedford, why not arrest Houst in New York?" James asked.

"The government's priorities were the Union soldiers Houst bribed. Houst paid for his connections; his arrogance convinced him he was untouchable. Once the government tracked three of the soldiers Houst paid, he disappeared. They hired me to flush him out."

"Maybe you're working angles, too," I said.

"In your state, a fair accusation, Miss Evie. I'm working for Katie, you."

My stomach churned at the question looming over us no one asked. "Uncle Augustus . . ." I couldn't hold my tears. "Why would Houst wait all these years?"

"Evil men wait a lifetime to get even," Delly said.

"I asked my uncle, Delly. You haven't answered. Why did Mama pay Delaney Houst?"

"*Ma petit chère*, we thought Houst dead until Bedford tracked him in New York. Houst depleted his money and influence. Something or some-one lured him back to go all in and pursue Westland. That something was Essie Mae. A young woman now giving speeches in New York City, we believe Houst saw Essie and knew well her face, a face from his past."

"Who?" Essie asked, trembling.

"Your mother."

"Isabel." Essie caught her breath. "Houst knew my mama?"

"He worked at Westland when Isabel worked here. Houst is the sort that would notice a woman as beautiful. In Katherine's words, it was difficult for men not to notice Isabel."

"Want me to ask the menfolk to leave, James?" Delly asked, scaring me.

"No," Essie said, tears in her voice. "I will hear this with my family."

James buried his head in his hands. I couldn't stop dread from covering me. Evie sat tall in her chair, staring at Augustus.

"Augustus, please." James motioned for him to continue.

"The news I received in Mobile was from the woman, Lila. Houst joined the Southern rebels, failed Confederate leaders bent on destruction of blacks, progress in education, equality, and to hurt unionists—white Southerns who supported the Union."

"Us," Lil said. "The rebels are the enemy of freedom. Why the soldiers come."

"Uncle, you said they caught the men who torched Tom's barn."

"Not all of them. We can attest to that. So far, none of the fires at Westland have been large enough to cause real damage, as if set by a juvenile as a warning."

"Uncle, please, what does this have to do with Essie?"

"We believe Houst was blackmailing Katherine on the knowledge Essie Mae is your half sister. I am sorry, child. She is not. Essie Mae is not your sister, Evie."

Essie burst into tears. Sky dropped his chin onto her lap. She shooed him away.

The room, quiet.

"Legally, Katherine was Essie's guardian. Katie adopted you, Essie Mae, when you were fourteen, to ensure your future."

Delly settled Essie's sobs, rocking her and whispering in her ear.

I remembered the night I spoke with James when he said *Essie always knows.*

Essie gathered herself. "Thomas mentioned . . . oh, Lil . . . you knew. Who is my father, Delly?" she asked, indignant.

"Don't know, child, that the truth, but it ain't John Winthrop. And nobody know except me. So if you wanna let hell make ya angry, here I be. Doc Jones said Isabel already three months pregnant when John take her."

"Raped."

"Yes, child. John ain't the only one who do the evil thing to Isabel."

"Houst. Is Delaney Houst my father?"

"Shame is, nobody know, child. Nobody."

"Dr. Jones comes into the middle of it again," I said. "What's he to do with this?"

"He tend to Isabel," Delly said, wringing her hands. "He be the only one who knew she already with child 'cause she almost lose ya once, Essie."

Essie gasped. "It would've saved us, you."

Delly shook Essie now. "Don't ya hear? Katie treat ya like her daughter. You home."

"Home?" Essie eyed us in disbelief. "Westland could never be my home birthed in such ignorance, passivity, and violence."

"Whoa, Essie Mae," James said. "Are you blaming Katie for this?"

"I'm not one of your fillies, James."

"Katherine never knew," James insisted.

Bedford hushed the room. "Please, sit down, everyone. Augustus and I don't have all the answers, Essie Mae, but the danger lies because Houst believes he is your father, a secret he will kill to protect."

"Kill me?"

"After the war, Houst built a sweet scam, impersonating treasury agents stealing small plantations across the South with his rebel friends. Houst fears enough, having a daughter born of a slave, would be his ruin among them and his death."

Essie ignored Bedford, her tearful gazed fixed on Delly. "How, Delly?"

Bo stepped in and answered, "I told ya a crazy runaway slave rape you mama; it was Houst under the willow."

A chill swept through me, recalling Mama's last words. "Westland, where its willows hold secrets, until the night air sweeps through their leaves, scattering them in the wind and into our ears. Essie, Mama tried to tell me."

"Ain't like that," Bo shouted. "Houst don't force Isabel like John in the evil way. Isabel weren't right, Essie Mae. She all woman. All I say on that now. Don't make me say no more."

Essie raced for the door.

Delly held her.

"Snips and pieces. It isn't enough!" Essie screamed. "Now I know: no man raped Isabel; she was a whore! That's what you won't tell me. Why would Katie tell me John Winthrop was my father?"

"To protect ya, Essie Mae," Delly said. "Keep you girls together, always. John woulda killed her. He'd a drown Isabel's baby."

Bedford walked Essie to the back of the study. She bent over to catch her breath. "Slow breaths," he whispered to her. "It's all right." When Essie Mae settled, she drank the water Delly handed to her. Delly kissed her cheek and left her alone. No one spoke. Essie sat with us again, but off on her own, opening the curtains, letting the sunlight shine into the dim, cold study.

"This doesn't matter, Essie Mae," I said. "You're family."

James kneeled beside her. "That's right, darlin'. Katie adopted you years back."

"That makes this right?" Essie whispered. "Houst will never come back now. Westland is lost because of me. I never needed John Winthrop as my father to love Evie or you, James."

"Houst *will* return," Bedford said. "Showing up now . . . he's all in."

"He'll be the wrong kind to them that hate us," Bo said. "He won't stop till he get her. And Essie Mae ain't gonna stay here."

James rose. "Calm down now, everybody. This ain't easy, but we stick together."

Bedford said, "Houst believes he's paid the right Union soldiers—he hasn't."

"Essie, Katie love ya more than you understand," Delly said. "Since Katie's grand wedding to James, and when Mr. Wilcox built most a Sweet Water, newspapermen like writing bout Katie. They don't know bout our quiet ways after John die how we living and learning, black and white. They write bout Essie Mae and her speeches, too."

"The announcement of Mama's death would lure Houst to Westland."

"And a big party celebrating the mistress of Westland." Delly knew how to usher pride in our hearts and cool our tempers.

"That's why a country dance," I said. "But how could Lila step a foot on this plantation?"

"Katie know if them newspapers don't write bout her, Lila visit and Houst come with her. Katie believe Lila tangled with Houst, suspect he blackmail Lila, too. Lila's daddy spend his filthy money to keep Grant and what he do to Essie Mae outta the newspapers."

"Lila spread lies about Mama being a traitor." I checked on Essie. She sat motionless, gazing out the window. "Lila's the one writing us threatening letters."

Bedford perused a letter and tucked it back in his jacket. "No, Evie, this threatening letter was *for* Lila." The sound of shackles made Essie jump.

Bedford set them on the floor. "I found these in Essie's garden the night of Katie's party."

Silence.

"Houst isn't the only one who knows Westland and Essie's past."

Bo covered the chains with a blanket. "Get em outta here."

Augustus grabbed them and started to leave.

"Wait," Essie called. "Thank you," she said to Augustus. "I don't blame you. I don't blame any of you. It's all right." Essie took a deep breath, turned to Bedford, and asked, "It's Trailer isn't it? He was here."

"No, Essie," Bedford said. "I would know, but Lila was."

"I know it's Trailer, but why would he risk it? He wasn't like the other men . . . the kidnappers. I told you, Trailer saved me."

"Did he? One need only hear your speeches, Essie Mae, to know all about your fear of the old African man, one of the slaves Grant stole and locked in the wagon with you. You glimpsed a man in the carriage Mars drove; it could've been a woman wearing that yellow hat."

"Could've been anybody," James said.

"Then what do we do?" I asked.

"We wait," Bedford said. "Houst is holding another card: River Koontz. The government almost claimed Koontz's farm abandoned until James stepped in. But there is the question of Koontz's son, Evie."

"Son?" Essie and I asked together, astonished.

"They hadn't a record Koontz's boy served in the war," James said. "Hell, I reacted the same way."

"Do we know him?" Essie asked, eagerly. "River's son?"

"It's Trailer, darlin'," James said. "Trailer is River's son."

No one made a sound for a minute. Delly closed the curtains, but Lil flurried about the room, flooding the study in sunlight.

"I don't believe it," Essie cried, shaking.

I rushed to her. "Essie Mae . . . I don't know what's true. But I trust James and Mama. Mama died using her last breath to see this ends. It has to."

Essie stepped back, looking at me in horror. "Did you know Trailer was River's son?"

"Never. Before you blame Mama, remember we left. So much has changed, so much we don't know. Mama was ill, and what mattered to her was seeing us home again."

"Too much for a heart to sort, Essie Mae, but ya gotta give forgiveness a chance." Essie squirmed out of Delly's embrace and mine.

"Forgiveness?" Essie shouted. "You lied to me! You all did. You made me believe in something that saved me. That made me stay and watch over you. Thomas was right. I could've had my own life, away from here . . . and stuck with my own."

Delly bowed her head. "Shame on ya, child. You go on thinking blood make a family, it don't. You sisters in heart and spirit and need each other more than ever now."

Essie stood defiant, glaring at us as if we were strangers, shaking her head at Bedford, in her eyes, the worst of us. "I understand it now. Grant didn't devise the plan to kidnap me; Houst did. This Houst uses everyone. He's threatened Lila's family, why she came here. He threatens Trailer; perhaps he's mixed in this, too."

Essie pleaded with James, "You said Lila came to warn us, that she knows where Trailer is hiding. Maybe it's here. Maybe Trailer isn't a part of this; he's the one trying to warn us. Maybe he's tired of running too and has come back home . . . to his father."

"Why do you give Trailer so much room?" I asked.

"Because for all I know, he could be my father!" Essie ran out of the study.

"Let her go," Delly said, stopping Bedford.

Bedford stared down James, me. "No. Things are going to change around here."

"I've had enough of your decrees and interference," I yelled.

Quiet, Bedford slowly turned to me and said, "You don't let people you love run away."

He chased after Essie.

"I'm going to my room," I said, exhausted. "What makes you think Houst will return to Westland, Uncle?"

"This." Augustus dropped a hunk of gold the size of an egg on Mama's desk. "That man Essie calls Santa Claus, Mars, who you saw at the party, works for Bedford. Mars spied Houst holding a nugget as this when he first arrived to work for him."

"I've seen this. Mama used to keep one on her desk. She said it was fool's gold."

"Who gave it to Houst?" James asked. "He thinks it's from Westland. Damn stories."

Augustus exhaled. "I don't know. Houst is back in hiding now. Most likely, whatever contacts he has left, warned him soldiers arrived at Westland, he'll believe, to stop the arson."

Augustus sorted his papers, readying to leave. "We'll see if Houst files a legal claim for Westland. We'll assume that was him at the party. He showed himself to warn us; his resources, though thin, stretch wide. What the charlatan doesn't realize, we shall claim the government has already seized this plantation. I have the writ, false, of course. He'll not know the difference."

"Our ace, little lady," James said, "Houst doesn't know me or that I'm a Northerner who sided with the Union. Bedford said Houst thinks he's paid the right agents, so when they confiscate Westland, it's his."

"Oh, James." I held him tight.

"Darlin', one last ribbon to tie this mess, Westland stands because of one man."

"Me."

I turned to the familiar voice.

"William?"

I ran into his arms.

23.

ESSIE MAE

The bluebell sky bowed to kiss a meadow of yellow asters. My legs stretched in an overdue race as a colt bursting from its corral, free. I looked back. *Alone.* I relished the fresh air washing my cheeks, heat surging through my legs. Aged and tired, my legs couldn't keep up with my heart.

In the city, I scanned for pickpockets. Walking in nature polished my rusty skills in observation. *Listen,* Evie reminded me. *Breathe.*

Koontz's creek rippling in the distance, moist earth and evergreens. I opened my eyes to the walnut tree marked with our childhood carving. *Gray and blue shingles,* Evie said of its bark. I only saw its scars from the buck that rubbed it. My legs gave way in front of two conjoined crabapple trees. *Essie and Evie.*

"We didn't ask for this."

But it the way it is, child. What you gonna do? Leave her. Leave us?

You don bleed like we do.

"Shut up!"

You ain't nobody. You ain't white. You ain't black. You nothing.

You don't go on believing lies, Essie Mae. Taught ya better than that.

We prick our fingers and press them together. There. Now I got your blood; you got mine. We're sisters, Essie. Evie's childhood promise, declared in love, comforted my broken heart.

"Bo, why didn't you tell me?" I dropped my face into my icy palms, chilling my flushed skin, sobbing.

"Essie!" At the faint call, I hid inside a forest glen. *Breathe. Honeysuckle, fresh linen, pines.* The only fragrance rivaling my roses: Westland's pines after a rain.

I trudged onward to River's farm, the wet grass soaking my stockings and boots. The earthen smells comforted me through the years when I found no arms of compassion or understanding. River Koontz was as cold as the rain on the outside, but inside, his heart longed for the warmth of love and tenderness.

Our unspoken bond.

River could not see me, so he could not judge. I refused to see him as he was, but how I judged. *Trailer . . . River's son*, I thought at every step, chills wracking my body.

Trailer is River's son.

As I neared the path to Koontz's footbridge, a front of gray cumulus clouds served as a warning. I was too far from Westland now to take shelter, too far from the truth to find peace.

I reached the footbridge over his creek facing Koontz's farm, planting myself on the log bench he made years ago. The tears I held in on the train, hillside, and in the study escaped in a steady stream. My hands caressed the smooth arm of this tired seat, recalling Delly's letters sharing her gossip and tall tales with River as they sat here. "What secrets do you hold, old man?" The monotonous, gurgling water over the rocks quieted me. A paw print in the mud caught my eye. "Wolf? Cougar? Dog." I decided. "Sky? Are you there, boy?"

The drizzle stopped. The sun's warmth held me. I lounged on River's bench, drying my dress in the sun. Crunching leaves, snapping sticks, announced his arrival. "For the grandson of a Cherokee Indian, you're stealthy as an elephant."

"Hardly presentable," he whispered.

Sebastian. "You followed me?" I fixed my gaze ahead. "I thought you were Sky, Bedford."

"For a savant slash genius, Sky's smart, but I'm certain Bo hasn't trained him to talk."

"I heard panting and scampering. I kept looking for that dog."

Bedford tilted his head like Sky and smirked. "I'm not sure how to take that. I simply wanted to hand you this."

I turned around, mustering a chuckle at Bedford standing under the shade of a lemon parasol. *Snip a humor like a tiny ray a light in a cave, child. You gonna find hope again*, Delly bellowed in my thoughts. "It doesn't match your suit," I said. "Thank you."

"I'm not laughing, Essie Mae."

"I know. But I must, or I'll fall to pieces. I did a few minutes ago."

He wrestled with closing the parasol, staying behind me in the woods. "I confess, I saw you."

"Ah, your elephant march was you revealing yourself."

"Yes, Miss Essie."

"Do I call you Bedford or Sebastian now?"

"Whatever you wish."

"You don't have to stand behind me in the shadows."

"I am sorry, Essie Mae."

"I haven't entered the woods since—Bo and Delly forced me to hide in this forest when I was a child. No one thinks a little girl would possess the strength to climb a tree. I did." I stared at the footbridge, imagining a canopy of wisteria, water lilies below, young River and Polly in love. I shut my eyes at Bedford's soft breaths; mine skipped frantically as a broom across this bridge.

"Essie?" he whispered.

"I miss the forest, its minty fragrance, the shower of colors in the trees at sunrise and starlight illuminating a dirt road in the distance, calling me to linger. Does it lead to a cottage with a little family, a welcoming fire, and stew, or something else?"

His footsteps, hollow on the bridge.

The sun warmed me. I fanned my violet dress, wrinkled and moist. "I no longer wander idyllic dirt roads. I cower at the songs of coyotes and crickets, fearing them. It was a road as this where Grant took me. I was neither slave nor free, but something in between. I've taught many former slaves who said God made them free. Regardless of outward bondage, in their hearts and minds, they lived free. Their spirit would be free should they die, bound. My quest now. Not a slave, not free . . . to understand true freedom of the heart, mind, and soul, and how I might embrace it someday."

"Embrace it now."

"And when I at last quiet my mind, a chill comes, not a pleasant breeze tickling my skin after a rain, but one that wracks me from within, stinging my arms, causing such dread, I need a blanket, though it isn't cold. I need the warmth of something, someone, to bring me back."

Bedford's tender touch left my arm. I hadn't even known he held it. He draped a shawl across my shoulders. I tucked myself in it.

His soft steps faded.

"Did you know?" I asked, stopping him. "That John Winthrop was not my father?"

"Not until this morning." His low, mellow voice invited me to trust him. "You must understand, Augustus is legally bound to Katie's wishes and confidence."

"It has never mattered if Evie was my sister. We treated each other as such, regardless if anyone understood or approved." I looked away.

"I have always understood, Essie Mae, I needed to work three times as hard as any man to earn your trust."

"I've tested you. You have never quit." The rippling water calmed me. "Katie adopted me to ensure my future. I am her legal heir?" The softness returned to my voice.

Bedford walked closer. "Yes."

"All right."

"Miss Essie, you have a say in Westland's future."

"It's not about money. Katie gave me a seat at the table." Bedford neared the bench without a sound. The frill of the yellow parasol passed over my boots. I reached for it.

His hand held mine.

I slid my hand from his, covering up in my shawl. "I matured faster than most girls, to stay alive. Westland makes me feel vulnerable and small." I walked to the other side of the bridge, staring at the creek below.

He followed.

"Westland was our own world, Sebastian. I found my voice in New York."

"Such courage, telling your story, opening minds to learning—true freedom."

His words ignited my faith. I gazed at the water, inviting him to me. His arm pressed against mine; my hand entwined with his again. We leaned over the railing.

"I know what that lemon parasol represents," I said, "frilled in lace, a mother-of-pearl handle. I've seen what greed and poverty invite. Men held me in a cage, my black skin, gold." I squeezed the railing, flinching at his touch. "I *never* required luxury, but safety and peace."

Sebastian exhaled and swirled his palms together in a soft whirl as Evie when she was nervous. "When we first met, I smiled at your whispers of hope in a hopeless world. She's still in you."

"That child? No, Sebastian, they beat her out of me. I strive to see light in a dark world."

Sebastian grabbed my hand and passed it under a ray of light, back and forth, sunlight dancing across my brown skin as threads of gold. "Katherine used to say, no matter how anyone tries, you cannot keep out the light. It will shine through the smallest crack . . ."

"And illuminate the darkness." My eyes closed at his touch, his hand still waving mine in the sunlight piercing through the branches.

"You are that light, Miss Essie. It's all around you."

His handkerchief slipped under my chin. I wiped my tears. "I must go to Richmond," I said.

"Yes."

"You will take me with you?"

He nodded.

"You won't let James or Bo stop me?"

"You're a grown woman capable of making your own decisions. They won't interfere."

"I need to face my past . . . him. I can't live with She anymore."

"We travel to Richmond on my terms." His monotone voice reminded me of the strict Bedford Jarrell. "No running off, talking to strangers, no Lady Pinkerton heroics."

I stared into his eyes, unafraid. "You have my word."

"One thing more . . ." He flipped open his jacket, hand to his hip, the silver pistol at his side. "You threaten everything Houst has spent a lifetime to build. You embolden him."

"You're using Westland to call his bluff."

"Houst always worked alone. Bribing Union soldiers was his greatest misstep. The government will never cease until they find the traitors. They want them all."

"He wanted me to see him. Have you ever met Houst?"

"I've relied on descriptions from Delly and informants."

"Sandy hair, a thick build, ruddy cheeks . . . charred, red hands, Evie says it is my odd obsession since my abduction, noticing people's scars." I rubbed the purple swirl on my wrist; he stopped me from covering it.

"By God, that was Houst. Burns from the night he torched Westland's cotton."

"Is Houst my father?" I needed to see his eyes when I asked it.

He didn't blink but raked the white streak in his hair. "We have no proof or legal claim. Yet, Houst appears convinced. Essie, I'm traveling to a small town outside Richmond."

"Ashland . . . where Grant stole me."

"One man may offer us answers. Dr. Jones."

"A busy night for Katie's family doctor, delivering two babies, Isabel lost, Houst burned . . . a slave auction. It makes sense now, Dr. Jones's curious words to me after Katie's funeral."

"What did he say?"

"He apologized, stared at me, and said I looked like Isabel, and he would have done anything to keep Katie safe."

Sebastian raised an eyebrow. "Katie was a striking woman, and Dr. Willow Jones is a dashing man. In solving a crime, nothing and no one is without reproach."

"A strange twist of fate; Dr. Jones recently married Jeanie, the Irish woman who cared for me after my ordeal. Evie said Dr. Jones never previously married, dedicated to his calling. I don't begrudge his happiness."

Sebastian paced. "Your family loves you. I have never seen such devotion. I know what it's like not to know where you come from."

"Thank you, Bedford."

"Sebastian. It's still confusing?"

"Not one bit." I looked toward Koontz's house, rethinking my visit. Sebastian followed my gaze and moaned, agreeing seeing River in my state was an awful idea. "Will James be safe if you leave?" Dizzy again, I sat back on the log bench.

"Houst believes soldiers watch Westland for his arrival. He's disappeared and won't risk traveling. Time is on our side. Evie and Lil will go to Paris."

"Evie made her decision then. And Trailer?"

He sat beside me. "Lila told James, Trailer is hiding out near Richmond in Ashland."

My heart skipped. "I don't believe her. But if it's true, what happens if you find Trailer?"

"When. I'll arrest him."

At the mention of Trailer, I rose, looking at River's farmhouse again, resolved. "I need to visit River Koontz alone. I'll return to the house in an hour."

"You're trembling." He lifted my shawl back over my shoulders. "You should rest."

I shook my head and handed him the parasol for his walk home. "If you linger, wait for me at this footbridge. I don't want River to hear you, know you're guarding me." I spotted shimmering gold in the water. "Look, fool's gold, pyrite. Crystals fill that sharp rock." Sebastian slid down the hill, plucked it out, and handed it to me. "River will like this."

"He's blind."

"River Koontz sees clearer than anyone I know."

"I hope you gain the answers you seek." His ominous tone frightened me.

I handed him the rock. "No matter what happens, I will always remember your kindness."

"I had hoped you would always remember me." He leaned in and softly kissed my cheek. His nose lingered on my skin.

I slid away. "Sebastian . . . who brought the slave shackles into my garden? How did a painted man get so close? Few know of my rose garden."

"James cut the new path around Westland that curves behind it."

"You know every inch of Westland."

"I've walked the grounds with James several times, yes." He tugged his earlobe.

"And you found the chains."

I hurt him.

"Essie . . ."

"No one is above reproach?" I folded my arms, scrutinizing him now.

"I never meant to sully Katie's memory. I . . ." He passed the rock over and under his fingers like a poker chip. "I follow leads. That is all."

I stopped his hands from fiddling with the rock and clasped it between his palms. "Miss Katie isn't a lead; she was as my mother."

He checked his watch and motioned toward River's home.

River stood at the window, looking our way as if watching us.

"He's blind, remember," I said, the fool's gold magically appearing back in my hand.

"Doesn't appear so, Miss Essie. A curious note, upon my arrival, Lil whispered to me, Evie shares the blame for telling Grant stories about gold hidden at Westland."

I clapped my hand over my mouth. "Oh, Evie. Childhood stories about her father. Grant didn't know she was boasting folklore to impress him."

"Westland was near bankruptcy years before the war. How did Westland survive when many plantations failed, especially without cotton?"

I lowered my head, watching Sebastian's boots shuffle away. "The settlement."

"You're not angry Augustus settled with Grant's family for a hefty sum for what Grant did to you?"

"Katie's business savvy tripled it. I begged her not to take it, but I respected her decision. She dreamed I might attend college and live well. John took everything from her. Evie's never done without."

"And Westland? You could have easily watched it fall."

"So Bo and Delly would be destitute? Why aren't you interrogating Grant's father? He would love me to disappear. I'm a constant reminder of Grant's sins."

"Grant's crimes transformed his dapper father into a feeble man."

"And Miss Katie into a grave."

"Many say I'm a gifted poker player, Miss Essie. I know how to play Houst's game. I'm not easily distracted by shills."

"That is what frightens me most." I hurried toward Koontz's farm and looked back at a smug man holding fool's gold.

Bedford held it to the light and tipped his hat.

I impressed him with my own sleight of hand, or was it worry?

24.

EVIE

The Civil War had stolen younger William. Though silver strands streaked his black hair, shoulders rounded, and swaggering gait lost, he rocked on his heels, flirting, his eyes flashing the mischief I loved.

"Your sunflowers brightened Mama's study, her favorite, next to roses," I said, reserved.

William smiled; his dimples made the smitten girl inside me resurface. "I bought them from a flower seller in Sweet Water who insisted on yellow roses."

"I'm happy you won. Essie's roses suffered blight this summer."

"If anyone can bring them back, it's Essie."

"Who will bring back Essie Mae?"

We left the solemnness of the study to walk James's path around Westland.

"Mama insisted no black in mourning. Your sunflowers scolded me to change my dress."

"Sometimes society's expectations are irreverent and destructive."

"You speak of the war."

William stood closer, straightening my collar. He smelled of cedar and violets. "You wore this green calico dress when I proposed to you at my father's estate. You insisted no fuss or frills." His fingers grazed the nape of my neck, thrilling me.

"I remember." A blush warmed my cheeks.

"You look stunning, Evie."

"And you look well, William."

"Take a turn, Miss Evie." William offered his arm, reminding me of James.

"I've missed this fragrance, rain soaking the fields at Westland."

"I forgot how beautiful it was here. How is Miss Essie?" He tucked his hand in mine as we overlooked Mama's orchard.

"Mama loved the harvest. The fruits of our labor, end of a season, and rebirth of the next. Delly says, if you want flowers you have to bust up the soil; the ground can take it, can you?" I picked up a stick and pitched it. "Essie's shattered, William. The past few years, she's teetered on the edge of a world I know not."

"She's strong, Evie, and will find her way home. I did. And you?"

"Something happened to me when Mama died. Despite Augustus's news, purpose has overcome my grief. Honoring Mama has made me see Westland in a new light."

"Much has changed in this valley for good."

"We have new neighbors, a young couple from Vermont who started a dairy farm. Lil thrilled them with her ideas for chocolate cheese, even a blueberry cheese. Imagine."

"Miss Lil will convince them to start a factory in no time. Northerners flock south now."

"Aunt Lil sings reinvention. This new world at Westland gives me hope."

We strolled a few moments in silence. I led him off the path to the brick walkway leading to the new greenhouse. Sky found us.

"And who are you?" William greeted him. "Evie, that dog means to herd you home."

"Bo's reminder he's watching. Go home, Sky, find Bo."

Sky ran off.

"Sky's watching or Bo?" William pressed a finger to his lips, squelching his laugh.

"Both."

We stood in front of the cottage. I slid my hand across the white picket fence, forgetting the rain. William lifted my hand. "Here." He patted it dry with his handkerchief.

"You always took care of me."

"A splendid greenhouse." He peered around the back, admiring the glass structure. "My mother misses our home in Virginia, what's left of it," he said, heavy-hearted.

"I'm sorry, William. The war took everything from you and your family."

"Including you."

His limp, an injury from the war, had worsened. He winced at every step. Catching himself, he stood taller, doing his utmost, hiding the pain. A black glove covered his gnarled hand. The scars of his past made me wonder if he noticed mine, darker, deeper.

I searched for Sky, forgetting I dismissed him. *Like William.* "Would you like to see inside? Essie cultivated a new rose. Oh, it is a wonder."

"I knew she would someday."

"She's named it Miss Katie. Lil's convinced Essie to show her new rose in London."

"And Conrad?" William slapped his glove in his palm at his rudeness. "I apologize, Evie. This is no day for my sarcasm or bitter regrets."

"I don't regret falling in love with you, William . . . but our situation changed. When I saw you in New York after the war, the girl in me came alive. London was a chapter in my life."

"Is that chapter over?"

"The war changed you, closed you off to me. You're still afraid to let me in."

William stood on the cottage's porch steps, offering his hand. "Show me."

Once inside the greenhouse, I closed my eyes at the humid warmth. The scent of tropical ferns and orchids settled my heart.

"You still close your eyes in a garden?" William nudged me.

"Always. Lil boasts this orchid smells of chocolate. I smell vanilla, red wine, and lemon in Essie's roses, but not a whiff of chocolate in this orchid."

"I do." William inhaled the orchids Lil arranged in her hothouse parlor. "Not."

His hand slid up my back; our past surged inside me. "Can young love resurface so quickly?" I said, breathless.

"Yes," he whispered, pecking my ear. "I will open my heart to you. Why I've come."

"Honey." I rushed to the back door. "I want you to meet her. The stables . . . fine horses."

He couldn't expect us to come together so tidy and swift. I waited outside on the terrace. His shadowed floated toward me, looking over his shoulder at the wonder of new roses.

"Of course, Evie," he said, defeated for now. "I am sorry at how things ended."

"Reconstruction . . . a fitting word now."

After a tour and story of Essie's new rose, we strolled on the path past Essie's garden to the stables. "It's a miracle you kept Honey," William said, impressed by her. "James has a fine lot. During the war, soldiers confiscated horses. Honey would bring two thousand dollars."

"Our quiet valley didn't see much fighting. Most in these parts stood against slavery and secession. James . . ." I stopped myself. *Mama wouldn't reveal much because I didn't ask.*

"They keep pretty belles away from horrific news, as well they should."

I snapped around at his statement, thinking of the off-putting Astra spouting these words. William lowered his head, discerning his truth was no compliment.

"We could ride the trail to the bridge if you like." I swallowed my defense.

William's smile; he adored me still, and I, him. "I have little time. I leave for London."

"Must you so soon?"

"My reward, you asking." His eyes took me in.

My heart raced.

"You're different, Evie. This trouble, James thought it best I explain my role. We were engaged; Augustus needed a statement regarding my activities during the war to save Westland."

"Do you remember Mama's garden? It's so vibrant now."

William held my hands, gazing into my eyes. "All right, Evie. We have words to say."

On the short walk to Mama's garden, William spoke of his family, their move to New York, longing to return to Richmond someday.

"Will you rebuild?" I asked, searching for the key to the gate, distracted by another forgotten in my pocket. I showed it to William. "I found this gold key under a willow."

"A treasure from the past?" William pointed to a key inside the gate's lock, turned it, and caught his breath at the garden's blossoms painted in raindrops. "A sanctuary for you and your mother. My sympathies, Evie."

"She spoke of you often." I led him to Mama's bench under the pergola of pink roses.

William wasn't ready to sit. He splashed his hand in the fountain's pool, snatching a handful of floating petals. I watched him, thrilled inside, confused, remembering our last kiss swept up in love.

He explored the stone walk to the magnolia path. I gasped, thinking of that odd woman, Astra, wondering if she sneaked inside the garden. *Delly sent the help away.* William explored ahead of me, disappearing behind the junipers. I followed him, stopping at the old potting shed.

"It is here," I whispered.

The walls of the shack covered in ivy, forgotten, its windows dirty, except one. I jimmied the doorknob. *Locked.* I rubbed the glass and peered inside. The shed, clean; fresh bulbs, new roses, and pots of dirt filled a table, and strangely, a stack of writing paper and red ribbon. Shovels and tools lined in a row. A book awaited its reader, resting on an elegant iron chair.

"Someone has used it." I pressed my face to the glass, straining to see more. A pitcher and basin of fresh water, a basket of Mama's pears, strands of yellow ribbons, two cornhusk dolls, a whittled wooden dog . . . the toys of my youth. I spotted something else, but I couldn't be sure. On the edge of a shelf, Lil's gold match case, the oddity in the shape of bloomers.

At William's call, I hurried back to Mama's bench, twiddling the key in my pocket. I examined it, looking back toward the potting shed. My mind swirled with this morning's confessions: *Essie, Bedford, Mama's dealings, Delly's truths, Lil's reserve. I could think it funny, Lil sneaking out here to smoke her cigars. But what of the other items? Lil said the potting shed sat unused for years.*

"Dreaming?" William startled me; his hands caressed my arms. "You're cold." He settled beside me, warming me, lifting my left hand, stroking my finger devoid of his engagement ring. "A rich man could enter the war for a year and quit," he began. "My father demanded Southern loyalty and service. It wasn't my war. I was a traitor to my family."

"What did the war do to you?"

"Rather, what did I do in the war, darling? We were not slaveholders. Father argued it was a matter of honor. The North shall not tell the South how to live. Blind fools all."

I shifted in my seat at William's unchecked temper. *He still could not tame it.*

He calmed his spastic breathing, removed his jacket, watching me as he laid it over the back of an iron chair. "My scratched eye, useless hand, limp, when I heard Essie speak of the horrors she endured, sweat soaked my clothes. I fled the theater a coward."

"I suffered battle scars of another kind. Here I am. Mama's words comforted me."

"But not her deeds."

"Forgiveness isn't easy but necessary, William, vital to living free. We each contend with it in our own way."

William nodded to Mama's bench, inviting me to join him. I did. "They sent me to fight Indians in the West. I refused. If not for Father, I would be in prison. Lil found me."

"Lil rarely discussed her war efforts. She worked tirelessly using her influence."

"You really don't know how connected your aunt is, do you?" William scanned the garden, ensuring we were alone. "A secret order, the Peace Society, offered me protection for deserting the Confederacy."

"Essie and Lil's midnight whispers. Lil said Mama hid deserters who found Westland."

"Lil contributed to a secret network in the South to infiltrate Confederate ranks, aiming to deter secession and the escalation of war. I fought a different war, Evie, against them." I stayed quiet as William caught his breath. "We infiltrated Congress to end the war."

I held back tears, proud. "I wished I had known, hiding news from pretty belles, indeed."

"There was a plan on Christmas day in December 1863 to lay down arms; others swore oaths not to fight the enemy. We were responsible for the surrender at Vicksburg."

"It's incredible, but makes sense now. Lil's soirees in New York City were . . ."

"Meetings. Evie, I swore never to reveal its secrets to anyone."

"Lil spoke of special handshakes and signals to identify secret soldiers. I thought she was balmy." I snatched a long stick and tapped it on my right foot. "Was that right?"

William retrieved his jacket, pressing his lips into a smile.

"Sit with me." I missed William's body warming mine, the caress of his strong hand, desire in his eyes admiring me as attractive, mature, and whole. He caught his stare, searching the rambling roses overhead. "Mama closed this garden for years, as I have done to you. Thank you, William, for all you did, spoken and unspoken, for my family and Westland."

"We did our utmost to bring about swift peace and war's end." William hung his head, stroking again my empty ring finger. This time, he placed a violet on top and let me go. "James waits for me. I wish we had more time."

My heart sank, leaving the magic of Mama's garden.

"Will I see you again?" We paused at Mama's willow. With Bo's horrid confession regarding Houst and Isabel, the tree no longer enchanted me. We quickened our steps.

"I hope so. Be at peace, Evie."

"William, so much of my life has been unfair."

"I must track down a book. Men's lives are at stake. I can say no more. Soon. I promise."

"The book Mama kept on Confederate deserters? Bedford said she didn't."

"And I never said she did." William checked his watch. "I must go. Delly invited me for Christmas." Joy returned to his voice.

"Good. I'll have something to look forward to."

He held me tight as we walked home. *Home.* The word sat warm inside me.

"I've been looking for you two," James said, smiling at our clasped hands. "William, I'll wait at the carriage."

William's finger grazed the deep red scar near my right eye.

I jerked away from that touch. "Scars remind of us of pain we rather forget."

He rubbed his wounded hand. "No, they remind us we're alive."

"William, you know I can offer you no children, at least none of our own. I'm no housewife, spending the day baking and flower arranging . . . I cannot sew."

"Neither can I."

"I might write or paint! I have ideals, independence." My confession hadn't moved him.

"Then you and my mother will hold lively debates on a woman's right to vote."

"Something has happened to me these years away. I have Lil's brass and don't belong with giddy, gossiping ladies in overdone parlors. I could pretend, but I no longer wish to."

"That is why I fell in love with you. Christmas then," he said, holding me.

"Christmas."

I watched him walk away, hoping he'd return. "Perhaps, I may even take up wearing trousers!" I called.

He stopped and rushed back. "I never meant to hurt you."

"Nor I, you."

His kiss, loving and warm, filled the hole in my heart missing Mama, desiring him.

"William," James called, a smile in his voice. "Crack on, man."

William left me with one last kiss . . . and a decision.

"I know a fine tailor in London who fashions a crackerjack pair of women's trousers!" he called, tipping his hat.

"Nursing a lonely heart, Delly, isn't better than a broken one, for it refuses to feel."

A shower of fall leaves fell upon me. I looked up. The gray skies hadn't dissipated. I saw sunlight shimmering through the clouds, regardless.

"This is what forgiveness feels like, Mama." I remembered the gold key in my pocket and held it in the light. "Forgiving ourselves most of all."

I waved at William as they drove off, making the key flash in the sun, knowing what I had to do.

25.

ESSIE MAE

Musty wood and cloves hit my nose, entering his dim house. His back to me, puffs of dust floated in rays of sunlight as he opened the curtains. He knew I stood inside, making me wait, creepy, uncomfortable, the way he liked it.

His soft snickering made me uneasy. Evie warned me River's behavior had changed. *Spells and temper; sweet one instant, gruff the next.*

I held my breath, waiting for him to turn around. I scuffled my feet, announcing my presence. Ignoring me, he hummed and grunted, arranging teacups and saucers on a new tea table in front of Miss Katie's flowered settee.

I smoothed the wrinkles from my violet dress, damp from the rain. "Don't you think you've ignored me long enough?" I asked.

"Still sassing like that Evie. Hello, Smiles," he said, his back to me.

"Hello, River," I squeaked.

"Why you crying, child?"

"You won't welcome me. I shouldn't have come. I'll go."

"Wait." He turned around slowly and dropped a teacup. His eyes to the ceiling, he stopped me from racing to him to clean the shattered porcelain. "That us," he said. "Busted?"

"Are you all right?"

He lowered his head, then looked up, staring into me, his left eye crystal blue, teary.

"Glory be," Koontz said.

For a moment, I thought Bedford was right; River could see me, really see me.

"I'm a mess," I said, jollier, fluffing my curls. "I got caught in the rain."

I wanted to sweep up the porcelain near his shoes. He stood stuck in the middle of his little home. A pot of spearmint tea permeated the air. Delly's blueberry bread, sliced and served. I left him alone. He'd move sooner or later, or maybe his knee got stuck like Delly's did after a rain. He wouldn't want fuss or embarrassment, cradling him in my arms, hobbling to a chair.

I wandered to the front door, reacquainting myself with the old front porch, a fresh coat of white paint on its deck, gray-blue spindles as at Westland. "Bo's been painting. I can't wait to see your garden. Evie says your roses grew plentiful this summer despite the drought."

He reached me; his hand caressed my shoulder.

My tears fell.

He gently turned me around to him and hugged me.

We wept together for what felt like minutes, mere seconds. I missed unspoken words. If this was all I had with him, his first tears moistening my shoulder, it satisfied a deep void within my heart, River's genuine love.

He swallowed, cleared his throat. His weathered hands trembled, guiding my shoulders, nudging me back in front of him a little. I gasped when his eyes squinted, staring directly into mine, the filmy cloud over his left eye—clear.

"Lord, child, you're as beautiful as your mama."

"You see me?" I held my breath, embracing him again. He squirmed and wriggled away. "You see me?"

"Now, now." I fell into his tenderness, rocking me as a child, stroking my hair. "Not like ya suppose." River gripped my arms, his boney fingers hurting me a little. He nudged me back, gazing at me once more. I could scarcely see his smirk through my tears.

"I prayed dear Lord, jus once, let me see Essie Mae's face. Today's the day."

"I don't understand. How?"

"Come on in the house. Help me."

River never asked for help.

My visit shook him and me.

I lit a lamp after helping him into his rocker and covered him with the quilt I made for him our first Christmas. "You kept my sunburst quilt." I fanned it out, remembering the trip to Sweet Water with Miss Katie, helping me pick fabrics and colors.

"Course, you sewed it for me and said Evie helped ya. I feel the crooked stitches and get to hooting 'cause they hers. Some nights, feeling for them stitches, make me fall asleep."

I let him settle, noticing his trembling hands, as mine, shaking uncontrollably now. We both needed quiet. I escaped into the kitchen, catching my breath, my wits. *Useless.* I held onto the table, trying not to faint, overwhelmed by unanswered questions, our past.

"I got caught in the rain," I called, pouring our tea.

"More likely, ya wanted to. We all do. Dry days without ya, Smiles. So dry and sad."

"I'm here," I whispered.

"And you tell Delly I did my ablutions twice, knowing you visiting."

"That's a record." I set his teacup on his side table. His hand wasn't ready to lift a cup.

"Been rocking on my porch thinking all these years, what two girls hanging round a mean old cuss like me?"

"Evie used to say you were our challenge. I said we didn't have a daddy, none that raised us, nor a grandpa to intrigue and offer wisdom like you did."

He pressed his lips together. "Hmm," he moaned, pleased with my answer, tousling his mop of wiry gray hair, thinking. "Suspect Polly say, Lord drop ya on my doorstep 'cause ya need somebody, and I need ya, too."

"That's nice, River." My nerves twisted inside.

"Hmm." He blew his worry across the top of his teacup. "I told Evie, I suspect you come round asking questions."

I glanced at him, answering with a slurp.

"Ah, the smell a cinnamon makes me feel like a boy." He lifted the cup to his nose, closing his eyes, savoring his steaming brew. "Everything so sad . . . bitter without you sweet girls. Evie gets my goat sometimes; I get to snapping at her questions," he warned.

Courage anchored me until I spotted tears trickling down his cheek. I rushed to him and kneeled beside his rocker. "How do you see me, River? You're pretending now you can't."

"Knew you be beautiful 'cause you radiant like the sun on the inside." He set his teacup down, staring out the window, rocking. "Pretty as a rose." His hand found my face without flailing. His rough fingertip traced my cheek to my chin. He edged back, his smiling eyes absorbed in mine. "I see eyes the color of autumn grass, green and gold." He inched closer, his nose almost touching mine. "Why, child, you got my gold flakes in your eyes."

I held his hand to my cheek. "You do see me." My toughness crumbled. "That's how you danced. Lord a mercy, River. They don't know, do they?"

"Womenfolk. A man can't answer all them questions at once. Doc thinks my right eye past saving. See blurry some days, not like I used to. Yes, Essie Mae. I can see your pretty face."

We didn't embrace as long. He nudged my hands away, slumping back into his chair. I sat across from him now, my face washed with a shower of tears. He blew his nose into his hanky.

We sat staring at each other, silent.

"My heart hurts." River swirled his palm over his chest.

"I'll fetch Dr. Hodge."

"Not like that, child."

I sat, my eyes fixed on his.

"Old man like me used to living alone, so when Doc Jones come round after all these years, saying newfangled doctors say I might can see again, I shooed him away. He say my accident years ago ain't permanent . . . 'cause I used to see everything perfect when I a young man. I scare Doc, too. I say I'd kill him he ever step a foot on my land again."

"Why would you say that? Dr. Jones came to help you."

He squinted and felt the air. "You still there, child?"

He was right. He could scarcely see, or perhaps, what he wished me to believe.

"No games, River. It took a lot of courage for me to come today."

"Brave woman like you don't need to bolster courage. God set it in ya the day you born."

"Why did you chase Dr. Jones away?" I pressed my body to my seat, suppressing flight.

"'Cause he kill Polly."

I held my tongue.

"I know Evie tell ya bout my wife."

"Yes. Polly's stories are delightful. You thrilled Evie by trusting her with them. She needed Polly, River, to keep on after losing her mama."

"Sunshine writing yet? She promised me she would." The boy in him returned, sitting on the edge of his seat, clapping.

"Last night, I saw her writing in my garden."

"Oooo, good story bubblin' then! Wanted to save your roses, but nobody visit in months."

"They kept busy caring for Miss Katie."

He fidgeted. "I don't visit em 'cause I know what that's like, watching the one you love most on this earth, that make sense a life, breathe her last breath. Ain't a thing to see."

His way to get to me to leave, I told myself. *Dark words.* "It's been a long time, River."

"Delly and Evie spoil me with sweet talk, not you, Essie Mae. You're the one person in this world I'd sit up with, tend to ya in need." He carefully patted his eyes with his hanky. I never saw a man cry so much, except James on the hillside, burying Katie.

River swallowed, walked to a window, unsteady. "I love you, child."

I stood next to him, gazing at the apple cove I played in as a girl. "I lingered at your footbridge . . . I'm not myself, River . . . I . . ."

"I think I see a shadow with ya. That a man or a tree?"

"Bedford."

His hoot cracked the tension. "Take my hand. We'll sit a spell on the porch." We walked outside. River kept his head down, feeling for his rocker. "Good eye makes me dizzy. I get two surgeries. When the bandage off, I see colors, specks a light, a face now and again. Most days, nothing. Glory be. It ain't pretend were it, child? You here?"

I patted his hand; he would never let me hold it. "I'm here. Let's sit. The sun feels good." Face to the sky, he took a deep breath. Though questions clawed at my heart, I marveled at him, smiled at his slicked hair, pressed red shirt and usual coveralls. I knew when he needed small talk, and when the door opened for deeper subjects. "You smell like lemon verbena."

"Dagnabbit! Delly switch my lye. I tell her, make a soap that smells like cedar and straw. Straw a good smell, ain't it?"

"Fresh straw, I suppose. River . . ."

He dropped his head, squinting at his shoes, making his feet remember his jig from Katie's party. "Fetch my straw hat on the table yonder. I make that table for a man and his wife. He don't fetch it yet. Drizzle fine, don't like storms, you?"

I ignored his second warning, forcing a smile I wondered if he could see.

Koontz slapped the straw hat on his head, pinching at his front pocket for the harmonica bobbing inside. "No, suspecting it ain't time for a tune."

"No, it isn't."

"Years, child," he said, reading me. "We had years. Few minutes ain't gonna hurt."

River held me hostage, his harmonica blaring.

I left him, meandering in his garden.

"You stomp on my lavender I pick for Delly. I hear ya! Come on back now."

"Why? You won't talk to me. You barely want me here. I feel it."

"Maybe you jus feel an old man gets scared too. I dread this day, Essie Mae."

I raced up the porch steps. "Why?"

"All my damn secrets shoot up from the earth, spent years, tampering em down."

"You knew my curiosity and appetite for questions . . . especially about Isabel."

"Nobody say that name round here."

"Why not?"

He exhaled. "You don't come to show me your roses, nor ask bout mine, nor tell me funny stories bout New York or even good ones bout your school. You start with a heavy *River* . . . my name said with a load a questions, suspicion, doubting, and all the ugly things churning in my mind . . . years we don't talk bout. But that Delly harp, they talk bout us."

"They scream."

"Cuss and clamor and torment. You think I'm dumb. Jus 'cause I know all them words don't mean I gotta use em." He hovered above me now, hands to his hips, daring me to leave.

"I see we are both not ourselves. River, I never feared once you would hurt me, you're making me afraid now."

"Good! Then maybe these strangers can spout the words we be avoiding all these years. Bes get it out now." The boy in him crushed; his younger self revealed a lightning flash of Polly's inflamed husband defending her honor, his family.

River always respected my strength before him, but I loathed absorbing a manipulative man's temper. I let him cool and wandered the porch, admiring his crafted tables Evie described, inlaid with seashells, mother-of-pearl, and gold flakes. "Does Evie know you can see?"

He tucked his arms into his body, hiding his lips like a child refusing his medicine.

"You're overtired," I said. "I should leave."

"I told Sunshine I see colors, but they don't come together yet."

"All these years, a chance to see—you're punishing yourself. You allowed a surgeon to fix one eye because when you saw for the first time, it frightened you."

"You're damn right it did."

"Will you tell me about your son?"

He used to sense my fear and sorrow without seeing, by a whisper. Now, he studied me, seeing clearly despite his claim. "Who told you bout him? Them government folks?"

"No, you just did."

26.

ESSIE MAE

"He's dead, ain't he?" River asked.

We sat together in his makeshift parlor, sipping tea and nibbling blueberry bread, though my stomach soured anxious for the truth.

"No. At least, we don't believe so."

"*We*? Hmm."

"Why didn't you tell me?"

My presence opened a floodgate of tears locked within him. River gazed at me as if he could see again, tears sprinkling his cheeks. He didn't bother to dry or hide them. A wheezing groan; he rested his hands in his lap, settling their shaking. A small green book bobbled between them. He placed it on the table next to him, sinking into his chair with a sigh.

"Can't see ya like I first did. Maybe I didn't see ya at all. You wearing violet, child?"

"Yes. You saw me."

"Remember it the rest a my days, you in the sun, smiling. It settled my quivering heart."

"Trailer saved me. Does that ease your mind?"

"Nope. You gotta believe that so you don't go wishing he was dead instead a my wife or your mama Isabel. If Trailer saved ya, he wouldn't a let Grant steal ya. If he saved ya, it wouldn't have taken three days to keep ya caged with them men in that camp."

"Stop."

"If my son saved ya, you'd be married by now, three children giggling and stealing my apples. I suspect my son didn't have the guts to save you 'cause I didn't save him."

I started to speak, but he held his hand up at my breath.

"Don't ask, listen." The small emerald book he clutched offered him courage. *River Wild*. He hugged Polly's storybook into his chest. "Katie gimme words to ponder years you been away: bes make my peace fore God take me home." He dropped his straw hat over his eyes.

"Don't hide, please. It's just us."

River brushed the hat off his head; it floated to the floor. "Ain't gonna remember exactly. Hell, some days, I don't know I'm living here nor how to garden. I fight it. I do."

"I understand."

We settled back into our chairs. "Every morn, I thank God for my wife, but Polly birth a son, and when he come into his own, he nobody we know breaking our hearts."

"Was it Isabel?"

His glare frightened me. Tried from memory, it failed, rolling the whites of his eyes. "Your heart's thumping against your chest like my palm on the side a my chair. Thump. Thump. Thump."

"You're scaring me."

"Good. 'Cause this ain't no story time, girl."

"Don't call me that."

"You think I'm some sweet old man all these years? You tolerate what you knowed bout me. You don't know what I've done."

"I don't care who River was twenty-five years ago. I know who you are to me today."

"No. I could never scare Essie Mae. Evie stay away at my fits, but you kept on a coming, softening my heart again. I tell ya a secret. I'm afraid. Afraid if I look back, my heart will turn to stone, dead, like Lot's wife in the Bible. Take a long time for it to feel again."

"I won't let that happen."

"But maybe it'll happen to you."

The smell of the old farmhouse reminded me of girlhood. I inspected his improvements, softened as Koontz. Sunlight overtook the dingy, dark atmosphere of my youth. A moist breeze through the opened windows carried the scent of rain and spices from pouches swaying near spotless panes. My heart calmed, pleased a woman's touch thawed the coldness in River's home. *He was blind, yet he fixed up his home for us . . . for Polly.*

An oval garnet rug highlighted his new parlor, confirming River could see well enough when he wanted not to trip over it. A vase of yellow mums and plum roses decorated a table. I inspected the roses. "These are new," I whispered.

"Say what, child?" he mumbled, closing his eyes, feigning sleep.

"Periwinkle means sweet memories," I said louder. "Where did you find lily of the valley at this time of year? A return to happiness."

"Somebody leave that bouquet on my stoop. Figure it was you."

"Delly more likely."

"Evie baked my wife's apple pie for ya. You ain't lived lessen you taste a Polly pie. Got ham sandwiches; say you'll stay for lunch. Then I know ya forgive me for the words we say."

"My stomach's wracked. I couldn't eat a bite . . . yet."

"Ya gimme hope. Go on, ask that young feller, Bedford, to join us."

He surprised me. River gloated.

"You met Bedford?" I asked. "He never told me."

"Sure enough. Augustus come visiting end a summer warning thieves trying to take my land. Augie's an uppity Frenchman but honest." The old River reappeared, slapping his leg, forgetting our row. "Makes my heart leap, seeing ya swaying and whispering with Bedford on my bridge. That man follows ya like a pup. What Evie do to that dog? Sky smells like jasmine."

"Lil," we said together.

"Near my new sofa." His boney finger pointed to a wicker basket braided with pink ribbons. "Can't see where 'tis. Look in that basket; bring me the frame wrapped in pink silk."

Sweet and sour, mad and forgetful. I promised myself, marching indignant to his home, I would forgive no matter the outcome. River's blind acceptance and love, extended to me as a girl, saved me. I forgave his past prejudice, ignored rumors. I knew his faults and secrets; he knew mine, yet we needed each other, pillars of our unspoken bond.

"You quiet thinking, child? Don't like the feeling in this house now."

We jumped at the yipping and scampering outside his front door.

"Sky comes visiting round lunchtime," River said. "He don't bark much."

"I'm afraid he's looking for me." I opened the door. Sky wouldn't enter. He licked my hand and ran off toward the footbridge. Bedford waved, the lemon parasol twirling above his head. He disappeared back into the forest, Sky by his side. I needed Sky to stay. "He's gone."

"What's that?"

I reluctantly walked back inside, shivering in a cold sweat as if waking from a nightmare. I dabbed my moist brow with Delly's old hanky, soft and worn, still smelling of lemon blossoms.

I didn't want to stay for lunch. Maybe Koontz was right about my heart. Since visiting Westland, I craved the solitude of a strawberry farm. I glanced at the table. Softness returned as I eyed three plates set for lunch. *You stubborn cuss.*

I forgot the frame wrapped in silk, resting in my hand. "Is this Katie's?" I asked.

"Polly's. Open it."

I collapsed in my chair at the sight of an old photo. A tall blonde stood next to a striking young black woman; the black woman's eyes and smile, wide and carefree—resembled mine.

Koontz caught the frame before it hit the floor. "Looky there. I see that in time."

"I'm sorry. Is that . . ."

"That's your mama, Essie Mae. Isabel's hugging my wife Polly."

I held my breath. "I've never seen a photograph of Isabel. Thank you."

"It's yours."

I didn't treasure it as I should, but searched it again, confused by my indifference. "I've imagined Isabel for years. Somewhere along the road, I stopped wondering. She's a stranger."

"Maybe that's the answer you seek." He closed his eyes and leaned his head back, smelling the air. "Wish you bring me your orange roses; they smell like clover honey."

"I don't blame you or your son."

"Polly use people she loved in her stories. *River Wild* ain't bout me but Trailer, my boy."

My heart skipped at the tenderness in his voice.

"The plum dragon, telling stories," he said, proud, "flying children on adventures, be Isabel. Polly say Isabel got a gift for storytelling too. Polly taught your mama to read."

"Isabel meant something to you then."

"At one time. I ain't no slave killer nor owner like folks gossip when you small. When Polly die, Doc say I go crazy. Set my mind against black folk 'cause they kill her and blind me."

"You never told me how you lost your sight."

"For good reason."

"Did Trailer love Isabel?"

"No. True love a wonder; Trailer don't know this love. Hate don't poison my heart till the day I see a nude Isabel splashing in my creek. Polly say it weren't my fault—what happened when that girl nearly drowned. I figure it weren't . . . most days."

I stood awestruck, ready to run. Forgetting he could see, I sat, regretting I started this.

"The wrong woman to a man like finding gold dust. Trailer can't have Isabel, but he get the fever, seeking her out against my wishes. His last year a school, he leave the college I scrape and pay for, breaking Polly's heart 'cause professors say words like brilliant bout my boy. When Trailer come home that summer, Isabel start showing a child, saying John Winthrop do that."

"John wasn't the father." My confession shocked him. "What happened at the creek?"

River slammed Polly's book on the table.

I stood my ground, swiping it off the table, placing it on the mantel. I poured him a sip of whiskey. His soft moan turned into wheezing; he couldn't catch his breath. I soothed his back as Bedford did mine. "Shh, slow breaths," I said. "Drink this." I sighed at his grin. "It will be all right now. I won't judge you, River. You never judged me. Not once."

"Child." He puckered his lips and blew out a breath like puffing a cigar. "Whooeee. That's my good bourbon."

"Damn right it is, old man." I swigged a sip.

A flush painted River's cheeks. "You remind me ya full grown. Sometimes, in my mind, you still that little girl." He held his glass out for a refill. I topped it. "False courage."

"Lil says one sip of courage with the enemy might have ended the war sooner. You're not my enemy, River, don't act like it."

"Polly shine a rainbow a gifts, but no gift at mothering a wild son. She tried till Isabel come a stealing Trailer's mind and heart. True love don't do that."

I grabbed two blankets, tucked him into his, and sat across from him, bundled in mine. "I haven't any delusions about Isabel. She's a ghost to me."

"Maybe we the only two sane folks in this valley. Folks whisper, River Koontz balmy, but I don't lose all my memories. Wish I could. Ain't easy for an old man to confess his sins. Still smell the foul stench a that woman slinking down there near every week, same hour, so the men could watch her frolic in my creek."

"Isabel?"

"John's men clean up flowery on the outside, but filthy as a dog rolling in the mud. Isabel a good girl, but when Alex send her away, she come back all woman. She ain't right."

"Delly hid the truth and shared only good stories about my mama. I knew better, River."

"Don't know what was wrong with Isabel. She tempt em, wading in the water, showing herself to any man spying. I never spied her, except on the day I search for Trailer, he down there hiding, ogling her. I fetch him, catching myself watching too, 'cause Isabel slip and disappear underwater. Creek deep that year, you know the drop that dumps into a pond gets deep."

"Cool swimming hole on a summer's day," I mumbled, remembering.

"Maybe it longer, but it only take a second for Trailer to catch the evil skim across my eyes and my foot move nary an inch toward the house, not the creek. Wish I blind then."

"You didn't save her?"

"Didn't have to; Bo noodle Isabel outta the water like a catfish. Essie Mae, my boy weren't wrong when he see my evil thoughts. Don't make me say it."

"You don't have to." I wasn't used to the old man's eyes following me. He squinted as I turned the photo of Isabel facedown in my lap.

"Trailer forget he'd a bolted away not caring, till I grab his sleeve to drag him home. Isabel all right, I tell him, 'cause Bo carried her away. Hear Dr. Jones say, Isabel ain't right in the head fore or after the accident."

"A concussion . . . she lost oxygen?"

"Her mind shocked since she see her daddy die in the hills. After the creek, Alex don't let Isabel work at my farm. She lie, tell him she see me spying, make her do that lewd thing. Fetch Trailer is all. She see my shotgun fore she slip. Weren't gonna do nothing but scare young'uns into right living. Isabel don't slink round my place after that. Her wiles pervert my boy."

"Isabel couldn't swim. What was she doing in the creek alone?"

"Polly wonder the same thing, then she know. 'Isabel hasn't been taught to respect herself, River,' she said.' First time Polly ever go against me. Dirty show for men. Trailer still wanted Isabel. They all did."

"Trailer continued seeing Isabel, didn't he? Maybe they were in love."

River wiped his mouth and shook his head. "My son could've been somebody, but he wasted away on the drink and mischief with Houst 'cause Trailer can't wed Isabel the summer he come home from school, see she with child. And he know Polly and I won't ever approve."

"At eight years old, I visited your creek and met a man sneaking around your place. He told me he was sorry and needed to see me just once. A thick, red scar sliced his cheek from ear to chin. It frightened me, so I ran. When Augustus said Trailer was your son, I remembered."

"Don't know who Isabel be for years, child, till Willow come round poking his nose in. You didn't exist 'cause Katherine hid ya as a babe. Doc Jones couldn't even save my Polly, so he ain't welcome on my farm, but he come that night. Suppose I shoulda been thankful."

"The night I was born? River, Isabel acted in that way . . . she had no choice."

"Hmm," he grunted.

"John Winthrop kept her like a dog. Katie looked the other way!"

He snapped his fingers at me. "There 'tis. You ain't the only one who needs blame to give ya peace."

"How did Trailer get the scar across his cheek?"

"I give it. Too many damn scars round here. We called it the Westland Fires, night John burn Katie's cotton fields. Katie come home from school same year as Trailer, running Westland like her daddy. Fever sweep through the Black Belt. Some say yellow fever, others, smallpox, a reckoning for the foul business conducted here. First, some slaves at Tom McCafferty's die; he set em all free. Then his maid and her boy get sick. Katie nearly lost her baby. Isabel, too."

"And Polly?"

"Fever take her. Doc Jones say I go mad. Don't remember much after I say goodbye to my Polly. I'm told I was a wicked man, treated Isabel dreadful 'cause she came back to us, promising to heal Polly, saying she got a gift."

"She was a girl."

"She all woman pregnant with you."

I walked to the window. Storm clouds melted with my anger. Compassion overtook the sun.

Koontz continued, "John get his chance to run things when Katie bedridden for months fighting fever and pregnant with Evie. After Katie's daddy died, Katie hired men and women, black, white, at Westland like Alex did. She don't know John's ways behind her back. Suppose I was bitter at Alex for stealing my chance to buy more land, strike gold, so I stay quiet. Ain't my place. Polly died. I turn to stone."

"What about Houst?" I asked, sitting across from him.

"Houst a cardsharp come back to Westland, crowing. He tell John to keep paying Bo, Delly, Ned the closest help to Katie, so she don't get suspicious at what John doing."

"Slaves. Katie had to know the cotton crop increased. Somebody worked the land."

"You know this sad past. Ain't repeating it now. Katie died trying to make it right."

"Augustus said the night of Westland's fires, John ordered two young men to torch the fields, Houst and . . ."

"My boy did it to spite me." River slumped in his chair at the weight of his memories.

I couldn't picture the frail, weak boy River described. Trailer stood tall and muscular, intimidating before Grant, fearful and kind-hearted, alone with me.

"Trailer never knew who I was?" I said to myself. "He couldn't have known." I couldn't trust my memories like River. Perhaps my recollection, as River's, was a dream.

"On the night you girls born, the stars sang and the moon wept. We all shoulda been singing. Hardly know John, till he raise hell. Maybe I rain down hellfire that night too 'cause I don't do nothing to stop it."

"It's not your fault."

"Willow Jones stopped it. If it ain't enough foul business, Trailer show

Houst my gold. Houst plotted for months, when I weak and forlorn, to steal my land. But I ain't blind, yet."

"What happened?"

"Houst plan to steal my gold and farm that night, but Isabel had you, died, and John turned a monster like me when I lost Polly. Neighbors get word Katie gonna banish John again this time for good 'cause she nearly lose Westland, till Augustus arrest Houst. John lost a fortune gambling in St. Louis. Houst saved John's life, so John owed him. Don't know bout that."

I stayed quiet.

"Night of John's slave auction, Doc Jones saved my life—and you. Can't do nothing for Isabel. Two male slaves flee the auction with a sickly mama and boy, woman near death. Tom sent the women and children to my farm to hide em. I a grieving madman, child. Ain't close to nothing like myself. I hated them to come here. Didn't want em, you hear?"

"Delly told me you blamed a slave for killing Polly."

"I blamed Isabel, blamed em all; Doc Jones, mostly. He promised me Polly would live. I knew better, still had hope." River covered his ears, then felt for his glass of bourbon. "A drop."

I poured it.

"That's what I never confess. Your mama the woman I keep to nurse Polly. So it's my fault I bring the shame into my home that steal my son."

"Alexander Wilcox sent Isabel away after Luby died because she was a child."

"When she matured into a young woman, Alex take her back. She lived with us. Alex felt guilty, but Ruth don't want her."

"A wrong influence on Katie; they were secret childhood friends."

"Isabel loved Katie like Katie her girl, a doll. Isabel always coming back to this farm 'cause nobody want her, but she find someone—Trailer."

My thoughts swirled. I didn't want to hear more. River couldn't stop now.

He took a breath and continued, "Them two slaves come to rob and kill me. They beat me near death, knock my head with something, and hurt my eyes. Only remember cold, pitch-black, eyes bleeding, blind. First soul come to help me, I slash with my knife."

"Trailer."

"I hear the men who beat me, still at my farm, shouting, 'Kill him. Kill him.' I scramble for my shotgun, start shooting and the screaming stopped except my own. Come to learn, my gun don't do a damn thing. It be Doc Jones shot dead two slaves come looking for their wives and children. They get my pistol and say they'll kill me."

"Lord in Heaven."

"Last thing I remember, a sickly woman die, and Willow scurry to get the women and children safe. Never see him again. Not till the year you save Evie. Willow stayed and cared for you girls, then Doc Jones disappeared till Katie get ill during the war."

I hadn't any tears left. I stared into his bloodshot eyes. "Is Trailer my father?"

River wouldn't answer.

I fetched a cold rag for his eyes and one for my throbbing head.

He exhaled at the comfort. "If Trailer your daddy, he woulda stayed, even against my wishes. He wouldn't a left Isabel, least of all let John take her."

"Who is my father? Houst?"

River scowled at the mention. "Isabel be what my wife call an unholy woman, Essie Mae. Isabel learn the tricks when she young 'cause Houst teach em to her. When Alex sent her to Sweet Water, Isabel meet Houst, and the street urchin use her for cons."

"What tricks?"

"Lewd tricks to get a man to look. She picked pockets to start. When she older, the rush a hot temptation surge a power through her when she win a man's affection and money."

"River, do you know who my father is?" I pressed.

"No," he said, exhausted. "One man might."

"Dr. Jones. I'm what I imagined all along . . . nothing. No one. Daughter of a wh—"

"Don't you utter that word in my home. You got more faith in them dirty thoughts than all you done to survive this life?"

"No, sir."

"If you believed you're nothing, you woulda gave up years ago. You're smarter than that, child. That's why you come to me now. 'Cause you don't wanna spend a life regretting the past, wasting away like I did, alone. We ain't alone no more, are we child?"

"I can't judge you for staying blind when you had the medical chance to see. You punished yourself for what happened."

"At first, Polly don't think Willow a doctor. Years ago, she imagine she see him in a circus passing through Sweet Water, shooting trick shots. One evening, Delly sneak my sour mash, spilling how Willow carry guilt round James 'cause Willow was an Indian fighter in the war. Like I said, Willow cut and run after the night you were born."

"But he came back as Katie's family doctor again. I remember him."

He rolled the tension from his shoulders. "Willow returned after John died."

"That's what Willow meant when he said he would've done anything to keep Katie safe."

"Word was Willow Jones loved Katherine. Set to ask her to marry him when she graduated college, but John Winthrop come with her. Doc Jones slunk away."

"Delly never said a peep regarding Willow Jones."

"Polly thought Willow was a prince in her stories. Willow a dandy more than a doctor, buying up my unsold apples at harvest. What he do with all that fruit?"

"He gifted it to Mrs. Bixley for the pies she sold for a living after her son died."

"Where'd ya hear that?"

"Delly sneaks cherry wine, too."

Despite a cloud of heavy, sordid confessions, our bond, broken then cemented back together, felt stronger, closer.

"Delly says the storms of life make things whole again, River. Maybe that's what this is."

"Nobody need a twister to bring life."

"I'm sure of it more than ever. Houst threatened Trailer he would come after you; that's how Trailer got mixed up with Grant."

"Last I remember the night you born, soft hands smooth my hair and put a wet rag over my bleeding eyes, whimpering and whispering. It be my son and an older woman. 'Go,' Doc Jones said, breathing hard. 'I told Katherine I'd get them on the steamer.' That's all I remember."

"The women and children to safety? The slaves?"

"Don't remember. I tried and tried. Don't wanna remember. My son left me there to die like he suppose I was gonna do to Isabel the day she nearly drowned. I ain't seen my boy since."

"Delly says regret is a poison that kills faster than any plague."

"Healing and good change come to this valley 'cause round these parts, we all regret not a one of us say, you wrong, and make John Winthrop pay for all the death and hell he bring to this land."

"After all these years, would you want to see your son?"

"No!"

"Why?"

"'Cause he hurt you."

"You cherished true love once. Trailer shared it with Isabel. And I don't believe in your heart you thought evil about your son marrying a black woman. I think you worried they wouldn't have a chance, and you wanted to protect them. You turned into a tyrant. Trailer didn't understand you don't have a gift with softness, but you love, and he rebelled against you, loving her in spite of you."

"You're the only one I know, be bleeding in the grass, looking up at the man who stab ya, thinking it ain't his fault somehow. Polly call it mercy. I call it a miracle how God made your heart, child. Don't ever wanna hear you say you're nothing long as I'm living, ya hear?"

"Yes, sir."

"You hate me, child?"

"Never."

"Essie Mae . . ." His voice was hoarse, a raspy whisper. He downed his water as I swallowed his truth. "If I knew Trailer was your daddy, I'd a told ya fore you left for Richmond when you nineteen, and you'd a never been taken. Never. 'Cause I'd a never let my daughter leave like Miss Katie let you girls go all by yourselves."

"I don't blame Miss Katie."

"You do. Me too, for a mess a things; blame myself most of all. But what we both gonna do bout that now? Katie gone, so it best our bitterness get gone too. What are you gonna do, child?"

"Find your son."

27

EVIE

Essie and I rode the trail to the covered bridge over Chancers Creek in silence. I treasured riding Mama's palomino for the first time in months. Riding Honey, cantering through the wind, felt free as the night I danced at Mama's party. Entering the meadow, Essie struggled, holding back her filly while Honey walked the trail at her pace. My mind needed slow and steady, nature's song. The afternoon sun split golden shafts through the trees. I glanced at Essie. She waved her hand in the sunlight, watching gold threads flicker across her brown skin.

"What are you doing?" I asked.

"Nothing." She caught herself, embarrassed, as if I read her secret thoughts.

"We can turn back if you're tired. You haven't slept much ... or dreamed."

"Sister, when I sleep, I do my utmost not to dream."

We paused on the trail and traded smiles.

"And you are my sister, Essie Mae. Nothing will ever change that."

Leaves drifted to the ground in a swirling waltz.

Essie closed her eyes, inhaling autumn. "I've missed this."

We loosened our grips on the reins, settling into the saddles, our horses walking alongside each other now.

I shook my head in disbelief. "River can see."

"Dr. Hodge confirmed River's sight in his left eye is fragile. Evie, River saw me."

"I get goosebumps picturing it."

"I never thought a blind man would fear seeing again."

"I thought I imagined River wiggling his fingers goodbye. I suspected something. River didn't say if he'd go through with the next surgery. Dr. Hodge holds hope."

"We all do." Essie chuckled. "River didn't need his sight to see through us."

"That strange old cuss knows us better than anyone, doesn't he, Essie Mae?"

"Yes, he does." Essie's coy glance lightened my heart. "William's returning for Christmas?"

"I thought I needed answers. None of them matter now." Essie's chuckle fell behind me as I daydreamed about William, his touch, kiss.

"I'm happy for you, Evie."

Honey found her prance. My stomach knotted, thinking of Mama. *"When I was a girl, I dreamed of riding in a circus,"* Mama whispered in my thoughts. *"Dr. Willow Jones filled our heads with daydreams about the circus, especially when we wouldn't take our medicine."*

"What did Doc Jones know about the circus?"

"Plenty."

Honey shimmied at the sight of two does, waking me. "There, girl."

"Evie, what are you snickering about?" Essie sighed as we passed the cottonwood trees.

"Mama's dream of riding in the circus."

Essie scrunched her forehead. "River said years ago Polly saw Dr. Jones as a young man trick shooting in a circus traveling through Sweet Water."

"Bunk. If Dr. Jones is a sharpshooter, I'm a tightrope walker," I shouted, nearly slipping off Honey.

"Lord a mercy, Evie! You still can't ride."

Essie's laughter was my favorite sound next to the rain.

"I bet you five dollars, Honey could beat that filly today," I called. "Come on, Honey."

"You owe me for Bo dancing with January. Evie, wait!"

Honey's spirit ignited mine as we raced through the meadow, leaving Essie behind, the only way I could ever outrun her. I circled Honey back, swishing through a field of dandelions. "Follow us, Essie." Honey slowed to a trot. I watched our shadows bouncing across the grass as a light snowfall of dandelion fluffs tickled our noses.

"Evie, you're crazy," Essie said, catching us. "Whoa, Jasmine."

"But I am a better rider."

We exhaled our troubles together.

Our race ended at the covered bridge over Chancers Creek. We tied off the horses and took in the view. Essie wouldn't walk inside the dark bridge. We stood at the bank, pitching stones.

"I told William I'm going to start wearing trousers."

"Tell him you smoke cigars, too. That'll win him."

We listened to the rushing water. The current mesmerized Essie as it rippled over the flat rocks. She walked away, pulled a pink object from her saddlebag, and hid it behind her back, returning. "You look so much like your mama, Evie. I always wondered if I resembled mine."

"Mama said you did." Quiet, we watched the horses savoring a bed of clover. "Essie, Uncle Augustus should have never told you about John Winthrop."

"No, I'm glad he did."

Essie's hazel eyes still captured me. "We're family. I don't care what anyone says."

"I love you, Evie, but that's not entirely true. I have always understood my place."

Her truth pierced me. "I know what it's like to lose yourself . . . and lose you. I haven't understood when it counted. Bedford is right. Things must change. They will. I promise."

"Why didn't Miss Katie tell us about adopting me?" Essie focused on the bank, watching the current erode bits of earth. Curled leaves floated past us as canoes. Sunlight bathed the trees in linen. The water melted into gold. Essie's hand folded into mine. "Droughts change everything," she said, letting go. "A flood of memories haunted me on the train and here. I must face them. Do you understand?"

"You're leaving." I saw us sinking with the rock I pitched in the creek.

Essie's eyes, red and moist, pleaded for compassion. "It's not only regarding my father." She fiddled with the object behind her back. "I crushed River with my questions about his son."

"No, you released him."

Essie's sparkling eyes thanked me. "I purposed to forgive, but I didn't tell him."

"You didn't have to."

Essie wandered to a patch of thistle.

"Essie, you have something with River I don't. You are as a daughter to him."

"Evie . . . what if Trailer . . ."

"James used to say sometimes the answers we seek bring more hurting and questions. If we let the why of tragedy rule us, we will never live free."

Essie revealed the secret behind her back and handed it to me. "Open it."

I did, marveling at a photograph. I recognized Polly as the tall blonde from a portrait I found at River's. The young black woman holding Polly resembled Essie. I searched Essie's eyes, stunned.

"That's my mama, Evie."

I caught my breath. "Isabel?"

She nodded.

I gazed at the photograph and handed it back, bewildered by Essie's blank stare.

Essie shrugged her shoulders. "I don't know what to think of her, Evie."

"I can tell you what you shouldn't." Essie raised her chin, glaring. "You're not her."

Essie glanced at the photo again, me.

"I can say that to you because I used to worry I would be like my father someday, controlling, evil, a drunk."

"Why would you ever think that?"

"Because he was my father; I have his blood."

"Evie Wilcox, that's the dumbest thing I've ever heard."

"And what of you and Isabel?"

Essie stomped through the grass to Jasmine and tucked the photograph into the saddlebag. "You tricked me."

I grabbed Essie's hand and pulled her to a massive tree stump. "Do you remember this?"

"You used to stand on it reciting Shakespeare."

"And you gave speeches about our futures and freedom." Arm in arm, we strolled back to the creek. "Grant stole the forest from you. Will you let Isabel steal the creek?"

"No." Essie's hand trembled in mine.

"One night, Delly marched me to Ruth's Lake. We sat on the dock fishing, waiting for the full moon to rise so she could see Westland aglow in Katie's blue, she called it."

"I would've liked to see that."

"A peach sunset rippled atop the water and Delly said, 'Child, sometimes, it's not the family we're born into, it's the family that finds us, the ones who save and care for us.'"

"Stand by our side."

"You have your own life. We've been together since we were six saving each other."

Her fingers lifted a strand of my hair and twirled it behind my ear. "You have changed."

"I thought answers about my father would bring me peace; they don't. Purpose does . . . forgiveness. But no one explained forgiveness is a process, not a breath."

"Evie, a lifetime of unspoken words ricocheted in that study. If I don't find out about my father and who's threatening Westland, Bo's right, Westland, secrets, and pain, will follow me."

"Ned had a son." I swallowed my tears; they slipped away from me. "Mama worked tirelessly to find him. At the Morgan's, you can be someone else. I've longed for that, too."

"You heard Lil, the war isn't over in the South. The rebels ensure it."

Heaviness dropped on me at Essie's words. "Freedom isn't free." I wandered back to check on the horses, fidgeting to leave. "A storm's rising."

Essie stopped my fingers from tugging a thread on my sleeve.

I turned to her. "I know what my family is saying. I have a child's mind. I don't grieve her . . . young Evie. A broken girl makes a broken woman."

"We don't have to stay broken."

We smiled together, knowing this was our answer.

"Evie, your sight is a gift. Thunderclouds lumber as elephants; crushed paper opens like a flower. Never let them take it from you. Wear your trousers; write your stories . . . dream."

"Thank you, Essie."

Essie distracted herself, stroking Jasmine's cheek and checking the sky for a storm. "Evie, Lila told James, Trailer is hiding in Ashland."

"What?"

"I'm going with Bedford to face him."

"How can you be so foolish? You're protecting River, aren't you?"

"I don't know what we'll find in Ashland. I only know I must travel with Bedford." Essie rattled it off so matter-of-factly.

"Essie Mae, look into my eyes and tell me you trust Bedford."

"Implicitly." Her eyes rolled away when she said it.

"James will worry. We best ride home."

Essie stood her ground. "Bedford will see to my safety."

"He's in love with you. I've seen the way he looks at you."

Essie turned inward, facing the forest. "Fool talk. This is about our lives, not love!"

I folded my arms, examining her. Essie's boldness collapsed as she buried her thoughts, staring at the woods.

"What of Bedford's life? Is this how you use his generosity and good-will?"

Tears trickled down her cheeks. She shook her head forcefully, *no*. "I have to stop running," Essie shouted. "Slow breaths," she told herself.

I left her alone and calmed Honey. "You scared Honey. Essie, what's wrong with you?"

"I'm sorry." Essie rushed to me. Her hand swirled upon my back.

I stepped away.

"For six years, I floated between a white and black world, Lil's world. What of my own?" Essie asked. "What is it? Where?"

"With me and your family." I stared at her in disbelief.

"You said I deserve to live my own life."

"Yes, *live*! Not risk it in a town with the man who abducted you."

"That's not fair."

I snapped around to her. "What is your obsession with Trailer? You remember him as someone else. I was there. I don't care if Trailer is River's son. He's a criminal."

"Stop."

"No." I pointed back and forth between us. "This . . . truth is what will heal us now. Trailer is an accomplice to the crime of stealing you to sell you, a free black woman, into slavery for profit."

"I wasn't free."

"If you believe that and going to Ashland will bring you back to me—go." I threw my hands up and ran to the horses.

"Evie, wait."

"Essie, you're wrong in this. Your memory betrays you."

Essie grabbed me, holding me tight. "They won't divide us. This is what they want."

"Sometimes, I wonder if it's what you want," I whispered in her ear.

She let me go. "In our school, mixed children outnumber blacks. In Paris and New York, my skin color goes unnoticed. Here, I can't breathe in nature, the safety of my youth. When I see a forest, I tremble. The smell of a campfire sours my stomach. In the night sky, I see the old African. I've been running from him, myself, for six years. I am tired."

I chose my next words carefully, holding my tears and judgment. "Essie Mae, do you feel guilty for living in this family, for Mama raising you, for being sisters?"

"I don't know."

"Because you can't hate the white in you without hating me too."

I saw hope floating down the river, but when Essie held my hand and dried my tears, she saved it, sneaking hope into my pocket before it dissolved underwater, leaving us for good.

"I could never hate you."

"What's in Richmond that will help you solve this?"

"Jeanie, the Irish woman who cared for me; she married Dr. Jones, who cared for Isabel. Dr. Jones is the only soul who knew Isabel was three months pregnant when John raped her."

"Dr. Jones left so suddenly after Mama's funeral."

"Katie adopted me when I was fourteen. If she knew I wasn't John Winthrop's daughter, why did she still pay Houst? She knew, Evie. I don't know why she told us we were sisters."

"Oh, Essie, couldn't Westland be our home? I've at least pondered it now."

"If my going will protect Bo, you wouldn't think twice, would you?"

Dread overcame me. "What about Bo?"

"Houst knew everyone's secrets. Don't you think he had ways of knowing Bo killed your father? This has to end. You'll go to Paris."

I glanced at the trees, bluffs, and tall grass for spies. Essie followed my gaze. "For years, I wondered who told Grant where to find us? How did he know we would walk the road to Ashland? Mama was the only one who knew our plan . . . and Bedford."

"Katie hired Bedford to end this. What is *this*? I'm finding out no matter where it leads."

Our tender embrace made everything right again.

"Essie, John Winthrop had a weak heart. The drink killed him. Dr. Jones attested to that."

"Interesting. Willow Jones appears in every tragedy at Westland."

"I'm scared. James risks Westland with Bedford's scheme to trap Houst. Bedford assured me Houst showed his hand at Mama's party, hiding in the carriage. Houst hasn't the men."

"Don't think Houst doesn't hold the will. Come, Sister, I'll tell you a story."

We mounted our horses and headed home. *Home.* A word I dreamed would sink into Essie's heart as one of her rose seeds deep in the soil, watered, and blossoming in the sun.

Our giddiness at the start of our ride dissipated as our horses walked side-by-side.

"Before the war," Essie began, "Thomas met a poet named Mingo. Thomas said many believed Mingo was so intelligent, he would have become a star."

"A Shakespeare or Balzac?" I asked, tears in my eyes.

"Yes. Mingo's gift and intelligence made his owner suspicious. He had Mingo arrested and locked in a slave prison to be sold. His crime?"

"Writing poetry."

"On the walls of the prison, before Mingo escaped to run back to his wife, he wrote his last poem. That night, Mingo escaped his cell. The blood-hounds caught him."

"He died."

Essie nodded. "I must leave, Evie. I have learned too much. Perhaps, I haven't learned who I am, but I know who I will never be again."

"Essie, what was the poem Mingo wrote in prison?"

"A man, who learned of Mingo's intelligence and gift, visited that prison to answer the same question. I memorized his poem, to remind me of the price Mingo paid so I may learn."

"Good God! And must I leave them now,
My wife, my children, in their woe?
'Tis mockery to say I'm sold!
But I forget these chains so cold,
Which goad my bleeding limbs; though high
My reason mounts above the sky.
Dear wife, they cannot sell the rose
Of love that in my bosom glows.
Remember, as your tears may start,
They cannot sell the immortal part.
Thou Sun, which lightest bond and free,
Tell me, I pray, is liberty
The lot of those who noblest feel,
And often to Jehovah kneel?
Then I may say, but not with pride,
I feel the rushings of the tide
Of reason and of eloquence,
Which strive and yearn for eminence.
I feel high manhood on me now,
A spirit-glory on my brow;
I feel a thrill of music roll,
Like angel-harpings, through my soul;
While poesy, with rustling wings,
Upon my spirit rests and sings.
He sweeps my heart's deep throbbing lyre,
Who touched Isaiah's lips with fire."

28

DELLY

I rise fore the rooster crow and the sunrise show its glory. Can't stop thinking bout my girls . . . leaving. James awake, too, rustling round in the study.

"Got warm cornbread and honey," I whispered.

James fall asleep again and lift his head off Katie's desk. He wear his new square spectacles, rooting in them papers, making sense a nothing, then rummaged in a drawer.

"I'll fetch my coffee."

"Delly, stay." He stretched, moaned, and pulled us two chairs near the window. "Katie loved watching the sunrise." He held my chair out like I a fancy lady, motioning for me to sit.

I shoo his silliness away, but relish the rest. "She fancy pink sunsets too."

He stared at me, waiting for some kinda answer, one he scouring for in them papers.

"Mr. James, I ain't never seen you scared, and you won't start now."

He leaned back in his chair, his burly chest rise and fall. My heart skips 'cause his smile chase that spirit a fear clean away.

"Fear ushers in common sense," he said, winking. "Nothing wrong with being afraid, Delly. Just can't let it rule ya."

"Go on, twiddle them thumbs. Houst doing a fine job tossing that common sense round."

James snorted like a bull elk. "I don't fear Houst. I stay awake, fearing complacency at the threats he makes to our girls."

"They ain't girls no more, and you can't guard Essie Mae forever. You spend years beating yourself bout the harm that come to both of em. Weren't your fault."

"Wasn't it?"

I waved my hands at him. "Oh, Lord. Strong, bold man like you ain't kidding Delly." Sad to see my words slap the jolly from him.

He plucked a splinter from his rugged hands, hiding his eyes from mine. I rub my swollen knuckles and show him my blistered palms; he show me his, and we release our chortles.

"James, you ain't afraid a no con man come to do us harm. You never was—you afraid you fail Katie. You take a bullet fore you dishonor her name."

James chewed on his lip like a wad a chaw. "You have to let me do this my own way."

My silly grin put him at ease. "Oh, I will." Can't help gloating too.

"She told ya."

"Why wouldn't she? Bes get used to believing, Houst nor that scrawny cat River don't hold all the cards, Delly do. But you can trust me." My turn to sigh like the wind. "I know how to play this game; sad game 'tis, too. Miss Katie don't leave Westland to Houst, hmm?"

"Never."

"You think Houst out there?"

"Don't have to see a skunk to know he's around, just a matter of time."

"Why don't Houst face ya like a man? He still a weasel coward like when he a boy. River fill Essie's mind with all kinda notions. Poor child. Ain't even questioning if he telling the truth."

"I suspect he told most of it."

"He hid from us he can see some; we knowed." I rise with my temper, straightening paper on Evie's desk, picturing her showered in sunlight scribbling a story.

James pulled me back to our window. "River's still blind, Delly, till his good eye keeps. It wasn't our secret to tell now, was it?"

"Supposing not. The girls don't know half a what we fight through during the war."

"Like to keep it that way." James shuffled back to Katie's desk, flipping through papers.

"Don't know nothing bout legal papers and you wrecking this study to find em."

"Bedford and the law are on our side now."

"Never thought that a question." Lingering in Katie's study ain't pleasing to me these days, so I tug on him to leave. "Cornbread's hot."

James removed his spectacles, piercing his eyes into mine. "Delly, I need you to talk the girls into leaving for a time until I sort this out. Lil's convinced Evie to go to Paris."

"You sure bout that?" My glare soften his.

"Essie Mae's filled with questions. I'm counting on Bedford to help her find answers." James walked me to the kitchen. "I can't make Essie stay. None of us can."

"But you could ask."

I serve my cornbread, singing inside, watching him gobbling it up, grinning. First time in months, James sit with me, jawing. Wish we crow bout the rebirth that come to Westland.

"Delly, this time it can't be up to me. Do you understand?"

"I understand Essie Mae and Evie got no idea what home means."

James thinking, massaging an old wound on his hand.

"We all got em," I said. "Scars." His icy stare gimme a shiver. "Thick, red, flat, thin, most fade to nothing in time, excepting them on the inside we think nobody will ever see. Scars show a curiosity, like them knickknacks on the shelf. Some so private, we afraid somebody gonna ask, and we can't trust ourselves with the answer."

James smirked, shaking his head, closing that red knot in his fists. "Hard work—life, beat up these hands. Some scars are nothing, Delly."

"Never to a woman."

"I won't trick Essie into staying," he hissed his warning.

"Love. See, Essie can't figure out her place, but love abides here. Grant stole more from her than what we see on the outside, stole her trust a white men, hard journey getting it back."

James glimpsed the last of the sunrise. "That mantle doesn't fit on me, Delly."

"Why I says it. You know bout that ache . . . Indian blood in ya."

"Hmm." James opened the back door, breathing in crisp air. "Some folks don't trust people, not for what they look like, but the deeds they do or not. I'm not much on words."

"You right to stick me."

"Delly, you love so big. I never fault ya."

"You think folks round here fancy a black woman giving the master a the house what for, learning his daughters, scolding his highfalutin sister-in-law that forget I used to change her sheets 'cause she wet the bed when she too old?"

He shook his finger at me. "Living here without Katie's buffer, few facts you need to get straight. I'm not your master, and I don't give a hang what folks think about me."

"Then why you keeping all these secrets, chasing em away with whiskey?" James jumped back as if I bit him. "Don't mean to stick ya."

"Sting."

"Oh, Mr. James, queen bees don't sting."

"And rattlers don't bite."

"Now we a pair, Queen Bee and James the Rattler, sound like an Evie fable."

"This isn't make-believe. Thanks for breakfast. I best get on patrol, men waiting."

I handed him his lunch basket and canteen. "You scout the wagon trail again for Houst?"

"Every morning." He slap his hat on his head, tucking it down, hiding his eyes. I spied his crinkling blues. "I respect your words and deeds. Watch my girls," he said, low and quiet.

"Yes, sir."

"Delly, you've carried a significant burden . . . we're thankful."

"She tell me too. I miss Katie something awful."

"If it wasn't for sitting in the light of Heaven, I'd say Katie misses us, too."

"Why, Mr. James . . ."

His peck to my cheek chased my sorrow. My old heart can't take too many surprises, and it take a whole lot a nonsense to make me blush, but I feel the tingles rising on my cheeks. And I think I'll wake the girls with a hymn a thanks to the Lord, sitting beside His still waters, far from that shadow a fear and death.

I contemplate all morning, nary doing a chore: Good Shepherd leads me beside the still waters, but God don't make me sit. That up to me. I settle, *I'll lead, Lord, up to them in the end.*

Earthquake I set to rumbling, rattle Westland, splitting this dry land.

We broken but the Good Lord know how to put His creation back together again.

Essie and Evie visit the stables again, fancy remembering Katie and Honey. My stomach jumps as if I gussied up going courting with Samuel, my long-lost beau. I swallow my pride with a sip a sweet tea, letting it chase the sour taste a my past away. Losing Katie, stir my girlhood memories that nearly vanished. Today, they bittersweet; my snip a lost love come calling.

I sweep the porch and a strange song spill out. "The big bee flies high," I sang. "The li'l bee makes the honey. The black folks make the cotton. And the white folks get the money."

"What's that you're singing, Delly?" Essie Mae sneaked up on me, laughing.

"Isabel used to sing that walking to the creek and gardening." When I say the word creek, Essie eyed me as if I curse the Lord's name. Evie and Essie sat on a step. "You girls look tired."

"Where's James and Bedford? We have to talk to them." Evie rolled her eyes from mine.

"James on patrol. Bedford in the study. What bout talking to Delly?" I sit between em. We squeeze together. "Years since we share this step." They drop their heads on my shoulders.

"Tell us a story." Essie press her cheek to my arm, saying them God words to help me start.

"You wanna hear old Delly's story?"

"What story?" The zeal in Evie's voice calmed my fretting.

"Mine."

They jolt their heads up, staring at me like I got roses growing outta my ears.

I patted their bony knees to help me rise. "Bedford gimme God's wisdom to ponder when he say, you don't let people you love run away. Secrets in Westland's soil out but one—mine."

God drop a stillness, His quiet.

I breathe deep and step into the house. They follow, hushed, holding my hands as we walk to the parlor. Last time they this still, we enjoying a rare snowfall tickling our cheeks. I sit on my soft rocker, smoothing its fancy cushion. Evie close the parlor door. Essie sit on Katie's new lilac settee, staring. Evie poured the tea, respectful, quiet. Essie's whirling breath over her steaming teacup could've lulled us to sleep.

I served my gingerbread. "Weren't my place when ya two leave the first time to Lil's in Richmond, but I got words to say fore you do it again."

"Bedford told you," Essie Mae said, bothered. "My mind's made up."

"Minds like beds. They never stay made up. Bedford bring good change round here."

"He gets the idea he runs things," Evie sassed. "Big law degrees and detective business."

"Lord a mighty, Evie, sass come flowing outta you like ribbons in the wind, easy."

"Bedford gives Evie a harder time than us," Essie said.

"He jus ruffle Evie's feathers like Lil do mine. Good changes bring healing." I rock. They sipped and slurped. "Is that what you two doing? Running away?"

"No, ma'am," they said together.

I look behind me for Lil saying them fine voices. "Difference is, you young women out to find yourselves. What I learn bout freedom: you gotta fight to get it, fight to give it to yourself, and fight to keep it. What you gonna do?"

Evie and Essie peck my cheek and sit near. Evie pressed her lips, trying not to cry, her emerald eyes shining.

"Days I sit in here with Katie, days I earn; days I free. She free, too, even if for a time."

"Did you blame Mama?" Evie asked, staring at her shoes.

"Suppose I blame a whole lot a folks for hateful things. Blame ain't nothing but a word now. James say an excuse to go on acting bitter and hateful, blames himself for plenty. I make my peace with Westland. Bes do the same, or that darkness will follow you wherever you live."

Essie quiet then asked, "When you first arrived at Westland, did darkness follow you?"

I shifted in my chair, tucking myself in a throw 'cause my past shivering through my body. "Daisy . . . the li'l flower plays second fiddle to the queen of flowers, roses. But a Daisy make Delly whole, give her hope she a good woman . . . a mama."

"A child?" Essie Mae gasped.

"Darkness don't follow, it cloak me. Doc Jones say I lose my mind. He don't mean it."

Essie crinkled her brow. "Dr. Jones again. You make him sound like part of the family."

"You set yourself against him, but he was," I said, proud.

Essie don't like it, focusing out the window. I wait till she look at me again, Evie, too.

"My Daisy. Oh, girls, I young and pretty—and born free North on a li'l farm to a stern mama and a sweet papa. I love a man, Samuel. It weren't right 'cause I too young, not much in years, but life, an immature child. But Samuel a bold man. Peacock like Miss Lil, strutting and cawing, winning my attention."

"Samuel loved you." Evie's wide eyes dreamed with me.

"Daddy won't let us marry. I go against my sweet papa and marry Samuel in my heart. Now I scared 'cause I gonna have a baby. Then something strange happened."

"Your daddy accepted you," Essie said, always smart, knowing the story fore I finish.

I join Essie on the sofa. Evie did, too, squeezing together, leaning on each other. "Mama and Daddy sing like I give em a gift. They don't want me to run away nor do a bad thing."

"And Samuel?" Evie asked.

The words stuck inside me. "He left," I whispered. "Daddy babied me. Oh, he babied me. But I too sick, Daisy born too soon. She live long enough a showing me God's miracle."

"Delly," Evie whispered. "Did you . . ."

"Blame God? No, child. Blame makes ya crazy. Whys too."

Essie dried her tears. "How did you find peace?"

"My heart don't come together for a long time. Samuel return. I don't wanna marry or see nobody. Mr. Wilcox sent Daddy a letter, offering to hire me. Daddy don't want me going South."

Essie shook her head in disbelief. "I don't know what to say. I always thought . . ."

"I was born a slave? No. Mama born in West Africa, brought here on a slave ship. She sewed fine French dresses for her mistress. Her mistress set her free. Mama and Daddy marry and open a small dress shop, selling Mama's fashions. Daddy don't enjoy farming, but he do it for her, us."

Evie wept softly.

"Evie, Alex woulda fought all by hisself the men who bring slavery to this land."

"I don't understand how Grandfather insisted Mama marry a man as my father."

"Alex don't know. World full a John Winthrops. I watch the one woman I love more than my own mama, die, trying to make things right. Evie, you nearly died . . . Katie did."

"It's hard to reckon with, Delly. Slavery isn't a sin to forgive and forget."

"We never forget. Bes learn from it. Guilt kill ya mama. I ain't watching it kill you."

"I never said I want to lose Westland." Evie stood now, fight flashing in her eyes.

"If you can't see the changes that matter at Westland, you living blind, punishing yourself for another's sin. Shame 'tis, when so many lose they lives to give ya one."

Evie stared at me sorrowful. "And when my father arrived?"

"I stronger then. Don't let my mind wander in the sad past. You gotta decide now."

"What, Delly?" they asked together.

"When it's over. Evie, you Granddaddy Alex used to say Westland like no other place. Trees taller, grassland greener, and the sky hold sapphire nights and bluebell mornings. Some folks look at all I been through, but I say even broken instruments can still sing."

We all let out a breath, tired. Evie wandered to the fireplace. Essie Mae, the window.

"Evie, child!" I clap, waking us. "Did ya know Alex gave River that silver harmonica?"

"No." Evie wiped her sniffles, snatching that snip a joy.

"And Essie Mae, you Granddaddy Luby, Alex, and River used to sit on the front porch, blowing harps, whistling music in the night putting Westland to sleep."

Essie perked up, soaking in a pleasing word bout her family.

"Won't forget the time you girls throw dirt up my nose, giving me an aching back that still bothers when it rains. And Polly taught Lil to sing like an angel. Wish Lil sang more."

I relish Evie's laughter. "Delly, what does all that have to do with staying at Westland?"

Essie set her gentle hand on Evie's cheek. "Stories, Sister. Delly wants us to remember Westland isn't land, it's stories. Wondrous, wretched . . ."

"Loving," I finished.

"I'm so sorry about Daisy." Essie Mae held me. Evie's arms stretched, hugging us both.

"Only other soul I tell be Polly. She write Daisy in *River Wild,* calling it a tribute. My heart nearly together then, whole when Essie Mae born. See, it take a lifetime, but I'm here."

"And Westland's home," Evie said.

"You girls don't need me to tell ya what Westland is or can be. Katie be Westland's heart. She weren't perfect, maybe that's part a the lesson. Living with ourselves when we the worst but do all we can to change and blossom. Forgiving don't excuse evil, it lets it go and speaks forth, you ain't gonna kill me nor my dreams . . . nor my sweet memories. Daisy."

My girls rush me like when they small. We hug, but not clinging—for courage, strength.

In no time, a rainbow gonna shine over us, but not till the storm brewing burst its rain forth in darkness and lightning. Now all the secrets, wondrous and wretched, come a busting out the sad earth, the Alabama sun shining its rays on the truth.

One of em missing. Buried in the rich black soil, it come sprouting up. But I don't discern if it be a weed or flower. I don't know jus yet till it grow a li'l more.

29

ESSIE MAE

Evie ran to the stables, waving a small cowboy hat banded with a pink ribbon. *A genuine Stetson, Boss of the Plains hat.* I smiled, recalling Lil showing us the ad, spoiling James's surprise. *It took him months to find gifts for you girls. When they arrived, his blue eyes sparkled for the first time in months. Act surprise for Lil. James needs a well of joy. It's up to us now.*

I pretended I hadn't spotted the pink hatbox waiting for me on the stone bench under Katie's magnolias. "Essie Mae, meet me here in an hour," James said.

I finished packing for Richmond and left Evie, James, and Bedford to the business of Westland for a stroll with Delly. I mulled over Delly's confession. *Daisy. A child.* In Delly's fashion, she harvested joy, weaving through the orchard, giddy with Bo's January. In the distance, I spied the odd woman, Astra. "Proud pears," Astra babbled. I felt sorry for her. "Koontz grow pink pears yonder," she called.

Delly shooed her away. "River knows the roses and pears. James gonna sell em."

Evie was right. This was a new Westland I hadn't known, progress.

Nelly, a young Irish maid, tossed me an apple. "Good to see ya again, lass. We'll have tea when you visit my Aunt Jeanie in Ashland."

I stumbled at her mention. *Bedford never said our trip was a secret.*

"Hope ya stay, missus," January said. Her authenticity forged our instant connection.

Astra waved her basket above her head, dropping pears, sending January scrambling.

"Clumsy child, clumsy women. Lord, what we gonna do round here?"

I would remember Delly's belly laugh in the orchard all the way to Richmond.

🌿

I sat on the stone bench, waiting under the magnolias for James.

He joined me. "You've shouldered a heap on this trip home, Essie Mae."

I stroked the pink silk band on my new riding hat, thinking of Miss Katie, and tried it on.

James tilted it over my brows, nearly covering my eyes. "Might not be the rage in those fashion magazines, but I had it made special."

"It's perfect. Thank you, James." I tucked my hat into its box. "Delly gave us much to contemplate."

James's eyes smiled. "That's her gift." He stood and offered his arm. "Shall we?"

We walked his new path around Westland. When we reached my garden, he stopped and breathed it in. "Katie loved this walk, especially in the moonlight. It reminded her of—well, that was years ago."

"You were going to say when you visited Katie in John's absence. You loved her so, James. There's no shame in remembering."

James's squint made me grin. "I've missed your smile."

We reached the stables. James released my hand. He held it throughout our walk.

Evie waved to us. "Yep, she's busting to know what we're talking about," James said. "Evie doesn't keep company with gossiping ladies, but—"

"She fancies gossip. Thank you for not opposing my trip with Bedford to Ashland."

"A lot of talk about *places* around here, but not the open spaces I roamed as a young man. The place you're pondering is where you fit in . . . where we belong."

"Evie told you?"

"She didn't have to." James waved at Evie. We lingered a few yards away. "Your letters changed. Katie noticed." He paused and looked back toward the house. "I'm chopping that old willow near the house, Essie. It's unsafe. January says it brought blight to Westland and your roses." I didn't question the resolve in his voice. "Katie would agree. Change is nothing to fear."

"It's difficult to absorb."

James hesitated, unable to find his next words. He tipped his hat back, searching for my eyes. He found them. "You're a stunning woman, Essie Mae. Katie was so proud of you. When you recited your first speech for us in the parlor, I couldn't stop clapping."

"Why didn't Katie tell me about the adoption?"

"World of hate out there never made sense to me. A little girl wants to dream a big dream and gain an education. Shouldn't matter what her skin color is, should it?"

"No, sir."

"But it did to a lot of folks. This valley's changed. I'm not a man of learned words."

"Yours are the words I remember most."

"I don't tell my story because, well, I don't know it. What I remember ain't a history worth boasting. Men aren't open like womenfolk."

"You could try."

"Since you were girls, you whispered about my Indian blood. Hell, it's true. My mother ... *ishki*." He closed his eyes as his ears savored his Choctaw word. "Was Choctaw."

"*Ishki*," I repeated, to his delight.

His sly glance made us both smile. "I can still see her long black hair, glistening in the sun as she stood waving goodbye to my father. Handsome woman. John's mama ..." James swallowed the unpleasantness of his words. "Know little about John's mother. She wasn't good to him or me. Yeah, what you're thinking is right. We didn't have the same mother."

His confession shocked me.

James rubbed his mustache, looking toward the corral. "I don't know what you're walking through, Essie Mae. My boots don't fit ya, and I bet ya five dollars yours don't fit me."

"I lost all my money to Evie."

"I lose my bets with her, too." James tipped his hat back again, his eyes moist. "But this old half-breed knows what it's like to float between two worlds, a white one and Indian."

"I don't like that term ... half-breed."

"You shouldn't. Nobody should."

"How did you choose?"

"I didn't."

I couldn't be angry at James's simplistic answer. He wasn't a man of letters as Bedford, yet his brief response deposited deep into my spirit. I demanded more. A lifetime of secret shame, prejudice, abuse . . . I deserved more. But even as I contemplated thoughtlessly pressing him—his whispered wisdom found its soil, its roots already sprouting inside me.

He stroked my hand. "Essie." I scarcely heard his muffled whisper.

"I'm here."

"You're home. Westland will always be your home."

"Two worlds collide soon enough, and that isn't a bad thing?"

"Many worlds exist out there that people wanna push ya into, but it's not their place. No more than you asking them to buy you a ticket to a destination they choose. It's your journey, isn't it?"

"Thank you, James. I'll remember that."

"You're family. The world that counts is the one that brings you peace. Seem to recall Delly saying something about that, do you?"

He didn't wait for my answer because he wasn't the one who needed to hear or know it.

I did.

30

ESSIE MAE

Once a mineral springs resort for Virginia's elite, the war degraded its renowned racecourse into a Confederate training ground. The Civil War ravaged Ashland. As Sweet Water, the town's reconstruction was equally a marvel. New churches, white picket fences, and storybook cottages lined the quiet end of Main Street.

"I remember the races," I said. "Lil took us on a special train to Ashland. Ladies a flutter in pastel hats and dresses, a flurry of betting, the grandstand and clubhouse, brimming."

"Ashland boasts a new gambling house," Bedford said.

"Um-hmm. As a poker aficionado, I'm surprised you never ran into Houst."

"He would have made me remember him."

Gone was the girlhood inquisitiveness of my past as our train pulled into Ashland's small station, the depot Evie and I never reached on that moonlit walk fleeing Lil's.

"Evie held a lion's courage, making us walk a road to a station she didn't know existed."

"Looking into your case, Essie, I'm convinced Grant knew your plans long before you left Lil's and followed you."

"How?"

"You remembered a stranger outside Lil's home the night you fled."

"I was never certain. It was Lila, wasn't it?"

"That's why we're here. We're going to find out from a boy who saw you the night Grant kidnapped you."

"I don't remember a boy ..." A flash of a boyish face startled my memory. "Blond hair? Surely not the daft boy who held me with the brute."

"Regardless, he's a young man now."

"Will he remember me?"

"His mother does—our first stop."

Bedford's motions blurred as he loaded our satchels into a carriage. Main Street spun in a whirl of strangers. White circus tents and a caravan of painted wagons dotted the hub of Main Street, alive with a festive crowd ogling the sideshow.

"I hear circus music," I said, steadying myself.

Bedford smiled at my foot tapping to the lively tune. "The distraction, our fortune; we're unassuming arrivals among the tourists. You may even enjoy a respite at a carnival, Miss Essie."

I playfully rapped his knuckles. "Why, Mr. Jarrell, focus."

My lightheartedness surprised me until our carriage neared Main Street's dead end, a ghost town surrounded by woods. Signs of life: a park and garden, gravel walks, and gas lamps; an inn stood alone at the end of the street. *Belle's*, a newly built yellow two-story house with Nantucket blue shutters and a spacious front porch festooned with fake ivy.

"Strange, a new inn, a circus in town, and no guests," Bedford said, walking up the steps.

"Potted flowers would add charm."

Bedford pointed to a row of potted blue hyacinths.

I snubbed them. "Ironic."

"I know this . . . hyacinths mean truth." His grin changed into a grimace when he spotted my hands trembling. He didn't coddle me. Instead, inspected the back porch and nearby woods.

My stomach tumbled like the clowns greeting us at the station. "Couldn't we register at the hotel first?"

Bedford's fist hung in the air, pausing to knock. "We could, but we're here, Essie."

I held my chest, my heart pounding as I left him on the porch, walking back to the carriage, soothing the tired white pony. "You need sugar and a quiet meadow, too."

Bedford's hand fell upon my shoulder, tender, warm. "I'm here, Essie."

"Sebastian, why did you stay in New York after Thomas left? It was more than waiting to escort me to Westland, wasn't it?" I boldly asked, learning to find comfort in his pale blue eyes.

"You ran a school. Miss Evie returned home. You needed help."

"Did you know of Houst then?"

"Yes."

"I see."

"Lass, it is you," Jeanie's Irish brogue greeted us. "I could spot your smile in that circus crowd yonder. Essie Mae, how are ya, lass?" Jeanie stood on the porch. Her porcelain hands suctioned to her hips, hair in a beehive of copper curls and shamrock green ribbons. "Forgive my yard's appearance. I'm no gardener."

"Miss Jeanie." I offered my tentative embrace.

"Miss Essie is an expert gardener and cultivates her own roses," Bedford said.

"Aye. I meant to see you speak in New York when Willow visited ya."

"I never knew Dr. Jones came to see me in New York."

"He'll tell ya all about it, but he's not here." Her eyes shifted to Bedford. "Willow promised to retire after the war. He's busier doctoring than when we met."

I lost my footing, disheartened by Dr. Jones's absence.

Bedford snarled, swiftly checked his pocket watch, and shoved it into his pocket. "This won't do, Mrs. Jones. Dr. Jones gave me his word. We traveled all this way—"

Jeanie frosted Bedford's burn with air kisses to his cheeks. "Cool your heels, lad," her voice velvet. "Call me Jeanie. It's no excuse, Mr. Jarrell. I'll tell ya what I know, what I can, Essie Mae. Jonesy promised his appearance by suppertime."

"Appearance?" Bedford huffed. "We didn't come for a circus, Miss Jeanie." Bedford removed his hat and nodded, dropping the disappearing Willow Jones for now.

"You know why we're here?" I asked. "Has Nelly arrived?"

"Oh, no." Jeanie waved off the idea, ushering us into her parlor, pursing her lips at Bedford's sullenness. "My niece visits her mum in Maine. Jonesy required his privacy now, suffering one of his spells."

"Spells?" Bedford asked, intrigued.

Jeanie scuttled to the tea table, doling out cakes on a tray. "He frets so. His work calms him, senseless, all that pressure healing folks and minding orphans until he finds them homes."

Jeanie's words muffled in my ears. I paused at a painting, reuniting with an old friend.

"You remember the portrait of the actress in the feathers," she said, standing behind me.

"I stared at her for hours, wondering if I would ever smile like that again."

"Ah, a mischievous grin at that. Poor dear, no young lass should relive *That*."

That. One word transported me to Lil's salon in Paris, her guests discussing the Union fighting the evil in the South. *"How did you endure your kidnapping, Miss Essie?"*

"'She' was birthed during my recovery at the home of a kindhearted woman, Miss Jeanie, who nursed me back to health. Jeanie referred to my imprisonment and torture as That. That happened to She. And She wasn't me."

"And so, by disassociating yourself from the trauma you ..."

"Trauma? Evil. I reserve judgment and chastisement, but nameless evil is easier to excuse, ignore, and forget for those who haven't survived its wrath. Diluting unpalatable words as rape to taken; slavery to servitude or 'a way of life'; evil to mistakes, placates evil, setting it free to roam and lull many to sleep. Until one day, That becomes acceptable and tolerated, even profitable. Until That leads a nation to war with itself to free men, women, and children from the bondage of evil which surely has a name: slavery."

"Miss Essie?" Bedford's soft touch brought me back.

I welcomed this recollection. It rushed through my being, providing courage.

They watched me snub the painting, no longer beguiled by the courtesan's grin.

"I'll fetch the tea. Ya don't strike me as a teetotaler. Wine, Detective Jarrell?"

"Tea. Please, call me Bedford."

"Aye, a contrary streak in a man is attractive. Ah, but you're handsome without it."

Jeanie slowly approached, her eyes admiring me from head to toe. "Jonesy was right. You're spectacular, deary." She held my wrist, tracing its deep purple scar. Her finger found another, only I could see, near the corner of my mouth, and another, a slash behind my ear.

Jeanie wore sensuality as a diamond necklace, center stage for all to see. She caught the habit, backing away. After all these years, I closed my eyes, welcoming her mothering touch, pure and safe. Her peck on my cheek calmed my nerves.

"No shame," she whispered in my ear. "I know your scars because I soothed them, my girl." Jeanie walked to a vase of white daisies and tucked a flower in my hair. "All better?"

"Yes."

"You're among friends and welcome in my home." She sauntered out of the room.

Arms folded, Bedford stood in the middle of the parlor, sneering at the gaudy paintings of an actress and a few nudes on a corner wall by the fireplace.

"I know what she was," I said, reading him. "It was a long time ago."

"You trust her? I'm not so sure."

"Jeanie hasn't said one word yet."

"Oh, she has." Bedford walked to the mantel and studied a photograph of a boy.

He examined the parlor again, snickering at a red velvet settee with gold-fringed pillows, worn but once elegant. Lace fans decorated the wall behind a rose tufted chaise longue. The edge of another portrait, hidden behind a red velvet curtain, made us blush. Bedford folded back the drape: the painting was of Jeanie partially nude, reclining on the same chaise longue.

Astringent musk and gardenia perfume covered the scent of tobacco. The heady fragrance from a vase of red roses cooled my blush.

"A rose petal soothes a sour stomach," Jeanie sang, returning. "I'm not sure what candied violets do, but I brought some and my shortbread. Do you remember my shortbread, deary?"

"I should. I ate enough."

"Good."

I stepped back, aghast, as Jeanie slapped my belly. *Such vulgarity*, Lil whispered in my thoughts. Gentility and reserve, infrequent guests at Belle's Inn.

"Your new home is lovely. Why Belle's?" I asked, enjoying a cookie.

"In honor of my sister, the Good One, Mum called her."

"Evie mentioned you met Dr. Jones at Westland during the war," I said.

"He met me. After your horrific ordeal, Essie Mae, I left that town. It was time."

"Why we're here," Bedford said. His gaze pierced into Jeanie since we arrived. He scrutinized her fingers rattling on the pianoforte and twiddling the ribbons in her hair.

She knew, smirking, flirting. Jeanie waltzed to him and flipped his vest, missing its middle button. Bedford grinned while she inspected him and threaded her finger through the white streak in his hair. He flicked her touch away, clutching his vest.

I sat watching their show.

Jeanie noticed her nude portrait on full display and swiftly closed its curtain. She tamed the once flirtatious young madam, flinging her shawl, covering herself to the neck. "I run a respectable place," she said, refilling our teacups.

"Naturally." Bedford nodded to me.

Jeanie winked at Bedford and tossed her lace shawl onto the chaise lounge.

"Miss Jeanie, we have much to discuss," I said. "Forgive my forwardness."

"Truth cuts in this parlor. James told me why you've come, deary. You'll stay here?"

Bedford cleared his throat before I could answer. "I've secured rooms," he said, stressing the *s* in *rooms*. "At the new hotel."

"Busy, if that's what you need, lad."

"Precisely."

"Jonesy and his melancholy, we'd be booked with circus folk. I rather keep a quiet inn. Jonesy coaxed this circus to Ashland. He loves a traveling wagon show, where he got his start."

I choked on my tea.

Bedford shook his head *no* when Jeanie wasn't looking. *Wait*, his eyes insisted. *Why?* I wondered. *For Dr. Jones.* Bedford's scowl reminded me of his conditions for this trip: I remain silent during his interrogations. And so I did.

Jeanie's laugh startled us. "Your own wee performance in my parlor."

"Who was Delaney Houst?" Bedford asked her, sharply.

"Who wasn't Houst? A cardsharp, swindler, twisted sod. I never hid who

I was, but Houst could be anybody, pleasured in ruining lives. He worked alone, except for the girl."

My posture stiffened.

"What do you know about her?" Bedford asked.

"A phantom. Came to work for me in my younger days and vanished."

"What did she look like?"

"Blonde wig, brunette, Moroccan, Spanish, I don't remember. Many brown-eyed exotics came and went." Jeanie's fingers fluffed her ribbons.

"Go on." Bedford studied her.

"I heard about a young rancher winning at the tables, gambling houses, making his way to my establishment. Houst met the girl there and left, kept her as a pet, hidden."

"That's more than I know. How long was the woman with him?"

"I don't keep track when they leave. The night James busted in with you, Essie Mae, I had long left that . . . *work*," she spit it out in disgust. "I had a son."

"How long ago was that, Miss Jeanie?"

That did it. I cringed, watching her wilt.

Jeanie rose and searched out the window, the street barren. "My mum spoke sharp truth with a honeyed tongue, making it go down easy. Aye, the church wouldn't let her preach, so she visited me and preached to my girls. One by one, they left until I was nary alone. Mum paid me a final visit."

"What did she say?" I asked.

Bedford coughed, seething at my interruption. *We break a stone wall by force, steady pressure, surprise*, he instructed.

I rescued her.

"No words, a look. Mum reviled my red velvet walls and black lace curtains, lectured on the rank of spirits and tobacco, and found my nude portrait, enthralled." Jeanie laughed. "Mum turned from the painting; her eyes popped open. 'Jeanie, my girl,' she said. 'It's beautiful.' I rocked my boy in my arms and listened. That life was over for me. I moved here after the war, wiping the dirt off my boots from that filthy town."

"I'm sorry for stirring up the dust now," Bedford said.

"Essie Mae, James told me to cut to the truth. Lad, you're smart enough to figure one reason John hired Houst—Houst had something on him. Me."

"John Winthrop came to your . . ."

"Establishment. Not me, understand? If Katie knew John—"

"She knew," I said. "John abandoned Katie before Evie was born. When we turned thirteen—she banished John from Westland. We thought for good."

"Sad 'tis. James dreamed of marrying Katie ever since I knew him."

"Back to Houst," Bedford said, focused.

Jeanie slowly blinked, searing regret into the picture of her son. "John and Houst blasted into that mining town in over their heads in a high-stakes game with a real player. Friends of mine caught John cheating; they roughed him up. Houst brought John to my damn place for mending. I tended John's wounds long enough for that bastard to beat one of my girls."

"Go on."

"James caught word; first time in years he saw his brother. I thought James would kill him. Gossip floated like fireflies in Lil's circles. Everyone knew John left Katie, but James. After that, James watched—guarded—Katie, years before Evie was born. Katie was awful lonely. I thought James and Katie married."

Bedford finally relaxed in his chair. "Katherine Winthrop was already married to John."

"Hell of a marriage. John was at my house when Katie wired Lil about Isabel's rape. Lil sent help. No cause, but they aimed to jail Bo for the trouble, or worse."

"Heavens. Where was Houst when this happened?" I asked.

"At Westland. After that, John kept Houst close. Houst had a *friendship* with Isabel."

"What about your son?" Bedford checked his watch, my signal to stay quiet.

Jeanie snickered, masking dread. "Lad, you've been cordial, letting me dance around my boy. Beaut of a watch. Why don't you two enjoy the carnival? We'll continue this at supper."

Though I owed Jeanie my life, I couldn't soften this blow. I needed answers to save Evie, Westland, and myself.

Quiet, Bedford anchored in his chair, motioning for me to sit. "Jeanie, what did your son know about the night Grant kidnapped Essie?"

Jeanie exhaled. "I heard Lil was ready to pay a hefty ransom to the rat. I couldn't let that happen. Big mistake paying Houst; once is all the devil requires. He would've killed her."

"So, it was Houst who arranged the abduction?"

"Yes." Jeanie stared into my wide eyes and nodded. "Truth cuts in my parlor because I spent a lifetime running from it, like you, Essie Mae." She poured herself whiskey mixed with milk and spices, and raised her glass to Bedford.

He declined.

Jeanie strutted to her portrait, shaking her head, toasting the brazen model. "We act a fool when we're young and in love. A famous French artist painted that, my boy's father. I thought he'd marry me. We all think that." Jeanie absorbed my hollow stare. "You've traveled miles to speak to a worn Irish lass who held a man's gaze once. Now, she's happy to cook stew for her husband, who travels exhaustively—running from himself. We visit Ireland next spring. I may not return."

"Why wouldn't you return?" Bedford asked.

Jeanie ignored his question. "Quinn. I gave myself a new name to spare my mother shame. Jeanie Quinn until Willow Jones gave me his. Is that what you seek, deary . . . a name?"

"Yes."

"I can't give it to ya because I don't know your father. Maybe I can offer peace until Jonesy arrives. I owe James my life." She shot Bedford a side-glance. He couldn't hold it. "I've lasted this long because I know how to keep my trap shut."

"Jeanie, please help us."

She stroked my hair. "Deary, I'm tough, but your screams in the night sent a terror into me as if the devil had come to stay. I knew they'd haunt you. I couldn't mend those wounds."

"Nightmares."

"Yes." Jeanie collapsed onto the chaise lounge. She flung her shawl to the floor. "Bedford promised to spare my son. He's a gentle young man, slow . . . a difficult birth."

"I'd like to speak with him," Bedford insisted.

"My boy ain't coming. See, he rarely speaks. Things like this don't set right in his mind. Sweet boy nearly built this house himself. We don't want trouble."

Jeanie's bluster dissolved, transforming her into a frightened, protective mother.

"Trouble won't come to you," I said.

"After you left my care, a man with a slashed face visited me with questions and threats."

Bedford sat on the edge of his seat. "Trailer?"

"Yes. Thick red scar on the right side of his face, ear to . . ."

"Chin." I stared into her.

"He asked about you, Essie Mae." She draped her lace shawl around my shoulders. "You keep it, deary. I told Trailer I didn't know ya. He threatened to hurt my boy. I said I didn't have a son, but he knew. He wanted to know where to find ya. By then, the war started. I never said a word, never saw Trailer again."

"You didn't turn him in?" Bedford asked.

Jeanie stayed quiet.

"How did Trailer know about your son?" I asked, to Bedford's disapproval.

"My boy was there, Essie Mae, the night Grant stole ya."

Silence.

"He repented. They used him! He wasn't with that gang. They said they'd pay because you were a runaway. But when my boy saw Grant hit a woman, he ran. He's seen it before."

"Evie."

"My boy ran to me when Grant brought ya to that camp, telling me your location."

"That's how James found me."

"Aye."

I never saw Jeanie cry.

"Houst threatened my boy about me. I made my fresh start. Carny threats weren't gonna run me off this time."

"Carny?"

"The circus, how Katie's father found Houst, gave the boy a chance. Katie was like her father, giving wayward folks, like me, a fresh start." Jeanie's past overwhelmed her.

I took Bedford's hand. "I'd like to leave now."

Jeanie offered a thankful embrace. "A few hours, love. By then, Willow will return."

"All right," Bedford reluctantly agreed. "Until this evening." He tipped his hat. "I'll wait in the carriage, Miss Essie."

"Deary." She stopped me. "Sebastian . . ."

I turned around, surprised by her reference.

She nodded. "Fitting you end up with him."

"You're mistaken. Mr. Jarrell means to solve my case. After six years, he is close to finding all the men who hurt me so we can ensure they never hurt another again."

"Pity. You only seek justice."

"Shouldn't I?"

"Yes, but now I'm broken, lass, that for six years, your life remained as stuck as mine."

"Stuck?"

"Aye, the past. Go on. *Bedford* is waiting." She stopped me at the door. "God saved ya, child. Don't waste your life seeking revenge. It withers a dashing young woman."

I nodded, pausing at the bottom of the steps. "Jeanie, how did Trailer act when he saw you that night?"

"Like your father."

"Was he?"

"You'll have to ask him."

"Is he here . . . in Ashland?"

"I don't think so." She caught her fingers twirling her hair ribbons and smiled. "Willow will know. Go. Let the past be just that, even if for a few hours. Enjoy the circus. It's a good one." She shivered at Bedford's steely gaze. "I pray Mr. Jarrell is on your side, lass, don't you?"

Before I walked away, she caught me in her arms.

I wanted to kiss her cheek; the beauty mark Evie swore was a painted heart of melted chocolate. I didn't. I rarely gave anyone, outside my family, affection.

She patted my hand and said, "It will come one day, in pieces, but soon."

"What, Miss Jeanie?"

"Trust. And when that happens, you'll open your heart again to love. Visit and tell Jeanie all about it, aye?"

I rushed to Bedford, eager to take in the sights of the circus.

I welcomed a slow carriage ride toward the festivities.

Bedford finally spoke, "I thought it best we stay in the busy part of town."

"Alone?"

"In Richmond, I learned Lila's tip on Trailer went cold."

"Are you positive?"

He stroked my hand. "It cost me, but I'll know more after a visit to the proprietor of the general store here in town. Perhaps, Jeanie is right. Until we speak with Dr. Jones, I don't see the harm in a little entertainment, do you?"

"My head's spinning. You don't fancy diversions. You frown upon them."

"The spirit of this lost resort town awakens me, Lady Pinkerton." He flipped open his watch, grinning. "Learning about this circus might help us understand our carny, Willow Jones."

"Jeanie made no secret of his past. River was right. Dr. Jones was in the circus. Evie will never believe it."

"Look there . . . scoundrels." Bedford pointed to three men holding a small crowd captive with a card game. "I should break that up. Damn nuisance."

"You mustn't. Lord a mercy, a rare display of temper befitting Delly, Mr. Jarrell."

Bedford halted our carriage, gaining the men's attention. He whispered in my ear, "The oldest con in the book."

The men returned to their crowd.

"Any sign of Houst in that gathering?" In Virginia, the fall chill sharpened my senses. I scanned the shops and streets for Trailer, noting every tall, muscular man. Thin, jagged beards played tricks mimicking Trailer's slash down his cheek.

"Calm yourself. You don't think Trailer would risk the open, do you?"

"I don't know what to think, Sebastian."

"Let me do the thinking on this trip . . . at least momentarily."

"You almost broke Jeanie."

"My intention. You're too close. I should visit Dr. Jones alone."

"Not on your life."

"I'm interested in what Jeanie didn't say, never revealing her son's name. She's protecting him."

"He's simpleminded. I don't want to crush Jeanie or her son."

"Jeanie lived six years in solace. And you? Think of that before you ease her conscious again and interrupt my questioning."

"I'm sorry. She saved my life as much as James."

"Let me do my job. Dr. Jones won't act as guilty or accommodating."

Our ride resumed. The con men stared at Bedford as we passed.

"What's the oldest con in the book?" I asked.

"Three-card Monte, a confidence game. A cardsharp shuffles three cards; his victim attempts to pick the money card."

"Like the shell game Evie liked to play in Richmond."

"She did?"

"Once."

"The stout man in the suit serves as the trusted businessman; he butters the crowd. His partner in the Stetson, the unwitting rancher, is the cardsharp. The third, wearing the red tie, an insurance man who traps his mark by winning a few games. On a train, he engages in friendly conversation to earn his mark's trust."

"Mark?"

"The victim they trick into betting a large sum to pick the money card. The insurance man moans he's never won the game. Instantly, his luck changes, and he swears to the mark he's discovered the secret to winning."

"He reveals it to the mark. They let the victim win a few games, building his confidence."

"And hook him into making a final large bet."

"Only to clean him out."

"But when that mark, the strongman over there, figures it out—it's going to get ugly. Good, the sheriff arrives. It never takes long. It wasn't prudent for me to interfere."

"You always get your man, is that it?"

"Let's be thankful Evie's in Paris, and you're with me."

"You must win."

"Yes. If I don't someone will die. And it isn't going to be me."

31.

EVIE

My traveling trunks hidden on the porch, I watched Mama's willow fall at Westland. Bo and his men had already hauled off the branches.

"That wood ain't good for nothing, excepting brooms and flutes," Bo shouted.

A draft horse tugged the willow's rotted stump out of the ground to a swell of jubilation. I hadn't a tear, only for Essie and the secret unearthed that Houst had violated Isabel underneath it.

"That's not why Bo's chopping down that willow," Delly said.

James stayed quiet on the subject as he tossed a few willow branches into the bonfire on the eve of Essie's departure. She whispered her thanks for the gesture. He showed us the willow's blight and crack in its trunk from a summer storm declaring, "Katie's daddy planted plenty of willows at Westland, time for this one to return to Mother Earth."

Bo promised to fashion a plaque from my grandparent's carved heart holding their initials and promise of true love. No one fought to save the tree. That willow wasn't Westland, we were, and on the trip into Sweet Water I told Lil I couldn't leave James alone again.

"I'm proud of you," Lil said. "Figure you might change your mind. Your Aunt Lil's battling her own small war. Hang the steamer. I'll visit Mobile and help Augustus."

"What about Paris?"

"Paris delays the inevitable. It will be there next spring."

A trusted friend of Mama's agreed to drive me home.

The men carted off the remaining logs toward the river. I greeted Bo with a tray of glasses and a pitcher of Delly's lemonade I found waiting in the kitchen. The house was empty.

"Why, Miss Evie, what you doing back?" Bo asked, surprised. He shooed his men away.

They swarmed me instead with well-wishes, then raced to the iron table to chug their lemonade.

"Don't bust them glasses," Bo said. "Back to work. Go on, now."

"Thank ya kindly, Miss Evie," they called, leaving.

"James hired young ranchers for this job. Hardworking, but ain't much on manners when you gone, Miss Evie. You forego Paris another week again?"

I marveled at the sight; the past burned and whittled to ashes and saw-dust at Bo's feet.

The flash from the gold key I found under the willow caught his eye. It dangled from a chain around my neck. "This key guided me back home. I couldn't leave you now."

"Pleasing, you singing that word home. I forget to give ya this." Bo pulled a napkin from his pocket, unfolded it, and handed me a necklace holding a wooden locket.

"How did you know I'd come back?"

"Not knowing, hoping, Miss Evie."

At Bo's whistle, a bounding Sky wiggled and hopped, greeting me with kisses.

"You've been in the fields with James." I plucked burs off of Sky's scruff.

"With Lil gone, Sky no parlor dog."

I admired Bo's gift, a wooden mosaic in the shape of a heart, and slid the locket open. A four-leaf clover rested inside. "You made this?"

Bo nodded. "Lil say add green dye to save the shamrock's color. I seal it with a shine like my tables. That's the clover ya find me."

"Thank you, Bo. It's beautiful."

Bo wiped the sweat off his brow, showing off the cleared land, ready for its fresh start. "Careful now, don't trip on the brush, Miss Evie. Like to drink that lemonade instead a wear it."

"Weeks ago, I stood under that willow, thinking about my grandparents and Mama. But years of happy memories couldn't erase a horrific one."

Bo hid his thoughts, tossing a branch into a kindling pile. "Glad it gone, past healing."

"Nothing is past healing. You taught me that."

"You gonna serve that lemonade or make my jaw water, staring at it?"

I fetched two glasses.

"Suppose James know what he want," he said, back to work, raking leaves.

"I've missed many changes at Westland, haven't I, Bo?"

"You notice the ones that count. James gonna have a fit seeing you back. Ain't safe here."

"Where is he? I thought the soldiers arrived by now."

"Some do, staying at that couple's dairy farm, the rest making camp a few miles away."

"Is James with them?"

"He was mending fences this morning. Might be at the house by now. He won't leave Miss Katie's study."

"All right."

"James ask me to build his gazebo straightaway. Strange, like James plan it months ago. Painted spindles and rails tucked behind the greenhouse. Find supplies in the carriage house too."

I laughed. "Sounds like Mama's doing."

"Says he'd like Essie Mae to see it when she comes back."

"How wonderful!"

"Miss Lil with ya? Delly and January at McCafferty's. We got that barn raising in a week. Lumber finally arrived. Shipments slow, if they come at all."

"Lil's gone to Mobile to help Augustus sort Mama's affairs. I'm going to find James."

Bo stopped Sky from nipping at the leaves as he raked them. "Evie, James worse than before. He's fixing to visit the soldiers' camp. Help things along, he say, and I can't stop him."

"Bo, it's going to be all right. I promise. How about I cook my special breakfast for supper, seeing how Delly won't be home tonight."

"Fine, long as you don't burn the bacon. Rain coming, best crack on and finish."

I headed toward the house. "That reminds me, another Jane Austen novel is missing from Mama's library. Would you know anything about that?"

"Took Edward long enough to propose to Elinor. Why folks waste so much time?"

"A fitting lesson, isn't it?"

"Go on now. Got work to finish. Storm's coming."

"How I wish you hadn't said that."

When I returned to the house, my trunks were missing from the porch. I walked into the study, finding James, resting his head on Mama's desk, asleep.

"James," I whispered, nudging him awake.

"Darlin', you'll miss your train." Confused, he rubbed his eyes and shook himself awake. "What are you doing here?"

"Young Bear brought me back. I invited him to stay. He's catching up with Bo."

"You should have gone, Evie. You can't stay here."

"I'm sorry for the trouble." I walked to the door. "I needed to come home, James. Bo said the soldiers are here. I need to fight with you for Westland."

"Come here, Evie."

I sat beside him, staring at the aged letters strewn across Mama's desk.

"You remind me more of your mama every day."

"Six years ago, I begged Mama to let me leave Westland, knowing I could never return. Despite war, sickness, tragedy . . . abuse, I came home. I'm home, James."

"*Chuka.* Home. I like the sound of that. You haven't called Westland home in years."

"*Chuka.*"

He kissed my cheek; his mustache still tickled.

"I shouldn't have left you and Mama. I'll have to live with that, but I couldn't live with leaving you alone again, fighting by yourself to keep something that's more a promise to Mama than it was a part of your heritage or birthplace."

"This whole earth is our heritage and birthplace."

"I knew you'd say that."

James swiped through the papers on the desk, revealing a crumpled telegram. "Augustus found a buyer . . . for Westland."

"Oh, James. No."

"Calm down. I suspect with you ditching Paris, Lil's going to Mobile to stop the sale."

"When were you going to tell me?"

"Delly said she never saw me afraid. She's wrong. The first time I saw a woman, Jeanie's girl, beaten by John in a town outside Richmond, I was afraid, facing evil—my own—for wishing my brother dead. Afraid when your mama married him, me, loving Katie so. I ran not because I feared him, but myself in what I might do to him."

"I understand losing Mama has stirred up feelings, but we promised each other years ago we wouldn't look back. It's not your fault. It never was."

He rubbed his mustache and nodded.

"Are you afraid now, James?"

He shook his head and shuffled to the window, carrying the world. "In a blink, the willow's gone." He reached for my hand. I held his, standing by him. "You girls mean the world to me. Is it wrong, ensuring you live the rest of your life safe, away from trouble?"

"Selling Westland won't do that, James. I thought running away with Essie to Richmond would give us freedom. I thought leaving Lil's would keep us safe."

"When did you get so wise?"

I perused the letters on Mama's desk, noticing Jeanie's signature. "It doesn't feel right rummaging through Mama's private letters."

"Don't have much choice." James swiped up the stack. "I have to get a message to Bedford, see that he settles his business and avoids lingering in Ashland."

My gaze caught the colored glass on Mama's curiosity shelf near my writing desk. A small gold key nearly matching mine sat inside a tray on my desk. I searched underneath near the brass waste can and Delly's sewing basket.

"I know what's missing! James, I might have good news when you return."

"Missing?"

"Mama's strongbox. She used to let me play with it when I was a girl. She gave it to me for my treasures, paints, and all the curiosities I used to inspire my stories. Maybe it's nothing, but it should be right here." I pointed to the floor at the side of my desk. We stood staring at the faded carpet around a perfectly worn square of vibrant red swirls and gold flowers.

"You find that chest." He held up Jeanie's old letters. "Jeanie fancied writing Katie. Don't think she meant for me to read these, but under the circumstances . . . seems Houst had a habit of burrowing himself in abandoned mining towns. Easy money, low risk."

"Was Jeanie the contact Mama used to pay Houst?"

"I don't know. Before you arrived, Sal sent word of a hullabaloo at a played-out mining town near fifty miles away. Marshal said same game; stranger arrives at their village and stirs a ruckus, winning at the tables. This appeared as something more."

"Houst?"

"And a lady. Worth a trip. I was leaving before you came."

"Sleeping. I stirred you awake?"

"Got a mind to send you to Mobile with Lil. Things get sticky, you promise to heed me?"

"Yes, sir."

"I'll be back in time for Tom's barn raising. Bedford and Essie Mae should be, too. You find anything, darlin', you send word to Lil through Tom McCafferty. He'll get it to her."

"You do trust Tom."

"With our lives. Time to visit our soldier friends and send my wire to Bedford."

"What will you tell him?"

"My daughter has come home."

32.

ESSIE MAE

When we dropped our bags off at the Ashland Hotel, its quiet courtyard tempted me to leave the detective business to Bedford, stay behind, and rest. But I hadn't traveled all this way to Ashland to sleep.

Driving toward the circus grounds, Bedford complained about the con men and their three-card Monte swindle. We stopped at the general store, which looked empty as the streets, except for a curious little girl standing outside before her easel painting a boy's portrait.

"A worthy likeness," I said to myself. "See our young painter in front of the store?"

"Poor girl. She's probably with the circus."

"Bright girl. She wins the business of this block all to herself."

The boy's mother handed the girl money and happily retrieved her painting and son.

"Wait here," Bedford said.

"May I at least stretch my legs, Mr. Jarrell?"

"If you must."

I pointed to the girl, catching her spying. "Do I have permission to speak with her?"

Bedford rolled his eyes and nodded toward another man standing in front of a restaurant.

"Yours?"

"I'll return in a few minutes." Bedford eyed the curious girl. She ducked behind her easel. "I'm craving licorice. You?" he asked her.

"Thank you. No, sir," she said, painting.

"A smart setup you have there, miss," Bedford said, entering the store.

"I'm not a miss. I'm a girl." She held up a painting of a meadow and sunset.

Her portraits captured me. "You shine a talent and so young." I glanced through the store window. Bedford spoke furiously with a clerk.

"Portrait, miss? I'll paint ya, if you'll let me. I paint fine portraits."

"How old are you?"

"Doc says it don't matter. I paint fine."

"Doesn't matter. Do you attend school?"

"Yes, ma'am."

"Are you with the circus?"

She cowered behind her easel. "I don't like it there, too many scary faces. I know faces."

She didn't look like a runaway. Her brown hair in a shiny braid, she twisted in a green cotton dress, reminding me of mine when I was young. Her shoes, dingy; she noticed me looking and swiped them off with a rag.

"I'm sorry," I said. "It's not polite to stare."

"Oh, but it is. It's how I make my money." She held up a charcoal sketch of me.

"How did you . . . so that's how you lure folks, huh, child?"

"Portrait, miss?" she parroted again. "I'm not a vagrant."

"You have some schooling, don't you?"

"I stay at Belle's with Doc Jones and Miss Jeanie."

"With your parents?" I knew better than to ask, but I had to know if she was telling the truth about Belle's.

"Mama's gone. Daddy died in the war. Kin far off don't want me. Doc trying to find me a family. Jeanie ain't much for keeping kids. She got a grown one who acts like a child. Sweet as pie named Amos."

Amos, Jeanie's son. "How much for a painting?"

"How much will you pay?"

"Ten dollars."

"Golly, that's the price of three portraits. You a beaut, miss. I'll paint ya fast, but fine." She squinted at me, back to her sketch, scribbling my chin on the page.

"How would you paint me?" I stretched to peek.

She flipped her notebook closed and hid it behind her easel. "In that pretty pink dress with the cream lace tickling your neck. Your skin is the smoothest, pearliest skin I ever saw. Maybe the color of a brown baby rabbit in the sunshine."

"Is that right?"

I couldn't help chuckle when her little fingers reached high to lift my chin, studying me. "Near dried soil, but that don't sound pleasing. In the sun, a cup of English tea with a splash of milk. That's it! Your gentleman friend, he's an Indian, ain't he? I see the red under the green in his skin. But he got the blond hair and that strange white streak like a lost ribbon."

"You see all that?"

"Oh, miss, I see everything. 'Tis my business . . . colors . . . to see. Hope ya don't take no offense. My skin's peach with too many freckles. I paint em away."

"You can do that. I have business with Dr. Jones, but maybe I'll sit for you tomorrow."

"Golly, I'll remember you, miss." She rubbed at the purple plop of paint on her chin. "I'll start right now from my sketches. Jeanie says God gave me a gifted memory for faces. I'll never forget your golden eyes and the shamrocks dancing inside them. No, ma'am."

"Will I see you at Belle's for supper?"

"Yes, ma'am."

"Essie Mae . . . you may call me Essie."

"Pretty name. What does it mean?"

"I'm told, star."

"I'll paint the pearl on your cheeks as starlight."

I handed her my money. Her grin unsure, stiff. "Go on. It's yours."

"You trust me?"

"Yes. What's your name?"

"Dorothy. Friends call me Dottie. You can too if you wanna. Don't know what my name means." Forgetting her business, she tapped and shuffled, impressing me with a brief dance.

"I do. I have a student named Dorothy. It means gift of God."

"I didn't know I was that special."

"You do now."

"Miss Jeanie's making chicken pot pie and silver cake for dessert. She makes silver cake on birthdays with thick almond icing. Miss Millie's gonna take me to the circus after, so I'll stay outta your hair. That's what Jeanie said. You just arrived."

"You know an awful lot for a little girl."

"I study all the new faces in town, miss." Dottie pointed to the depot across the tracks.

"All?"

"Yes, ma'am."

I looked through the window, searching for Bedford. He stood at the counter, still talking to the merchant. *Don't speak to anyone. What harm could it do?*

"You all right, Miss Essie?"

Dottie was ten or eleven, but I found trust in her innocent brown eyes. "Dottie, have you ever seen a man with a scar on his face from ear to chin?" I spit it out, embarrassed. I walked over to look at her sketches.

"Oh, yes."

My heart fluttered. I slowly turned to her, my eyes shifting to Bedford's man, staring right at me. "You did?" I whispered.

"He frightened me."

I rushed to her so fast; she cowered behind her easel again. "I'm sorry, Dottie. It's important."

"Do you know him, Essie? The scarred man?"

"When did you see him last? Think, child."

"Near a year ago on my birthday. Jeanie made me a silver cake."

"You haven't seen the scarred man since?"

As children do, joy resurfaced, reminding me of Wren. *Wren and Abigail,* I thought, tucking the idea away for now. Dottie busied, painting at her easel, annoyed at the passing crowd and business I made her miss.

"I see everybody, Essie, entering Mr. Abel's store. Nowhere else to buy goods for miles, especially liquor. Men around here need it. And the women hoard the dress goods."

I grew impatient now, but I reminded myself Dottie didn't know me. I may have trusted her, but Dr. Jones taught her well to remain cautious of strangers.

"You shouldn't be out here alone, Dottie."

"I'm not alone. Mr. Abel always sits with me when he ain't got customers. Ma, we call her Ma, at the pharmacy, keeps a keen eye out." Dottie pointed across the street.

I turned around to a husky woman standing outside her shop, watching us the entire time. Dottie waved to her. The woman waved back, nodded to me, and wobbled back into her shop.

"I remember." Dottie swallowed, searched around, ensuring no one was near. "The scarred man," she whispered. "He bought a lady's sunhat. Strangest thing, 'cause I don't see no lady with him."

"A woman?" I knew it was foolish, maddening, but I pulled out the frame wrapped in pink silk, my hands shaking. Dottie touched them; her icy fingertips made the hair on my arms stand up. Her little hands slipped the pink silk off the frame and she stared at the photo of my mama.

"Have you seen her?" I asked, my voice breaking.

"Yes," she said.

My heart quickened.

"Where? When!"

Dottie pointed at me.

As I released a sigh, her tiny finger wiped the tear off my cheek. "I can't paint you crying, miss. You're filled with light."

"Thank you, Dottie. You've been a tremendous help to me."

"You got a family?"

Compassion steadied me as I looked into her eager eyes. "Yes."

"Do they look like you? They must be beautiful."

"Oh, child." Little Dottie didn't know what to make of me, but she craved loved and absorbed every ounce in my embrace.

"You're lucky to have a family to love."

I pinched her pudgy pink cheeks. She giggled. "I had to check and make sure you're real. Someone I love, near a mama, would say you be an angel, child. An angel."

"Maybe I'll meet her . . . your family someday. Is Mr. Jarrell your husband?"

"No. Why would you think so?"

"His eyes sparkle like gemstones when he looks at you, aquamarine. The Doc give Jeanie an aquamarine ring. Sometimes she lets me hold it, and I paint eyes that color."

A bell chimed. Bedford stood outside, grinning at us. He spotted Dottie's sketches, tipped his hat to her. "Ready, Essie Mae?" Bedford asked, hopping into our carriage.

I kissed Dottie's cheeks, flushed and warm. Love melted my heart as her nose nuzzled my cheek.

"I won't forget you," she said.

"You won't have to, Dottie. I promise. I'll see you at suppertime."

"I believe your promises, Essie Mae."

"You owe me a portrait."

"It'll be ready. Maybe two?"

I waved, but Dottie was quick back at work painting.

"What was all that about?" Bedford asked.

"Your news first."

"We need a break and I'm hungry."

"A distraction. All right, Mr. Jarrell. I'll play along."

Between a gaggle of blushing wives and the showmen trumpeting their attractions, one could cringe or applaud sideshows without entering the tents. A man who eats fire! The lady snake charmer. Lucky Lydia, the woman who eats glass. The tallest thin man, Giant George, who dances gracefully in oversized shoes next to a miniature poodle in a tutu.

"Why attend the shows if you can see them now for free?" I asked, taking in the sights.

"Freak attractions entice you to pay for a seat in the big top."

"I could gain as much excitement with my nose in an adventure book."

"Could you gain clues?"

I perked up. "That's why we're here?"

"Not precisely. Dr. Jones is a patron of this particular traveling circus. Why?"

Behind the wagons and tents, a show of ballerinas in pink tights and clowns in half makeup, scratching their baldheads, orange wigs in hand. "Anastasia almost slipped doing that damn somersault on the chestnut horse again. I told the boss she wasn't ready," a man said.

"If Jonesy doesn't pay us this week, we're done." A woman with long white hair wearing a butterfly costume trudged past.

"Jonesy?"

"Shh." Bedford squeezed my hand.

I eavesdropped on every grumble now.

"Where the show happens." Bedford pointed to a man making sugar glass.

"I wonder if the glass-eating Lydia fancies lemon or vanilla."

"Ya ain't supposed to be back here, gent," a strongman called.

Bedford flashed a pass. The strongman whispered to another and left us alone.

"The candy butcher," a tattooed woman said, making me gasp.

"A candy butcher is a seller of red lemonade and candy." Bedford offered me his bag of popcorn.

"What did you show the strongmen back there?" I asked.

"If you knew the secrets to all the tricks, you wouldn't see the show."

"Um-hmm."

"I have a special pass today."

"Your gun?"

"No, Miss Essie. Today, I'm an inspector of sorts."

"I see."

After a tall man tipped his hat to us, I realized, Bedford had an in, and the purpose of our intrusion backstage at this circus: searching for Houst and Trailer.

"You already know they're not here," I said, looking.

"Better you remained all smiles and agog."

The gathering of half-costumed clowns, led by a dwarf, hustled to confront us.

"We're blown. We'll search the games." Bedford nodded to the tall man; he stopped the carnies from confronting us. "You promised no Lady Pinkerton."

"Why bring me if you don't want my help. Lord a mercy, I can't help it if you give yourself away. You're distracted."

"No. I'm enjoying this with you."

"What?"

"Romance."

"Indeed."

Bedford found a flower seller, bought a pink rose, and handed it to me.

"Don't you ever give up?"

"You said it yourself, Miss Essie, I must win."

A flush warmed me. "I can't picture Houst or Trailer playing children's carnival games. Let's see the wagons."

"Essie Mae, wait!"

For the first time in weeks, I felt free, skipping as a child through the circus sights: lights, balloons, acrobats, clowns, and musicians. I headed for the line of vibrantly painted wagons, searching behind me for Bedford. Forgetting myself, swept up in celebration, terror stopped me.

I lost him.

"You shouldn't be here," a man whispered.

A lion's roar startled me. I peered around the back of a tent to the sight of a row of white horses and women sparkling in silver costumes. I circled back to the freak show again. This time, it frightened me to view it alone.

My heart stopped.

"Essie."

At the sight, I ran into the nearby woods.

"Essie!"

I broke my promise to Bedford, but I couldn't stop running. My foot hit a log, and I stumbled, tumbling across the grass. I hadn't fled as far as I imagined. The colored wagons and crowd blurred between the branches.

Footsteps.

I scrambled to stand, lurching back into the woods, the shadows. I ripped a sleeve, my flesh, on a branch. I imagined a hand gripped me.

I didn't imagine the voice.

"Go back. You shouldn't be here."

"Trailer?"

The hand slid off me.

"I'm Amos. I remember you. He said if I wore this yellow cowboy hat and scare ya, get ya to leave, he won't hurt Mum. Go home . . . Essie!"

I screamed.

No one heard it over the crash of music and revelry.

"He's running away. Sebastian! Please. Trailer? Amos!" I fell to the ground, flailing for the light. "Please."

A scuffle of softer steps. He slowly approached.

"Essie. I'm here. It's Sebastian, Essie."

I curled into a ball at the base of a tree.

He hid with me.

"I heard a man's voice. I did, Sebastian. I thought it was Trailer."

"Wait here."

I clapped my ears at the gunshots. "Sebastian!"

He raced through the woods behind me, then to the street. "A man with a scarred cheek," he said to someone, winded. "No."

"Guarded the woods all day like you ordered, boss. Nobody passed me. Nobody."

Bedford returned. "Essie, no men came into these woods."

"I heard gunshots."

"The circus. The games."

I curled up tighter. "Maybe they hid in the forest before your man stood watch. He sounded like a child, said the name Amos. Dottie said Amos is Jeanie's son."

Bedford disregarded my news. "Did you see a man?"

"No. I only heard a voice, but a hand grabbed me."

Bedford picked up a broken tree limb. "A fresh break. It ripped your sleeve. You're bleeding. That's a deep cut."

I hadn't felt the sting until he held my arm. "A man was here. He warned me to go home. He knew my name. I'm not crazy!"

He kneeled beside me. "It's all right now." For the first time in five years, Bedford's voice trembled.

"I'm sorry," I whispered, my voice not my own. "I'm so ashamed. I'm sorry."

"It's all right." His hands slid under my body, unfolding my arms and limbs. He checked my arm and tied his kerchief around my wound.

I swiped the dirt off my dress, sitting against the tree. He waited for his invitation, moved closer, and sat beside me. I tucked my chin to my knees, avoiding his stare. "You weren't going to walk us past those wagons. You knew. The chained man . . ."

"It's an act, Essie. He's all right."

"The African man, painted, held in a cage, wild. His hands rattled the bars. He stared at me so . . ."

"We shouldn't have come."

"I shouldn't have fled. Raised by wolves, saved by Indians; locked in a cage for money."

"It's a show, a novelty."

"Not to me."

"What can I do?"

"Listen." I reached for his hand.

He helped me stand. We walked along the edge of the woods, the town in view.

I inhaled my pink rose, finding solace, sliding my hand into his. "Three days . . . two dirty hands, four, eight—dirty men, dirty desire, greed, lust, a place in the woods, my lost sanctuary. I do not have the heart to tell Evie the smell of evergreens sickens me. I loathe the sight of a forest cove and a bed of pine needles; the sounds of a creek used to soothe me. The smell of James's bonfire, the smell of men, their touch, looks, whispers—fill me with dread. But I'm relearning, waking to their comfort."

"Good."

"You've helped by bringing me here. I'm sorry I ran."

His gaze stayed on me as we exited the woods to an isolated walk back to the hotel.

"I once knew who I was in the speeches I gave, Sebastian. I believed my words. I professed the men who stole my body didn't take me with it. They did. Bit by bit. I am thankful. I do not remember them all. Grant's abuse was enough. Do you understand?"

"I understand he's dead and you're alive. It doesn't make you less, it makes you more."

"More what? Desirable, wanton?"

"Beautiful, brave, strong, pure."

"Pure? Is it possible?"

"It is to me."

"Sebastian, I long to feel again, not shame or grief. I used to spy James stroking Katie's cheek." Sebastian pulled me into our carriage. His hand brushed my cheek, my lips. I fell into his tenderness. "And smiled at the innocence of her blush at James's touch, her desire." I closed my eyes, remembering. "His kiss, tender, soothing; it made her right, something in his kiss."

"Love."

"Love is childish."

"Not when it is real."

I stopped him from holding me. He inched back, respectful. I raised his hand to my cheek, searching his eyes for trust. "Jeanie's expecting us."

"Yes."

I placed my hand on his chest, moving inside his vest to feel his heartbeat. "Sebastian." I moved closer, grazing his lips with mine, wondering what he felt when I kissed him.

"Essie, I will never imagine what life was for you, but I will believe what it can be, good, purposeful, and safe."

He kissed me under the moon cast in Katie's blue, and I closed my eyes, feeling safe, free, and loved by a good man for the first time.

33

ESSIE MAE

"I'm sorry I missed you this afternoon. I hear you met our little Dottie and had a fine time at the circus." Dr. Jones acted cordial all evening, too cordial. I rubbed my injured arm Bedford had bandaged, hiding the unsightly bulge under my shawl.

Dr. Jones readily spotted pain as Delly did mischief.

One annoyance rattled Willow—Bedford's pistol. Whenever Bedford's hand neared it, Dr. Jones flinched, smiling at his own hand landing on his hip as if he too wore a holster under his jacket. Bedford hadn't forced the subject of Miss Katie, Westland, Houst, or Trailer. He didn't have to. It hung over the dining room, shading Jeanie's dazzling table setting.

Bedford sat patiently, puffing a cigarette. I never witnessed Bedford smoking, except for a hazy memory of a pipe with the newspaperman, Mars. Bedford tossed the flirtatious, protective persona he wore with Jeanie and simply watched—me.

His stare changed since our kiss.

I relished it.

Willow Jones embodied Westland all by himself, sitting at the head of the table, making me feel small. A power Willow didn't know he possessed. Or did he?

"Many visit me for answers, hope, and healing," Dr. Jones said at the start of dinner.

Bedford played contortionist, arching around the truth, restraining himself from confrontation throughout the meal. The grotesque display dropped a false peace over Dr. Jones, who, perhaps by now, assumed our visit was an overdue reunion with Jeanie. Lil was right. Willow remained a dapper man, he knew, tall and thin, typically clean-shaven, but tonight he wore a peculiar sliver of a mustache and thumbprint goatee resembling a swashbuckler in a play. He looked younger than his sixties, commanding the room as soon as he swaggered into it.

Dr. Jones clung to the distraction of Dottie's presence. Bedford wished the child left an hour ago. I made matters worse by mentioning Wren and Abigail to Dottie. Talk of a new sister and life in Mobile preoccupied the meal.

Before my eyes, a magic trick befitting the circus, I had distracted Bedford. He relaxed, enchanted by Willow's memories of Westland and prattling charming antidotes of when I was a child. With every tale, wielding the gift of his soothing, tender voice, it was as if Dr. Jones had given Bedford an elixir to lull the beastie asleep.

At Dottie's departure, the charming Willow lost his brilliance.

For a humble inn, Jeanie dressed the table for formal dining akin to Lil's affairs: silver candlesticks, crystal glasses, a tower of fruit, gold urns stuffed with pink and red roses. "Love, we don't have twenty guests, though royalty, only two," Dr. Jones said, clearing the dishes.

Jeanie slapped his back, then tossed him an apple. "Show them your juggling, aye?"

Willow squeezed the apple as if he wanted to throw it at the wall. "My wife thinks she's a duchess. She's queen to me."

Jeanie smoothed the edge of the lace tablecloth, a woman who spent a lifetime dreaming of acceptance and elegance from a society who judged her harshly. In Ashland, Jeanie accepted herself, proving it was never too late for grandiose opportunities and dreams. "Next year, we'll build cottages near the springs. The well-to-do will flock again, and Belle's is ready for them."

Willow glided back into the room with the tea service. Jeanie behind him with a large cake, missing two slices. "Dottie couldn't wait."

I faked a laugh.

Bedford stayed quiet, studying Willow.

Willow rubbed his temples, bothered by pretense. Jeanie pranced in a garnet silk gown with black fringe fit for a ball, rubies sparkling around her neck. I wore the elegant yellow gown, Delly insisted I pack, for Jeanie.

"Bonnie dress," Jeanie said to me, pleased, spinning Lil's pearls around my wrist.

Bedford and I stared at each other from across the table. Willow's sing-song of the Wilcox's genteel past at Westland rang hollow, embellished with as much opulence as Jeanie's table.

Let him stew, Bedford said on the train.

"*Miss Katie and Evie trust Dr. Jones implicitly.*"

"*Why all the guilt and secrecy?*"

"I'm curious, Detective Jarrell," Willow shouted, making me jump.

Bedford noticed and sat beside me. "Call me Bedford, Dr. Jones."

"Willow." Tipsy, Willow squinted at Bedford. "What motivates you in your line of work?"

Bedford opened his watch; my signal to stay quiet. "Miss Essie will attest, I don't dance. I'd be flinging hay at that circus. Not an artistic talent in my bones."

Willow lit his pipe and offered Bedford another cigarette. Bedford declined. "I once knew a woman," Willow continued, "who, later in life, discovered she had the voice of an angel. Imagine what she could have accomplished in her youth."

"Why in her youth?" I asked, forgetting myself. Bedford let it pass, focused on Dr. Jones.

"The stage is cruel that way. The circus is not. Young, old, the circus accepts all into the family. Belle, the elder angel sings."

Jeanie laughed from the next room. She popped in. "My sister and her moment of fame. Oh, she'd still be traveling in that wee circus if she hadn't thought better of it and hitched herself to Ben." She offered coffee, pushing my plate of cake in front of me. "You boast a handsome figure, Essie Mae. Go on, I baked it special."

My stomach wanted sweets like a child castor oil, but I choked down a hunk. *Divine.*

"There it is," Jeanie purred. "That smile. Sweets always calmed ya."

Jeanie waved Willow's pipe smoke away with her kerchief, snatching it from his hand as a naughty child. A flash of temper burned across his face. "Not in my dining room." Jeanie's kiss cooled his blush.

"Son, you read people as a fortuneteller reads cards," Willow continued. "So do I, in a way. But it's those tells I've missed that haunt me. You?"

"Tells?"

"A mild fever a child shakes in minutes ends their poor life. Monsters who walk this earth as gentlemen. Ladies as temptresses, feigning innocence, yet, in the dark revel in lewd behavior."

At the slam of a window, Jeanie left the room.

"Love," Willow called. "Excuse me."

Bedford and I sat in silence. A few whispers and whimpers later from our hosts, Jeanie and Dr. Jones returned, sitting quietly as if nothing happened.

"Forgive me," Willow said, swirling his napkin.

Jeanie rose and stroked his cheek. "Best I leave ya now," she said, taking her exit.

"You may recall, Essie Mae, I am a doctor of few words. I relish my quiet life and work."

"You were nothing but kind and gentle at Westland."

"Oh, I can't string words like you, Essie Mae."

"In his crude way," Bedford interrupted, "Dr. Jones is saying, disease never lies."

"Right, son. It exposes every secret. Except one, the psychiatric wreaks havoc in my work. A healthy man convinces himself he's dying. A woman swears delusions will harm her, staying locked inside a house while she and her beautiful garden withers. Essie Mae, believe dear Delly would preach at me now."

"Lord a mercy, Willow, she would. For God has not given us a spirit of fear, but of love, power, and a sound mind. I cannot recall the verse, to Lil's imagined chastisement."

"I can't either. We know it where it counts. In here." Willow patted his heart.

Bedford rolled his eyes.

"You taught us that long ago, Dr. Jones."

"I tried."

Bedford pressed his praying hands to his lips, watching Willow stuck in the past. "This quiet life you seek, Dr. Jones, roared before your time at Westland."

"You've done your homework, son. The circus."

Jeanie appeared, racing to close the windows on this warm night.

Our travel, lingering task, and fright from the circus exhausted me. *Focus, Essie Mae. Don't quit now.*

"You'll speak more freely in the parlor," Jeanie said, eyeing the windows again.

Dr. Jones took her cue. "Yes. Privacy." Willow held out my chair and offered his arm.

"I'll be in the kitchen." Jeanie winked at me.

Bedford stayed behind.

Once in the parlor, unlike our visit with Jeanie, alone with Willow, I sat stiff in my chair, covered in my shawl, chilled.

Dr. Jones noticed. "Warm night, but I'll light a fire."

"No," I snapped.

Bedford entered.

"You often had chills as a child," Dr. Jones said, leering toward Jeanie's nude portrait. "Katie worried. You needed iron pills, remember?"

I didn't know what he was talking about and only nodded.

"No, you wouldn't," he said. His charm resurfaced. "But you got yourself in a pickle pilfering spoonfuls of Katie's blackberry jam."

"Yes, my weakness."

Bedford leaned back in his chair, amused.

"More so, for the tummy ache cure, my homemade cream soda. A marvelous, smart girl."

"Katherine Wilcox trusted you with her life," Bedford said, shocking him.

"Yes." Willow turned instantly sullen. "We all know I failed her on that account." He exhaled, ridding himself of the weight of unspoken words. "Essie Mae, Katie hoped you would visit me. And your friend, Abigail Fitzpatrick in Mobile, prospective mother to Dottie, kismet."

"I didn't mean to speak out of turn. I was so excited to tell Jeanie and Dottie." *A distraction*, Bedford wailed in my thoughts.

"I trust you, Essie Mae. Naturally, we'd like to meet the parents. Talk of Abigail's Irish mother won Jeanie."

"Abigail's son died in the war. Her daughter, Wren, is seven, bright and sweet."

Willow's eyes glistened, staring at me as he did the day of Katie's funeral. "Perhaps, Dottie and Wren will need and save each other as you and Evie."

Bedford tapped his foot, eager to resume his interrogation. But in our grief and hell I've endured, finding a family and home for Dottie served as a silver lining.

"I'll wire Abigail tomorrow if it's agreeable," I said, nodding to Bedford.

Bedford finally spoke. "Abigail is an upstanding woman, Dr. Jones. Her husband, a rising star in politics. It's my business to know the people who get close to Katie's family."

"Yes. I'm aware. Why you're here now."

"Dr. Jones . . . what can you tell me about my mother?" I asked.

"Katie said you were smart, but I hadn't calculated you'd return here to find out."

"Is this why you moved to Ashland?"

"He moved here for me," Jeanie said, standing at the door.

Willow's temper boiled over. "I've never hid behind a woman. I'm not about to start."

"Yes, sir." Jeanie left.

I sat astonished by Willow's flash of anger and Jeanie's submission. Bedford smiled, entertained.

Willow brushed his hand through his salt-and-pepper hair. "Forgive my manner. I'm tired. My wife understands me."

"Fretting? Spells?" Bedford said. "We're all tired, Dr. Jones. Let's to it."

Willow noticed my trembling hands. He held one. "Jeanie's right. That trembling isn't from what you suppose, Essie. In stress, you've always needed a bit of sugar for your blood."

I took the candy he offered.

Bedford rose and opened a window, anxious at Willow's avoidance.

"If you're not worried, then he's not here," Willow said of the opened window. "Houst." Willow offered me a blanket. I waved it away, not him. My smile softened him. "We'll do anything to protect loved ones. Jeanie means well. It's her instinct."

"I was grateful for her mending, Dr. Jones."

Bedford cleared his throat at my constant interruptions until he saw my hands shaking.

"Does your heart flutter, Essie Mae?" Willow asked.

"Sometimes."

"You poor girl. You deserve tranquility."

"And answers."

"I'll do my best."

"I owe you my life, Doctor . . . the bullet wound in my shoulder. One night, I heard you whisper regarding an infection . . ."

"I rather not speak about that night."

"Why?"

"Because I was a coward. I should've never left Westland. Where do I start?" He glared at Bedford.

"That circus in town," Bedford replied, unmoved.

Willow circled the parlor, closing the window again, asking Bedford to sit. Willow stretched across Jeanie's chaise lounge, her portrait in full view. Noticing, he threw the drape closed in disgust. "My wife cherishes her fame. I've run from mine." He laughed, out of place, time. "A windjammer is a circus musician. A talented, drawing clown will clear near a thousand dollars a week, and a traveling circus is a wagon show. That far back, son?"

"As far as you need to go."

"I'm beholden to Katie's last wishes. I broke my promises to her in life; I refuse to in her death."

"Westland's in trouble," I said. "My life is at stake, Willow, if we don't find Houst."

"Houst wouldn't hurt you."

"Strange. He orchestrated kidnapping Essie Mae." Bedford leaned in.

"Is Houst my father, Dr. Jones?"

"Only Isabel knows." Her name stuck to the back of his throat. "How do you know Houst ordered Essie's kidnapping?"

"Jeanie told us."

"Oh."

"What does that mean?"

"She told you what she heard. It doesn't make it fact."

Bedford jumped from his chair and marched up to the played-out Willow. "Are you going to give us answers, Dr. Jones? Because if you're not, you've wasted our time."

"I haven't been able to come to terms with Delaney and what he's done in years, why I stayed away from Katie. I thought it best."

"Why, damn it?"

I held Bedford back.

Dr. Jones walked toward Bedford. For the first time, we saw the gun at Willow's side, a pearl handle, gold-tipped. Willow snatched it from his holster. Bedford's hand clutched his. "Don't do it, son."

"I'm not your son." Bedford stepped back.

Willow snickered, flashing his gun, spinning and twirling in a marvelous sideshow.

Bedford wasn't amused.

"Let's all take a breath and sit." Dr. Jones holstered his gun. "All right?"

Bedford had placed his body in front of mine. My arms wrapped around his back, clamping his chest. He released me, gingerly placing me on a chair as a doll.

Willow tossed his gun on a table. "It's not even loaded. I suspect you saw that. But now I know where you stand. Good." He yawned and stretched on the sofa. This cocky man wasn't the soft-spoken, mild-tempered Dr. Jones I knew. "Used to have a fancy rig, red vest and boots, hated that costume. I'd give anything to wear it one last time and perform with my family."

Bedford examined Willow's gun and chucked it back on the table. "The circus?"

"You didn't travel to Ashland to hear about my past glory. I practically raised Houst . . . and Isabel." He locked the parlor door. "I was so proud of Katie and her odd family everyone called it, bonded not by blood or race, but love and acceptance. The circus, society's castoffs, *freaks*, were my family . . . once."

"You had exemplary parents," Bedford said, envy in his voice.

"Yes." Willow choked on the word. "A wayward son too proud to return home." He walked to the mantel, staring at an old photo, piquing Bedford's interest. "Me, the sad bloke next to the dancer. How many fool boys leave good families for folly?"

"Are you a dead shot?"

Willow removed a rifle from the wall and looked down its sight, aiming it toward the window, then at Bedford. Bedford didn't flinch. "Trick shots and killing men, two different skills." He returned the rifle to the wall. "When I met Alex Wilcox, he convinced me my hands were meant for something else."

"A surgeon?"

"Yes, but I hadn't the discipline or money for medical school. My father taught me to shoot, and, alas, I sing a dandy's ballad: a woman stole my heart. A dancer. I joined her circus, to my father's consternation. She left me in Sweet Water. I was seventeen and alone."

"Alex found you?"

"Yes. Polly Koontz visited Sweet Water to sell her stories and visit her sister, Hazel. Hazel ran a home sheltering lost and found children she called them. I reunited with my parents, worked for Hazel as her hand that summer, and met three other children: Isabel, Houst, and Trailer. I was the oldest, and we were inseparable until I started college."

"Where did Houst come from?"

"Houst was a grunt in the same circus, an enigma. He hid his sleight of hand skills until the boss let him swindle the crowds for big money. When Houst cheated the boss, they left him in Sweet Water. Away at school, I learned Hazel tried to reform Houst. But he corrupted Isabel, teaching her cheap tricks for coins. Rumors swirled regarding young Isabel and men. Against Ruth's wishes, Alex brought Isabel, now fourteen, back to Westland."

"Did Houst follow?"

"No. Alex wouldn't hire him. Houst disappeared, drifting from circus to circus. I hadn't seen him until he returned to Westland with John Winthrop as an arrogant, bitter young man I scarcely recognized."

Unlike at dinner, Willow avoided my eyes now. He rose when I walked toward him. So did Bedford, following on my heels. I stood in front of Willow, the rifle on the wall overhead. "Is Delaney Houst my father?"

Willow morphed back into the compassionate Dr. Jones, caressing my arms, his tender blue eyes slick with tears. "I don't even think Isabel knew."

"Trailer? John Winthrop?" I screeched the desperation I held all evening. "You're a liar!"

"Poor dear. When I saw you on the stage in New York, you took my breath away you resembled her so. Now, you look at me with those strange hazel eyes . . . I cannot guess for you. There is no way of knowing for certain, but your father is white."

Dr. Jones caught me before I fainted.

Embarrassed, I waved him off, crumbling into my chair.

"Perhaps Essie should rest, Bedford. I'll have Jeanie take her to a room."

"No," I said. "I'm not leaving."

"Isabel's behavior ruined many men. I'm sorry, Essie. Your gift or curse, dear child, is you know the answers to the questions you ask, a gifted child, an intelligent woman. You always knew, didn't you?" Willow asked.

"River said something was wrong with Isabel to make her . . ." I glanced toward Jeanie's portrait, shifting my gaze to the floor.

Bedford hadn't cleared his throat or checked his watch. Respecting my need for answers, he let me continue.

"A woman who used men? Promiscuous. There was an incident with Isabel *bathing* at River Koontz's creek."

"River confessed it."

"Yes, well then, you know Isabel wasn't the same after that. She had deficiencies and trauma as a child, which worsened the brain injury. However, I couldn't be certain, but I believed Isabel suffered from a split personality, the medical term, dissociative identity disorder. One minute she's as a thoughtful child, the next a lewd woman without morals or control."

"I don't believe you," I said, my body curling into itself.

"For pity's sake, Dr. Jones, you're scaring her. Isabel was her mother."

Willow rushed to me, kneeling beside my chair, trying to get my attention. "Essie Mae, Isabel's mind was damaged, perhaps at birth. I don't know how her mother died, and the tragedy of losing her father, Luby, added to Isabel's trauma. But she learned because she had intelligence beyond her years, like you. Polly made her well."

"I have no more questions." My voice monotone, mind absent.

"I promise you. Right now, your mind seeks the pieces of a puzzle. It will come together in time." Willow shook his head, admiring me. "A wonder, your mother suffered so, yet you, a genius. Your mind's only limit comes from you."

"And if it doesn't come together? Will I go mad, like my mother?"

"Never. Isabel played a dangerous game, using her wiles, bathing as she did. Did River say Houst also watched her that day?"

"No."

"He didn't save her."

"Bo did."

"No. I did." Willow retrieved his pistol, running his finger over the pearl handle. "I followed Isabel after River alerted me to her behavior. I had planned to treat—save her . . . somehow. Bo helped me get Isabel back to the house to care for her so it wouldn't—"

"Look like you had done something."

"I couldn't let Alex send Isabel back to River. Polly had died; River was mad. Isabel wasn't safe with him alone. And there was the incident with Katie's sister Sally at Ruth's lake."

"Sally almost drowned too," Bedford said.

"Because of Isabel."

"Why Alex sent her away the first time," I said, shaken. Chills swept through my body.

"Alex sent Isabel away because he couldn't trust himself."

Bedford edged his neck back at Willow's claim. "Convenient, Dr. Jones, no one is alive to rebut your accusations."

"Think what you will, Detective. I'm telling the truth."

"What about you?" Bedford asked. "A handsome man, Isabel by every account a Venus."

"Preposterous."

"Was it? You happened to be at the creek watching Isabel, too, yes?"

Willow didn't answer.

"Did Katie know John wasn't my father?"

"No. She always believed John was your father until recently." Willow sneered at Bedford, who now stood at the window, staring into the moonlit woods. "I told Katie the truth. She deserved peace."

"I thought I did too. Evie's right. More answers, less peace."

Willow joined Bedford at the window, strangely putting his arm around his shoulder. "Yellow fever struck our valley. Helpless. It killed Polly, some hands. Alex was weak, Ruth weaker. Katie returned from school, mature and beautiful. Yes. I loved Katherine once, not as I do Jeanie. I promised Alex I would watch over Katherine, and I failed."

"What does this have to do with Houst?" Bedford unlocked the parlor door.

I gathered myself to leave.

"You don bleed like we do."

I stood stuck in the middle of the parlor.

Bedford raced up to Dr. Jones and grabbed his collar. "What is this?"

Jeanie burst into the parlor, coaxing Bedford off Willow. "No, Sebastian. This is why you brought her to us."

This is why you brought her to us? "What does she mean, Sebastian?"

"Doc knows what he's doing," Jeanie said, ignoring me. "Trust Jonesy."

Dazed, Bedford pulled me along and snapped, "You do. I don't."

"Please." Jeanie tugged my arm from Bedford's.

"They don't bleed like we do, do they, Essie Mae?" Willow asked.

I shrugged off Jeanie's grip. "Why would you say that?"

"Careful, Dr. Jones."

"River's bullet into your shoulder, types of wounds: perforating, laceration, burn, rupture, hemorrhage. In Essie's case, she was lucky old River didn't blow her little shoulder off. One inch. The infection alone, she should have lost her arm and there was the severe nerve damage in her neck. You couldn't speak for a few days. Adrenaline carried you that night."

Bedford gasped. "My God."

I can't speak, feel anything now.

Dr. Jones's voice lost its warmth, horrifying me. "If you hadn't been on River's horse, his horrendous aim, bullets would've blazed over your head like fireworks. Heaven forbid, a few more inches, into your skull."

"Is this necessary, Doctor?" Bedford whispered.

I hear you.

"Some watered wine; you were a brave, strong girl. I took care of you. You trusted me once, Essie Mae."

I cowered near Jeanie's portrait as Willow walked closer, extending his hands. He stopped, waving his hands for me to calm as if approaching a flighty horse.

"What does that have to do with now?" I asked.

"Trust. I understand men have broken it for you. I have always taken care of her."

"Tried and failed, but I blamed none of you but—"

"Your father because he shouldn't have left you."

Cautious, I sat back in my chair.

Dr. Jones pulled an armchair and sat in front of me. "I've been shot a time or two," he said. "Once, as a boy, by my own gun. At first, it burns like a hot coal, then the nerve endings grow numb; shock sets in. If you're lucky, the bullet travels clean through, like it did to your shoulder, Essie. Complications of fragments and . . ."

"Scars."

"Scars can feel as painful."

"They never fade."

"Yours didn't, did they?"

"You know they haven't."

Bedford stepped closer when Willow leaned into me and rested his hand on my knee.

I let it linger. "Why didn't you tell me you came to see me in New York?" I asked him. "You never saw my speech. Miss Katie sent you to consult with the Morgan's doctor regarding my condition, didn't she?"

Willow nodded, shifting his eyes to Bedford. "I came to New York to kill Houst. Is that plain enough for you?"

Quiet.

Bedford walked closer, standing behind me now, enlivening Willow.

"You don't want to know the truth," Willow shouted. "Essie Mae, you remain blind as River. Yet, how you run wild, free."

"Free," I whispered to myself. "Free!"

"Child, many died, so you might live. If you only knew; we dreamed for you."

I leaned into Willow now, brushing away his hand. "Nightmares! You've always made us suspicious. You acted too perfect, Dr. Jones. I saw you. You returned to Westland after John died. Your jealousy of James struck you blind. You slithered to Katie in the night. I saw you try to make love to her, and she spurned you. You laughed and laughed, and you *ran* without saying goodbye to us, didn't you?"

Dr. Jones rose in a rage and tossed his chair.

Jeanie screeched, scooping it up like a pet.

"Your mind is playing tricks, Essie Mae," Willow said. "As it's doing right now. As it has done these past years, hasn't it? You're hallucinating and hearing voices."

"I saw plenty. I saw too much."

Willow calmed himself with deep, quick breaths, clinging to the mantelpiece, the photo of his past.

"So did Evie, didn't she?" I asked.

Bedford held me.

"Don't you dare." Willow hissed like the old African.

Bedford gripped Willow's arm, stopping him from approaching me. "That's enough."

Willow eyed his gun on the table, me.

"It's empty," I said.

"A wise woman once told me, it's not the families we are born into; it's the family that finds us, the ones we create."

"Don't. Delly isn't here to rescue you."

Dr. Jones's age arrived. Gone was his swagger and charm. He exhaled and sat again in front of me. "Do you want to live, or do you want to waste everyone's life avoiding the truth, as we did? People died, so you might live, Essie Mae?"

"My mother died, and I might as well have died with her. And you killed her. That is the guilt you carry, the guilt that drives *you* mad."

That stopped him.

Dr. Jones glowered at Jeanie, walked to her portrait, opening its curtain. "You're wrong. If you believe, you standing in this parlor, our home is for nothing, I can't help you. Why did you come to me? Why are you torturing me by bringing up my past?"

"Because I deserve the truth!"

"You don't deserve a damn thing if you won't fight for it."

"I'm tired of fighting. I can't, don't you see?"

"Trembling hands can still accomplish much good. A troubled memory, will sort itself out. Your heart hasn't changed, has it? No, because you're risking your life for the ones you love. So have I."

"You protected him, you coward. Delaney Houst was as your brother, as James protected John." I faced him, wanting to slash that dirty portrait.

Jeanie had closed its curtain and collapsed on the sofa in tears.

"And that's it," Dr. Jones said, comforting his wife. "Blame will get you nothing, girl."

"Don't call me that." I rushed toward him.

"Why, girl?" He stood in front of Jeanie, protecting her as Bedford had shielded me.

I searched the parlor, unable to see Bedford. The room pinwheeled in a red and white haze; crystal chandeliers flickered before my eyes.

Dr. Jones's hands steadied me, cradling my body as a newborn. I imagined him plucking me from my mother's wound, bloodied, screaming. But his hands felt warm, safe, despite my mind telling me he was anything but.

"Because I have a name," I said louder. I pulled away, standing on my own. "I am a woman. I am not Isabel. I am not my mother. And I am whole. I. Am. Free."

"That's it, Essie Mae. Good."

The thud of our bodies collapsing in our seats resounded in unison.

Jeanie was the first to rise, finally opening the window. A cool breeze swept through the parlor, scattering the dust of our past.

"Whose side are you on?" Bedford asked Willow.

Dr. Jones violently grabbed Bedford, snatched his watch, and opened it. "Hers!"

The room spun in a swirl of red and black; runny paintings on the wall. I crumbled onto Jeanie's seedy chaise lounge, laughing, crying . . . screaming.

"My ears won't stop ringing. It's too loud. Dr. Jones, make it stop."

He pressed a cool rag to my forehead, steadying me upright. "You slept for an hour."

"Am I still in the parlor?"

"Yes," Jeanie said.

"I'll ready my carriage and take you back to the hotel."

"No, Dr. Jones . . . Willow," I said, coming to myself. I pleaded with Bedford.

Bedford didn't hesitate. "Essie is strong enough."

I welcomed Willow's company now. I couldn't sort out what happened yet, but I felt something had lifted.

"It's coming back to you," he said. "In pieces, but the truth is coming to your mind. It will travel fast now. You may not absorb it."

"Doctor." Bedford stopped him from approaching me.

"All right. I'm here to help." Willow handed Bedford his hat. Bedford refused to take it. Willow snickered. "You're reading Houst all wrong, son. The villain isn't Houst, it's your own mistrust of each other, including me. That's Houst's gift. Take the blackmail and shuffle it with distraction."

Bedford whipped around at Willow's statement. "What did you say, man?"

"Desperation. Distraction. The Take. The oldest con . . ."

"In the book. Three-card Monte." Bedford turned to me. The shock on his face sent terror through me. "Houst needed to appear unafraid, making his brief appearance at Westland, and he used Lila to do it. First, he needed to know Westland survived the war."

I sipped the glass of water Dr. Jones handed me. "Patience," I said, right-headed. "Houst knew how to bribe the right lawmen then, but the war changed the South. The law shifted."

"Shuffle," Dr. Jones whispered, scaring me.

"Dear God," Bedford said. "Westland, Essie . . ."

"Evie. Oh, Bedford! It's Evie . . . she's the money card." I took hold of myself, remembering. "But she's on her way to Paris. Evie's safe with Lil."

Bedford held up the wire from the general store. "She didn't leave, Essie Mae. Evie stayed for James. She's at Westland."

"What will Houst gain by taking Evie?" Dr. Jones asked, skeptical.

"Ransom. Gold."

"You're the one," I screamed at Willow. "You and your talk of family. You protected Houst all these years. You could've stopped him! What was your cut from his filthy blackmail money? You spited Katie for rejecting you. What did you get, you bastard? Money. Revenge?"

"Essie, no. Dr. Jones helped us," Bedford said, trying to calm me.

I fought them both. "Leave me alone. Why are you protecting him?" I felt my mind shifting. *Like my mother*, I thought, horrified. *Like my mother!*

Jeanie entered at my screams. "Drink this, deary. You trust Jeanie. We're here to help, not hurt you. You trust Jeanie."

"You went too far," Bedford said.

"No, lad. She'll be all right now."

I reluctantly sipped the fizzy white drink, the parlor spinning. Her perfume turned my stomach. I closed my eyes at the sight of the smug Dr. Jones. "I bleed now, old man."

"Essie, I didn't find out about Houst blackmailing Katie until you did. Believe me, if I could have found him by now, I would have. I've hired every wagon show I could think of to locate him. The circus was his perfect hideout."

Jeanie held me, soothing with her mothering touch. "I've watched my husband spend a fortune, searching for this man. Before you think one way, lass, Katie's the only woman I've been jealous of all these years. And yet, she helped me and Jonesy live again."

"I promise." Dr. Jones's soothing voice came back in focus as a gentle wind reminding me of the noble doctor of my youth. "It's all I ever wanted for you. So much so, I could stop you both right now."

"You could try," Bedford said, keeping an eye on the rifle.

"Why would you do that, Willow?" I asked.

"Because you two have a chance at life. If you return to Westland, he'll take it and this will all be for nothing."

"Why didn't you tell me you saw my speech in New York?"

"I told you. I didn't come to see you, but to kill Houst. It's the last time I saw him. I was too late. I knew he'd try to find you. With your name in the papers . . ."

"Houst did," Bedford said. "Come, Essie, we need to get to the station. We must leave now."

"I'm going with you." Willow kissed Jeanie, grabbed a pair of hidden pistols, and dashed upstairs. "I will meet you at the depot."

I pulled away from Bedford and ran after him. "Wait, Dr. Jones . . . River said, on the night I was born, the night River was struck blind, he heard you say, 'I told Katherine I'd get them on the steamer.' Who?"

"Isabel and Trailer."

34.

ESSIE MAE

"Poor dear."

I crumpled as a rag doll onto the bench at the depot, waiting for the train's arrival. A slip of a cloud drifted in the night sky; a golden halo around the moon.

"Essie." I dreamed Bedford's caresses smoothed my skin, stroked my scars. His whisper chilled my ear. "You're safe, darling. Safe."

I awoke in a moment, an hour. I hadn't known. My body wilted on a bench. My neck lopped over, my eyes drowsy, spying my satchel. The train's whistle howled in the distance.

"I don't believe a word Dr. Jones said, do you?"

"He's not here, Essie. He didn't show." Bedford tried to wake me. "He's no part of this now. We are—together."

"All aboard!" the conductor called.

"Come." Bedford lifted me and helped me onto the train. "She's all right," he said to Sal.

"Miss Essie," Sal said, taking my other arm.

The last thing I remember, closing my eyes to walnut panels, cobalt velvet curtains, and a green silk duvet.

"Sebastian," I whispered.

He sat next to my bed, his eyes heavy. "Yes, Essie Mae." My name sounded sweet from his lips, sweet and silky as honey.

"Show me your watch." I strained to keep my eyes open, but I clearly saw his grin as he opened the back. I sighed at the photo. "I knew."

"Sleep, Lady Pinkerton. We'll arrive at Westland soon."

"I knew."

"*Chulosa.* Peace."

"In my rose garden, the night Lila came to Westland, you promised you wouldn't let any harm come to me, and asked me to trust you. Why did you bring me to Dr. Jones?"

"Because you deserve to live free of him."

"Trailer? The old African?"

"No . . . all of them."

35.

EVIE

For the past two days, I awaited Essie's return, falling asleep to a snare drum of rain pinging across the glass roof of the greenhouse Mama hoped would usher in new beginnings. I clutched mine, rushing outdoors. The morning sun stretched across Westland, swallowing the dew. I tilted my face to the sky, savoring its warmth.

"No more hiding," I whispered, wondering if Mama could hear me. "No more running."

Resolve quivered through my body, anchoring me to Mama's Westland. "*Chuka.*" James's Choctaw word watered my spirit. "Home."

Westland was quiet, everyone anticipating James's return and Houst's whereabouts. Young Bear brought the welcomed news of Essie Mae and Bedford's arrival posthaste.

I fiddled with the telescope stationed under Bo's new gazebo. "I can't wait for Essie Mae to see it."

"How you know I coming?"

"I trained my ears to warn me of your march, Delly."

Delly labored up the steps and sat on the swing. "Don't know how ya look at stars and swing, but it calming. Katie's mama Ruth loved stargazing."

"You can't swing and look through a telescope. You view the stars standing. And that swing doesn't belong in here. Where'd it come from?"

"Bo surprise me with my Christmas gift early. Cut-out hearts in the woodwork, see?"

"It's marvelous."

"Bo gonna haul it to the back porch after Tom's barn raising. James say we can't go traipsing off to the gardens right now, so I ask Bo to set it here till Essie Mae come home."

The elms almost bare; gold and copper leaves carpeted a path to Mama's garden. "Home. I understand now, Delly."

"Good." She slapped her hands into her lap and closed her eyes. "You gonna stop planting strawberries out a season, worrying old Delly? No more muttering to yourself bout what you gonna do? I enjoy seeing ya playing with Sky in the yard. You look happy, child."

"I am, even during this storm."

Delly sighed. "Child, you fretting the stormy sea like Peter. You ain't getting it in here." When Delly pressed her belly, she meant her spirit. "You will." She closed her eyes and sang to Heaven, "Yea, though I walk through the valley of the shadow of death, I will fear no evil; for You are with me. Your rod and Your staff, they comfort me."

I looked through the telescope at a blurry blue sky.

"Fine spot for a wedding, hmm?" Delly asked.

"Fiddle-faddle." I stared at the ceiling, pointing to the straw stuffed in the rafters.

Delly grinned. "Fine wedding chapel and home for a fat mama robin. And don't you look at me 'cause I past the age caring."

"I didn't."

"You don't need no pretty li'l lips to sass me. Them buggy green eyes do it for ya." Delly patted the swing, inviting me.

I snuggled next to her. "I'm worried about James."

"We all battle Houst in our minds now. The way he like it."

"James wouldn't have left us alone if it wasn't safe, right, Delly?"

Delly tucked her finger under my chin as she did when I was a girl seeking my attention. "As long as you keep looking back, don't matter who leave or stay, you ain't never gonna feel safe. Sooner or later you gotta trust and live life."

Live free. "I'm writing in Mama's garden today. I don't feel like a party."

"You know what James say. You to stay in the house."

"He also asked me to find Mama's strongbox. It could mean everything."

"Don't mean nothing. Why you mama give it to ya when you a girl. All you do is stuff it with them newspapers and toys."

"Toys!" I popped up, jostling Delly. "That's it, Delly. I could kiss you." I did.

"Go on, get! Bo already at McCafferty's. Young Bear's gonna stay and watch ya. Tom's wife, Astra, waiting for me to bring my cakes. Bes go." Delly scrunched her forehead and looked at her shoes—her tell for hiding a secret.

I eyed her as she sauntered up to me, fixed my collar, and flipped the gold key around my neck, abandoning the fight to keep me in the house. Tom's carriage arrived. The driver helped Delly fill it with food baskets and cake boxes.

All I could think about was Essie, James, and the disappearance of a strongbox.

The potting shed.

At James's request, I hadn't visited Mama's garden in weeks. I couldn't resist remembering the odd disturbance of the potting shed in Mama's garden, my old toys, Lil's gold match case, the book on the chair waiting for its reader, and the key around my neck. In the flurry of Essie leaving for Ashland, I hadn't thought to badger Lil about it.

My heart quickened, seeing Mama's garden gate wide open. "I should've brought Sky. Where are you, boy?" I walked inside.

Storms scattered the last of fall's glory; sticks and wilted blooms covered the stone path; the pergola of pink roses withered and done. I brushed the pile of dried petals off Mama's bench, startled at the sound of her voice.

"Where's the black girl seem stuck to ya?" Astra said, shielding her face with the green scarf attached to the same sunhat from the first day we met.

"Astra? What are you doing in here? You're supposed to be at your barn raising."

Astra hid in the shadows, raking leaves. "Folks fancy romancing in a garden, sniffing roses, cooing bout colors, but they don't do the work. We do. Where's that girl?"

"Essie Mae?"

Astra inched into the sunlight, wearing a lilac party dress covered with a garden apron. She slid back into the shade, huffed at my inspection, and curtsied. "I ain't fit to meet her?"

"We've caught you spying. Bo said . . ."

"Sugar! Bo said—you run things now, girl. What you say bout it?"

"I came here to find peace, not you." I turned my back to her, staring at the fountain stuck with curled pink rose petals.

Astra crushed an armful of dried leaves into a barrel. "Dead things give life."

"Go away," I mumbled. "Why are you gardening in a party dress? You're balmy."

"Whooee, Katie say you a ball a fire. Can't figure what that mean till I rile ya."

I set my journal aside. "Why did my mother hire you?"

"Maybe she do. Maybe she don't. Next time Delly bark bout stormy seas, ask her if she'd get out the boat and walk on the water? She like telling, but she don't like answering."

"You don't make sense. Your eavesdropping is going to get you into trouble, Astra."

"My eavesdropping gonna save your life."

I ignored her and sketched Mama's lavender rosebush.

"Wanna help is all." Astra shuffled her boots in the leaves. "Delly getting on; you don't wanna see it. Other day, she hold one a my pears say it an apple."

"That's a story."

Her cackle chased the crows. "It did be my pink pear." Astra dropped her rake and gloves onto a pile of leaves. "My tricks ain't working to bring ya no smiles. You forlorn, miss?"

"I need quiet and miss Essie. She's arriving any day."

"Nobody visits this garden for quiet 'cause Katie talk too much in here."

"Talk?"

"She whisper." Astra kept her distance. "Her roses talk, too, saying I thirsty, too much sun today, I'm tired, so tired."

"Like you?"

"No, ma'am. I'd work all day. Work keep my mind sharp and body strong."

"You've done a fine job. You surely brought comfort to Mama. We're thankful."

"Why, Miss Evie, that's the first soft word you speak to me since you come home. But then, I don't give folks much reason to speak kind words." Astra picked up a small shovel and started digging near Mama's lavender rosebush. "The big bee flies high," she sang. "The li'l bee makes the honey. The black folks make the cotton. And the white folks get the money."

"Why aren't you home with your husband Tom, Astra McCafferty?"

"You think using my full name make me tell ya? Well, maybe I will. Maybe I won't."

"You're trembling. Your hand . . . it's burned."

She scrambled to find her gloves, grimacing as she shoved them on.

I spotted thick scars around her wrists. "You best let the doctor mend it."

"No doctor gonna mend anything this time."

"Why are you here?"

"Tom say I can stay away, miss. I . . . I don't take to crowds. People don't like me."

"You sound like River."

"Ain't nobody sound like that daft old bastard."

"How do you know?"

"Tom try to do for him. River snubbed us like most, judging I'm a black woman not fit for marrying no white man. Bo don't tell ya bout my sad days 'cause they keep pretty belles away from horrors."

"Stop it."

"Katie don't fancy sitting with me when the roses dried up. When she young, she see a blue spider; stopped visiting her garden for weeks."

"Dried roses in a garden aren't pleasing, especially when they look sickly."

"You talking bout that girl . . . Essie's roses behind the barn. Bo shoo me away, but I sneak in there. Near bring me to tears that fungus swallowing them roses."

"Go home, Astra."

She started digging again. "Dried petals be handy. I know things, miss. Bet I could conjure a use for every fold in a rose. Rose petal jam, rose honey, rose syrup." She shoveled and pitched dirt furiously now, the hole deep enough for a root ball of a small tree.

"That's enough. You're gonna kill Mama's lavender roses if you keep digging like that."

"You in a lather today like Katie when she missing her true love. No need for melancholy bout dried roses if they ain't sick. Ain't no use for sick things. Rose beads and potpourri." She eyed the key dangling from my necklace.

I hid it under my collar. "If you won't leave, I will."

Astra threw a pile of dirt blocking my path. "You ain't leaving, Miss Evie, 'cause you still wondering bout me."

I searched behind me for the rosebush, shrub, or tree she was planting and found nothing but an empty wagon and her barrel of leaves.

"Supposing Tom's serving beers now. I tell him wait until after the build so the men don't nail the roof on crooked." Her green scarf flittered in the wind. She peered at me as she walked to an iron table set with two glasses and a pitcher.

"Who's the other glass for?"

"You." Astra poured the orange drink and handed me a glass.

"What's this?"

"Something that'll calm ya. Peach honey tea. My mama's recipe, but I add smidgeon a pear and rose syrup."

I sipped the tea, surprised by its refreshing flavor. "It's good." I sat on Mama's bench, feeling sorry for Astra, an outcast.

"Pleasing, ain't it?" She walked toward me, nearly sitting on the bench across from me, reconsidered, and dipped her hand in the fountain, staring into her handful of rose petals. "Old medicine man tell me rose water be purifying." She downed the rest of her tea like a shot of whiskey and slammed the glass on the table, keeping her back to me. "When I young, I chase a peddler's wagon near a mile. Steal five dollars from my missus. I was gonna give it back. Bought all his rose water and wash every inch a me so I purified. Delly say God do that with a whisper a believing, but I don't know that prayer."

"Hogwash. If you know Delly, she'll pray it over you and make sure you know."

Astra sniffled, picked up her shovel, and smoothed the fresh mound of dirt. "Can't fool, Miss Evie, no ma'am. You right. But I don't believe it. I can't 'cause I do too many sinful things. My mind say I'll never be right, not for what I done." Her voice changed, deep, dark.

"I should go back to the house. Young Bear's waiting."

"And that dog. Where's the gray collie? Sky don't like me."

"Sure he does. Unless you hurt him . . . or me."

"Rose water, honey, and butter make a tasty roasted chicken. I recite a poem when your mama restless. 'You that exhale so sweet an odor, are you the rose?' 'No,' the leaf replied, 'I'm no rose, but I lived near her, hence the sweetness I possess.' Miss, I know things."

"Enough!" Astra had intrigued me, but I needed to search the potting shed, alone.

She reared up at my shout, twirled, and curtsied again. I couldn't stop watching her. She waved me off and resumed her digging.

Why are you digging that hole?

"Tell ya my secret, Miss Evie. Secret potpourri, Damask rose petals, orange flowers, lavender, pine needles, marshmallow flowers, mint, be your mama's favorite. Lull her to sleep."

"Why are you doing this?"

"Never needed Bo nor no mongrel to protect me, this pepperbox my friend a long time." She revealed the pistol from her apron and stuffed it back into her pocket. "You need not fear me, girl. Doc Jones taught us to shoot well enough, don't he?"

I scrambled to the gate, stopped by her words. "How do you know about that, Astra? Nobody knows about that?"

"Ah, Doc teach ya too, don't he?"

"I've never told a soul, not Essie, Bo, not even James, I can shoot." I eyed her, unafraid.

She looked away, tugging her green scarf across her face. "You think you hold secrets round this place, girl? Nobody do. Secrets be the ghosts howling in the night . . . howling now. Ain't no storm rising. It the dark things we stuff away, screaming, nagging, chasing."

"I'm going to the shed. You best be gone when I return. I'm not afraid of you."

"You hiding a pistol too 'cause Willow don't never teach ya to turn your back on a stranger pointing a gun. But I ain't no stranger. We friends. Miss Evie," she called, bringing me back. "That li'l gold key ain't for the potting shed!"

My breath skipped at a flurry of movement at the edge of the juniper trees. I marched back to Astra. She stood over a small metal strongbox that sat in the hole she dug.

"Calm yourself, girl," she said.

I sidestepped her touch. "You found it."

"It find us."

"I used to lose myself for hours, imagining what was inside that strong-box until Mama gave it to me, sharing her childhood treasures. 'Yours now,' she whispered." I looked over my shoulder as if Mama stood there.

"Help me lift it, child."

We each grabbed a handle and, with a final tug, hoisted it from the dirt.

"What's in there, rocks?" *A pirate's treasure chest*, I imagined, slightly smaller, the metal box embellished with brass hinges and flourishes. I brushed off the dirt from crumbling inside, turned the key, and opened the lid. "Heavens."

"Seen many treasure boxes in my lifetime." Astra stepped away. "A few moist kisses and a sultry voice set a man aflame to prove his worth . . . mine for the taking. Jade boxes, gold, silver caskets, but wooden crates tucked under the bed hold the most."

Skeptical, I examined her, the strongbox. Astra squirmed as a child antsy before me. She snapped her gaze toward the gate. A flock of swallows landed in the trees. "Mama trusted you?"

"See, I know things. Knowed where it be the whole time. Truth is we're both still here."

"Both?"

"That box and me. Ain't ya gonna read it?"

It should've been my hand to pluck the scrolls tied with red ribbons.

"Was Mama here . . . in the potting shed? I saw red ribbon and paper."

"Host a folks and memories live in that shed, girl. I'll watch the gate. You go on now."

The scrolls shook in my hand. I searched down the path to the magno-lias. The path to the potting shed cleared of brush, the antiquated structure in sight.

Its door open.

I ran and stepped inside, overcome, picturing Mama sitting at the table, writing her words. "I can't, Mama. I can't."

Astra stood at the potting shed's door. "You must, child."

She closed it, locking me inside.

36.

EVIE

I sat at the table, staring outside through cloudy glass panes in the door, Astra no longer in view, the air in the potting shed stuffy and warm. My hands shook, imagining Mama here. The tabletop cluttered with soil, pots, new life ready for planting. I traced my finger through a trail of dirt, pausing at a thumbprint left behind in a pile of black soil.

The past held me captive. I cringed at Astra's singing while she gardened without a care.

Singing ceased.

The wind whispered.

Worn turquoise paint flaking from the walls bordered another freshly painted pink, the color of rose water. Weathered garden tools meticulously arranged in cubbyholes, and hanging on the wall, drying lavender swayed from the ceiling. Ivy snaked up the windows, frightening me. The clouds hid the sun, casting the shed in gray.

Two scrolls teetered in my hand. One, a crisp letter rolled and tied with a red ribbon like a royal decree. Mama's handwriting on the outside:

For Evie.

The other, a fragile thin half-sheet, water-stained, torn, also rolled and tied with a red ribbon marked:

For Sebastian.

"Bedford?"

Mama's letter aside, I slipped off the ribbon from the scroll marked *Sebastian*, watching it drift to the floor, and unrolled the delicate paper that read:

Birth Certificate
Child: Sebastian Alexander
born in New York on February 3, 1838
Mother: Katherine Evelyn Wilcox
Father: James Winthrop

"Oh, Mama."

37

KATIE

My Dearest Evie,

No mother desires writing a letter of regret and confession to their children. As I sit here in this potting shed, surrounded by the hope and thrill of planting new life, I imagine many mothers have contemplated the task. Yet, remained silent.

Silence—an easy act that destroys many lives.

I am forever sorry for my silence.

If you are reading this, you are still my mischievous girl, and I am glad for it. I pray a trusted friend planted enough clues, luring you here to my secret garden, to remind you of happier days. My last letter held my wish for you, the key to happiness. I knew you would find it. This strongbox holds the gold and papers you need to keep Westland. I am proof one cannot live well with such secrets. Delly warned us the only good that comes from secrets is when we go on and tell them. Some secrets are so painful one only longs to forget, least of all confess.

Pain and love seeded this garden. How can pain and love grow together in this sanctuary? Why do roses have thorns, my darling? My father created this garden for two girls to thrive in secret—one white, me, one black, Isabel. Its tall fence shielded us from hate and his prejudice. Pink rose petals dance in summer, scarlet in fall, and those surprising rebels shining on their own. As Isabel and I to my father, you and Essie Mae to me, those rebel roses, blooming in their own shades apart from their mothers. I could not build a high enough fence to protect you.

My father arranged my marriage to John, though I loved James. Years before you were born, when Daddy died, John abandoned me. I threw myself into Westland. James and I fell in love again in this garden. John repented, longing to return, but something had happened. I became pregnant with James's child.

I confided to no one, not even Delly. When I grew ill, Dr. Willow Jones and James discovered my secret. I turned to my mother's sister, Aunt Charlotte, whom you know from Paris. Aunt Charlotte arranged for my stay in a country cottage in New York. Westland faced threats. My pregnancy would ruin my father's name and Mama's aristocratic French family, who still held a place in Alabama's society in Demopolis. None of this mattered, for my son had died. I convalesced in Paris under Aunt Charlotte, who refused James's letters.

At my aunt's insistence, I never saw my baby save those first few moments I held him in my arms. James's claim our son had lived turned into an obsession, dividing us. I returned to Westland, broken, focusing on Westland's success.

Willow Jones demanded Augustus complete my divorce from John, and I marry Willow and forget James, in his eyes, the miscreant who ruined me. When I refused Willow's proposal, he left Westland, my secret in his hands. Dr. Jones returned when you were born; misery accompanied him.

I never forgot the rush of life and love that overcame me, holding my son in my arms. Two years ago, a young man entered my chamber with news my son had lived, and I may hold him in my arms once again.

After recovering from the birth and loss of my son, John returned to Westland. Aunt Charlotte arranged our reconciliation. What could I do? I hadn't known what Aunt Charlotte had done, misguided and cruel, ordering her doctor to take my baby and place him with another family. Now my aunt is frail, and I had not the heart to confront her. When you face the end of your life, the past is a vapor. All you long for is one more day in the present.

After the war, when my illness progressed, James confessed his secret. I had not hallucinated my boy, now a young man, had visited my bedroom at Westland. I shuddered at the streak of white in his sandy hair, a birthmark I had only seen once before, his cornflower blue eyes, and swagger as James's. Sebastian had come home.

James's obsession paid off. He found our son when Sebastian was five. James's Choctaw mother raised the boy until a young man. Augustus secured Sebastian's education and position in law. The able clerk turned detective known as Bedford Jarrell is indeed my son, Sebastian, your brother.

For two years, I treasured my son, but I missed my daughters. I could not tell you, my darling. Bedford needed the blackmail to continue to confirm Houst was still alive. I did not foolishly pay Delaney Houst to keep Essie Mae's birth a secret, nor for the truth I believed John was her father, but to protect you from your mother's shame and illegitimate child.

I underestimated Houst's patience. A drifter my father took in as a boy, who returned with John, a charlatan. As many frauds, after John's death, Houst claimed John owed him a substantial debt. Without proof, Augustus refused payment. Houst sent me threatening letters, claiming knowledge of my love affair with James. A bluff I regrettably confirmed by paying Houst in gold for his silence. He never knew my son's identity or that my baby had died. I could not risk it. And there was the matter of Bo. I will say no more regarding this.

When the government threatened to seize Westland and discovered my payments in gold to Houst, I fought until my last breath to ensure your safety. Bedford revealed the horror of what Houst did to Isabel under the willow tree, and that Houst believed he is Essie's father. I do not know the veracity of his claim, but as my adopted daughter, I resolved to end this, hiring and holding the highest faith in my son. James agreed no matter the cost, even if it meant losing Westland, threats against my family would cease.

You and Essie Mae will have many questions that deserve answers. I cannot give them now. Evie, I leave a portion of Westland to my son. I leave him Westland to free you of it, and to give him what he should have received years ago. I have taken care of you, James, Essie, Bo, and Delly. Westland is your decision now.

Now, I see your shining face and dainty finger soothing my tears that stain this page. I have faith in the love my father planted long ago, faith in the One who created this all, and pray Westland and my Evie thrive.

No one can force you to stay, my darling, but I share my last truth to help you decide.

Westland holds more than hate and broken-heartedness. It houses the rich soil to grow amazing things, blossoms that healed us, brought us together, a firm foundation on which to build. One may start over, if one dares to try.

Forgive me, Evie. Forgive me for the pain of your father. I prayed every day for God to soothe your heart, replace painful memories with joy and life. For, if my daughter does not live, then I truly failed. You have a brother, and Westland is your home.

Stay with us, Evie. Stay.

Love,

Mama

38.

EVIE

For the first time, nature's solitude frightened me. A film of tears blurred the potting shed's door, now cracked open. I hid Mama's letter and the birth certificate under the pile of dirt and searched for Mama's strongbox.

Astra kept it.

I ran outside. She sat on the bench across from Mama's under the pergola, swinging her legs as a child, a traveling bag at her side.

"It was you. Where's Mama's strongbox?"

"It's safe."

"You planted the tulip bulbs up the drive and placed the yellow ribbon I gave to Essie on her garden bench and under Mama's magnolias. The cornhusk doll, new roses, freshly painted green benches, all you, Westland's secret gardener. Why?"

Astra kept her head down, staring at her swinging boots. "Some call the blight in a garden a burning, and fire the only way to get rid a disease."

"Astra, how could you. You set the fires?"

She rubbed her burned hand. "Only way to get the law to come, girl. She needed me to 'cause nobody doing a damn thing to save anybody round here."

"Who?"

Astra turned away and removed her sunhat. Her green scarf floated across my shoes.

I saved it.

"Woman tell me a story when I small," Astra said, "'bout a snake who devoured the land until one winter the snake spotted a glittering gold stone. In his greed, he slithered into the hills to find it. He couldn't eat or drink and lost sight of night and day. He searched and searched for that glittering gold stone only to be caught and frozen in a great storm, freeing the people of the snake that came to steal everything."

"Is that what you came to do, steal?" I walked closer to her, searching for the strongbox.

Astra laughed. "If I did, I woulda left last summer."

"That's how long you knew about Mama's strongbox?"

Astra grabbed the shovel and pitched dirt back into the hole she dug earlier. "The li'l bee makes the honey. The black folks make the cotton. And the white folks get the money."

The hairs on my arms stood up. "Delly said Mama hated that song."

"I know. I sing it to rile her."

I examined Astra's green silk scarf; the edge decorated with tiny blue paisleys. "Where did you get this scarf?"

"Still thinking I'm a thief, Miss Evie?"

"Your voice is different . . . you don't sound . . ."

"Like a half-wit? That's what ya called me. Balmy." Astra kept her head down, busy shoveling dirt. "My scarf is from Paris. A gift . . . from my daughter."

I offered it to her. "I didn't know you had a child."

She snatched it back, tying it around her neck. "Maybe I did once. Maybe they stole her."

She noticed me edging toward the gate. "My friend had a scarf like that. Mama liked it so much; she sent it to her from Paris. Mama wouldn't part with it."

"She would if I ask her?"

"Why?"

"'Cause it's all I got to take in the sweet smell a my daughter."

"What daughter?"

"Essie Mae."

I caught my breath. "You're lying." I spied the scar on the left side of her face, ear to chin, like the split on the top of a bread loaf.

"Doc do the bes he could." She grabbed my hand, swiping my finger over her scar.

I tugged it away and walked back to the potting shed. *Mama's garden maze—my way out.*

Astra clutched her shovel and followed me. "Ain't ya tired a running, girl?"

We stopped in front of the shed. "I'm not running."

"Weren't no time for stitching. I can still hear the old man's screams in my dreams when they smash his head and eyes." She picked up the rake nonchalantly back at work.

I grabbed it from her. "I don't know who you are or what game you're playing. Get out. Now! I'll call for Sky. He'll make you leave. Sky!"

Astra cowered, searching behind her shoulder toward the garden's entrance. "You'd never say that if ya see what them hounds do to me."

"You scared me."

"I don't believe in keeping ugly things away from belles like you." She grabbed my cheeks and turned my head to the light, swiping her finger across the red scar near my eye.

I jerked my chin from her grip. "Are you part of the ugly, Astra? What old man? What are you talking about?" I prayed Sky heard my call. *Run, Evie!* I stood stuck, beguiled, terrified. *She knows things about me no one else knows. How? Why?*

Astra held her lip, inspecting me. "Maybe I was part of the ugly once. Nobody wanna teach a black girl like me nothing back then. Toss me like a wilted weed in the trash bucket. Trash . . . that my gift, child. Knowing what I was, but not knowing what I could be."

The grass and sky spun in a whirl, making me wonder about the tea Astra served earlier. I rushed inside the potting shed for a pail. "Leave me. Can't you see you've made me ill?"

"There, girl. Smells like Katie in here, roses and jasmine." Astra sat in the chair, smoothing my hair like Mama.

"I don't want you here," I whispered. "I don't want to know anything more."

Astra stood over me, crying now.

I jumped up to leave.

She blocked my path. "They say my wicked ways steal men's souls. I get the rose water, Miss Evie, to purify myself. Then I meet Trailer, pretty boy, good boy."

That stopped me. "What do you mean? You're mad."

"Doc say I got the skin make thick plum scars like a licorice rope. Scars fade on pretty white skin like yours. Not on my daughter neither. Oh, she got the terrible scars. I spy em."

"Your daughter? Astra, let's go back to the house. We're both confused. Sky! Sky!"

She slapped her hand over my mouth. "I see that girl's scars, pink, purple, and brown like a bruised apple."

I wiggled from her grip. "Essie Mae?"

"No, she got no name. She That Girl like me. When I a child, I don't even know I gotta name for a long time, so I call myself That Girl, 'cause that's what Miss Ruth call me." Astra stood before me, arms folded, smiling. "Won't hurt ya. You ain't leaving. You curious bout me."

I shook my head. "You won't let me leave."

Astra stood aside. "I won't keep ya, but you bes stay. Told ya, my eavesdropping gonna save your life—if ya trust me like Katie. Evie's a curious, frightened thing today."

"I'm not a thing."

"Fussbudget too. Bo get me he know I here. He sting like a hornet when he wanna. Purr like he giving out the honey, then *swoosh*, dive in to bite."

"Bees don't bite."

"They sting. Hurt like hell. I watch a woman die right fore my eyes, wiggle like a worm, then she go to Heaven."

"I don't believe a thing you say. You make up stories."

"Bewildering gaze wiggle across your face like that woman on the ground."

"Stop it."

"Don't ya wanna know who blue woman be?"

"No," I whispered, peering back at her.

"My mama." She lifted her chin to the sky as Essie and I knew.

Lord in Heaven, I knew.

"Truth be, my mama don't die from no bee sting. She die 'cause Daddy beat her."

"Astra . . ."

"No, that ain't true. Daddy kind sometimes. Mama kill him. Maybe I do it. I remember rain. I hate the rain, do you?"

"No. Rain brings me peace."

"Rain brings death. It killed my daddy."

"Luby?"

"Doc say, when I see Daddy fall off the cliff, I go mad. I ain't insane. Polly tell me I could be somebody someday no matter I black as the soil. She say, good, that's the soil that gives life. Why don't we grow beige flowers? Only with a frost. That's the color of my girl, ain't it?"

"I don't know."

"See, you staying, Evie, 'cause something rolling in ya mind. How do I know bout you learning to shoot and why did Katie trust me with that strongbox?"

"Yes."

Astra pointed to two garden seats. I wandered to one, searching for Sky. We sat on the stools under a sprawling oak. She lowered her head. Tears dripped down her skin into the groove of her scar. "He say go to creek after sunrise, twice a week . . ." She swiped her tears. "Wash with rose water, then I clean. Maybe I know men be watching. Maybe I don't."

"I need to get back. James will be looking for me."

"No, child. James gone. I know who you be—me—'cause I see me in your eyes."

I left her, returning to the potting shed. "I'm no sad child, Astra, nor a sad woman. You stole my toys, planting mischief. Why?"

"Do what I'm told. Been doing that since I'm eight, till I leave here, till they send me away, till they steal me . . . and her."

"Who?"

She raced up to me. "My baby!" Astra's scream pierced through me. "I figure it take forty years for that rose water to purify me. Katie say it weren't no rose water, but God and forgiving. She the only friend I had in the world. I leave Westland so John don't kill her nor my baby. That's why I leave. And I gotta live with it the rest a my days."

"You're not right, Astra. You need help."

"Nobody wanna give it to someone like me. But I come here to keep a promise to someone I love. I learn what love be too late, child. Maybe it's too late."

"It's never too late to love."

"Then maybe you love me someday. You close your eyes at Westland, child, you can hear all them secrets a moaning with the wind. Sins Katie wants buried with her, and it break my heart to know em. I. Know. Things."

"You're Houst's woman, aren't you? The woman who swindled with him in New York."

"Paris, the circus, gambling houses . . . wear me a feathered dress like a flamingo. I float in looking for a swell, mine in minutes." Her chocolate eyes, wet with tears, failed to hold my gaze. She rubbed her hands together, sloughing off the crust of dirt. Her green scarf flew across the grass as she fell to the ground, sobbing. "I can't do it no more. I shouldn't have come, Katie," she whispered. "No courage. I'm old, worn, sick, tired."

I kneeled beside her and wiped her tears. She snatched my hand, frightening me, and held on. Quiet, we walked to Mama's bench under the pergola of roses. She sat beside me as a child, squeezing my hand so tight it stung.

"It can't be," I said, tears rising in my voice.

"It can if you want it."

"Does Delly know? Bo?"

"Katie don't want em to know. Never."

"How?"

"Listen and don't look at me with them judging eyes."

"You hurt a lot of people. You were dead. You'll hurt many more."

"No time for explaining. Your mama trusted me; you best too if you wanna stay alive."

"I don't trust. I never did."

"Girl, everybody at Westland hide something from somebody to keep em safe. Even you now. Don't fetch James. Gimme time. I'm not asking. I'm telling."

"What are you going to do?"

"James protected Katie. Katie protected you. I protected Essie Mae. Ain't no different now. You protect me till I see my girl. She here. She looking for River but it gonna be me she find. Please, child."

"Why should I do this for you?"

"'Cause I love Katie more than anyone in the world. Look in my eyes. You know it's true. I keep my baby safe, hiding, letting her go like Katie tell me. It kill me inside."

I could barely see her through my tears. "I don't believe you. I don't . . ."

"Go on then. Run, child! Hide yourself in Katie's garden. They won't find ya here." She snapped around to the garden's entrance, back to me, tears streaming down her cheeks.

I held my breath, eyeing the vibrant flowers in Mama's garden, the letter in my pocket, the woman before me now. *Trust.* "I don't understand. Are you in trouble?"

"He's already here. I know it."

"Houst?"

"Fool woman, this ain't where he told us to meet." A man stood before us holding a shotgun, his faced slashed with a thick red scar across his right cheek.

I gasped. "Trailer?"

"You ain't supposed to bother me. You promised," Astra shouted. "I'm handling this."

The man grabbed my arms and shoved me on the path, lifting my feet off the ground.

"Who are you?" I asked. "James will never pay! Do you hear? James will never pay."

"I'm Trailer, River Koontz's son." He stepped into the light. His scar shined in the sun.

"You won't get away with kidnapping me like you did Essie Mae. The law will make you pay. They know you're coming. The soldiers are . . ."

He stopped, turned me into him. "I'm not taking you, Evie. I'm hiding you from him. Come on."

"From Houst? Where is he? Essie!"

"Fool woman followed me back to Westland. Stupid doctor told; that's what happened. Stupid fool. Can't do much about that now." Trailer shoved me inside the potting shed and locked the door. "Stay down," he yelled. "I'll stall him," he muttered to himself.

"Let me out! Let me go to her." I ducked at the glimpse of Astra, swirling her hand across Trailer's back, whispering in his ear. Trailer looked back at me, motioned toward the trail to Koontz's farm. "Lord, please keep her safe. Keep Essie safe."

"Houst come to steal ya. He'll burn this place down they catch me. Do what we say."

"Why are you doing this?"

Trailer didn't give a glance at Mama's strongbox. He ran toward the secret trail to River's footbridge as if he remembered the way. Astra ran the short route to River's farmhouse.

"What's going on? Let me out!"

He'll burn this place down they catch me. Do what we say.

When they left me alone, I saw the top of his fury head. He barked and growled, jumping at the door. "Sky!" He popped up again, clawed at the soil. "Get back, boy."

I grabbed a shovel, broke the glass, and unlocked the door. "They're at Tom's. You won't know where that is or how to fetch Bo. Wait. The azalea bushes. Come, boy."

I found Bo's rifle and ran faster than my legs would let me.

I ran.

39

ESSIE MAE

"We're home, Essie."

I awoke to Bedford's whisper.

"It's quiet," he said, scanning the grounds. "That's good."

"Is it?" The first thing I noticed as our carriage entered Westland's gate: the new white gazebo where Miss Katie's willow once stood. "Lord a mercy. Would you look at that."

"Hmm, perfect spot for a wedding, eh?"

"Indeed. Whose wedding, Mr. Jarrell?"

A peck to my cheek his answer. "James wired everyone's at Tom McCafferty's today. Evie is with James. We shouldn't worry now."

"Evie doesn't know?"

"It wasn't my story to tell . . . not yet."

As we walked into the house, I closed my eyes, inhaling the smell of Delly's gingerbread, imagining her warm hug. "Let's skip Tom's barn raising. I'm tired."

"I agree."

Two of Bedford's men appeared in the dining room. I nodded at them and walked to a window, glimpsing a flash of a soldier's blue uniform. "Are the soldiers here?"

Bedford held up his hand, quieting me, listening intently to his men.

"No harm in a walk?" I asked, hopeful.

One man raised his voice.

"Of course, Essie. Stay close. I'll be in the study." Bedford continued whispering with the men. Distracted, he hadn't argued to keep me home or under his guard.

I sneaked away.

I needed to see River.

"Essie!" Bedford called.

Jasmine was fast. I took the carriage to bring River back with me. It was time we all became a family again.

River's farmhouse appeared as quiet, his front door open. His rocker on the porch teetered as if River rushed inside. "You old cuss!"

Quiet.

I smiled at the colored streamers draped over the railing and above his front door. He painted a sign in pink crooked letters. I couldn't stop my tears, picturing River seeing, painting. It read: *Welcome Home, Smiles.*

The homecoming he wished we had before our trouble.

The porch held a woman's touch. *Evie.* Small pumpkins and potted marigolds decorated each step. A posy of pink roses rested on the rocker next to his—my seat. I spotted something else, a ragged wreath of mugwort and juniper hanging on the door, the one Lil rejected. "Clodhopper superstition," she said. "Mugwort and juniper do not protect us from evil men."

A fresh wreath sat on River's seashell table, yellow and red roses, violets, and sprigs of periwinkle. I inhaled its perfume and hung it on his door, tossing the mugwort. "It can't be." I breathed in the roses again. "Miss Katie's roses. Who made this?"

"Me. *My* roses."

I slowly turned around, startled by her delicate voice. A woman scurried under the shade of an apple tree, her face covered in a green scarf.

"Do I know you?" I called. "Have you come for River's table?"

The woman ignored me and started picking apples.

I recognized her now. "Astra?"

"No, miss."

"Why are you picking River's apples? River!" I called toward the house.

"He ain't here, child. They all at Tom's barn raising. Tom, my husband. Not by law, but I live with him after the war. I'm his wife all the same." She curtseyed, scrunching her fine lilac dress covered by a worn, dirty apron.

"River knows you? Please, stop picking his apples." I paused at the bottom of the porch steps, hesitating walking any closer.

"You look like the sun rising on a spring morn in that yellow dress, blue ribbons pleasing. Ya fixing to go to my party?"

"Why aren't you there, Astra? Why are you picking River's apples?"

"They'll rot. He like em sour for his cider, too sweet now." Astra stepped into the sunlight and untied her scarf. A gust of wind snatched it from her. It was too late for her to chase it. It whipped in the breeze, flying toward the creek.

She let it go.

Hand to her hip, her other smoothed the soft curls off her forehead.

I gasped and dropped the frame hidden behind my back. Glass shattered on the step.

Astra rushed to clean it.

I backed away.

"Don't fear me," she whispered.

I flinched at her touch.

"Please. I'm no ghost like ya suppose, child." She stepped aside.

I kept my eyes down at her boots, trembling, leaving the photograph of my mother in the grass, watching the wind flutter it into a pile of leaves. When I finally looked up, her brown eyes, slick with tears, gazed into mine.

We said nothing.

She raised her chin to the sky.

I saw me.

My button nose, the arch in her brows, high cheekbones; she turned, revealing the other side of her face. A jagged scar cracked her left cheek wrinkled and curled around the edge of her lips, reminding me of Trailer's.

"I used to be a pretty belle," she sang, swiping her curls again. "No. I weren't no belle, a fetching girl once." She draped her long black braid over her shoulder.

"Who are you?" My throat felt stuck with jam. I couldn't stop shaking my head, peeking at her, trying to glimpse the photo I lost. I didn't need it. I had studied it on the train to Ashland and back home, tracing her grin over the glass, her hand clinging to Polly's. "It can't be."

"It can if you want it, child."

I recoiled as she reached for me. A fresh burn seared the top of her hand. "You died giving birth to me," I said. "You're not real."

She blew a warm breath across my face. "See, I'm real. I died giving birth, leaving you. Lord, child, you shaking like a skinny willow in the rain."

I took a deep breath, brushed myself off, eyed her, skeptical. "Bedford warned us, after the war, swindlers crawling everywhere like spiders after a rain."

"Night crawlers more likely. Sure enough, folks ripe for the picking. Too much lawlessness for the lawmen to lockup. Sing like a ditty, don't it?"

"No."

"Land sakes, you got Delly's glare. You wrong bout the law. A whisper the owner a traitor, win a plantation in the South. That's what he thinks."

"Who?"

"You'll know soon enough."

"An accusation of treason nearly stole Miss Katie's Westland."

"I beg him not to. Katie too smart for that con."

"Is that what this is, Astra?"

She shook her head and hid behind the apple tree.

"You think I'm afraid of you," I called. "You're afraid of me. Why?"

She bid me come to the spot Evie and I hid in as girls spying on old man Koontz. The evergreens served as River's fence line hiding his farmhouse. Bo cut down two dead pines, providing a clear view of the footbridge over River's creek. I knew every hiding place to spy on old Koontz, the hills above, the tree line, berm, shrubs near his porch, and the apple cove Evie and I played in as children. I scanned my hideouts for movement, leaves rustling, impressions in the grass as Sebastian taught me. The forest was still as my breath.

"Did you make that rose wreath?" I chased after Astra.

She circled the tree, evading me, giggling as a child. "You don't wanna know me," she said, breathless. "I'm gonna leave."

I spotted a traveling trunk and satchel behind a bush. "Are you going on a trip?"

She took a deep breath. "I find me six benches hidden round Westland, in the gardens, woods, Ruth's Lake, by the creek, though I take to water like a fat cat, that mean I hate it."

"I understand."

"River gotta nice bench under his apple tree yonder, li'l splintered. Sit with me?"

"I've only smelled roses like this once before, a rosebush of yellow and red roses in front of Miss Katie's home. That is until Sweet Water, yellow roses tinged with red at a flower shop and one in the center of a sunflower bouquet in Miss Katie's study."

"Like I said, *my* roses. That's my flower shop in Sweet Water. I tell Mr. William buy Miss Evie my yellow roses, but he don't want em, like nobody want me."

I fell on the bench under the apple tree. "Isabel?"

She edged her neck back, searched toward the evergreens, and sat next to me. "More fitting you say mama, huh, child? Say it once for me."

"I don't . . . I don't know you." I shivered as her hand pressed on my back.

She tried again, two taps afraid she would break me. "You do. In your dreams. In that picture yonder fluttering in them leaves."

Dread hit me, but I didn't run. I faced it, her. "Make me understand . . . believe."

She sat on the edge of the bench, squinting at me. "I look at you and see me as a girl a pretty boy love once. You look at me and see you as an old woman."

"You could be anyone, Astra."

"You spy the good side a my face . . . you believe." She lifted my hand to her smooth cheek, and placed hers on mine, stroking it, seeing my face for the first time. "My whole life men take what ain't theirs. Two girls, only good in my world. One had golden hair like Evie. This girl love flowers and running in the woods. Her daddy send her away 'cause the bond we have be a sisterhood like you and Evie. Too much love for him to understand 'cause she white, and I black. Katie saved me. He stole her away 'cause he want that love and kinship."

"And the other girl?" I stood to leave.

She tugged my hand as a child, making me sit. "You." She let me go, rocking herself, staring toward the creek. "On the night you born, yellow fever steal many. I weren't no fit mama, Essie Mae. Jonesy say, only way to keep you alive is I go on leave ya."

I looked back at the carriage.

"Bo and Delly don't know," she said. "I died the night you born, only way to save em."

I studied her every movement. Her fingers flipped her dress; she tugged her earlobes, staring at mine. She spoke in circles for a moment. *Pears. Roses. Katie's last wish.*

"What was that?" I asked, squeezing my eyes shut, trying to focus. A splinter pricked my skin. I thought it was a splinter until she smiled, shoving something in her pocket. My mind played tricks. Lightheaded, warmth surged through my body as if I guzzled champagne.

"Your mind racing 'cause you tired a life and them taking us. I need a smoke . . . a drink. Let's sneak inside River's house and sip his nasty cider. He still make it?"

I nodded, eyeing her apron pocket again; something weighted shifted inside.

"Think Bo know. Bo love me once. Katie . . ." Tears overcame her. "Jonesy weren't sure Katie survive Evie's birth. I don't know what to do. John go crazy."

My body edged closer to hers. "You left me? John Winthrop believed you died. By all accounts you did, Isabel. Your death drove him insane."

"He already crazy, a drunk. Houst drove John mad, like he do me, like he trying to do to you, child."

"I've heard about you and your stories, Astra. This isn't funny."

"I ain't Isabel no more? You pondering if you should stay or leave, girl. You look back at the carriage twice. Katie say no good looking back."

We both snapped around at rustling behind the berm.

"A tom turkey. Ain't that funny," Astra said, relieved. "Look at him puffin his feathers like my husband."

I stood, uneasy, pointed to the carriage, and offered her my hand. "Tom asked me to fetch you and bring you home. He's waiting."

She looked me up and down and laughed. "Girl, a lie gotta sing without blinking or gulping. Delaney says bluffing an art."

"And you've seen the best?"

"Maybe you go on lie to yourself I ain't who I say. Maybe ya should."

"Why aren't you at your party? Where's Evie?"

"She safe, girl."

"I didn't ask you if Evie was safe."

"I ain't no half-wit like they say. It's an act. You know all bout that."

"You're talking nonsense . . . stalling. Why?"

"My missus teach me. I know things, but mostly we act like we don't 'cause white folks don't like no black slave knowing nothing."

"No slaves here."

"All kinds."

"Enough. I'm leaving."

"You hard like me. Good you ain't no easy mark, least I know you fight in this world, not roll over on your back, hide, run away like we did."

"Men will arrest you if you don't leave, Astra. My last warning." I stomped on my mother's photo, rushing back to the carriage. Jasmine twitched and bobbed her head. "There, girl." I paused, scanning River's garden.

"When you born, you got a red star on your forehead, still do!" she called.

I stopped, picked up the photograph, and walked back to her.

She puffed her chest out like the turkey, smirked, and sat on the bench, expecting me.

"No one has ever noticed it." I took my seat. "Not even Delly."

"See. I know things."

"No. You don't know about me. My mind . . ." This time when her hand grabbed mine, I studied it and traced the shape of her fingers. It felt softer than it looked. Dirt crusted her knuckles, but her palms felt soft and warm.

"Don't let him make ya crazy like he do me, Essie Mae. My Essie Mae. You know, don't ya? Know it inside. You can't look at me and think I ain't real, nor her."

"I've dreamed of finding you, mama." I swallowed the word, sharp and bitter as whiskey.

"Isn't that something? Your heart knew I was still alive. You knew."

I let go of her hand. "What happened?"

40.

ESSIE MAE

Now that River could see, he cleared the hedge Evie and I hid behind as girls. The berm above, still a shelter with an unobstructed view of his barn; I eyed it again.

Isabel wrung her hands.

I quieted them, as Evie did mine.

"Katie and Jonesy say it to protect ya," Isabel said. "Don't remember everything, child. My mind plays tricks, too, but ya ain't crazy. You don't let em tell ya you crazy."

"Dr. Jones said you were born with a . . ."

"Nobody know. Jonesy act like my papa when I a girl, but when you born, he take ya and warn us, we to never return to Westland, or John will kill Katie, Evie and you."

"We?"

"Houst, Trailer, and me best never come back. We cause enough grief in this valley, and you and Katie deserve peace. I ain't no fit mama. Jonesy say I the wrong kinda woman. Westland a monster, ain't no sweet land for raising nothing, few roses is all."

"You're wrong. I know it now. Isabel . . . is Trailer . . ."

"Your daddy?" She sighed. "I spy me a pretty boy once from that grassy berm you keep watching. Trailer work his inventions in the barn and sleep in the sun on the porch, jig, too."

She showed me, hopping and jerking her body. I wasn't sure what to make of her, but I believed Dr. Jones now. Amidst sweetness and sorrow, danger simmered inside her. I felt for the pistol in my pocket, the one Sal had given me. I couldn't remember if it was loaded.

"Willow said I twisted men's minds with my wicked ways," she said. "They twist mine."

"What about Trailer?"

Isabel stared at River's front porch, remembering. "Trailer's mama sit on the porch steps, writing. She teach me reading and writing. River don't like it, 'cause she act like my mama."

"Polly?" I asked, astonished.

Isabel bowed her head, pressing her fingers into a tent, engrossed in the feat of billowing them together like a jellyfish. "I lived with em. Polly let me help her write a story bout Daisy and River Wild. I'm the plum dragon." Isabel covered her scarred cheek when she smiled. "You ever love somebody, Essie Mae? Feels like you sinking in a bed a rose petals on a cool spring day; it hurt, too. You ever ache like that, child?"

"Yes." I lifted her burned hand. "The fires."

"Had to—only thing bring the law here. You gentle with me?"

"I never blamed you."

She left me and held herself up under the tree. "Pity like a bucket of weeds, useless." The smooth side of her face still revealed a beauty. Her scar, our horrors, fused, sinking in my stomach. "Abandoning my baby a pain that never leave."

"The night of the slave auction, you escaped and left me with Bo and Delly."

"Willow's doing. John feared Bo. Bo kept ya safe. Don't recall how I got to Paris."

"Why did Willow call you the wrong kind of woman?"

She sat next to me again. "Be pleased ya call me mama again. Suppose it too much to ask. We don't got much time."

I searched the grounds, still no movement in the brush. The horse stood quiet at the carriage. I could even hear the ripple of the nearby creek.

"Jonesy say I tempt men 'cause I yearn for loving. I only love one man, till he leave me."

"River's son, Trailer."

"You all lit up inside. Maybe your hazel eyes scare the truth outta me." Isabel darted her eyes to the berm, barn, and house. "Trailer a handsome man with a head a corn silk hair. We stay up all night under the stars, talking bout his inventions. River called him a do-nothing boy. Trailer my first . . . love and things." She bowed her head, clicking her thumbnails together.

"What things?"

She giggled. "Loving. But it weren't nothing like what them other men do, taking me."

"Rape?"

She puffed a breath buzzing her lips. "Foul word." Her voice changed deeper, older. "Strange, yellow rapeseed flowers sway in fields all round Westland, hundreds—all that lemon against the blue sky." She stroked a sky-blue ribbon dangling from my sleeve. "Trailer say rapeseed called Brassica napus."

"Do you remember what happened with Delaney Houst under the willow?"

Her fingernails dug into my arm at my question.

I snatched it away.

"You forget the men who rape you, girl?" Her voice, cold, dead.

"Some."

"No, child! But your mind's powerful, tucking that torment away. One day it'll spill out without your say." She left me to pick apples again.

I stopped her, held her hand as a child, leading her back to the bench.

"Delaney and Trailer fought over me since they young. Houst and Willow like my brothers, the only family I got. Jonesy watched over us like he our pa, till he leave for college. I lived in the foundling home Miss Hazel run in Sweet Water. Charitable woman, but she can't tame Houst."

"Why did you stay with him? Are you with Houst now?"

Isabel fetched her trunk and satchel from behind the bushes. "Houst discover I love Trailer. Houst think he raise me when Jonesy left, but when I'm a woman, Houst steal me under the willow 'cause I tell him me and Trailer leaving. Houst ruin me so Trailer won't want me."

"What about the creek, bathing for men?"

"Don't remember. I dream I'm drowning and hear Bo and Jonesy whisper I dead. Doc pump the water outta me. Delly scold I bes get right bout Trailer 'cause no white man, especially no balmy River, gonna let his son marry a black girl."

I pressed in. "Did you love John Winthrop?"

"No." She swiped her mouth in disgust. "John woulda drowned you in the river."

"Dear Lord."

"John catch a sickness for me, found out bout Houst and me under the willow. John want me since he come to Westland after them days Katie love James. I see it."

"See what?"

"Katie and James loving each other like a slow waltz. She tell me. Katie love me like her sister again in the secret garden I tend for her."

"Why would Katie claim John was my father?"

"Houst threaten Trailer and lie telling me Katie send me far away and kill my baby. Shoulda never believed Katie do no such thing. But she took ya."

"She saved me."

"John returned. We all surprised Katie let him stay. She promised not to tell John bout what Houst do to me. Doc say I already pregnant. I don't mean to deceive her. I figure fore John hurt me, I give him my body so he think you his. Maybe then they let me keep ya."

"Now, that lie didn't sing, did it? You're blinking and gulping. Who are you?"

"Keep running! I'm telling the truth. Trailer told River bout our baby. Trailer say it his."

"You're lying. River said Trailer didn't know he was the father. Things would be—"

"Different? Maybe I don't remember it right. I told ya."

"You don't know who my father is, do you?" My turn to walk away.

"How's a slave gonna fight for her baby when she can't fight for herself? Jonesy, River, and Trailer had a falling-out bout me. River blamed me for his son leaving school. Polly died a yellow fever, making us all insane. You don't know all that old man done to me."

"River loved Polly with an ache we'll never know."

"So did I."

"You're incapable of understanding true love. You wouldn't have abandoned me."

Isabel revealed a pistol and pointed it at me. She spotted my hand feeling for mine, snatched my gun from my pocket, and threw it near her photograph in the leaves. "Katie boast you so smart, but you're a dumb jackass, girl, letting me talk bout all this fluff that mean nothing now."

"Don't do this for him."

"I'm doing it for me. I promised Katie."

She shoved the pistol into my chest. "You trust me, child," she whispered. "Today, you bes decide ya gonna trust somebody . . . trust Mama. Trust like never before."

She labored, grabbing the trunk, pointing the pistol in my back as we walked in the open toward the barn. "You ain't the past and you ain't a name, you a woman," she shouted. "No shame acting like one. But you ain't. You scared, letting folks lead you round like that dog, Sky. But that mongrel don't follow nobody. He lead, like you will again someday."

"What about you?"

"My time's over. I a ghost returning for Katie so you and your pretty man live life."

"What pretty man?"

"Sebastian. Nobody get nothing in this life for free. It cost more than money. The cost hard to pay, but today, I gonna pay it for my daughter like I shoulda done years ago."

I swallowed my fear, keeping my gaze forward. "He's here, isn't he, Isabel?"

She shoved me onward. "All that talk bout forgiving," she shouted. "Hell, that's what my papa thought. Might be me sitting here in a French ball gown, diamonds dressing my neck and rubies pinching my lobes 'cause that's my goldmine. But here I be, a beauty once till that crazy old man slash my face to pieces in the night, tried to calm him from that beating is all."

"Willow told the truth. You left me to catch the steamer with Trailer."

"Houst said if I get him the gold . . . he'll leave you alone."

"Don't do this! Katie spent her entire life paying him. Houst will never leave us alone."

"He was only gonna take Evie to escape the soldiers, get himself on the ship to Europe. He knows they're here, watching. He said Katie's Aunt Charlotte will pay. She paid before."

"It won't get that far, Isabel. Why would you risk coming back now?"

"To kill him." Her whisper sent a chill through my body. "Doc say we do it his way. Let us."

"Willow?" I whispered.

"Essie Mae, you remember the day you free? You give them speeches like you do but it never come."

"What?"

"Freedom. This be it, child." She looked toward the grassy hill where we saw the tom turkey, the berm in view of the barn.

"Who's out there?"

"Me." A short, stocky man walked through his plume of smoke and pitched his cigar.

Delaney Houst hunched over as an overworked hand at the circus in Ashland. His fingers knotted and curled worse than River's. He smirked at me, as if his smile held a boyish charm.

"You look like hell, Delaney," Isabel said, turning her pistol on him. Isabel lost her childish voice. "Always hiding under that yellow hat, lemme see ya."

"You ain't no flower." He tossed his hat at her feet.

Isabel laughed. "You think I'm a fool, Houst?" she called to the sky.

"What's going on?" I spotted red makeup on the man's cuffs. "Your hands."

"That's right, child," Isabel said. "Where is he, Silas? You think I'm stupid?"

Clanking chains.

We froze.

"You don bleed like we do."

"Stop it, Delaney." Isabel shielded me.

A short, muscular man stepped out of the barn through a plume of cigar smoke like his decoy. Only this time, he flicked his cigar at Isabel's feet, lighting the straw on fire.

She stomped it out. "Fool. Wanna burn the place down?"

"That's the general idea. Silas, go back in the barn. See to our *guests*."

"Don't listen to him, Essie Mae."

"That her?" Houst asked, leering at me.

I spied his hands, burned and gnarled. One appeared stuck, curled in a fist, his gun hand.

He shook it open. "Isabel," he said, disappointed. "I knew you'd come here looking for him. You running on me? I took good care of you, didn't I?"

"Sometimes. Don't look at me like that. Compassion left you long ago, Delaney."

"How Jonesy figured it. Willow's damn circus found me. I wasn't fool enough to draw on him, but he made sure I never did again."

"Lucky he didn't kill ya after what you did to me."

Houst tossed the chains, glaring at me now, clicking his teeth like Evie's father. "You agreed to meet me at Westland, Half-wit."

Isabel clutched her pistol. "Don't call me that." She turned the gun on Houst, then lowered it. "That damn detective showed up. Figure the old man's farmhouse safer."

"You find the gold?"

"Over there, in the trunk. We don't need Evie, Delaney. Nobody's here. Just leave."

"You think you're running this, Isabel? Where is it? The deed."

"I haven't found it yet. I was about to."

"With her?"

Sandy hair, ruddy cheeks, short and solid as a bull, he was the man I saw hiding in a carriage the night of Katie's party. His red, broken nose, gnarled as his fingers, looked fresh. Despite her gun, he strutted to Isabel, savoring that his presence made her cringe, and swiped the yellow hat.

I glared at him as he slapped it on his head. "How could you?" I asked Isabel, groggy.

"You drug her? Yeah, she looks it. You said she'd be sleeping by now."

Isabel winked at me and laid me down on the grass. "Yeah."

Houst lifted Isabel's satchel. "Feels like gold. You said you'd bring Evie."

"You promised me time with my daughter. I ain't risking my life for nothing this time."

"Daft woman, maybe Essie ain't even yours. You don't remember a damn thing."

"She mine."

"That's all I needed to know." Houst cocked his gun, pointing it at Isabel. I rose, shielding my mother.

"Essie Mae, no!" Isabel pushed me aside. "Stay out of this."

I stood between their guns. "You won't shoot me, Houst. Soldiers are everywhere. You have no way out."

"Ah, she speaks," he said, amused. "Most of the slaves I captured got their tongues cut out, and I did it." He holstered his gun and swatted Isabel's away.

"Houst ain't nothing but stories, Essie Mae," Isabel shouted.

"Why did you come looking for me?" I asked him. "You could have lived anywhere."

He scratched the back of his neck, contemplating me. "Not with you on my back."

"That's the problem with gamblers," Isabel said. "Delaney can't quit. You ran a good game during the war, Delaney, but you can't let Westland go till you destroy it."

Houst shoved Isabel aside and searched through her satchel. "Heard they burned Westland during the war and the Union would seize it like the others. John owed me. It should be mine."

Isabel stood toe-to-toe with him. "I told ya years ago, ain't no gold in them hills, fool. All them folks you wait to get even with are dead. John, Katie, Alex . . . Isabel."

"Jonesy." Houst snickered. "You never could bluff, Half-wit. Isabel's you."

"No. You killed her years ago."

"I ain't going back to prison. Got me a ticket outta the states. I'm taking it."

"I'm not your daughter." I was used to men ogling me, but when Houst did it, I was She in the woods all over again.

Isabel grabbed him.

He shook her off, stopping himself from drawing his gun on her again.

Isabel held him close. "Take the gold and go, Delaney," she whispered.

"You ain't my daughter, huh?" Houst asked. "She tell ya that? You sound like her, look like young Isabel, smell like her, too."

"Essie Mae, don't listen. Still the same con." Isabel kept her pistol in his sight.

Houst kept his holstered. Standing before her was enough to make her cower. He inched closer to me, shaking his fist open, but it clamped up.

His gun hand is useless. I could best him. I closed my eyes at the thought. Images from the night Grant took She in the woods played in mind. I thought it then, too.

"Isabel ever tell you about that old man?" Houst asked. "Maybe he raped her."

Isabel blocked him from me. "You did."

"All these years later, you're still confused about that night, sugar. Are you telling fables again, Half-wit? I took care of you, didn't I?"

"I'm not leaving with ya, Delaney. You're dying. Seen enough death to know. Can't even hold a gun."

"That ain't no sure bet, Isabel."

"You won enough in that last town. Take the gold. Move on. I'll buy ya time."

I grabbed her. "Isabel, no."

She slapped me to the ground. "Stay down!"

"And when they find out who and what you are," Delaney said, soft and smooth. "You think they'll welcome you back? You think River won't kill you the first chance he gets. What about Jonesy? Nobody wants you, Half-wit."

"I live with a good man now." Her eyes widened as she realized she spilled her secret.

"Why I torched his barn. He ain't for you, Half-wit." Houst rocked on his heels, enjoying this, glowering at Isabel, repulsed by her scar. He leaned into her and kissed it anyway.

She slammed his chest, shoving him away.

He laughed. "You shoulda stayed in Paris, Isabel. You ain't nothing but trouble, always were. You came to me! I ain't leaving ya this time. Let's go."

"You a worn-out cardsharp ain't bluffing me. Hands no good. Can't hold cards or a gun." She raised the gun to his face. "You raped me, made them think I damaged. I followed you to hell and back. Never again."

"You didn't complain until I found Trailer for ya. That the kind a daddy you want, Essie Mae? Trailer's a drunk who sold ya to Grant for a bottle of whiskey."

I buried my face in my hands, spying the chains on the grass through my tears. I thought of grabbing them, throwing them at his face. I couldn't touch them. Isabel's shoes brushed my dress. *I could topple her and run.* The grass buried me now.

"You're no man," Isabel shouted, shaking her pistol in his face. "You're an animal fit for a cage. You locked my daughter in a cage!"

"Careful, girl. I ain't fool enough not to have a man on you. Put that thing away."

I followed Houst's gaze to the berm. No one.

"Years ago, you took something from me and you never looked back," Houst said, checking his watch. "I saw you with him. You were already pregnant when you were with me, weren't ya? You turned John against me, put me in prison."

"You ain't taking Evie, Delaney. That ain't the plan. One last thing I gotta do." Isabel kept her pistol on Houst, and pitched a torch, setting an apple tree ablaze near the barn.

"What are you doing?" I screamed.

She grabbed my arm and held me back. Isabel was stronger than I expected. Rage filled her eyes. "Don't need no soldiers. I'll do it."

"You ain't playing." Houst slowly raised his hands. "You drawing on me, Isabel?"

"You woulda let me die in that creek yonder! I show my flesh for nickels and dimes when I a young woman. You gambled it away and left me with nothing but dirt and filth."

"You're crazy. Always been. Come on, sugar. We're going back to Paris like we planned, living high. All them fancy things you want. I'll take care of you now."

"You stole my baby. You did. Delly say an evil man wait a lifetime to get even—should've said a woman."

I approached Isabel and rested my hand atop hers, lowering her gun.

"How long ya got, girl?" Houst asked me. "Before you turn crazy like your mother?"

"A powerful man, who can destroy you with one hand, raised me. You hate I'm Trailer's seed, but I don't come from a man, a woman birthed me. God gave me life. No man will take it away. You tried once. Here I stand."

Houst folded his arms and scoffed. "This ain't no stage for speeches, girl."

I slapped him. "You're nothing to me. No one. You lose."

"Have I?"

"Amos Quinn," I said. "Do you hear that dog barking? The law's right behind him."

"Amos? Nobody will believe Jeanie's daft boy."

"You were there the night Grant took me and beat Evie. Amos saw you. He'll testify he watched you pay Grant. Was the African real or from the circus? No . . . he was real." I turned away from Houst's smug grin.

He walked closer, cocking his head, studying me. "There it is." His crooked finger landed on my nose. "You don't even know, girl. No fun living like that, is it? Mind . . . twisted."

I covered my ears at the voices of the past, his voice.

"Leave her alone," Isabel said.

"I'm not afraid of you." I looked behind me for Sky and Sebastian.

Houst grabbed my face, turning it toward the barn. "Maybe you're not, but *she* is. Boys!"

A woman's scream sounded from the barn.

Another.

"Hear those screams, girl?" Houst laughed.

"Evie!"

"No, Essie Mae," Isabel shouted, racing after me. "Wait!"

I ran toward the barn. Flames engulfed it now.

I halted at the gunshot.

Isabel fell to the ground. Houst held the gun.

Another shot.

Sky wrestled Houst to the ground. In a haze, Evie emerged from the berm, holding a shotgun. A wounded Houst managed to rise, aiming his pistol at me in his gnarled hand.

A final shot.

Willow Jones emerged from the brush and killed Houst.

We rushed to Isabel.

"Mama!" I screamed.

In the chaos, soldiers encircled Houst's dead body. I glimpsed Sebastian and James rounding up three men from the barn, Silas, a dwarf, and a tall, thin man from Ashland's circus. Sebastian's men swarmed the farmhouse. Bo called the soldiers to douse the flames.

"Trailer?" I heard Evie ask.

"Trailer's out there?" I asked, shivering. "He's here?"

Sebastian threw up his hands in disbelief. "Carnies. Little Jack, Dallas, and Silas, all Houst had."

"River's safe," Dr. Jones said to me, tending to Isabel's wound.

"Mama," I said, holding her. "Mama?"

"You say it like ya love me. Do you, child?" Isabel gasped. "So soon?"

"Be still, Mama. Dr. Jones?"

Willow shook his head, doing his best to stop Isabel's bleeding. Evie held me as I held Isabel.

"You don't grieve me, you hear?" Isabel whispered. "I do it all again for you, child. My life ended long ago. You live now."

"Isabel, you promised to lure Houst to the garden," Willow whispered. "It was supposed to be Katie's garden."

"You still handsome and smell like violets. This time, I do it my way. Had to, Jonesy."

"Shh, Isabel," Willow cried.

Isabel reached for Willow. "Tell old River . . . I'm sorry. I saved your roses, child, your new ones. Oh, they wonders . . . in his garden. And Trailer's inventions."

"Shh, save your strength, Mama."

"I strong, child, but . . . I use it all to face Delaney."

"You knew Houst was coming to burn down River's farmhouse?" Willow asked.

James stepped in. "Isabel led Houst away from Westland, long enough for us to get him. Willow's right . . . we all agreed to meet in Katie's garden. I'm sorry, Essie Mae. I'm too late."

"No, James," Isabel said, finding a burst of strength. "On time." She smiled. "You don't grieve me. This nobody's fault. My plan. Mine."

"Isabel." James lowered his head and whispered a prayer.

"Lord, child, get her in the house," Delly said softly, surprising us.

"Delly, leave me. God form me from this soil. It's where I belong now. Essie Mae . . ."

I cradled Mama in my arms.

"I said no good thing grows at Westland—I wrong 'cause it bring you."

"How'd an evil thing like this come to be?" Evie cried.

"What's evil bout saving someone you love?" Isabel asked.

"Isabel, stay quiet." Willow leaned down and kissed her softly.

"Always bossing," she said. "Essie Mae, I give you your name, but Katie an angel to you ... now she finally home, me, too. Oh, the roses, child. Can you smell em?"

Her hand fell limp in mine.

Mama closed her eyes. I only heard the crackling fire. James shouted for the men to work hard and douse it. It was too late, too late for many things.

A drop on Evie's cheek, tears and rain. Sprinkles and plops we would have danced under as children. I looked down at the peaceful face of a mama I never knew. How life was unfair to the lavishly dressed and rag wearers, black, white, male, female, adult, child, ignorant, genius, slave, and free. Delly's hum turned into wailing, a soft hallelujah in the rain. James ushered Evie away, always. Her hand tugged my arm, slipping off my sleeve at a rumble rattling the sky, my heart. I let her go, all of them, closed my eyes, my knees sinking into the soft earth, in need of rain. I smelled the roses on her skin, the gingerbread on her dress, death on her lips. With a last kiss, Bo's giant hands lifted her body like a fallen leaf. Sebastian draped a silk shawl over Isabel's face. A rose garden tucked her in forever sleep.

I do not remember walking. I remember nothing more, but falling into Sebastian's arms, hoping to wake to sunlight.

PART III

41.

ESSIE MAE

I spotted him standing on River's footbridge.

I ran. It's what I knew. I abandoned my mother as she had me. I could do nothing for her now. But I still had time to save myself... and my father.

"Trailer! Please."

He stumbled, hobbling into a forest glen I knew so well.

So did he.

I leaned my head back, forgetting myself, savoring the chill. The sounds of the forest wrapped me in warmth.

"Don't come any closer." His voice trembled.

"You're hurt. Let me see you, please."

"Houst shot Isabel?"

"Yes. There's nothing we can do now."

"This was Isabel's plan." He exhaled.

"Please, Trailer," I pleaded, coaxing this wounded animal from the brush. "Father?"

Tall, slender, worn and tired, he emerged. "What did you call me?"

I couldn't speak, staring at him: long wavy hair, clean-shaven. The jagged scar cracked his cheek as Isabel's. His face showed River's chin and arched brows, the small crook on the bridge of his nose . . . *like mine*. Trailer removed his hat, tousling his chestnut hair like his father.

"I called you Father." I offered my hand.

He clutched it, stepping over a pile of thickets. "Essie Mae?"

I nodded. "Let me bring you to River."

He let me go. "No. Do you want him to die, too? He's frail. I know." Trailer inched back into the woods, brushing himself off, throwing a hand up for me to stop following him.

I trudged on. "Willow told you. Did you know Isabel lived?"

He fell to his knees, tending his ankle. "It's not broken. I have to get out of here."

"You don't want to learn the truth?"

I recognized the worn satchel he clutched, River's, wondering when he sneaked inside the farmhouse to steal it.

"Hell, girl. No truth lives here. And I ain't your pa." He eyed Isabel's blood on my dress.

"You loved her . . . Isabel." I washed the blood off my hands in a puddle, eyeing his satchel. "Are you leaving with Katie's gold?"

"A handful of my father's; he owed me." He opened the satchel, revealing the nuggets, but I only saw a stack of papers and one of my new roses.

He wants to know about me. "River owed you?"

Trailer slapped his satchel closed. "I won't stand here explaining myself to a ghost. I am not your father."

"But you loved her. She said . . ."

"What did Isabel say?" He broke down. "We're not people, we're ghosts! I can't be a man because I let them do things to you. Do you understand? I'm a coward."

"You saved me."

"I didn't! I didn't know who the hell you were until I cleaned you up and saw your eyes—like mine. Barely knew who I was then, drinking. Wore that excuse out."

"My eyes saved me from those men, all except Grant. Then it stopped, almost as if Grant would set me free."

"I warned Grant if he touched you again, I'd kill him. I planned to take ya away myself, but he had too many men. Said he'd kill you and find that girl, Evie, no matter how long it took, and kill her too. I told Amos to fetch Jeanie. I ran once. Not then."

"James came."

Trailer found a boulder and sat. "Word swept through Ashland a gang of men were catching runaways for money. I volunteered to stop them. Guess I tried to make up for my wrongdoings until Grant took you. Saw ya the next morning. You looked like her. I died."

"I don't remember. Dr. Jones said . . ."

"Sure he did." Trailer stared into my eyes and held his breath. "I believe you don't remember. I do. I let Grant steal ya into the woods, knowing James was waiting."

"Then you did save me."

"No! Locked in a cage, was that saving? I won't speak on the rest." He winced, rising, searching the woods for his getaway.

I followed him deeper into the woods. "Only my body, Trailer. They didn't take me."

Trailer circled the cove, lost. "Isabel told me what Katie said, you and your troubles—nightmares. Isabel was never brain damaged or insane. You need to know. They tried to make her that way. I should've stopped it. Houst tried to do the same to you with his tricks."

"But Isabel had problems."

"Yes! What do you want? I gotta get out of here."

"Essie!" Sebastian called.

I grabbed my father's hand and led him to the trail only I knew. "There's a back road behind that line of evergreens; it leads to Sweet Water. I rode it once."

"Thank you." He squeezed my hand. "Why do you think I'm your pa?"

I stared into his eyes, seeing mine, a lifetime of pain and regret. "You were Isabel's first, weren't you? Only you know. And after three months, she told you about the baby."

"Yes. I loved her. That pig Houst found out. I traveled with my mother to Sweet Water. I came back and nearly killed him for what he did to Isabel."

"What of John Winthrop?"

"Isabel wasn't the same after she almost drowned in the creek. She was pregnant then ... with you. Nobody told you? She said she lost the baby. My father convinced me she tempted those men, the way she acted."

"She was scared, Trailer. Childlike. She didn't know how to act."

"I know it. I pleaded with her. Katie insisted on what we must do to save you. We agreed, but it went wrong. Isabel didn't know I told Katie I'd find ya and raise you."

"Those slaves beat and blinded your father. You didn't meet Isabel to catch the steamer."

"It all happened so fast. I was afraid. Maybe that's all I knew to do, run."

"You boarded a different ship. Dr. Jones helped you."

"Paris. The old lady wouldn't let me see Isabel. I tried. We planned to return to Westland. When Jonesy warns ya, he ain't bluffing. Did you know Willow loved Katie?"

"A different love. I have so many questions. Stay."

He looked at me fondly, tempted, then shook his head. "I'm not going to prison."

"Bedford would give you a chance. I said I would testify you saved me."

"And me," Evie said. "Are you all right, Essie Mae?"

"Yes."

Evie stood in front of me, noticing Trailer's injured foot, the satchel. "No one's here but us," she said. "They won't find us." Evie removed her scarf and handed it to Trailer. "Wrap your ankle tight with this. It's a long hike."

Trailer did. "You girls know the forest like I used to."

"We had to learn it," I said, searching behind me for Sebastian.

"Essie, Trailer hid me in Mama's garden to keep me safe from Houst. I knew you were at River's. I came when I could. Sky found me."

"You shot Houst," I said, surprised. "I saw you."

"In the leg. Sky did the rest and, well, Willow . . . I'm so sorry about Isabel."

"It's what she wanted," Trailer whispered. "Isabel was the only one who could flush out Houst. My crazy girl."

"You still love her. This is my father, Evie."

"Trailer Koontz." He grimaced as he rose, scrambling through the brush to leave.

"You won't see your father?" Evie asked him. "River's getting on."

"Someday. Jonesy said Pop might see. I never meant to hurt him . . . or you."

"River can see, Trailer, a little."

"I thought so. I begged Doc to try."

I whispered in Evie's ear. She handed me the money she had; I added to hers and stuffed the bills in Trailer's hand. "The first cottage you pass," I said. "Tell Mrs. Bixley it's an emergency and Bedford and the soldiers promised you a mount; they'll compensate her. You tell her Essie Mae gives her word. You tell her. You won't have any trouble from us."

"Trailer, you don't want to know your daughter?" Evie pressed.

Trailer hung his head, then managed a smile—a promise. "I'll find you. I am sorry."

"Wait, how will you find me?" I slipped from Evie's grip and chased after him.

He stopped me from walking closer. "Get that detective to stop following me . . . and Willow. I never ran with Houst. When Augustus clears my name, my Aunt Hazel in Sweet Water will send word." My daddy raced away, hobbling through thickets and mud.

"Trailer?" I called.

He paused and slowly turned around to me, taking me in.

"I forgive you."

He held his hand over his mouth and nodded. I watched him leave, aching to know my father, praying for the day he might return to know me.

42

DELLY

For two weeks, we drift round Westland like tissue paper in the breeze, looking in each other's eyes for answers and a place to land. When Augustus have the law take Houst's body and jail them circus folks and the Yankee soldiers Houst bribe to scare us and do bad things, we land.

I sit on Katie's rocker to feel her again, imagining the wisdom she'd speak now, mostly bout forgiving and loving. I rock, happy to see the last a the soldiers leave. Westland ain't no battleground bloodied and ruined, it mostly a garden of the flowers Katie love most—us.

Evie and Essie Mae laugh a li'l and play. Sky chase em like they his sheep. A soldier boy, too young for this work, wave goodbye to me, looking like a knight on his black pony, raising the gingerbread I give him for his journey. Something, how God bring folks together when we let Him. Now, with all the troubles, past, current, far away, all I see is Katie's smile, that, and the slip a peach in the morning sky, set me right.

At first, my spirit grieve I don't know Isabel be in this home. Nothing I can do. Isabel come back, made up her mind 'cause Katie need her again. Now they together forever. Though all them secrets burst forth, some settled, others nagging, I still say, most things in the past need the quiet, no cause to be waking em up.

"But you rattled the earth," Bo said, reading my mind, sitting in my rocker next to me.

For the first time, we sit rocking together on the porch like we a couple a swells.

Don't say cracks in the land don't hurt, but at least now the healing rain fall deep in the soil into the place that need it the most—our hearts.

"They waiting," Bo said.

"Like to sit here and rest all month if I could."

We sigh our troubles away together.

Bo grunted. "Don't even look like her, Delly, woman that come to Westland make me wonder."

I know who Bo mean, Isabel, but we fine with the unspoken words between us. "Um-hmm. Sebastian say one other know bout Isabel—Ned, your old hand."

"That night, Ned drive the wagon carrying Isabel's body, except it weren't Isabel."

"Katie knew John would never look at Isabel's body. Ned did, couldn't help lifting that blanket. Yellow fever raging in the valley, sad times, all them folks dying. Supposing Doc Jones find him a poor woman's body for Isabel and sneak Isabel to River's that night. I don't grieve her twice, nor fault Katie. We know John Winthrop woulda killed em both."

"Ned never said a word."

"Willow found out. Sebastian too."

"Katie set Ned up in a li'l house in New Orleans. Evie's poking round. I told her we bes leave Ned alone for now." Bo exhaled again. "James right, too many damn secrets. Supposing Sebastian run things now."

"You jus jealous 'cause Essie Mae grown and be gone again loving a good man."

"Essie Mae stay for now, all that counts. Mostly worried bout Evie."

"Next time someone say ain't no healing at Westland, look at my big man here, a shining them wet eyes befriending the mistress's daughter. Evie all right, strong like her mama."

"Strong like you."

I closed my eyes, feeling that big man's breath across my neck. He lean over, smelling sweeter than Essie's new rose, and kiss my forehead. "Wait for ya in the carriage, Delly."

"I can walk."

Sky raced up the porch steps and plopped at my feet.

"Looky there. Sky come and fetch me. Go on, Bo." I waved Evie and Essie Mae to me, soaking in Katie's Westland.

Always look different after a storm. My mind don't have the space to sort out all that happened here, but I gather come winter on a quiet snowy morn, it'll come together. Maybe I cry more tears. Maybe I sigh thankful. Until then, I celebrate my girls stay here with a load a living left, and my other two go home to find the peace that don't fall on em much in life. Whether it their own faults or the world's, don't nobody care now.

Whys be the confusion and heartache a life. God teach this old woman sometimes a why lead us to new friends and family to trust and love. Why lead us on a new path to travel, but we gotta learn another word God give us, courage. And I remember, Lord Almighty say He lead me 'sides the still waters, but He don't make me sit nor drink.

I rise from Katie's rocker moaning 'cause old Delly knows in her heart all the secrets bursting up out of this land won't be the last secrets flittering round Westland. Least now, we face em as a family. No odd family, I tell River . . . God's family. 'Cause God be the one who birth, keep, and save it. And I close my eyes a picturing Katie girl smiling, a thinking Good Lord let her light up Heaven again even for a blink, all by herself.

43.

ESSIE MAE

"It's not the family we're born into, it's the family that finds us, the ones who save and care for us."

"Stand by our side."

"Stay by our side . . . stay."

I fell asleep in Katie's rocker, waking to a musical voice. *Lil.*

"We have all worn out Katie's rocker, haven't we?"

"Good morning, Lil."

We watched Sebastian mulling around the stables, peeking back at us.

"Ah, a worthy gentleman waits to escort you to the hillside."

I wrapped myself in my shawl. "Evie requested alone time up there with James."

"I see." Lil joined me on the front porch. "We've hardly spoken since your arrival."

I stretched past her, spying Sebastian talking with Bo.

Lil followed my gaze. "Your secret love rekindles romantic memories of my dear Randolph. It pleases me." She caressed my shoulder and sat next to me.

A flush washed my cheeks. "Sebastian doesn't see me as I was, but who I can be."

She raised an eyebrow and grinned. "Yes, a worthy man." We rocked in silence, save the crickets underfoot. Lil closed her eyes, breathing in the chilly morning. Agitated by the sudden creak from her rocker, she rose, rustling in her almond gown, pearls pinging as she strolled. "You two would make a handsome sight twirling in a ballroom." Lil waved Sebastian on to join us.

"Do you miss your lavish parties, Lil?"

"My gatherings meant more to me than mere social events. You changed hearts, my dear. You persuaded many to fight for the cause of ending slavery.

Someday, Lil will tell you all about it. You sway as graceful as a sunflower in the summer breeze when you dance."

"Tell me now." I stood in front of her as that skittish young woman arriving at her home in Richmond during my first visit.

She jingled the keys on Katie's charm bracelet dangling from my wrist. "Stunning," she whispered, pressing my cheek. "Many heroes will never give a speech or hear their names cheered."

"You speak of William?"

"Sebastian . . . and you, my dear."

"You never knew?"

"No, child." She nestled closer. "I will not judge, or let anyone dishonor my sister's memory."

"Isabel lived in Paris. I may have passed her on the street, in a park."

"A garden? You have remained distant since my affair in New York City."

"I hadn't meant to run away."

She leaned on the railing, taking in Westland. "You've a sanctuary at the Morgan's. I am proud of your accomplishments. This will not stop you. I am sorry for Isabel, Essie Mae."

"I don't feel grief, Lil, but sorrow for her life."

Her eyes glistened with love. I was used to Lil's brashness. In this moment, I hadn't offered her my understanding of how deeply she missed her sister now. "We have much in common," she whispered, rushing past sadness. "And much to discuss regarding your future."

I nodded. "You treat me like your daughter. I'm grateful for all you afforded me."

Lil slapped her hands to her hips as Delly bobbling her head, making me laugh. "I have not made you, Essie Mae, neither did Thomas. And since he hasn't apologized for his abominable behavior in New York, I will. There is much you don't know about Thomas's past."

I clung to her as we walked down the steps. "Much he hasn't told me. We parted amicably. Perhaps, Evie is right . . . we are not women made for marriage."

"Posh!" Lil shimmied to find my gaze. "Ah, there it is . . . love. Something's afoot." We spied Sebastian popping out from behind a tree. Lil giggled at his giant wave.

We strolled toward the gazebo.

"The past jumbles in my mind." I looked through the telescope, focused on the horizon.

Lil turned it on Sebastian. "You're too wise and old for Lil's mollycoddling now."

I need it today.

Her hands, tender as a rose petal. "Our grief ushers in fond and tragic memories, Essie Mae. You will not contend with them alone. Evie's distance frightens me."

"You cannot continue treating Evie as your china doll. She's changed, Lil."

"Westland may save us yet. I am not made for the country, Katie," she said to the sky. "I'll away to London after the holidays and confront Aunt Charlotte. You and Evie will join me in Paris next spring, *oui?*"

"*Oui.*"

"My cue." Lil wiggled her fingers at Sebastian again. "Remember, a lady has every right to change her dreams. It doesn't mean we've given up. The important thing is to still have them."

"Yes, Lil."

"Your father . . . some paths lead to dead ends, and as we have witnessed, tragedy."

"Yes, but it is my life."

"That it is, Miss Essie. If you do not know who you are before you take this journey, nothing you discover will matter."

Sebastian appeared, clearing his throat for our attention.

I stood lost in Lil's tender gaze, absorbing her wisdom. She clutched my hand, then offered it to Sebastian. He flew up the steps to our laughter, capturing his prize.

"Nephew," Lil quipped.

Sebastian kissed her cheek. "Auntie."

"Adieu. I shall meet you two on the hillside. Shall I send the carriage?"

Sebastian cleared his throat again, crinkling his eyes at Lil.

"Ah, yes . . . you'll walk."

🌿

"I love her so." I watched Lil strut across the lawn, flirt with the driver, and depart to the hillside to Katie's memorial.

"Take a turn, Miss Essie?" Sebastian offered his arm.

"They're waiting for us."

"They'll wait a bit longer."

"Bo's right. You are Westland's boss now. What are you hiding behind your back?"

"Patience, Miss Essie."

We strolled the path to my garden. I hadn't wanted to visit it today. "It will never be like it once was," I said, peering behind his back.

He nudged my body forward. "Everything changes." His fingers threaded into mine.

"I wish certain moments could last forever. Evie's eyes, the first time she saw my roses. My garden stole her breath. She looked so proud at the wonder I made."

"Evie's eyes still shine for you. You don't notice."

"What of your eyes?"

"If you don't remember the way I looked at you the first time you boarded a train, I have no right asking you anything."

"I stared at my shoes, remember?"

"No, you noticed me." His fingers tickled mine.

"I certainly did not . . . that first train ride . . . not entirely."

"When did you discover my secret?" He stealthily held his surprise behind his back.

We left my garden and walked the trail to the footbridge over River's creek near his farmhouse. "We host a circus at Westland, carnival tricks, cons. Evie and I have tumbled and tripped through life as clowns, painting smiles on our faces while suffering silent horrors."

"If you succumb to despair, they win."

"You are right, Sebastian. I witnessed what despair did to Isabel, years wasted in shame, regret, and revenge. A slave no longer, yet bound."

"You spent years obtaining freedom, now we must live free."

"We?"

"We ran from our answers, fearing them, now they've arrived. What will we do?"

"You said we again."

Sebastian only grinned.

We sat on River's weathered bench, listening to the creek gurgle. The lingering smell of the fire wrestled with the pines.

"Things must change if I'm to stay here." I looked back toward Westland.

"*Chulosa.*" His fingers brushed my lips.

"Peace. Let's walk back. I've had enough of the past."

He smirked again. I spotted his secret bouquet as we navigated the forest trail home.

"Essie, for years I've traveled next to you listening to your hopes and dreams. Until one day, your dream ignited mine . . . to find my family."

"May I see your watch?"

He tucked it into my hand. "You knew in Ashland."

"I knew long before then." I opened his watch, comforted by Katie's photograph.

"How, Lady Pinkerton?"

I handed it back to him. "You must have known I saw Evie's grandfather's watch many times on Miss Katie's curiosity shelf. Why would you have it?"

"Evie asked the same question."

"You avoided showing me its photograph, your tears on the hillside at her gravesite, cornflower blue eyes and swagger as James's, hair fair as Katie's . . . Indian heritage. You even tug your sleeves like Evie and swirl your hands into the cicadas' whirl when you're nervous."

"I do?"

"Yes. How did you come to work for Augustus?"

"They shuffled me between homes. I looked all an Indian child when I was younger. My skin lighter now, blond hair, blue eyes, manners, and education, so did the Indian side of me, but in their prejudice many doubted a *savage* as I could learn, never Augustus."

"I am sorry I judged you, Sebastian."

"Katie never knew I lived, Essie Mae, and despite Dr. Jones's warning, I had to see her."

"Did you know Katie left you a part of Westland in her will?"

"Never. I understood your quest. I needed to see my mother beyond this tiny photo hidden in this watch, a token of a past and family I never knew . . . a family who hid me, too."

"You saw your mother in Evie, a sister you could have known. And me?"

"A love I could not hold."

"Sebastian, what chance will we have?"

"The one you're willing to give us. No one else matters."

"Not in the South. What chance did Isabel and Trailer have? We'll have to fight."

"Delly said the first sound we make entering this world is crying. We have to learn to sing. When a rose grows, what must it do?"

"Push through the earth."

"Everything in this life must fight."

"I'm weary, Sebastian."

"If you're tired of fighting, you're tired of living. I won't accept that."

We walked the trail to a wooden bench tucked under a maple. He eyed the bench, curious. I stroked it fondly as we passed. "Two little girls, a slave, and the planter's daughter, set out on adventures beyond this plantation."

"You and Evie?"

"Isabel and Katie. Your grandfather built this wooden bench like the others. Isabel re-painted them except for their bench in Katie's garden. Alexander Wilcox thought the only way to keep Katie safe was to hide her from the world."

"Like me."

"And me."

"Another . . ."

"Similitude."

I walked on. Sebastian lingered, lost in the bench's history. "I'm willing to fight for us. I am not my father who abandoned love."

"James found it in the end."

"I desire love for a lifetime, not a moment."

I hadn't meant to flee. "I cannot have children." I stared ahead as Sebastian kept pace.

He stopped me. "Your school . . . you have many children. And if we desire to have a family, we'll adopt."

"Westland isn't finished yielding its secrets."

"Life is full of secrets, Essie Mae, the surprises we anticipate, the horrors we ignore. When were you going to tell me about Trailer?"

I stopped at a carving in a tree, *A& R.* "We contend with our secrets now, is that it? I haven't told River . . . yet."

"Nor shall you, until we find Trailer again—and help him as Evie requested."

"Mr. Jarrell, you tricked me." We walked on. "When did you tell Katie?"

"During the war, when her condition worsened, James sent for me."

"It wasn't James . . . Evie pushed selling Westland."

"Yes. I came to offer my mother peace. For two years, we lived as a family."

"I didn't come to Westland for Miss Katie, but to expose secrets so Evie, *we,* might have a chance to live without them." I covered my face in shame. "I should've been here for Katie. I stayed away . . . angry, afraid. I loved her, Sebastian, blamed her . . . forgave."

Freedom bathed me.

I didn't care who saw us. I didn't care if Evie's grassy eyes caught us through the bare trees. I slid into Sebastian's warm embrace, sighing away my years of buried anger and regret. His gentle hand pressed against my hair, stopping my head from shaking. I couldn't look at him, but the carpet of rust and crimson under our feet, and inhale the storm on the horizon.

"I'm tired of not feeling."

His kiss washed over my lips. I hadn't control of the feelings I locked away. Feelings I told myself would never surface—*trust, desire, passion.* "Love?"

"Love," he whispered.

"I don't know how to love. I need to learn again."

"Let me teach you."

His kisses caressed my skin. Tucking my hands into his, he turned me to look at Westland through the trees' bare branches. My body rested against his chest. He swayed me as the breeze, gentle and graceful. His flowers presented at my feet.

"No one has ever taught you about good men," he said. "A man who takes care of the woman he loves. A woman he adores and sees in light and courage."

"Scars . . . deep, stretched, painful scars."

"I will soothe them." We darted our eyes to the sky as plump raindrops splashed upon our skin. "Let's go home."

"Where is that, Sebastian? Home?"

"With me."

I took the hand he offered, tugging him close, kissing his wet skin, his lips. And in the hallowed woods I swore I heard her giggle, Evie, the little white girl with sunbeams in her hair. I paused, searching for her, but as we quickened our steps toward the house, Evie stood, waving at us from the front porch as the little girl I knew ready for mischief in an old man's apple cove.

"I have so much to tell her."

"We do."

Sebastian paused at the gazebo, ushering me inside. The morning mist ended and sunshine stretched across Westland.

"Where did Jarrell come from?" I asked.

"I gave myself a name. Augustus tells me it is James's surname now. Imagine, a father taking his son's name, perhaps, a first."

"James Jarrell. Winthrop banished from Westland for good. Will you ever give me those flowers?"

He swallowed and kneeled to an echo of laughter in the distance, and presented his bouquet.

I breathed it in. "Honeysuckle . . . bonds of love." I nodded, impressed.

"Right." He smiled, proud, squirming as I admired the bouquet.

"Pink rosebuds?"

"Confession of love, carnation—pure and deep love, and yellow jasmine . . ."

"Yes, we know all about yellow jasmine. You made this bouquet for me?"

"Yep."

"One white rose?" I raised an eyebrow at his worry. "Silence?"

He plucked it out and tossed it. "You're forgetting my favorite, the cuckoo bud."

"What's that?"

He pointed to a posy of buttercups.

"Oh, Mr. Jarrell, and what is the meaning of the cuckoo bud?"

"Marry me."

"No."

Sebastian bowed his head.

I lifted his chin. "That would be this." I pointed to the sprig of ivy. "Yes."

"Yes?" He sprang up and lifted me off the ground, my dressing spinning in a whirl of glimmering light.

"Sebastian, you give me an amazing gift . . . a name."

"You always had a name, my love." He held my hand to the light, admiring the ruby ring he slipped on my finger.

"This is what it feels like, Miss Katie . . . love. Real love."

A breeze carried the scent of crisp evergreens from the nearby woods. I closed my eyes, held my breath, and took it all in, unafraid.

As my beloved held my hand, I dared to picture a wedding here, and, for the first time, my future. Nearing the house, I spotted one last gift from Isabel. Miss Katie's prize rosebush, blossoming with yellow and red roses, had vanished. In its place, a mature bush of my new roses, Miss Katie's pink tipped with lavender. "How?" I whispered, imagining Evie's touch.

It isn't time to question, but believe.

44.

EVIE

We gathered on the hillside to visit Mama, and now, Isabel.

"They have been apart long enough," I said, insisting Bo bury Isabel next to Mama in the resting place we made for her under the willow near our hillside. Tom agreed.

The hills lost their gemstone sparkle, but the rain stopped and the sky a cornflower blue. We finished creating our memorial to the belle of Westland. Lil planted bulbs and plants from Mama's garden, ready to bloom next spring. Bo's bench awaited James and me. The black iron fence protected their sleep, and a fairy-tale willow invited us to dream of new beginnings.

Essie's lavender rose petals blanketed Mama. Fresh yellow and red roses sprinkled Isabel. Weeks ago, in the secret hours, Isabel had visited Mama's grave to say goodbye, transplanting the red and yellow rosebush Mama had treasured that once enamored us in front of the house.

"Fitting," I whispered. "Mama's favorite rosebush rests with them now."

James tapped my arm as I dreamed. For the first time in months, we didn't need any words. We admired each other, tears filling our eyes—joyful, thankful.

My heart stilled at his wide smile. "Well, it's over, Katie. It's over," he said.

"Is it, James?"

He squeezed my hand, plucked a red rose from the shrub, and placed it on Mama's grave. "Think the storm's holding off until this evening. Cool front will clear the skies, making it perfect for stargazing after supper."

"You haven't wanted to discuss Sebastian. I understand why you held your secret, James. You always protected Mama and me."

"It's complicated, Evie. We need to let this set as a family awhile. Tonight is the time for reflection and truths all around. I invited River."

"He's family now. Secrets ... Westland's crop, no more."

James cocked his head as if he hadn't known Essie's secret. "Wish that were so, little lady. Human nature; you can't rid the world of secrets. Suspect in time, you would've told me you're a crackerjack of a shot." His sly grin made me snicker.

At the thought, I turned serious again. "I couldn't kill Houst, James. I could have."

"You wounded him when I had my aim. Sky charged and good Willow did the deed when Houst pointed that pistol at Essie Mae."

"Willow told you. He left again so soon."

"He'll be back. Doc said you could shoot. Little miffed, I wasn't the one to teach ya."

"You've taught me plenty. I suppose now we may bury the past, but . . . Essie asked me, making me wonder."

"What's that, darlin'?"

"How did you reach Westland so fast after Willow shot Houst? You were at Tom's."

"Was I?" He smirked and called me to him. I snuggled into his arms. "Sebastian had a decoy take my place. Far off, not a bad likeness. He sure riled at shaving his white beard. Said his wife fancied him looking like . . ."

"Santa Claus. Sebastian's man, Mars."

"Yep. We have years to talk, Evie. She gave us that. Years."

She was Mama. She was Isabel. Both women gave their lives so that we might live free. And none of us would ever forget that.

We watched Essie and Sebastian in the distance, holding hands, walking up the trail.

"James, do you wanna bet Mama's plan for the gazebo worked out this morning?"

"Don't have to bet. I can see their glow from here. Darlin', it pleases me to see you accepting your brother these past few weeks."

"Delly was right all along, an earthquake shook Westland, and we weren't ready for it."

"But we're standing here together, aren't we?"

I hadn't any more words, only love, as I settled in his arms.

James turned to Delly, watching her laugh with Bo and River. "Delly gave me a speech the other day befitting Essie Mae's talent. See, it never mattered to any of us that Delly didn't have schooling; she holds a higher wisdom." He jiggled the key draped around my neck.

"So do you."

James tipped his hat. "Delly said, only we can know when the sad things we've walked through are done hurting. Justice arrived, but you're still allowing the evil that men have done steal your mind. But I asked her, what if I'm the evil man?"

"And she shooed you away and threatened to baptize you in the creek."

"Yep." James's chest rose and fell with a deep sigh. He nodded at Essie and Sebastian's arrival. I only saw James. "I'm not one for speeches, little lady, but I figure if we let hateful folks keep us under, we haven't won a damn thing, and it ain't over up here." He pointed to his mind.

"Or here." I patted his heart.

"Sometimes we don't fight for strength or freedom," James said, "we have to give it to ourselves, and fight to keep it."

"How do we let it go?" Essie asked, walking up to us.

"Something in ya snaps a boldness," Delly said, squeezing her. "It one word, all I know, different for everybody."

"Delly, what was your word?" James asked.

"Enough."

We soaked it in as the breeze.

"Mama's word was forgive, wasn't it?" I asked James. "She wrote about forgiveness in her last letter."

"I believe it was," he answered, remembering. "Forgiving ourselves most of all."

"What's your word, Aunt Lil?" I asked, holding her tight.

"Love, dear. Always love."

"Essie Mae?" Lil asked.

Essie looked at us against the backdrop of our hillside and down at the crumpled photo introducing her to her lost mama. She tucked the photo in Isabel's roses, eyed us as a painter sizing up a portrait, and squeezed in the middle of James and Sebastian.

"Family. And yours, Evie . . . my sister?"

I stepped away, turning to Westland. The trees' fall glory faded, but a light shone over the drive to the front porch. It was what I wanted to see,

Mama rocking, waiting for us, rising to stand on the railing as a girl, her face to the sky, waving us home.

"Home," I said, strong and proud. "*Chuka*," I whispered to James and Sebastian. "Home."

River joined our rejoicing. At Lil's call, my family rustled away. Essie remained by my side. We stood looking out at the hillside like those little girls from long ago. She looked up at the clouds, pointing to a fluff and whispered, "It's a dog, old Pepper."

"Nah, it's a teakettle."

We watched Sky race in circles and settle at Bo's command.

"Evie Wilcox, you're trying to rile me."

"Maybe." I elbowed her, then grabbed her ring finger, giggling at the fiery ruby.

Essie sighed, turned to me, and handed me a small card. "This came in a letter from Thomas today. Harry Polk is a publisher from New York. He is interested in your stories, Evie."

"A writer." I held the card as a bar of gold. "Thank you, Essie."

"Miss Evie, you made that old man slip a tear, offering him a resting place on this hillside." We welcomed Bo's mellow voice.

River squeezed us together, nearly conking our heads. "Ain't too keen on using it jus yet." River's hooting filled the hills. "Odd family," he said to Essie Mae. "Odd family 'tis. And I tell ya what, nobody ask me, but my word be ... thankful. Woulda said hungry, but Delly will thump my ear."

Delly marched to River. "You ask me bout eating twice already. You can see me coming now, least most days, bes know this ain't no place for sassing." Delly grabbed his arm for their promenade. "Come on now," she said, grinning. "I got the fixings on."

"Hold on," James said. "River, you told me you'd like to honor Katie with a word."

I guided River to Mama's resting place. Essie held his other hand.

River scratched his stubble, pondering a moment. Essie whispered. I smiled. We never saw Koontz in a suit before. He took a deep breath and when he finally looked at us; he was all grin. "When Katie a girl, she fancy one a Polly's tales," he said softly, "a comfort that chase her tears away. I'd like to recite it if my memory holds."

"Please do, River," I said.

River bowed his head and whispered a prayer. He squinted and flailed for a moment. James took his hand and nudged him to continue.

"There once be a li'l girl named Flora," River said, taking us in. "Who danced in the meadow every morning, wearing frills and fluffs some say made from rose petals. Flora silky and soft and nearly float away; she danced so light on the slip of the wind."

Lil joined River now and wiped her tears. Delly close behind, until River squinted again, marveling at his little audience.

"When Flora smiled," River said, looking at Essie Mae, "the sun turned jealous 'cause Flora light the whole meadow by herself. One day, storm clouds hover, and Flora says she'll chase them away. But her daddy said, 'No, Flora, we need the rain and sometimes rain brings great treasures. Watch.'"

River broke free from Lil and Bo, and grew animated finishing his tale. "So Flora waited and waited until the rain stopped, and she ran to the meadow with her daddy to see the great treasure the rain brought. Flora danced under the rainbow she thought her daddy bring. 'See, Flora, he said, storms don't have the last say, do they?'"

"Thank you, River," Essie and I said together, holding him tight.

He wiggled out from our sniffles and hugs, searching for Delly. "Delly, you go on take my arm," River said. "*I'll* help ya down the hill. Fine day, don't need the carriage."

"Been walking this land one acre to the next, don't need no helping now," Delly sassed, "But I'll hold on, lessen you fall and stay laid up, making me tend to your chores all winter."

"Hee-hee, Delly. You sassing more than them girls."

"Meet you at the house," Sebastian said, leaving Essie with his kiss.

"That seals it, you two," James said, slapping Sebastian's back. "If sisters by paper don't satisfy you ladies, my son is making Essie Mae your sister-in-law, Evie."

"Indeed," Lil shouted. "A spring wedding . . . after Paris. You promised, girls."

"Yes, Lil."

"Fine voices. I'll give you that."

Essie waited until we were alone. Bo lingered at Isabel's grave.

"You coming, Evie?" Essie whispered.

"Yes. Essie Mae ... River doesn't know he's your grandfather?"

"In time, Sister. In time."

"Think I'll sit a spell and ..."

"Dream."

Bo waited for Essie. She would have much to tell him. No one took the carriage home, for it was a fine day for an autumn stroll. I watched them all, soaking in their laughter, a hoot from River, a screech from Lil, cautiously navigating the twists and turns of the worn trail home. A bonfire in the distance, its amber sparks floated in the air like fireflies on a June night.

Essie caught up to her Sebastian and rested her head on his shoulder. I thought of William and his promised visit at Christmas, Delly readying the house for the holidays, Essie a flurry in her new greenhouse, and memories of Mama and Isabel as children, wondering if they ever dreamed on our hillside. *You can now.* "A hillside where you can dream a million dreams, listen to the trees, how their leaves give great applause, Mama, if you close your eyes and listen. The clouds, they form wondrous shapes for us to become lost in for hours. Only on our hillside, Mama, nowhere else has Westland's clouds."

I looked toward Mama's resting place, then Isabel's, and the willow that guarded them. I glanced down at the dirt road winding the path back home and gazed again into the forest to the rugged trail leading to adventures.

And in the distance, I saw them hold hands.

ABOUT THE AUTHOR

MICHELLE MURIEL is the award-winning, bestselling author of *Essie's Roses*, *Westland* and *Water Lily Dance*. She holds a Bachelor of Fine Arts, magna cum laude, and worked as a professional actress, a member of Actors' Equity and The American Federation of Television and Radio Artists for twenty years, doing theater, voice-over, and commercial work. She is also a songwriter and musician. Michelle lives in Missouri. Connect with Michelle at MichelleMuriel.com.